D0261765

LANCASHIRE COUNTY LIBRARY
3011813778248 2

THE ROOT OF EVIL

Also by Håkan Nesser

THE LIVING AND THE DEAD
IN WINSFORD

The Barbarotti Series

THE DARKEST DAY

THE ROOT OF ALL EVIL

The Van Veeteren series

THE MIND'S EYE

BORKMANN'S POINT

THE RETURN

WOMAN WITH A BIRTHMARK

THE INSPECTOR AND SILENCE

THE UNLUCKY LOTTERY

HOUR OF THE WOLF

THE WEEPING GIRL

THE STRANGLER'S HONEYMOON

THE G FILE

HÅKAN NESSER

THE ROOT OF EVIL

Translated from the Swedish by
Sarah Death

MANTLE

First published 2018 by Mantle
an imprint of Pan Macmillan
20 New Wharf Road, London N1 9RR
Associated companies throughout the world
www.panmacmillan.com

ISBN 978-1-5098-0937-0

Originally published in 2007 as *En helt annan historia*
by Albert Bonniers förlag, Stockholm.

1 3 5 7 9 8 6 4 2

A CIP catalogue record for this book is available from the British Library.

Typeset in Dante MT by Palimpsest Book Production Limited, Falkirk, Stirlingshire
Printed and bound by CPI Group (UK) Ltd, Croydon, CR0 4YY

The town of Kymlinge does not exist on the map
and the Bahco adjustable spanner model number 0872
has never been on sale in France. Other than that,
the contents of this book largely accord with
the known state of affairs.

ONE

NOTES FROM MOUSTERLIN

29 June 2002

I am not like other people.

And I do not want to be. If I ever find a group where I feel I belong, it will only mean that I am getting blunted. That I, too, have been ground down to the bedrock of custom and stupidity. This is just the way it is; nothing can alter these fundamental conditions.

Perhaps it was a mistake to stay here. Perhaps I should have obeyed my first impulse and said no. But the path of least resistance is compelling and Erik interested me in those first few days; he stands out from the crowd, at any rate. And I had no fixed plans, no strategy for my journey. To go south, the only important thing was to keep heading south.

But now it is night-time, I feel less certain. There is nothing to keep me here. I can pack my rucksack at any time and move on and this fact, if nothing else, provides insurance for the future. It strikes me that I could actually leave right now, at this very moment; it is two o'clock, and I can hear the monotonous voice of the sea in the darkness, a few hundred metres from the terrace where I am sitting to write this. I realize it will soon be high tide; I could go down to the beach and start walking east, nothing could be simpler.

But a level of inertia, combined with the fatigue and alcohol in my veins, holds me back. At least until tomorrow. Probably a few more days after that. The last thing I am is in a hurry, and perhaps I will find myself drawn into the role of observer. Perhaps there will be things to write about. When I told Dr L about my plans for quite a long trip, he did not show much enthusiasm at first, but when I explained that I needed time to think and write about what had happened in an unfamiliar environment – and that this was the whole point – he nodded in agreement; eventually he also wished me good luck and it seemed to me that this genuinely came from the heart. I had been under his care for more than a year, and it must naturally feel like a triumph on the rare occasions when a client can be allowed out to run free.

As regards Erik, it was generous of him to let me stay here at no cost, of course. He claimed to have rented the house jointly with a girlfriend, but then they broke up and it was too late to cancel. I initially thought he was lying, guessed he was gay and wanted me as his plaything, but apparently not. I don't think he's homosexual, but I'm far from sure. He could be bi, Erik, and he's certainly a far from straightforward character. I assume that's why I can put up with him: there are dark corners in him that appeal to me, at least for as long as they remain unexplored.

And he's not short of money; the house is big enough for us not to get in each other's way. We've agreed to share the food bills while I'm here, but we also share something else. A kind of respect, perhaps I'd call it. It's almost four whole days now since he picked me up on the road out of Lille, and three since we got here. I normally tire of people in a fraction of that time.

⋆

But tonight – as I write this – I am starting to suffer my first real misgivings. It began with that extended lunch down by the harbour in Bénodet. I soon realized it would be a prelude to a trying evening. It's impossible not to notice such things. A thought even ran through my mind – once we had finally found seats in that noisy restaurant, and finally made the waiter understand our orders.

Kill everybody at this table and leave.

It would have been the simplest thing for all concerned, and it would have been no skin off my nose.

If only I had had the means. A gun, at least, and an escape route.

Perhaps it was just an idea born of the fact that it was so hot. The distance between intense heat and madness is a short one. We had moved the tables around and dragged the big parasols into various positions to create some shade, but I still ended up in the sun – particularly whenever I leant against the back of my chair – and it was anything but comfortable. Existence felt like one big itch. Pulsating irritation ticking towards some implacable point.

The whole enterprise was of course an act of sheer folly. Perhaps it was not the result of any one person's direct initiative, perhaps it was just a matter of general, misguided deference. A group of foreign fellow-countrymen happen across one another at a Saturday market in a small place in Brittany. It is entirely possible that convention demands certain sorts of behaviour in such a situation. Certain rituals. I loathe convention as much as I loathe the people who live by it.

It is also possible that I would not view a group of Hungarians round a restaurant table in Stockholm or Malmö in the same light; it is the internal dynamic of the group I find unbearable, while from outside it has no effect on me. Knowing and seeing through things is usually worse than being ignorant. Or pretending to be ignorant. It is easier to live in a country where one does not fully understand the language.

Take French, the language currently all around us, which appears at its most pregnant when one cannot fully comprehend what is being said.

But my thoughts never show from the outside, I let no devil cross my bridge. I curse inwardly but merely smile, and smile. That is how I have learnt to make my way through existence. *Navigare necesse est.* It could even be that others think me pleasant. Thoughts are not dangerous as long as they remain thoughts, that is of course a truth as good as any other.

And it is my principle never to say anything disagreeable.

So it was a question of two couples. I initially assumed that they already knew each other, that perhaps they were all on holiday together – but this turned out not to be the case. All six of us just happened to bump into each other amongst the market stalls in the square: home-produced cheese, home-produced jams and compotes, home-produced Muscadet, cider and crocheted shawls; it was quite possible that one of the women caught Erik's eye. They are both young and fairly attractive, so perhaps he even fancied them both, and he undeniably turned on the charm as we sat there eating our seafood and emptying one bottle of wine after another.

Quite possibly I did, too.

And then there was the strange Kymlinge connection. Erik has lived in the town all his life; apparently, the woman in one of the couples grew up there and then moved to Gothenburg, and the other woman has lived in Kymlinge since the age of ten. None of the three knew each other even remotely, but they all found this geographical coincidence irresistibly fascinating. Even Erik.

For my part, I found it nauseating in equal measure. As if they had all arrived on a coach tour and could now sit in this French village, revelling in the natives' customs and peculiarities and comparing them with people's behaviour back home. In Kymlinge and elsewhere. I drank three glasses of chilled white wine before the main course, a familiar sense of desperation trying to take possession of me as I sweated in the sun. An itch, as I said.

Where my own relationship with Kymlinge was concerned, I chose to stay silent. And I am sure none of the others knows who I am; if they did, it would be impossible for me to stay here.

Henrik and Katarina Malmgren are one of the couples. She grew up in Kymlinge, but they live in Mölndal just outside Gothenburg now. They're both around thirty, she works at Sahlgrenska hospital and he's some kind of academic. They're obviously married but haven't any children. She looks like the kind of woman who could, and would like to, get pregnant, so if there's some medical problem it no doubt lies with him. Dry and tense, slightly florid complexion, presumably burns fairly easily in the sun, perhaps he was enjoying the extended lunch as little as I was. He gave that sort of impression, at any rate. He probably feels more at ease in front of a computer screen or amongst dusty books than out with people; it's debatable how the two of them got together at all.

The other couple are called Gunnar and Anna. They're not married, don't even live together, apparently. They both had to struggle rather with their natural superficiality, trying to give the appearance of having thought things through and reached some kind of attitude to life. It didn't work very well, of course, and it would have been to both their advantages to keep their mouths shut, particularly her. He's a teacher of some kind, I didn't gather any more than that, and she works at an advertising agency. In some kind of client-facing role, I assume; her face and top half are undoubtedly her main assets. It also emerged that together they had just bought a horse to run in trotting races, or at any rate were in the process of doing so.

For some impenetrable reason, Katarina Malmgren speaks virtually fluent French, a capacity none of the rest of us round the table came anywhere near to possessing, and during our lunch she was accorded the undeserved status of some kind of oracle. We had at least eight different kinds of shellfish to eat, and she had detailed discussions with the waiter about every single one of them. Corks with pins in them for poking the reluctant inhabitants out of their shells; when you finally get the little muscular morsels in your mouth, you never know if they're alive or dead. As I understand it, you're supposed to bite through them and kill them before you swallow.

Erik took charge of the drinks; we started with ordinary dry white wine, but after three bottles we switched to the local cider, sweet and so lethally strong that we were all obliged to take a two-hour nap in the afternoon.

We accordingly went on to spend the evening at Gunnar and Anna's. They're staying about a hundred metres from here, along the beach towards Beg-Meil, another picturesque little house, nestling in the dunes. We sat on their terrace, all six of us, ate more shellfish and knocked back the wine and Calvados. Gunnar sang, too, and accompanied himself on the guitar. Evert Taube, the Beatles, Olle Adolphson. The rest of us joined in as the words came to us, and it was easy to start thinking of it as a slightly magical evening. Sometime around midnight, we were so drunk that there was talk of skinny-dipping in the sea. An enthusiastic quartet comprising the two ladies plus Erik and Gunnar set off with a bottle of sparkling wine and their arms round each other's shoulders.

I sat there with dry-as-dust Henrik; I ought to have asked him what he actually does, exactly what his field of research is, but I didn't feel like talking to him. It was more pleasant just to sit and sip the Calvados, smoke and stare out into the darkness. He made a few attempts to start a conversation about some characteristic or other of the people here in Finistère, but I didn't encourage him. He pretty soon lapsed into silence, presumably as uninterested in my views on assorted topics as I am in his. He seems to have some kind of integrity embedded in that dry nature of his, after all. It felt as though we were both sitting listening to our friends out there in the water in the dark. He had more call to strain his ears, of course; it was his wife, not mine, who had taken all her clothes off in the company of three strangers.

It is five years since I had a wife. I miss her sometimes but mostly not.

When the party returned, they were at any event modestly draped in towels, and altogether more subdued than when they set off, and I could not help feeling that they were sharing a secret.

That something had happened and they were concealing it.

But maybe they were just drunk and tired. And chilled – the

Atlantic in June is way below the twenty-degree mark. We only stayed half an hour after they came back. As Erik and I walked back along the beach towards the road to our house he had obvious difficulty staying on his feet, and he crashed out as soon as he got indoors and kicked off his sandals.

As for me, I feel surprisingly clear in the head. I'd almost say analytical. Words and thoughts have a clarity they can only possess at night. Some nights. I can sense the sea out there in the dark, and the air temperature must be twenty-five degrees. There are insects bouncing against the lamp as I light a Gauloises and slowly sip my last drink of the day. Erik is asleep with the window open and I can hear his snores; he must have at least two litres of wine in his veins. It is a few minutes past two, and it feels good to be alone at last.

The Malmgrens' house is in the other direction, on the far side of the Pointe de Mousterlin. Along this coastal strip there must be about fifty holiday lets, all told; most of them are a kilometre or so inland, of course, and maybe it isn't so odd that three of them should be rented by Swedes. As I understood it from Erik, they didn't all go through the same agent, but the others are basically new arrivals, just as we are.

Three weeks of potential socializing lie ahead of us. I suddenly realize I am thinking of Anna. It happens against my will, but there was something about her naked face and wet hair when they got back from their swim. And that guilty look. In Katarina's eyes there was something else, a kind of yearning.

I should have watched Henrik's face too, of course, for some sense of counterpoint, but I didn't. The observer role is not always that easy to maintain.

To live is not necessary, I find myself thinking. I don't know why that thought occurs to me.

Husks, we are nothing but husks in eternity.

Commentary, July 2007

Five years have passed.

Sometimes it feels like fifteen years, sometimes like five months. The elasticity of time is remarkable, and everything depends on the starting point I choose to view things from. Sometimes I can see Anna's face very clearly in front of me, as if she were sitting opposite me here in this room, and the next moment I can see those six people, including myself, from a great height; ants on the beach, milling around, performing their futile, meaningless gyrations. In the cold light of eternity – and in the trinity of the sea, the earth and the sky – our negligence seems almost laughable.

As if they really could have gone on living. As if not even their deaths would carry sufficient weight and meaning. But I have made up my mind and will carry out what has been decided. Actions must have consequences, otherwise creation goes off the rails. Decisions must be acted on, and once made they no longer need to be questioned. Carving these thin lines of order into the chaos is all we are capable of, and our whole duty as moral individuals resides there.

And they deserve it. The gods must know that they deserve it.

The first thing that strikes me, beyond that, is my own naivety. How little I understood that first evening. Those six people in their houses on the beach. I could have packed my rucksack and left that flat strip of coast the very next day; had I done so, everything would have been so different.

Or perhaps I never had a choice. It is interesting, of course, that I had that thought at the restaurant in Bénodet. *Kill everybody at this table and leave.* Even then, right at the start, there was something in me that realized what was going to happen many years later.

I have decided who has to be first. The order itself is not unimportant.

24 JULY – 1 AUGUST 2007

1

Detective Inspector Gunnar Barbarotti hesitated for a moment. Then he engaged the seven-lever lock.

This was not routine. Sometimes he didn't bother locking the door at all. If they want to get in, they'll do it somehow, was his way of thinking, so there's no point forcing them to do a lot of damage.

Perhaps thoughts of that kind bore witness to a kind of defeatism, perhaps they bore witness to a lack of faith in the group of professionals he himself represented; he fancied neither of those suggestions was particularly incompatible with his take on the world. Better a realist than a fundamentalist, after all, but there were no ready indications to point in either one direction or the other.

Such were his thoughts – and he wondered at the same time how the matter of locking a door could give rise to so much porous theorizing.

But perhaps there was no harm in having an active brain in the mornings? And in any case, since moving into his poky little flat on Baldersgatan in Kymlinge after his divorce five and a half years ago, he had never had any uninvited visitors – apart perhaps from a dodgy school friend or two brought home by his daughter Sara. We ought to think the best of our fellow human beings until they prove the opposite; this was the guiding principle that his optimist of a mother had tried to get into his head from when he first became amenable to persuasion, and as a rule to live by it was as good as any other.

And anyway, it would take a peculiarly dense burglar to think such a basic mahogany-laminate door as his could conceal anything worth stealing and selling. That was just being realistic.

But this time, he double-locked it. He had his reasons. The flat would be standing empty for ten days. Neither he nor his daughter would set foot there. Not that Sara had done so for over a month; with her school-leaving exams out of the way at the start of June, she had taken herself off to London and started a job in a boutique – or possibly a pub, but if so she was keeping it quiet so as not to worry her dad needlessly – and that was the way it was.

She was nineteen, and the sense of losing a limb when she departed was slowly starting to fade. Extremely slowly. The thought that in all likelihood they would never live under the same roof again was boring its way into his paternal heart at about the same pace.

But to everything there is a season, thought Gunnar Barbarotti stoically, shoving his keys into the pocket of his jeans. And a time for every purpose under the sun.

A time to live together, a time to part and a time to die.

He had started reading the Bible about six months before, on the advice of God the Father himself, and it was striking how often words and verses popped into his head. Even if You don't actually exist, dear Lord, he would think, one has to admit that the Holy Scriptures make a damn good read. Parts of them, at any rate.

And our Lord would agree with him.

Barbarotti took his soft-sided suitcase in one hand and a bin bag in the other and started down the stairs. He felt a sudden happiness spreading through him. There was something about walking downstairs, he had often thought, making your way at a decent pace down a pleasantly curved staircase – on your way out into the swarming diversity of the world. The true core of life was movement, wasn't that so? Just this sort of sweeping, effortless movement? Adventure waiting round the corner? And on this particular day, the windows on the stairs were open, high summer was streaming in, the scent of newly mown grass tickled his nostrils and the happy laughter of children could be heard from down in the courtyard.

A girl screaming like a stuck pig, too, but there was no need to listen to everything you heard.

The postman must have been a tango dancer in his spare time, for it was only an elegantly executed back step that preserved him from the swipe of the suitcase.

'Oops. Off on your travels?'

'Sorry,' said Gunnar Barbarotti. 'Going a bit too fast . . . yes I am, as it happens.'

'Abroad?'

'No, I'm making do with Gotland this time.'

'No point leaving Sweden at this time of year,' declared the unexpectedly chatty postman, waving towards the open window. 'Do you want today's haul or shall I put it through your door so you don't have to worry about it for a while?'

Gunnar Barbarotti thought for a moment.

'Let's have it. But no junk mail.'

The postman nodded, leafed through his pile and handed over three letters. Barbarotti took them and jammed them into the outside pocket of his case. Wished the postman a good summer and carried on at a rather more sedate pace down to ground level.

'Gotland's a real gem,' the postman called after him. 'More hours of sunshine than anywhere in Sweden.'

Hours of sunshine, thought Gunnar Barbarotti once he had left Kymlinge behind him and got the temperature in the car down to twenty-five degrees. Well, I've nothing against sunshine, but if it rains for ten days solid, I shan't be too upset about that, either.

Because it was a different kind of warmth he had in prospect, but the postman couldn't know that of course . . . *If two lie together, then they have heat: but how can one be warm alone?*

Lots of Ecclesiastes today, noted Gunnar Barbarotti with a quick glance at the time. It was only twenty to eleven; the postman had come unusually early, so perhaps he was off for a dip that afternoon. Barbarotti liked the idea of him doing that. At Kymmen or Borgasjön. In fact, he wanted everybody to do whatever they felt like today. He really did. A sigh of pleasure escaped him. That was how sighs ought to be, he suddenly realized. No need to give them actively, they should simply escape. That ought to be in Ecclesiastes, too.

He looked at his face in the rear-view mirror and saw he was smiling. He looked unshaven and a bit tousled, but the smile split his face virtually from ear to ear.

And why shouldn't he smile? The ferry from Nynäshamn was due to leave at five, the roads seemed as empty of cars as the sky was empty of clouds, and it was the first day of a long-anticipated trip. He put his foot on the gas, slotted a Lucilia do Carmo album into the CD player and thought what a joy it was to be alive.

Then he started thinking about Marianne.

Then he thought that really, these were one and the same thing.

They had known each other for almost a year. With a vague sense that time must be out of kilter, he reminded himself it really was no longer than that. They had met on the Greek island of Thasos last summer in optimally favourable circumstances – freedom, no responsibilities, an unfamiliar setting, velvet nights, the convenient time of the menstrual cycle, and a warm Mediterranean Sea – but it had gone further than a mere holiday romance. I'm not the type for holiday romances, Marianne had declared after their first evening. Nor me, he had admitted. Don't even know how they work, because when I stare into a woman's eyes I generally want to marry her, as well.

Marianne thought that sounded extremely solid and dependable. So they had carried on seeing each other once they were back on home ground. At regular intervals; two middle-aged, single-parent planets, that was how he visualized them, slowly and inexorably gravitating towards one another. Perhaps that was the way it had to look. The way you had to proceed, delicately but relentlessly building a bridge that was equal parts bravery and caution. Marianne lived in Helsingborg and had two teenage children, while he lived about 250 kilometres north of there – in Kymlinge – and had a daughter who had just flown the nest, plus two sons living beyond the borders of Sweden. So it could be contended that this was going to be quite a long bridge.

He felt suddenly downcast at the thought of Lars and Martin. His boys. They lived with their mother outside Copenhagen these days. He had spent two weeks with them at the start of the summer and possibly had one more to look forward to in August – but he could not escape his sense of gradually losing them. Their second replacement father was called Torben or something like that and he ran a yoga institute on Vesterbro; Barbarotti had never met him, but the indications were that he was a slight improvement on his predecessor. The latter had been a paragon of manly virtues until the day he became seriously unhinged and made off with a belly-dancing bombshell from the Ivory Coast.

What did I tell you, Barbarotti had thought at the time, but even then it had felt like a stale sort of satisfaction, well past its sell-by date.

And Lars and Martin had not seemed particularly upset by the prospect of living in Denmark, with the best will in the world he couldn't claim that. The question was, rather, why occasionally – in one of the most sordid recesses of his brain – he even *wanted* them to be unhappy there. Would his Cold War with Helena never end? Would he be hoisting faded, deranged 'I told you so' banners for all eternity?

It's my responsibility to make *them* happy, she was always insisting, not *you*. That's a thing of the past.

In another recess of his mind, he knew she was right. After the divorce, Sara had elected to live with him, and she was the one he was missing now. Not his ex-wife, nor his sons, either, if he was honest. Sara had saved him from the demons of loneliness for five years; it made it all the harder now, when she had left him and launched herself out into the world.

Instead, Marianne had come along. Gunnar Barbarotti was well aware that he had his lucky stars to thank for this – or possibly the potentially existent God, with whom he was in the habit of striking gentlemanly bargains.

I hope she understands what a void she's got to fill, he thought. Or maybe it would be best for her not to understand, he corrected himself a few moments later. Not all women were wildly enthusiastic about pandering to needy middle-aged men. Not in the long term, at any rate.

He realized his spirits were sinking – and that it was going to be bloody hard to keep his nose above water – and so, seeing a red light start to wink on the dashboard at that moment, he turned into the Statoil garage which presented itself so opportunely.

Petrol and coffee. To everything there is a season.

The ferry to Gotland was not as packed as he had feared.

Perhaps it was because it was Tuesday. Midweek. The wretched summer holiday invasion from the capital was concentrated at the weekends, presumably. Gunnar Barbarotti was grateful not to be spending his ten days with Marianne in Visby itself. He remembered with some distaste a week at the end of his marriage, when he and Helena had rented a shockingly expensive holiday apartment within the old town walls, at about this time of year. It had felt like staying in the middle of a malfunctioning amusement park. Yelling and puking and copulating young people in every little alleyway, impossible to get a wink of sleep before three in the morning. Christ Almighty, had been Gunnar Barbarotti's reaction at the time, if this is what they call vital tourist business they might just as well convert the royal palace in Stockholm into a bierkeller and brothel. Then they won't have to bother catching the ferry.

Their feeling of powerlessness had naturally been compounded by having three children to look after, and by the fact that the marriage was on its last legs. He remembered they had each given the other an evening to go out and do their own thing; Helena had gone first and come back at four in the morning, looking pretty pleased with herself. Not wanting to be outdone, he had spent the following night sitting alone on the beach down at Norderstrand with a carrier bag of beer, staying out until half past four.

But to be fair, as he walked home through the ruins and roses that morning, the town had looked beautiful, even he could see that. Bloody beautiful.

When Marianne had asked if he knew Gotland, he had limited himself to telling her about a couple of visits in his youth – Fårö island and Katthammarsvik – and not mentioned that awful week in Visby.

But this time he was going to Hogrän. The name meant 'tall fir tree', she had told him; it was a tiny village in the middle of Gotland, not much more than a crossroads and a church, but that was where Marianne and her sisters had a house. They had inherited it from the previous generation; a rather difficult brother had been bought out and the place was guaranteed to be free of any kind of troublesome tourism.

Because it was over ten kilometres from the sea, she had explained, the nearest bathing beach was at Tofta; the children generally cycled there a couple of times a week, but she didn't often go with them. And for the next few days, he was guaranteed an entirely child-free zone.

Peaceful is such an over-used expression, she said. That's a shame, because peacefulness is the very essence of Gustabo.

Gustaf, after whom the place was named, had built the whitewashed house some time in the mid-nineteenth century – and when Marianne's father bought it in the early fifties, the thing that apparently appealed to him most of all was its name. He had been a Gustaf, too, and the last five years of his life – after his wife died – had largely been spent there. Gustaf at Gustabo, Gustaf's Rest.

The bare necessities of life were all provided. Water, electricity and radio. But no TV and no telephone. You're not to bring your mobile, Marianne had instructed him. Give your children my neighbour's number, the farmer next door, that'll do fine. You're not meant to have the roar of the world in your ears when you're at Gustabo. Even my kids have learnt to accept that.

We usually listen to the shipping forecast and Poem of the Day, she added, they like that. Johan even drew his own map of Sweden with all the lighthouses marked on it.

He had done as she asked. Switched off his mobile phone and left it under a pile of papers in the glove compartment. If they were going to steal the car they might just as well have the phone too, he thought, and there was no seven-lever lock on either of them.

As the ferry drew close to the island, he went up on deck and watched the well-known silhouette of the historic town glowing in the final rays of the setting sun. Roofs, turrets and towers. It was so beautiful it almost hurt. He thought of something a good friend had once said: Gotland isn't just an island, it's another country.

I hope she's waiting there like she promised, he thought next. Wouldn't be much fun having to hunt for a telephone box and ring that farmer.

Did telephone boxes still exist?

She was waiting.

Suntanned and gorgeous. A woman like that can't be

waiting for a man like me, he thought. There must be some mistake.

But she threw her arms round his neck and kissed him, so presumably he *was* part of the plan, after all.

'God, you're beautiful,' he said. 'You mustn't kiss me again or I might faint.'

'I'll have to see if I can restrain myself,' she replied with a laugh. 'There's a kind of . . .'

'Yes?'

'A kind of . . . grandeur to all this. Coming to meet a man you love on a glorious summer evening. A man arriving by boat.'

'Mmm,' mumbled Gunnar Barbarotti. 'Though I know something even better.'

'And what's that?'

'Coming by boat and being met by a woman I love. Yes, you're right, it's pretty grand. We ought to do it every evening.'

'And how nice to have reached an age where one has time to stop and appreciate it, too.'

'Exactly.'

Gunnar Barbarotti laughed. Marianne laughed. Then they lapsed into silence and just looked at each other for a while, and he felt a lump start to form at the back of his throat. He dispelled it with a cough and blinked a couple of times.

'Bloody hell, I'm so glad I met you. Here, I've brought you a present.'

He fished out the little box that held the item of jewellery he had bought. Nothing special, a small orangey-red stone on a gold chain, that was all, but she immediately opened the clasp with eager fingers and put it round her neck.

'Thank you. I've got something for you as well, but that can wait until we get home.'

Home, eh? thought Gunnar Barbarotti. She sounded as if she meant it.

'Shall we go then?'

'Where's your car?'

'Out here in the car park, of course.'

'Right. Take me to the end of the world.'

And let me stay there until the end of time, he added silently to himself. Evenings like this could make poets out of pig dealers.

Gustabo was in the middle of nowhere. That was how it felt, at any rate, when you arrived as it began to get dark. Gunnar Barbarotti knew he would not have been able to find the way by himself. Possibly back to Visby, but not in this direction. As Marianne turned in through an opening in a stone wall after barely half an hour's drive, he experienced the pleasant sensation of not having a clue where in the world he was. She stopped beside a hedge of lilacs and they got out of the car. An outdoor wall lamp lit up the gable end of the white stone house, translucent summer darkness had started to fall on the stretch of grass with its few gnarled fruit trees and cluster of currant bushes, and the silence was almost as tangible as a living creature.

'Welcome to Gustabo,' said Marianne. 'Well, this is it.'

At that moment, a church bell struck, twice. Gunnar Barbarotti glanced at his watch. Half past nine. Then he turned his head in the direction in which Marianne was pointing.

'The church in the middle of the village. And we're next door to the churchyard. That doesn't bother you, I hope?'

Gunnar Barbarotti put his arm round her shoulder.

'And there are the cows.'

She pointed again and he noticed them, just a few metres away. Heavy, ruminating silhouettes on the other side of the garden wall.

'They're out in the field night and day at this time of year. The farmer goes out there to milk them rather than bringing them in. We've got our four points of the compass here. The church is to the east and the cows graze to the north. To the west we've got the yellowest field of rape in the whole world, and to the south there's the forest.

'Forest?' said Gunnar Barbarotti, looking round. 'You call that a forest?'

'Sixty-eight broadleaf trees,' clarified Marianne. 'Oak and beech and Norway maple. Finest hardwood, and most of them over a century old. Right, we'd better go in. I hope you kept your promise.'

'What promise?'

'Not to stuff yourself with food on the ferry. I've put something in the oven and opened a bottle of wine to let it breathe.'

'I didn't have so much as a jelly baby,' Gunnar Barbarotti assured her.

He awoke to see soft dawn light filtering through the thin curtains. They were moving gently in a slight breeze and a concentrated scent of summer morning wafted in through the open window. He turned his head and looked at Marianne, who was fast asleep on her stomach at his side, her naked back bare and her mass of chestnut-brown hair spreading across the pillow as if a fan had been casually opened and thrown down. He felt around on the bedside table until he found his watch.

Half past four.

He remembered looking at it when they had finished making love. Quarter past three.

So it was hardly time to get up and tackle the new day.

But nor was it a moment for just closing his eyes again, he thought. He turned back the sheet, got carefully out of bed and made his way to the kitchen. Took a couple of gulps of water straight from the tap.

Might as well pee while he was up and about, he decided, and continued into the garden. He stopped for a moment and happily wiggled his toes in the dewy grass. So here I am now, he thought. Stark naked, here and now. In the summer night at Gustabo. Things will never be better than this.

It had that grandeur to it. Even more so than arriving on the boat, and he determined never to forget this moment. He watched the pink dawn over the churchyard for a while, then ambled over to the broadleaved woods to relieve himself. He ducked his head as a bat zipped past. He was surprised; surely bats only flew at dusk?

He followed the stone wall and paused at the other points of the compass.

The cows. The field of rape.

He gave a shiver and went back indoors. Looked about him at the stylish simplicity of the place. Whitewash and brown wood, nothing more. His eye fell on his case, standing behind the kitchen settle, still not unpacked. There was something white protruding from the side pocket. He went round the kitchen table and saw that it was the three letters he had taken from the chatty postman as he was leaving home yesterday. He pulled them out and inspected them. Two looked like bills, one from the phone company, the other from his insurance firm. He stuffed them back in the pocket.

The third letter was handwritten. His name and address in black, written in scruffy, angular capital letters. There was no sender address. A stamp with a sailing boat.

He hesitated for a second. Then he took a knife from the knife block on the draining board and slit open the envelope. He took out a folded sheet of paper, opened it and read.

GOING TO KILL ERIK BERGMAN.
LET'S SEE IF YOU CAN STOP ME.

From the bedroom he heard Marianne mutter something in her sleep. He stared at the message.

The serpent in Paradise, he thought.

2

'What do you mean?' said Marianne.

'Exactly what I say,' replied Gunnar Barbarotti. 'I've had a letter.'

'Here? A letter came here?'

It was the morning of the second day. They were sitting in deckchairs under a sun umbrella looking out over the field of yellow rape. The sky was blue. Swallows were darting and bumblebees were buzzing; they had just finished breakfast, refilled their cups, and the only thing happening was digestion.

Plus this conversation. He wondered why he had brought it up. He was already regretting it.

'No, it came just as I was leaving home yesterday. I shoved it in the side pocket of my case. But then I opened it, this morning.'

'A threat, you say?'

'In a way.'

'Can I see?'

He pondered the fingerprint aspect for a moment but decided he was on holiday and went inside to get the letter.

She read it with one eyebrow raised, the other lowered; he had never seen her with that expression before, but realized it signalled a combination of surprise and concentration. It looked really rather elegant, he couldn't help noticing. She looked elegant in every way, when he came to think about it; apart from a battered old straw hat with a wide brim, she was wearing only a thin, almost transparent garment that hid little more than the glass in an aquarium.

Linen, if he was not mistaken.

'Do you often get letters like this?'

'No, never.'

'So it's not routine for a police officer?'

'Not in my experience, at any rate.'

'And who's Erik Bergman?'

'No idea.'

'You're sure?'

He shrugged. 'Nobody I can bring to mind, anyway. But it isn't a particularly uncommon name.'

'And you don't know who could have sent it?'

'No.'

She picked up the envelope and studied it. 'The postmark's illegible.'

'More or less. I think it ends in "org" but it's not at all clear.'

She nodded. 'Why send it to you, then? I mean, this must be some kind of lunatic, but why would he send it to you in particular?'

Gunnar Barbarotti sighed. 'Marianne, it's like I said. I really have no idea.'

He waved away a fly, regretting again that he had ever mentioned the letter. It was idiotic having to sit here on such a perfect morning and talk about police business.

But it wasn't police business, hadn't he just decided? Merely a momentary source of irritation . . . not worthy of any more attention than the fly he had just batted away.

'But you must have some kind of . . . what's it called? . . .

intuition? How long have you been a policeman? Twenty years?'

'Nineteen.'

'Oh yes, that's right, we talked about it, the same length of time as I've been a midwife. But there is a kind of instinctive sense you develop over the years, isn't there? I think I have, anyway.'

Barbarotti drank some of his coffee and thought about it. 'Sometimes, perhaps. But not where this is concerned, I'm afraid. It's been going round in my head all morning and not the least little idea has occurred to me.'

'But it's addressed to you. To your home address.'

'Yes.'

'Not to the police station. But surely that must mean he . . . or she . . . has some particular relationship to you?'

'Relationship is taking it a bit far. It only means he knows who I am . . . or she. Now let's talk about something else, I'm sorry I brought it up.'

Marianne put the envelope down on the table and leant back in her chair. 'What do you think, then?'

She evidently did not give up that easily.

'About what?'

'The letter, of course. The threat. Is it serious?'

'Presumably not.'

She pushed the straw hat right back and raised both eyebrows. 'How can you say that?'

He sighed again. 'Because we get a lot of anonymous letters. They're nearly all fakes.'

'I thought the police had a duty to treat everything seriously. If there's a bomb threat to a school, say, then I assume you have to . . . ?'

'We *do* treat everything seriously. There really isn't much we leave to chance. But you asked me if I thought this was meant seriously. That's another matter.'

'OK, sheriff. See your point. So you think this one is just a hoax?'

'Yes.'

'Why?'

Good question, thought Gunnar Barbarotti. Bloody good question. Because . . . because I want it to be a hoax, of course. Here I am in the paradise of Gustabo with a woman I'm pretty sure I love, and I don't want to be disturbed by some cretin who's planning to kill some other cretin. And if it does turn out to be genuine, then I . . . well, I want to be able to say I didn't open the letter until I got home from my stay in paradise.

'You're not answering,' she observed.

'Ahem,' said Gunnar Barbarotti. 'The fact is, I don't know. You can never say never, of course. Let's leave this for now.'

She leant forward and glared at him. 'What rubbish is that? Leave it? You've surely got to take some kind of action? Are you a detective inspector, or aren't you?'

'I'm on holiday in seventh heaven,' Gunnar Barbarotti reminded her.

'Me too,' countered Marianne. 'But if a pregnant woman arrived in seventh heaven and wanted to give birth to her baby, I would deliver it. You get me?'

'Smart,' said Gunnar Barbarotti.

'One–nil to the midwife,' said Marianne with a broad smile. 'Thanks for last night, by the way. I love making love with you.'

'There were a few seconds when I really thought I could

fly,' admitted Gunnar Barbarotti. 'But what an idiot I was to open this letter. Can't we agree to forget it, and I'll pretend to find it when I get home?'

'Not on your life. What if Erik Bergman's been murdered when you get back to Kymlinge, how could you live with that? I thought I'd met a man with morals and a heart.'

Gunnar Barbarotti gave in. He took off his sunglasses and regarded her gravely. 'All right,' he said. 'So what do you suggest?'

'You want *me* to suggest something?'

'Why not? Why shouldn't we have a bit of a job swap while we're on holiday?'

She laughed. 'So you'll look after all the pregnant women in seventh heaven?'

'Of course.'

'Were you there when your children were born?'

'All three.'

'She nodded. 'OK then. I only wanted to be sure no babies' lives would be put at risk. As I see it, there are two alternatives.'

'And they are?'

'Either we take this to the police in Visby . . .'

'I don't want to go to Visby. What's the alternative?'

'We ring your colleagues in Kymlinge.'

'Not a bad idea,' said Gunnar Barbarotti. 'But there's just one catch.'

'Oh yes?'

'We haven't got a phone.'

'We can get round that. We'll go and see the farmer and I'll introduce you. His name's Jonsson, by the way. Hagmund Jonsson.'

'Hagmund?'

'Yes. His father was called Hagmund too. And his grandfather.'

Gunnar Barbarotti nodded and scratched his stubble. 'Can I suggest something, in that case?' he said.

'What?'

'That you put on something a bit more substantial than that see-through handkerchief, otherwise Hagmund the Third's going to have a fit.'

She laughed. 'But *you* like it?'

'I like it very much. It somehow makes you look more than naked.'

'Grr,' said Marianne, forty-two-year-old midwife from Helsingborg. 'I suggest we go in for a while first. I've a feeling Hagmund won't be home for an hour or so.'

'Grrr,' said Gunnar Barbarotti, forty-seven-year-old detective inspector from Kymlinge. 'I think this rape field must be some kind of aphro . . . what's the word? . . . aphrodisiac.'

'Yes, that's the word,' confirmed the midwife. 'But it's not the field, you dolt, it's me.'

'Yup, you're totally right there,' said Gunnar Barbarotti.

Although an hour and a half went by before they made it across the road to the Jonssons', Hagmund turned out not to be at home. But his wife was there. She was around sixty-five, a stout little woman by the name of Jolanda. Gunnar Barbarotti wondered whether her mother and grandmother could possibly also have been called Jolanda, but he didn't dare ask.

At any event, the cheery woman refused to let them use the phone before she had plied them with coffee, saffron pancakes and eleven kinds of cake and biscuit – so it was not until after two that Barbarotti finally got through to Kymlinge police station.

As luck would have it, Detective Inspector Eva Backman was nesting on a ton of paper in her office. He was put through to her and set out his business in scarcely over thirty seconds.

'Fuck,' said Eva Backman. 'I'll take this through to the chief inspector and propose you break off your holiday and get straight back to work. It sounds serious.'

'You can consider our friendship terminated,' said Barbarotti. 'Holidays are no joking matter.'

Eva Backman roared with laughter. 'Fair enough. What do you want me to do, then?'

'I've no idea,' said Gunnar Barbarotti. 'I'm on leave. Just wanted to report a threatening anonymous letter like the responsible citizen I am.'

'Bravo, inspector,' said Eva Backman. 'I give in. Can you read out what it says again?'

'Going to kill Erik Bergman,' Barbarotti said obediently. 'Let's see if you can stop me.'

'So it's "you", singular?'

'Yes.'

'Handwritten?'

'Yes.'

'Addressed to you in person?'

'Yes.'

'Hmm, can you fax it over?'

'I'm at Gustabo,' said Gunnar Barbarotti. 'There's no fax here.'

'Go to Visby then.'

Gunnar Barbarotti hastily conferred with himself. 'Tomorrow, maybe.'

'OK,' said Eva Backman. 'So what's it all about, does he mean any particular Erik Bergman?'

'Search me. I don't know any Erik Bergman. Do you?'

'Don't think so,' said Eva Backman. 'Well I suppose I can check how many there are here in Kymlinge, for starters. Does it tell us anything about where in town the prospective corpse might happen to live?'

'All it tells us is what I read out just now.'

'I see,' said Eva Backman. 'All right then, if you fax it over tomorrow – including the address on the envelope – we'll see what we can do.'

'Fine.'

'In the meantime, you can put the original in a plastic bag and send it to us . . . I'll sort out this bit of unpleasantness for you, Mister Responsible Citizen. How's Marianne?'

'She's great. She's here with me now.'

Eva Backman laughed again. 'Glad to hear the two of you are enjoying yourselves. It's raining here. How is it . . . ?'

'Not a cloud in the sky,' said Gunnar Barbarotti. 'Right, I'll leave this in your capable hands and see you in a fortnight.'

'I wouldn't bank on it,' said Eva Backman. 'I'll be on holiday by then.'

'Bother.'

'These things happen. Incidentally, if I find there's a whole gang of Erik Bergmans, it wouldn't actually be a bad idea for you to look through them. Just in case you know any of them after all . . . would that be OK?'

'If it's not too long a list.'

'Thank you, constable. Where shall I send it?'

'Hang on.'

He put down the receiver on a bureau that boasted several

framed photographs and silver pots and returned to Jolanda and Marianne on the terrace. 'Excuse me, what's Gustabo's postal address?'

'Gustabo, Hogrän, Gotland, usually works fine,' said Marianne. Barbarotti thanked her and went back to the phone.

'You can fax the list to the police in Visby,' he said. 'And I'll do my faxing from there as well. I'm going to count this as eight hours' overtime.'

'You do that,' said Eva Backman. 'Kiss kiss, inspector, and regards to Marianne.'

Good, thought Gunnar Barbarotti, and felt the stirrings of indigestion from all the biscuits. That's that out of the way.

On their way out they bumped into Hagmund Jonsson. He was a man of around seventy, as tall and spare as his wife was small and roly-poly.

'Well well, so Marianne has got herself a man,' he said. 'And not a day too soon. So now you'll be living in the time of expectations as yet unfulfilled?'

This last sentence, delivered in a broad Gotland accent, had the ring of a Biblical quotation, thought Gunnar Barbarotti. *The time of expectations as yet unfulfilled?* They shook hands.

'It's like being back in childhood, isn't it?' Hagmund went on without pausing for an answer. 'The world and our lives are full of imprecise promises, of scents and premonitions we still haven't fully explored. Once we do, it leaves us empty. *Omne animal post coitum triste est*. So then we have to invent new expectations. And take our time in fulfilling them.'

'Never a truer word spoken,' said Marianne, pulling Gunnar Barbarotti out through the gate.

'Hagmund's a philosopher,' she explained once they were

out in the road. 'If you get caught in one of his conversations it can take several hours to wriggle free. What was that bit in Latin?'

'I'm not sure,' Gunnar Barbarotti had to admit. 'Something about feeling melancholy after making love, I think.'

Marianne frowned. 'I think that applies mainly to men,' she said. 'But they're happy people, Hagmund and Jolanda Jonsson. They've signed up for the first package holiday in space.'

Gunnar Barbarotti nodded.

'To prolong the sense of expectation?'

'I assume so. He's built his own telescope, too, out in the barn. It's a world-class one, apparently, but nobody's seen it since the newspaper sent someone round a few years ago. He doesn't let anybody in.'

'And how do you know they're happy?'

She sighed. 'You're right,' she said. 'I can't really know, of course. But it's important for me to imagine that they are.'

'In that case I'll agree with you,' said Gunnar Barbarotti. 'What shall we do now?'

'Are you already tired of sitting still in Paradise?'

'We can't make love more than two or three times a day. Not at our age.'

She laughed. 'No, you're right. I don't want you to get too melancholy. How about a longish cycle ride?'

Gunnar Barbarotti looked up at the clear blue sky and sniffed the wind. 'Why not?' he said. 'I'd sooner that than a space trip, at any rate.'

3

'What made you join the police? I don't think you've ever told me.'

'That's because you've never asked.'

'Fair enough. But I'm asking now. What made you join the police?'

'I don't really know.'

'Thanks. That's about what I thought.'

'What makes you say that?'

'Because men have this way of never knowing why things happen in their lives.'

'Damn cheek. How many men did you study to deduce that?'

'You're number two. Or perhaps number two and a half, though I never quite knew what to make of that physics teacher. But you've got to admit I'm right.'

They were lying on their backs under an oak by an old limestone church. It was four in the afternoon. The air temperature was about twenty-five degrees and they had been on their bikes for around two hours. Along pastoral highways and byways through the verdant countryside of high summer. Dry-stone walls, cornflowers and poppies. Low whitewashed buildings with climbing roses and Virginia creeper rambling over them. Black-and-white cows, larks high in the sky, indolent summer

Gotlanders snoring in hammocks, and little shops and stalls selling saffron ice cream and coffee to passing cyclists. Gunnar Barbarotti had no idea where they were in relation to Gustabo. And nothing could have worried him less.

'Things were more or less as they are now,' he said.

'Pardon?'

'When I decided to join the police.'

'How do you mean?'

'I had a sore bum. But not saddle sore in that instance. I'd been sitting on it for five years while I was studying.'

'Law at Lund?'

'Yes. I realized I'd have to sit on it for another forty years if I became a lawyer. A police job sounded a bit more mobile.'

'Fresh air and comradeship?'

'Exactly. A decent pension if you happen to get prematurely shot.'

'But were you right then? About being more mobile, I mean.'

Gunnar Barbarotti took a drink from his bottle of Loka mineral water and thought about it.

'Well, there's a fair amount of moving from chair to chair.'

She laughed and stretched her feet up towards the leafy crown of the oak. She wiggled her toes pleasurably. 'You could do what I do,' she suggested.

'And what's that?'

'Take away the chairs. I spend nearly all day on my feet.'

'Hmm,' said Gunnar Barbarotti. 'And you knew you wanted to be a midwife before you even left upper secondary, you say?'

'Earlier than that,' Marianne corrected him. 'We had a midwife from the hospital come to tell us about her job. I made up my mind the very same day.'

'And you've never regretted it?'

'Sometimes, when things go wrong. But it passes, and we know it's all part of the deal. No, I've never had serious regrets. It feels such a privilege to be there when life starts, and it never feels routine. They generally let me off the abortions, I'm glad to say. They're the hardest thing.'

Gunnar Barbarotti clasped his hands behind his neck. 'If a police officer had come to my school and told us what the job entailed, I'd definitely have chosen something else instead,' he declared. 'But you're right about it being a good thing that questions of life and death never become routine.'

'So what would you *really* like to do, then?'

He lay there for a while, listening to the drone of the bees. Gave the question due consideration.

'Don't know. I suspect I'm too old to train for anything else. So they'll have to put up with me. Though I could imagine myself as a country bus driver in these parts.'

'Bus driver?'

'Yes. In my very own yellow country bus with about eleven passengers a day on average. One morning service and one in the afternoon. Coffee from a thermos flask at the end of the route, in a ditch full of meadow flowers . . . well, something along those lines.'

Marianne stroked his cheek with her fingertips. 'You poor, worn-out middle-aged man,' she said. 'Perhaps you ought to apprentice yourself to Hagmund for a few days?'

'Not a bad idea,' mumbled Gunnar Barbarotti. 'Do you know if they need a farm hand?'

He was suddenly aware of how tired he actually felt. All at once it was virtually impossible to keep his eyes open; the deep green foliage of the oak, whispering in the light breeze, was clearly trying to lull him to sleep.

And Marianne's hand, which had now come to rest on his chest, was encouraging him gently but relentlessly in the same direction. He had not had much sleep last night, he realized, so it wasn't . . . it really wasn't anything to do with middle age, just to make that quite clear before he dozed off.

'That letter,' was the last thing he heard her say. 'You've got to admit it's rather horrible? Are you asleep?'

He dreamt about Chief Inspector Asunander.

As far as he could recall, he had never done that before, and he didn't really see why he was doing so now. Asunander looked exactly the same as usual. His eyes were close-set, he was small, dapper and bloody-minded, and the only slightly odd thing was that he had a riding crop in one hand and a torch in the other. He was angry, too, and walking round inside a big house, which at times seemed utterly strange to Barbarotti, at others entirely familiar – and in the latter case bore more than a passing resemblance to the police headquarters at Kymlinge. At any event, Asunander was clearly searching for something; there were plenty of dark nooks and crannies, which must be why he was equipped with the torch. It cast thin beams of light at distorted angles in the corridors that echoed to his footsteps, up grotesquely winding spiral staircases and through basement culverts dripping with moisture. Wasn't I lying under an oak tree in Gotland just now? The question ran through Barbarotti's head, and at that very instant he realized he was on his back in the dream, too, not in a peaceful country churchyard but under a bed in a dark room, a creaky old tubular metal bed with a horsehair mattress, and he . . . he was the one the chief inspector was hunting down. If he held his breath and strained his ears, he could hear the characteristic click of Asunander's dentures; he was very close now and Barbarotti knew the reason he himself was lurking under the bed was that he was guilty of gross neglect, having evaded his responsibilities, to put it simply, and now it was time for him to be held to account. Bloody hell, thought Gunnar Barbarotti, may the old git keel over with a blood clot or burn in . . . but then he changed tactics and sent up a hasty existence prayer to the other authority instead.

He was in the habit of doing this, though normally when he was awake. He had a so-called deal with Our Lord, in which Our Lord had to show his existence by heeding at least a reasonable proportion of the prayers his humble servant, Detective Inspector Barbarotti, sent up to him. Then points were awarded: plus points for Our Lord if Barbarotti's prayers were answered, minus if they were not. Just now, in this dream, at this moment beneath an oak in a Gotland churchyard in July 2007, God's existence was assured by an eleven-point margin, and that was the why and wherefore of the sudden offer of two points for not on any account letting the chief inspector discover his trembling subordinate under the bed, or under the oak, or wherever reality was currently being played out.

Dear God, it was only a little letter and I am on holiday, he quickly formulated his entreaty. After all, it can't really be that serious . . .

'I once knew a boy called Erik Bergman, in fact. It's coming back to me now.'

'What?'

He woke up. Opened his eyes and stared in surprise – and relief – at the shimmering green canopy of leaves. There was no Chief Inspector Asunander here. Just a midwife Marianne, lying there with her head on his chest. And the aforementioned oak, which was a distinct improvement. How long had he been asleep? Ten minutes? Or only one? Had she even noticed that he had dropped off? It didn't seem like it, she was still talking about that letter. No, perhaps he was just imagining he'd had a dream?

'I said I once knew a boy called Erik Bergman. What if he's the one who's going to die?'

Gunnar Barbarotti coughed to clear the sleep out of his throat and stretched his arms above his head.

'Of course it isn't. Was he a boyfriend of yours?'

'No, but we were in the same form at upper secondary. Not that he's at all likely to live in Kymlinge. That was it, wasn't it . . . this person whose life is in danger lives in Kymlinge?'

'Good grief, Marianne, how am I supposed to know? And nobody's going to lose their life at all. Let's not worry about this any more.'

She did not reply.

'It's only some nutcase. I'll go into Visby tomorrow and do my duty, but now I think my bum might fancy trying that saddle again. How about yours?'

'Never better. D'you want to have a feel?'

He glanced hastily round the churchyard, then did as invited. Just as she had said, it seemed to be in fine form. Phenomenally fine form, to be precise. It was enough to make a man lose his head.

'Right then,' she said, gently pushing away his hand. 'Let's go home and make some dinner.'

*

There were five individuals in Kymlinge who went by the name of Erik Bergman.

This could be seen from the list Gunnar Barbarotti received at the police station in Visby on the Thursday morning. The eldest of them was seventy-seven and the youngest three-and-a-half.

An acceptable name in every possible generation, it seemed. As he sat on a bench at the south gate of the old city walls, waiting for Marianne to finish shopping for some fresh vegetables, he went through all the potential murder victims.

The seventy-seven year old was a widower and lived at 6 Linderödsvägen. He had been a railway employee all his working life and had lived at the same address for the last forty years. He had no police record.

The second oldest was fifty-four and a relative newcomer to Kymlinge. He worked as a market analyst at Handelsbanken, and had been living at 10 Grenadjärsgatan with his second wife for the past two years. He had no criminal record either.

Barbarotti wondered if it was the wife or the address that was two years old. It wasn't entirely clear, but perhaps it was both.

Number three was a thirty-six year old living at 11 Hedeniusgatan. A single man, he owned and ran his own computer business, and had no skeletons in his cupboard as far as one could tell. Born and bred in Kymlinge, he had been active in the Kymlinge Badminton Club for several seasons, until a knee injury forced him to stop playing ten years ago, almost to the day.

Who the heck compiled this list, wondered Barbarotti. A ten-year-old knee injury? It must be Backman, having a laugh.

Erik Bergman number four was thirty-two years old. Like number two, he had recently moved to the town. A father of three with an address in Lyckebogatan, and a job at Kymlingevik school as one of the leaders at the after-school club. He did actually feature in police records, a single entry – the offence being an attack on an officer on the occasion of a football international at Råsunda stadium in 1996. In a state of extreme inebriation, he had shoved a hot dog complete with mustard, ketchup and gherkin into a policeman's face. He received a fine, which was only right.

Which left Erik Bergman aged three-and-a-half. No profession yet and no criminal record, but living with his single mother at 15 Molngatan.

Well there we have it, thought Gunnar Barbarotti, and yawned. So one of you is going to die, eh?

He had had a five-minute phone conversation with Backman while he was at the police station, too. Asked if they had taken any precautions.

Of course they had, Backman assured him. Asunander had taken the decision to have a radio patrol car drive past the various addresses twice a day to make sure there was no funny business going on. And incidentally, as far as they could gather, at least two of the Eriks were away on holiday. Numbers two and five.

But no warnings to those potentially at risk, Barbarotti had wanted to know.

No, Asunander had not judged it necessary. Just because you had a letter-writing numbskull to deal with, it didn't mean the police had to conduct themselves like numbskulls, he had pointed out. The cost of round-the-clock police protection was well known.

Once they had the actual letter in their hands, they would of course look into it more closely. And possibly arrive at a different judgement. Barbarotti had presumably put it in a plastic bag and sent it off as promised?

Gunnar Barbarotti confirmed this, then wished Backman a good week's work and hung up.

He folded up the list. Put it in his back pocket and thought he would probably have reached the same conclusion. He would not have taken more comprehensive steps either, if it had been his decision to make.

The fact that they were obliged to treat all threats as genuine was one thing. But it didn't mean you constantly had to pour in resources. Of course not. It was considerably cheaper in the long run to *take all developments seriously*, as politicians and diplomats had done since time immemorial. Internally, though never officially, the justification for this was that twenty out of twenty threats were false. The problem was when you got to the twenty-first.

That brought him to Marianne, the least and loveliest of all his problems. He hastily put all police matters out of his mind and went to meet her; it wasn't quite the same seeing her come out of the ICA supermarket with carrier bags as it was being met by her down at the harbour at sunset – but it was good enough. He felt his heart beating a little faster in his breast as she came into view.

I hope I shall be married to her, two years from now, he suddenly thought, and he wondered if it really was a thought or if it was just one of those constellations of words that the brain generated when it happened to be in action and the weather was good.

'How did it go?' she asked.

'Oh, splendidly,' he said. 'I've delegated the responsibility, so now I'm all yours.'

'Hah,' said Marianne. 'Do you want to carry both bags or just one?'

'Both, of course,' said Gunnar Barbarotti. 'Who do you take me for?'

4

'Are you reading the Bible?'

'Oh. I thought you were asleep.'

'I was. But when I sensed the bed was empty, I woke up.'

'Ah, I see. Yes, I read the Bible now and then.'

She closed the wine-coloured bible and put it down next to her teacup on the table. Leant back in her deckchair and squinted at him through half-closed eyes. It was Tuesday, the morning of the eighth day – that is, if you counted last Tuesday as the first day even though it was evening by the time they met up. But that was academic hair-splitting. Measuring time at Gustabo did not feel particularly important, thought Gunnar Barbarotti with a yawn, particularly time that had already passed.

Now, however, it was morning. The sky had started to clear after overnight rain and a thunderstorm they had watched and admired from the living room window. It had lasted from just after midnight until quarter past one, just over an hour, and the flashes of lightning across the rape field had been spectacular.

'So you . . . I mean, you believe there's a God?'

She nodded.

'You didn't tell me that.'

She laughed. Slightly uncomfortably, he felt.

'Well yes, I think of myself as a believer,' she said. 'But I don't exactly advertise the fact.'

'Why's that?'

'Because . . . because it embarrasses people. And I'm not a churchgoer. I don't like churches at all . . . not the actual buildings, that is, but the organized element. For me it's a private matter, if you see what I mean. A connection.'

He sat down in the deckchair opposite her.

'I understand. And I don't find it particularly embarrassing.'

'Are you sure?'

He thought about it.

'Yes, I really am.'

'But you don't believe in a god, I assume?'

'I wouldn't exactly say that.'

It was momentarily on the tip of his tongue to tell her the precise nature of his own relationship with God, but he decided to keep it to himself. They had known each other for nearly a year now – he and Marianne, that is, whereas he and Our Lord went back much further than that – but the time did not seem ripe for that kind of confidence. He was pretty sure God felt the same. They had a kind of . . . well, a kind of gentleman's agreement, to put it bluntly. A private matter, like she said.

'What does that mean?'

'What does what mean?'

'You said, "I wouldn't say that." What did you mean?'

'Just that I don't know. But I think about it now and then.'

She took off her sunglasses and gave him a look of slight concern.

'You think about it from time to time?'

'Hrrm, yes, that may not exactly sound . . . doesn't matter, anyway. But what about your own faith, then? Is it something you grew up with?'

She shook her head.

'Oh no. I'd probably have been kicked out of the house if I'd started on about religion. They were sort of Marxists, my parents, right into the eighties. My mother's dead now of course, but I'm blessed if Dad doesn't vote for the Left Party even now. Especially since Schyman bowed out, he rants on about her every time I see him.'

'And your faith?'

'Well, it kind of crept up on me, I suppose you could say. There's an old Persian poem that goes, "The victorious God treads gently in soft sandals of donkey skin", and that fits pretty well with my image of Him.'

'Soft sandals of donkey skin . . . ?' said Barbarotti.

'Yes. And it's to do with my job, of course . . . I need a centre of gravity. But it's a matter between Him and me, you see. I don't care about the facade, and sometimes I think . . .'

'Yes?'

'Sometimes I think it must be the Devil who invented religion, so it can put itself between human beings and God.'

'Did you think of that yourself?'

'No, I'm pretty sure I read it somewhere. But it doesn't make any difference, does it?'

'No. And the Quran and Buddha and Kabbalah?'

'A rose by any other name . . . Are you sure it doesn't bother you?'

'Doesn't bother me in the slightest,' Gunnar Barbarotti assured her. 'I detect some preconceptions about the spiritual qualifications of the Swedish police force. Anyway, you certainly don't need to read your Bible surreptitiously. I take the odd gander at it myself sometimes, too.'

She laughed and stretched her hands into the air. Palms upward. 'Take the odd gander at the Bible! Did you hear that, O Lord? What do You say to that?'

'I'm sure of one thing, though,' continued Barbarotti, in the grip of inspiration. 'And it's this: if He does exist, Our Lord, then he's a gentleman with a fine sense of humour. Anything else is out of the question. And he isn't all-powerful.'

Marianne grew serious again. She gave him a look that made him feel unaccountably breathless. Am I fourteen again, or what, he asked himself.

'You know something?' she said. 'When you say things like that, I almost think I love you.'

'It . . . it's a good job I'm sitting down,' he managed to croak, his tongue sticking to the roof of his mouth. 'Otherwise . . . well, otherwise I'd faint.'

At that moment they heard a cough and became aware of Hagmund Jonsson sauntering across the grass. He had a scythe over his shoulder and a dead rabbit in his hand.

'It never occurred to me that you'd netted a detective, Marianne. Congratulations. I never understand why they don't have the sense to jump out of the way of the scythe. Do you want it for your dinner?'

He waved the bloody rabbit.

'Thanks, but I don't think so,' said Marianne, averting her eyes.

'That wasn't my main reason for coming over,' Hagmund went on. 'My main reason is the detective. There's a telephone call for him. It sounded urgent.'

'Telephone?' said Gunnar Barbarotti.

Hagmund nodded and scratched the back of his neck. 'The lady and gentleman clearly decided to leave their mobile appliances on the mainland. That does you credit, without a doubt. But as I say, there's a rather eager female inspector on the line in my kitchen, and it might be an idea for him to come with me and talk to her. Sure you don't want this little chap?'

He dangled the rabbit in front of their eyes again. Marianne shook her head and Barbarotti got to his feet.

'I'm coming,' he said. 'Did they tell you what it was about?'

'Top secret,' declared Hagmund Jonsson. 'State security, most likely. I can't see them daring to shatter this idyll for anything less.'

He gave a knowing wink. Marianne wrapped her dressing gown more tightly round her and Gunnar Barbarotti followed the farmer out to the road.

'It seems your penfriend was serious after all.'

He didn't reply immediately. Fuck, he thought, I feared as much.

He gestured to Jolanda Jonsson to leave him on his own and close the kitchen door. And waited until she had done so. If they wanted to eavesdrop, then at least let them have the inconvenience of picking up a receiver in another room, thought Barbarotti.

'Are you still there?' Eva Backman asked.

'I'm still here,' Barbarotti confirmed. 'What did you say?'

'I assume you haven't forgotten the letter you got before you bunked off to Paradise?'

'No,' said Gunnar Barbarotti. 'How could I forget that? So tell me what's happened.'

She turned her head away to say something to a colleague, he couldn't make out what.

'Sorry. Yes, it's murder. A jogger found Erik Bergman's body out at Brönnsvik a couple of hours ago. The jogging track along by the river and up over the ridge, you know. He was out jogging too, it seems . . . Bergman, that is.'

'Are you having me on?' asked Barbarotti.

'No,' said Eva Backman. 'I'm not, unfortunately. There's a right old fuss here at the moment. What's more, the jogger who discovered the body happens to be a journalist by profession. Johannes Virtanen, if that name rings a bell?'

'I know who he is. But presumably the press don't know anything about the letter?'

'No, we've managed to keep that detail quiet for now.'

'Good. And which Erik Bergman are we talking about? I mean . . .'

'Oh yes, sorry,' said Eva Backman. 'Number three. The one with the knee injury and the IT company.'

'I see,' said Gunnar Barbarotti.

Which wasn't entirely true. He was keenly aware of a chugging in his brain, but it was more reminiscent of the engine of an old banger that was about to breathe its last than of any kind of thought process.

'Tell me everything,' he said, sinking down on a kitchen settle under a wall hanging bearing the artistically embroidered motto *Sufficient Unto the Day is the Evil Thereof.* Quite right, thought Gunnar Barbarotti. That's the way it is. And this day has scarcely even started.

'Found at 6.55 a.m.,' said Eva Backman. 'He was single, of course, but we talked to a guy who evidently knows him quite well. Andreas Grimle, he works at Bergman's company. Some kind of part-owner too, it seems. Anyway, he claims Bergman was in the habit of running that circuit two or three mornings a week. In summer, that is, before breakfast, between six and seven, roughly.'

'MO?' queried Barbarotti.

'Stabbing,' said Eva Backman. 'Sorry, didn't I say? Once in the back, a couple of times in the stomach plus a slash to the throat. He can't have survived for long. He was swimming in a pool of his own blood, more or less.'

'Sounds nice.'

'Certainly does.'

'Have you been there to take a look yourself?'

'Of course. Suppose we'll have to see what the crime scene investigators find, but we mustn't get our hopes up. The ground was dry and we know what that means. No footprints, no signs of a struggle, the murderer presumably leapt on him suddenly from behind.'

'But I thought he was running? Isn't it a bit hard to . . . ?'

'I don't know,' said Eva Backman. 'We'll have to think about that one. But he could have stopped him first . . . asked for help or something.'

'Could be,' said Gunnar Barbarotti. 'And who's been put in charge of the case?'

'Sylvenius is leading the preliminary investigation.'

'I mean the lead detective.'

'Who do you think?'

He didn't reply. He hardly felt he needed to.

'All right,' said Eva Backman. 'This is how things look. Asunander has left it in my competent hands for now. Though we've got everyone involved for the moment. Maximum show of strength. And I have a distinct feeling he's expecting you to step in tomorrow.'

'I'm on holiday.'

'If you resume your duties tomorrow instead of on Monday, you've got a week until the elk-hunting season.'

'I don't hunt.'

'I only meant it metaphorically.'

'I see. Was that the way Asunander put it?'

'No, it was just me, distilling the essence.'

'Thanks,' sighed Gunnar Barbarotti.

Eva Backman cleared her throat. 'I don't always agree with our dear chief inspector,' she said. 'You know that. But in this case I actually do. That was a personal letter to you. Not to me or Sorrysen or anybody else. It wasn't even addressed to police HQ. So it does . . . well, it does seem to be your pigeon. Though of course it'll be the whole group of us really. Like I said.'

Gunnar Barbarotti thought about this.

'Perhaps that's what he wants?'

'What?'

'The murderer. Wants it to be me taking charge of the investigation.'

'I've thought about that,' said Backman. 'Could be somebody you know, then?'

'Yes, but why?' said Barbarotti. 'Why should anyone be so bloody stupid that they'd expose themselves to the risk?'

'Stupid?' said Backman. 'I'm not so sure about that. More like cocky, I'd say. In any case, you'd probably better accept the challenge.'

Barbarotti thought about it for three seconds. He felt he had no choice.

'OK,' he said. 'You can tell Asunander I'll be there tomorrow morning. I think there's a ferry at five this afternoon, but if anybody pops up with a confession before that, I want you to let me know.'

'I've got a feeling that won't happen,' said Eva Backman. 'Unfortunately. And I'm sorry I had to break off your summer of love like this.'

'I shall be taking the other days I'm owed at a later date,' declared Inspector Barbarotti, and hung up.

In time for some elk hunting, maybe, he supplied silently.

What a morning, he thought, once he had left the Jonssons' farm and come back up to the road. It starts with Bible study and questions about the essential nature of God, then she says she almost loves me and I round off the whole thing with a bit of murder and elk hunting.

Marianne had few reproaches. Nor had he expected many from her.

'We had eight of our ten days,' she said when she had switched off the car engine in the car park at the ferry terminal. 'Perhaps that's all I can ask now I've fallen for a detective?'

'I shouldn't have opened that letter,' said Gunnar Barbarotti. 'If I hadn't found it until Friday, they couldn't have called me in.'

But he didn't know if he really meant that. It felt paradoxical, somehow; the notion that he was playing into the perpetrator's hands was hard to shake off. By opening the letter, reading its warning and passing it on. And then, by instantly leaping into the investigation? Wasn't that exactly what he – or she – wanted?

Why send a letter to say you intended killing somebody in the first place? Before you actually committed the act? Was there any significance to it? Or were they just dealing with a nutcase, someone it was a waste of time trying to understand in rational terms?

Impossible to know, thought Gunnar Barbarotti. No point speculating, not this early on.

But he knew one thing for certain: he had never experienced a case like this before. Come to think of it, he didn't think he had read about anything like it, either. The very fact of the perpetrator planning his deed was a rarity; the usual pattern was for one booze-fuelled party to lose his temper and make a fatal lunge at some other booze-fuelled party.

Or his wife or some other person who happened to have displeased him. But that wasn't what had happened in this case, he felt he could afford to assume that much.

'These days with you have been wonderful, anyway,' Marianne interrupted his thoughts. 'Shame you didn't get a day with those reprobate children of mine, too, though.'

It had been decided that they would come on the Thursday, giving the four of them an afternoon, an evening and a morning together. He had met them a couple of times before and it had all gone surprisingly smoothly. He liked Johan and Jenny, and if it had not seemed presumptuous to claim it, he would have said they seemed content to put up with him, too.

'Things are as they are,' he said. 'You'll have to explain that their new friend the policeman has got to get home to catch a scary murderer, that's the unvarnished truth of it, I'm afraid.'

'I think they'll accept an excuse like that,' concluded Marianne.

Then she kissed him and gave him a little push towards the car door.

The sensation of standing on deck and waving goodbye as the ferry put out from the shore was not a high point, noted Gunnar Barbarotti. Particularly not with his arrival a week earlier fresh in his mind. He found himself wishing he were a fourteen-year-old girl rather than a forty-seven-year-old detective – then he could have shed a few tears without suffering acute embarrassment.

But he wasn't. And being an airheaded teenage girl could prove rather a drag in the long run, too.

I hope there are going to be more weeks like this in my rudderless life, he thought when he could no longer make out the waving figure on the quay outside the terminal building. But I can bloody well do without the partings.

Then he went down to the cafeteria and bought himself a large plate of meat and potato hash with beetroot, and a beer to go with it.

5

It was quarter past nine and the sun had set by the time he climbed into his Citroën in the long-stay car park at Nynäshamn. For some reason he hadn't really understood, the ferry had gone at reduced speed, and the crossing had taken forty-five minutes longer than normal.

A dark drive home, he thought as he started the car. Three and a half hours' splendid isolation. He was not unaccustomed to solitude, but now it suddenly felt like a predatory animal, a shaggy beast that had been starving for a whole week and would now delight in sinking its teeth into him.

Before long, however, he had managed to make contact on his mobile with Inspector Backman. That was something, at least.

'You're my voice in the night,' he explained. 'The eagle has landed and requests an update.'

'I thought I felt the earth move,' said Eva Backman. 'Must have been that quake in the underworld. Well, I'm still at work, actually.'

'Congratulations,' said Gunnar Barbarotti. 'How many suspects have you identified? Am I ringing in the middle of the crucial interrogation? In that case . . .'

'We haven't really got that far yet,' Inspector Backman admitted. 'But we've started to narrow it down. We think we're dealing with a right-handed man between seventeen and seventy.'

'Great,' said Gunnar Barbarotti. 'We'll have him any day now. Are you sure it isn't a woman?'

'Could be a woman,' conceded Backman. 'But the knife went in with some force, so she must be strong and fit, if so.'

'And probably not seventy,' suggested Barbarotti.

'Fifty-five at most.'

'Tell me the rest,' asked Barbarotti.

Eva Backman sighed and launched in. 'Well if we start with forensics, the technicians have basically hoovered an area the size of a football pitch round the crime scene. I daresay they'll present us with their analysis sometime between Christmas and New Year. We'll have the pathologist's report tomorrow morning, but there won't be any sensational revelations in it. He died of those knife wounds, presumably within a minute or two. DNA doesn't seem to be an option. And then, well, we've started mapping out his family and his circle of friends, of course. We've got about fifty people to talk to, that's what I'm doing now. Deciding priorities. Which ones we're going to talk to, and in what order; he seems to have got about a bit, Erik Bergman . . .'

'What do you mean by that?'

'Nothing out of the ordinary. Bachelor with plenty of money, that's all. Liked going to the pub. Knew a lot of people . . . not a computer nerd, if that's what you were thinking.'

'I get the picture. What else?'

'We've got an expert profiler coming from Gothenburg tomorrow. There's something of a tradition of this sort of letter writing in the US, apparently. And a number of studies of that kind of murderer. It's pretty unusual here, of course, but this chap might have something useful to tell us. We'd better listen to what he has to say, at least. He's coming tomorrow afternoon, so you'll get to meet him.'

'Is there anything about Bergman having felt under threat or suchlike? Enemies?'

'No, nothing like that has emerged as yet. We've mainly been talking to this Grimle, the business partner I told you about . . . plus a few other good friends and the victim's sister. She lives at Lysekil, and I talked to her for an hour, but they don't seem to have kept that closely in touch. She's five years older.'

'Children?'

'Nix.'

'Parents?'

'On holiday in Croatia. But they've been informed. They live in Gothenburg, in Långedrag to be precise. They expect to touch down at Landvetter tomorrow afternoon. Well off, as you'll already have worked out; they wouldn't be living in Långedrag otherwise. Sold a big technology company two years ago and retired.'

'Ah, like that, is it?' said Gunnar Barbarotti. 'Any girlfriends? He must have had the occasional longer-lasting relationship? How old was he, in fact? Thirty-six?'

'Correct,' said Eva Backman. 'His age, that is. But when it comes to relationships there's not a lot to go on, apparently. He lived with a girl for a few months about ten years ago, but that seems to be it. To be honest . . .'

'Yes?'

'To be honest, I wonder if he wasn't perhaps a pretty unpleasant kind of guy. Picked up women and threw the cash around. Lived alone in a seven-room detached house with genuine works of art on the walls, a billiard table and jacuzzi . . . wine cellar and two cars.'

'Sleazy,' said Gunnar Barbarotti. 'The type who could aggravate a person, in other words?'

'Could well be.'

'To the extent that they felt like sticking a knife in him a few times.'

'Not impossible,' said Eva Backman. 'It could be as simple as that.'

'This Grimle, is he the same type?'

'No, thank goodness,' said Eva Backman. 'Very nice, actually. But then he's got a wife and two kids, as well.'

Someone came into Backman's office, and she asked him to hang on, which gave him a minute's thinking time. But the only thing that came into his head was a song title he recollected from the late eighties or early nineties . . . and even that he couldn't remember properly. *A man without a woman is like a* . . . well, what? It wouldn't come back to him. But the group was called Vaya Con Dios, wasn't it? And the title presumably fitted in with what Inspector Backman had just been saying.

Go with God? That was another kind of synaptic link, of course – hooking onto this morning's conversation at Gustabo. There are times, thought Gunnar Barbarotti, there are times when I think the human brain is nothing but an arena for a higher power to play patience in. That's the sort of brain they've given me, at any rate.

Now this was a new and rather surprising image. But after all, there were many possible combinations in a pack of cards, so the theory was, in a sense, self-fulfilling. Sometimes I really nail it, he noted with bemusement.

And sometimes a game of patience goes out.

'Mobile phone traffic?' he asked when Backman was back on the line. 'Has Sorrysen started on that yet?'

'Sorrysen's on holiday,' Backman told him. 'But he'll be in on Monday. Fredrikssen and Toivonen are handling the phone list for now. He had three, but I don't know what they've found out at this point. Nothing sensational, anyway, or they'd have told us.'

Three mobile phones, thought Barbarotti. Rather different from my paradise.

'The letter?' he asked. 'Anything to report on that?'

'No fingerprints,' said Backman with a sigh. 'Only yours and Marianne's . . . well, we assume they're hers. Standard envelope, standard paper, the sort you find in any printer. The pen was probably a Pilot . . . black gel . . . 0.7 millimetres. Available in roughly a hundred and forty-five thousand different retail outlets all over Europe.'

'The text, then? The way he wrote and so on.'

'I don't really know,' said Eva Backman. 'I think somebody claimed it was a right-handed person writing in block letters with their left hand, but I'm not sure. We sent it for further analysis today . . . when matters came to a head, so to speak.'

'OK,' said Barbarotti, and thought for a moment.

'I'm a bit tired,' said Backman. 'Maybe we can save the rest for tomorrow?'

'Good idea,' agreed Barbarotti. 'I expect I'll be sitting on my arse reading paperwork all morning. But . . .'

'Yes?'

'But if you can't give me the name of the murderer, at least throw me a little bone. What do you make of it yourself? Who on earth are we dealing with here, what type of person? I've got three more hours in the car.'

The line went quiet for a few seconds.

Then Backman came back with, 'Sorry. I wouldn't hold back from sharing even the slightest idea with you, but the fact is that I haven't got one.'

'Not a single teensy one?'

'No, that's what I'm trying to tell you. I've been working for . . . well, what is it now? . . . thirteen hours at a stretch, in round figures . . . and it all adds up to me knowing nothing more than that Erik Bergman was murdered.'

'Great,' said Gunnar Barbarotti. 'Good work, dear.'

And at that, Detective Inspector Eva Backman cut him off.

The rain started just before ten. It fell softly and persistently and the monotonous labour of the windscreen wipers made him sleepy. He stopped for petrol and a coffee once he reached Lake Vättern, and as he got back into the car he could barely resist the impulse to call Gotland. But it seemed entirely unreasonable to send Hagmund or Jolanda Jonsson out into the dark to knock on Marianne's door. He wouldn't be ringing for anything specific, but just to hear her voice. If she had had her own phone, he would have had her in the car all evening, he knew, but things were the way they were.

Oh well, at least her children were going to bring an emergency phone with them on Thursday, she had promised that; some rules simply had to be bent occasionally, and he would just have to be patient until then.

He ought to turn his mind to the coming murder investigation instead.

To the letter-writing murderer.

It all felt very odd. To say the least. Murder investigations did crop up in Kymlinge every now and then. A couple of times a year. Most of them were relatively uncomplicated, as he well knew; you could usually home in on the perpetrator/booze-fuelled idiot within a day or two. Murderers requiring protracted detective work were unusual. Drugs or alcohol were a major factor in nine out of ten cases, and the people involved were already known to the police in the same percentage of cases. The outcome of any investigation was almost always the result of steady, routine police work. If you were familiar with the procedures, you didn't really even need to think about it. At least, that was what Inspector Backman liked to claim. It takes no more intelligence to buy a cinema ticket online than it does to catch a murderer, she had asserted on one occasion.

This time she had said she hadn't got a clue. That doesn't bode well, thought Barbarotti. It doesn't bode well at all.

And yet the murderer had told them who his victim was to be. In good time. They had been given a week to protect Erik Bergman from his assassin. They had failed.

They had not even tried.

Gunnar Barbarotti hoped that this particular aspect would not get out to the press. It wasn't hard to imagine what sort of headlines they would come up with.

It was Asunander who had taken the decision, possibly in consultation with the prosecutor, Sylvenius, but Barbarotti had already decided he didn't blame them. He would have reached the same judgement himself. If they had known precisely which Erik Bergman was intended, then maybe they would have acted differently. In that case they would presumably have contacted him and tried to assess the threat in conjunction with him. In retrospect, it was easy to say that they ought to have done that anyway, but it was always easy to make observations in retrospect.

Nor was it police actions to date that were the focus of Barbarotti's thoughts on this rainy night. Quite the opposite, in fact. It was the actions of the perpetrator.

They really were bizarre. Why? Why the hell write a letter giving the name of your intended victim?

And why send it to him? Detective Inspector Gunnar Barbarotti? At his home address?

Was it just to tease them? Did it have any real significance at all? Did this person actually know Barbarotti?

And – last but not least – did Barbarotti know the murderer?

He had not found plausible answers to any of these questions when he finally parked outside his flat in Baldersgatan. Not even remotely plausible; it was twenty to one, the rain had stopped half an hour before but the streets had a wet sheen in Kymlinge, too.

Since it was past midnight it was now the first of August; it was his ex-wife's birthday and the whole town seemed to be in blackout mode as if in anticipation of an air raid. Why these two reflections should collide in his head was beyond him, but as he put the key in the lock he remembered the metaphor of a patience-playing power figure. He also realized how exhausted he felt – but still took the time to sort through the accumulation of newspapers, post and leaflets that lay in a drift covering half the floor of his cramped hall.

He separated it all into three neat piles on the kitchen table, and it was as he was hastily flicking through the letters which had arrived in the course of his week away that his fatigue was banished. It evaporated in a split second.

He had enough presence of mind to put a plastic bag over

his left hand before he slit open the envelope with a kitchen knife.

The lettering was the same, and the message as unambiguous as last time.

ANNA ERIKSSON'S TURN.

DON'T SUPPOSE YOU'LL STOP ME
THIS TIME EITHER?

Gunnar Barbarotti hesitated and held counsel with himself for half a minute. Wondered whether he could possibly be sitting in a deckchair at Hogrän, dreaming, but came to the conclusion that this was not the case.

Then he rang and woke Detective Inspector Backman.

TWO

NOTES FROM MOUSTERLIN

30 June 2002

The girl turned up out of nowhere. All of a sudden, there she was, looking at us with a crooked and slightly cheeky smile on her squarish face.

We were on the beach. All six of us; it was the next morning, and I don't know whether there had been some agreement made the day before that we would meet up, but Erik and I had scarcely got down to the beach and settled in our deckchairs before the Malmgrens came along on foot from the Bénodet direction and spread out their gaudy beach towels. Anna and Gunnar joined us only ten or fifteen minutes later and thinking about it now, I realize it must have been more or less by arrangement. Soon they had all sorted themselves out and started chatting in that desultory way people do on a beach; one clever comment at a time, with long pauses for thought. Supposed profundities but no responsibility for what they are actually saying; I pulled my cotton sunhat over my eyes and pretended to sleep, and probably needed it too, given that I hadn't got to bed until after half past two and had only had a few hours' sleep. Erik seems to be up early regardless of the night before, and woke me before nine this morning with coffee, bacon and scrambled egg; whatever else one can say about him, he's certainly a thoughtful host.

Perhaps I dozed off for a short while in my deckchair. I was hot, of course, but there was a pleasant breeze blowing off the sea; the distant cries of the seagulls mingled with the intermittent conversation, and after a while I could no longer distinguish one form of expression from the other. But I might actually have been asleep, in which case it was presumably the girl's voice that woke me up, its tone both childish and slightly abrasive.

Like an old soul in a young body, I remember thinking.

'Bonjour. Ça va?'

The others went quiet. Katarina Malmgren gave a laugh. 'Ça va! Bonjour petite.'

I pushed up the brim of my hat and studied her. A dark-haired girl of around twelve or thirteen. A red one-piece swimsuit, a blue straw hat with fabric flowers. A sweater knotted round her waist and a little rucksack on her back.

Sparkling eyes and a slightly mocking expression.

'Vous n'êtes pas français, hein?'

No, Katarina Malmgren clarified, we weren't French. We were Swedes. Holidaying in beautiful Brittany. The girl smiled her crooked smile again, and there was something instantly appealing about her, a sort of unabashed lack of inhibition, that could have been annoying had she been a year or two older.

But she was still a child, even though budding breasts were discernible beneath the thin material of her swimsuit. Katarina Malmgren asked what her name was.

'Troaë,' said the girl. 'Je m'appelle Troaë.'

It took a while for us to grasp the spelling of this strange name. And how to say it – roughly like the French pronunciation of the word 'train', but with a little 'o' inserted before the nasal final syllable, we were told. We all tried saying it, while the girl prompted, corrected and encouraged us. Gunnar and Anna in particular seemed to find this practice session great fun.

Troaë explained to us that it was not a common French name. She did not know where it came from, her father had given it to her, and he was an artist, living in Paris.

After all these preliminary gyrations, she put her little rucksack down on the sand and asked if she could paint us. I noticed there were a couple of little brown struts sticking up out of her rucksack and realized it was an easel.

'Paint us?' asked Katarina Malmgren with an artificial laugh. 'Why?'

The girl explained that she intended to become a painter, just like her father. But since she was at school all year in a drab Paris suburb, she had to use her summer holidays for practice. She thought we were an interesting collection of individuals and she had come down to the beach with that very aim in view. Finding a suitable group of people to paint.

She began setting up her easel. 'So you're on holiday here with your father and . . . ?' asked Katarina.

Not at all, it transpired. Troaë told them – if I understood her rightly – that in the summer she lived with her paternal grandmother who had a house outside Fouesnant. Just a few kilometres from the beach; her parents were in Paris, both her mother and her father, but they had divorced long ago and she lived with her father, at least most of the time.

As she talked she prepared her painting things: set up a canvas panel on her easel, backed about ten metres away from us, took out a box of watercolour paints, wetted various brushes with the tip of her tongue, it all looked very professional.

Gunnar asked in halting French if we had to keep still all the time, but the girl said that wasn't necessary, but it would be good if we didn't move too far from our present positions. I started to feel someone ought to have the sense to call an end to the whole charade, but no one else in the group seemed to object to being painted on the beach. Henrik, conceivably, but he presumably felt restrained by the others' jollity. I sank further into my deck-chair and tried to resume my doze.

In fact, everyone went quiet for a long time, it must have been getting on for half an hour, as Troaë stood earnestly behind her easel and painted her group of holidaying Swedes on the beach. For some reason, the previous free flow of conversation was inhibited by the girl's presence, even the women saying little. I think I must have dropped off for a few minutes, and the next time it was Anna who broke the silence.

'Lunch,' she said. 'A dip first, then a bite to eat. What do you say?'

'Hadn't we better get our artist's permission first?' asked Erik, and I could not tell from his voice whether he was tired of the whole set-up or still faintly amused by it.

Katarina called out to the girl. Asked how she was getting on and said we were about to go in the water and then for lunch.

She replied with something I could not catch; Katarina told us she was asking for two minutes more, that was all, then she was prepared to take a break.

'Cocky brat,' muttered Henrik, but was swiftly rebuked by his wife and Gunnar.

'I think she's delightful,' declared the latter. 'A proper little charmer. Can't you all see how attractive she'll be in five years' time?'

'You perverse creep,' said Anna, throwing her head back and laughing. The laughter was loud and affected. I was in two minds about whether to go back to the house after lunch; to find some shade if nothing else, and some peace and quiet for planning my future.

We held our positions until Troaë dropped a deep curtsey and thanked us for our patience.

'Can we see?' asked Katarina.

She shook her head. 'Not until it's finished. This afternoon or tomorrow, maybe.'

'Surely she doesn't mean we've got to model for her for days on end?' said Gunnar.

Katarina translated this for the girl, and we were told that a short session after lunch was all it would take.

She did not join us in the water, but came with us to the restaurant. I do not know whether anyone invited her, but if so, it would have been Katarina or Gunnar; but at any event, Troaë immediately grabbed Erik and walked arm in arm with him all the way to Le Grand Large, a little restaurant a few hundred metres east of the Pointe de Mousterlin. She pressed close to him, too, taking the occasional little hop, demonstrating classical ballet positions and chattering away ten to the dozen. Erik seemed flattered by the attention, pretended to understand everything she said and joked with her; at one point she leapt into his arms and kissed him on the mouth.

'Watch yourself,' said Anna with a strained laugh. 'That kid could be older than you think.'

Then she tried to jump up into Gunnar's arms as the girl had done with Erik; Gunnar was clearly unprepared for her antics and they both tumbled over in the sand. Troaë shrieked with delight, throwing herself on top of them, and a brief bout of uncontrolled wrestling ensued. Even Henrik took part in the rumpus; I was the only one to remain aloof and keep my distance.

When they were all on their feet again, laughing, getting their breath back and brushing themselves down to get rid of the fine sand, the girl announced that Swedes must be the most hilarious people in the world and that we were very welcome to adopt her.

'Oh, but we'd have to get your grandmother to sign a form first, in that case,' Katarina pointed out. 'No, no more wrestling, it's time for some lunch and a glass of wine now.'

She said the first part in French and the rest in Swedish, and was then obliged to translate in both directions.

'I'm sure my grandmother would agree to it,' said Troaë, looking grave for a moment. 'She thinks I have no manners and make far too much noise.'

She clung on to Erik's arm again and we continued on our way to Le Grand Large.

We spent the next two hours eating seafood and drinking white wine. It felt strange to be sitting beneath the pale-blue sun umbrellas in that big, boisterous group – now with the addition of a madcap young girl – as if it we were some kind of natural community. I was struck by the fact that I had only known Erik for about five days, the other Swedes for twenty-four hours and the girl for just a few hours. Yet there we sat over our food and drink, chatting and laughing as if we had known each other forever. I know that at the end of my treatment, as we were saying goodbye to each another, Dr L urged me not to be so sceptical, and I agree that this was part of my specific problem – but right here and now, on this slightly breezy afternoon, I still felt there was some justification for my doubt. Who were these people really?

Who *are* these people really, I ought to write, of course. How have I found myself in this cluster? What did we actually have to talk about as we poked around amongst snails and lobster and mussels and knocked back the chilled white wine? What were we imagining? As I write this it is late evening, and I am sitting out on the terrace with my thick notebook, just like yesterday. Erik is asleep indoors, or maybe reading in bed, but no, I think he's had too much wine for that. He isn't much of a one for books at all. He is not unintelligent, but he doesn't read. I'm wondering again whether I ought to just leave, but there's a sort of inertia to the situation itself, holding me back. The landscape appeals to me and that, too, somehow helps to keep me here. The heat and the flatness. The dunes, the low, half-hidden stone houses, the sea, there is so much space here. Maybe an element of tension, too, something unpredictable that I can't quite put my finger on; it feels as though there's something lurking beneath the surface of these people, something waiting to come to light, I can't help thinking. As if they need each other somehow, as if being in couples is not enough. This is particularly noticeable with Gunnar and Anna, of course; their attention is seldom focused on each other and it is as if they are constantly seeking collusion with, and affirmation from, the rest of us – even from the girl Troaë. Naturally I can't be sure what these observations are really worth, unused as I am to spending time with other people like this, and presumably there is some kind of boundary line, and the day will come when I can't stand it any longer. Simply that.

Anyway, Troaë sat with us at the table throughout, drinking

Coca Cola but also a glass of wine mixed with water, which she claimed was what she usually had with meals both in Paris and at her grandmother's in Fouesnant. She really did her utmost to entertain us, and even got us all singing together, which was something I had thought reserved for Swedish settings and a different sort of company. The girl sat between Erik and Gunnar and made sure to divide her favours between them as fairly as she could. If she kissed one of them on the ear, she immediately made sure she did the same to the other, and when we finally had the bill she insisted on paying her share, which of course she was not allowed to do.

We got back to our camp on the beach at around three thirty, and as we all sat or slumped in postprandial torpor in the pleasant offshore breeze, the girl went on painting us. She stood ten metres away from us with her feet planted wide apart and dug into the sand; her straw hat pushed well back and her pretty face veiled in concentration. Katarina Malmgren cursed herself for having left her camera at home, and I could understand why. There's something irresistibly attractive about the girl, a sort of unruliness and budding charm, difficult to guard oneself against. I don't know if this observation is correct, but I also got the impression that Anna grew much quieter in the course of the afternoon, as if some kind of rivalry was developing between her and the girl; the adult woman and the child. I may be exaggerating, not being used to concerning myself with the motivation and reasoning of strangers, but when Gunnar at one point attempted to slip his hand under Anna's bottom, he was discreetly but firmly rebuffed. She even snarled at him; Erik, too, noticed the incident and we exchanged a look of conspiratorial mutual understanding, as they say. This irritated me, for some reason.

The look, that is; the hand trying to find its way between Anna Eriksson's thighs is of no consequence to me.

After an hour or so, when everyone seemed to have had their doze – but with Troaë still working away doggedly behind her easel – the question of a boat trip to des Glénan came up again. They are a small group of islands fifteen to twenty nautical miles from Beg-Meil; Henrik and Gunnar had been talking over lunch about a trip there and the boats that run several times a day from a small harbour east of the point. But it's also possible to hire a boat yourself, and the two of them were clearly used to the sea, so the question now was what it might cost, and what other terms and conditions might apply. The plan, as I understand it, is for us all to go together in the next few days, and Anna and Katarina immediately chipped in with enthusiastic comments about an exclusive all-day trip with picnic baskets and bottles of wine and fishing tackle, and a private island without any other tourists, making it sound as though we were the select few, and I felt a sense of nausea creep over me at this sudden burgeoning of elitism, but I noted that Erik had nothing to say on the matter. Perhaps he is starting to get tired of these two couples, but with Erik, one never really knows.

The Glénan discussion was interrupted by Troaë, announcing that she had finished painting. That was to say, the picture wasn't finished, but she no longer needed us in position, she explained. Katarina asked again if we could see the result, but this was not allowed. Perhaps tomorrow or the day after, but on no account before the painting was complete and the paint had dried. The girl gathered up her things and crammed them into her rucksack; then she did something rather astonishing.

She informed us that she was going for a dip, and duly threw off her hat, took off her swimsuit and sprinted down the beach and straight out into the water, stark naked. The only one of our party to say anything was Erik. 'Fuck me,' he said. 'That was a surprise.' His voice came out a little thickly.

She was back five minutes later, unselfconsciously drying herself with a red towel, her small breasts thrusting, and you could see she had a pathetic little tuft of dark hair on her pudenda, no more than a hint; I felt she was putting on a show that trod a fine line between childish innocence and sophisticated acting. We were all stealing glances at her and I noted that nobody in the group could find the words to puncture the unnatural silence.

Then she put her swimsuit back on. Picked up her rucksack and hat and waved goodbye. Plodded up the slope from the beach, over the top, and was gone.

'Fuck me,' repeated Erik, and gave a loud and slightly artificial laugh. 'What a little madam!'

Gunnar joined in the laughter and before long, the others followed suit. Ten minutes later we called it a day, the Malmgrens setting off west – their house is a kilometre inland, halfway to Bénodet, apparently – while the rest of us headed east over the dunes. Nobody suggested getting together for dinner that evening; I could detect a weariness and a drowsy sense of saturation amongst the whole group, and as we parted from Gunnar and Anna below their house by the beach at Cleut-Rouz, we did so without promises in either direction. Erik was quiet and muted, as if brooding on something; we said little on the walk back to our house, and I sensed he was getting tired of my company, so when we got there I asked him outright. Asked if he thought it was time for me to move on and leave him.

'Christ, no,' he answered. 'But we're not married, don't forget. We've got to give each other some space, but the day I think I want you to go, I'll tell you.'

'OK,' I said. 'I'll probably stay a couple more days, then.'

'If you feel you ought to be making yourself useful, you can always cook dinner tonight,' he added. 'We've got loads of eggs, and I'd be happy with an omelette and some veg, what do you say?'

I nodded. We hung our swimming things over the patio rail and I went indoors and started rummaging round in the kitchen.

As we were eating, and having a couple of beers each, we talked a bit about the others. Particularly about the women. 'If you had to spend a night with one of them, who would you choose?' Erik asked.

He looked unexpectedly serious as he said it and I thought for a while before answering. 'Hard call,' I said. 'I'd really need to try them both before I could express an opinion.'

He evidently found this a thoroughly valid answer, roared with laughter and narrowly avoided spraying beer all over the table. 'Hell yes,' he said. 'Do you mean both together or one at a time?'

'One at a time,' I said. 'It's easy to lose focus otherwise.'

Erik nodded, but stopped laughing. That's the way he is, it's struck me in these few days we've been in each other's company; he can turn off his laughter in a split second. Switch it back on again just as fast, come to that. His states of mind have sharp edges but they don't seem to go very deep. 'You're right,' he said. 'Whatever we do, we need to keep focused. What do you reckon to Anna and Gunnar? Do they seem properly focused to you?'

'I don't know,' I said. 'To be honest, they seem pretty banal to me. Well, she does, at any rate.'

He leant back, propped his sandy feet up on the scuffed blue wooden rail round our patio and drank from his bottle of beer. 'People tie themselves for no good reason,' he said, trying to adopt a philosophical tone. 'That's where they get it wrong. They think you have to be a couple, but Gunnar and Anna would be much better with each other if they didn't have to pretend they're a permanent item. Don't you reckon?'

I shrugged. 'It's been a long time since I lived with a woman,' I said. 'So I'm not the right man to judge these things.'

Erik was quiet for a while. 'You know what,' he said, 'I quite fancy grabbing Anna for myself, just to see the reaction. What do you say? Might liven things up a bit.'

'And you're sure she'd be willing?' I asked, mainly because that was the question he was expecting.

'That's the impression I got when we went for our swim last night,' said Erik. 'And she seemed almost jealous of that kid girl, you noticed that, I bet?'

'She was pretty provocative.'

'Agreed,' said Erik, and laughed. 'But Anna didn't like Gunnar gawping at her, that was obvious. She thinks she's the one who deserves to be gawped at; it's a tendency most women have.'

I made no reply. This is just the kind of conversation I find hard to stand. That cod philosophizing, those cheap generalizations, those summings-up of paltry life experiences that so readily happen after a couple of drinks. You dumb jerk, I thought. You don't know a damn thing about life, and if I stuck a knife in your belly and twisted it and held up a mirror for you while I was at it, you'd discover the ignorance in your own eyes. That would teach you something.

I was taken aback by the sudden, articulate anger welling up inside me. After all, until now I had felt a kind of affinity with Erik, but now he engendered nothing but disgust in me.

'Though I actually find Katarina more interesting,' he said. 'You've got a different kind of femininity there.'

'Why not go for her instead, then?' I asked.

He just sat there, rolling the beer bottle across his forehead.

'It would cost too much,' he said in the end. 'Big investment and possibly no return on it at all. No, I'll leave her to you.'

'No thanks,' I said.

It was getting towards dusk now. A hedgehog came ambling serenely across the lawn and disappeared under the tool shed, and I thought that this could be his cue to ask me a thing or two about myself and my circumstances. But he didn't do it this time, either; we've been in each other's company for five days now and he still knows nothing about me. I gave him a name and a place that first day in the car, and that was all. I don't think I've ever met anyone so genuinely uninterested in his fellow human beings as Erik Bergman. It took me a few days to realize this was the case, but now I can see it clearly. If he'd started prying and bombarding me with questions about my background, it would scarcely have been possible for me to live here with him on these open-ended terms. On the other hand, one does wonder why he's letting me stay here at all. I have to admit that I can't work it out. If he's got any homosexual expectations, he's certainly concealed them well.

He drained his beer and lit a cigarette.

'I reckon we'll go along on that trip to the islands, anyway,' he said. 'If they sort out the boat and everything.'

'Could do,' I replied, and we didn't say much more after that. Just sat and stared into the deepening darkness, and after fifteen or twenty minutes Erik said he was tired and was going to turn in. I said I'd take care of the washing-up and perhaps stay up a bit longer, and he nodded and went off to his room. I heard him channel-hopping on the radio for a while, but he soon tired of it. I cleared away as promised and then took my notebook and another beer and went back out to the patio. I started my summary of the day; if Dr L knew how conscientious I am about my writing, he would be full of praise. We all have our individual routes to healing, he would often say. In your case, writing, recording what has already played out, is one of the more important components, possibly the most important of all.

I don't agree with Dr L on everything, but in this case I am coming to appreciate that his assessment is right. Words are what force us to choose our path.

It is half past ten. The sea sounds like the breathing of some enormous creature, out there in the dark. The insects flutter round the lamp. I feel whole and strong, and these people with whom I am temporarily associating do not touch me. They do not reach to my core, and as long as they stay on the periphery, I can handle them as easily as I wield this pen in my hand.

My last thoughts on the terrace this evening go to Troaë. I wrote at the start that she must be an old woman in a young girl's body; that was really just a phrase that came into my head, but when I think about it, I believe it comes quite close to the truth. Perhaps that is the way with reflections that present themselves without invitation, they often possess a weight and a pregnancy that their more artful and considered equivalents lack. An immediacy.

For there was something in that laugh, in the deft hands removing the swimming costume from the young body. The movements of experience, dancing over virgin territory; I wish expressions like that were not so easily accessible, and that they had the sense to keep out of my consciousness. The immediacy I was just talking about has no natural value per se, and I hope that girl is not going to turn up in my dreams.

Anyway, I shall go to bed now. The calm I feel within me is only superficial, and possibly a harbinger of storm and darkness, but I shall in all probability spend a few more days on this sun-drenched coastal strip.

Commentary, July 2007

I was so right to start with him. Rereading my account of that conversation with a person so utterly emotionally paralysed, I can only congratulate myself. Although I had no inkling that evening of what lay ahead, I still managed to put my finger on Erik's character; the sum total of goodness in the world had not been depleted by his death, in fact just the opposite. Not that I am driven by ethical considerations, far from it – but it does one no harm to be reminded of them. No one will miss Erik Bergman – it has taken five years to restore the balance that was disturbed in Mousterlin, to *start* to restore it, and the intervening years have been terrible. I have lost count of the nights when I awoke in a cold sweat after dreaming of the girl's body in my arms, lost count of the moments I have felt myself on the brink of a sheer drop of despair, ready to take my own life.

Yet it is not my death that will atone for what happened, but theirs. Actions must have consequences, and I am merely a tool for achieving that justice. It is all very simple and I do not intend to let myself be trapped; when I finally drove that knife into Erik Bergman's belly that beautiful morning, I could clearly feel the fresh air rushing into my own body.

Need I say any more?

1–7 AUGUST 2007

6

Christina Lind Bergman was a dark-haired woman in her early forties.

His immediate impression was that she seemed unexpectedly composed for someone whose only brother had just been stabbed to death. But twenty-four hours had passed, of course, and perhaps she had taken some kind of sedative. He also remembered that she was a doctor, and was presumably familiar with that sort of medication.

The first thing she said once the formalities were out of the way – having refused coffee, tea or water – seemed to indicate his assessment had been correct. She *was* collected.

'My brother and I weren't particularly close,' she said. 'It's just as well for you to know that. I realize you've got to interview me, but I can promise I shall have nothing to contribute. Nothing at all.'

Excellent, thought Gunnar Barbarotti. So we won't be going into this with unrealistic expectations, anyway.

'Uh huh,' he said. 'Do you think you could expand on that at all?'

Yes, she did think so. She rubbed something from the corner of her eye with the knuckle of her little finger and launched in.

'I'm five years older than my brother. It's just the two of

us. There's a bit too much of an age gap for us to have played together properly as children. When I was younger, I hoped we might get on a slightly better footing with each other when we grew up, or, well, I think that was what I hoped. But it never happened. Erik never grew up.'

She paused briefly, as if expecting some sort of comment on this assertion, but Barbarotti gestured to her to go on.

'No, he never grew up,' she repeated. 'Never matured. He's one of those men who keep the outlook they had on the world in their teens for the rest of their lives. Everything is a kind of game, people are toys you can discard when you get tired of them. Especially women. You might say they've stayed in the changing room after the boys' football match, those men . . . It sounds harsh and I don't enjoy saying it, but why should I beat about the bush?'

Why indeed, thought Gunnar Barbarotti, and shrugged his shoulders in a half-hearted gesture that he himself couldn't really interpret.

'Unfortunately, he's always had the money to be able to drift through existence on his own terms,' she went on without waiting for him to ask another question. 'Our parents have always bailed him out.'

'But his company's doing well, isn't it?' asked Barbarotti.

'Nowadays, yes,' said Christina Lind Bergman, and pulled a face. 'But I don't know how many millions Mum and Dad poured into it.'

'I see,' said Barbarotti. 'So you're saying your brother was some kind of spoilt yuppie?'

'More or less,' said Christina Lind Bergman. 'But he had no empathy, either, it's important not to overlook that detail just because he sailed through life with everything handed to him on a plate. No, I gave up on him years ago.'

'How much contact did you have with him?'

'None at all. We've even stopped seeing each other at Christmas. Mum and Dad don't come back home any more – they have a house in Spain now. And I don't know any of his friends, I'm not going to be the slightest use to you, that's all there is to it.'

'When did you last see him?'

She thought about it. 'Last summer. Though that was only by chance. I was in a cafe in Lysekil, where I live . . . and work at the hospital. He was on a sailing jaunt with some friends, and happened to come in. We just said hello.'

'Did he introduce his friends?'

'Only by their first names. Two guys, similar to Erik, as far as I could judge. Tanned and broad-jawed and a bit the worse for drink. I can't remember what they were called. Micke and Patrik or something like that, I think.'

Gunnar Barbarotti nodded. Nice family, he thought. Strong ties and all that. 'How do you get on with your parents?' he asked.

She raised an eyebrow. 'I don't see what that's got to do with the murder of my brother.'

'Perhaps you could answer anyway,' requested Barbarotti.

'Not all that well,' admitted Christina Bergman. 'To be honest, I see myself as the white sheep of this family.'

'Is that a fact?' said Gunnar Barbarotti. 'Well, I still have to ask you whether you have any idea at all who could have killed your brother.'

'None whatsoever.'

'And why?'

'You mean why somebody might have done it?'

'Yes.'

'Can't help you there, either. Not that I find it hard to imagine he might have treated someone extremely badly. And that person could have reached the end of their tether and stabbed him. But that's mere speculation and can scarcely be of any use to you.'

'You sound as though you aren't even surprised?' said Barbarotti.

'Of course I'm surprised,' she said. 'One always is, surely, when some kind of accident happens?'

No, thought Gunnar Barbarotti once he had escorted Christina Lind Bergman to the lift, ten minutes later, there was definitely no need for a sedative in her case.

'Guess,' said Eva Backman.

'Twenty-five,' said Gunnar Barbarotti.

'Wrong,' said Backman. 'The right answer's nineteen. But that's bad enough, I reckon.'

'Too right,' said Barbarotti. 'Can I see?'

She passed him the list and he glanced quickly through the rows of Anna Erikssons. 'Some have different spellings,' he pointed out.

'Three with a "c", one with only one "s". If we assume the murderer's spelt it correctly, that takes us down to fifteen. Do you think we should work on the assumption that he can spell?'

Gunnar Barbarotti tossed the piece of paper onto the desk. 'How should I know?' he said irritably. 'And what makes us so sure Kymlinge is the place in question?'

'I never claimed we were sure,' said Eva Backman, crossing her arms on her chest. 'The statistical data for this comprises just the one victim so far, which isn't a lot to go on, of course . . . though perhaps I don't need to tell you that? How was the sister?'

'Splendid,' said Barbarotti. 'She knows less about her brother than I do about the mating rituals of the pine weevil.'

'The pine weevil?'

'That was just an example.'

'Wherever do you get this stuff from?'

Gunnar Barbarotti shrugged. 'It's the creative process,' he said. 'Any old thing can crop up. So tell me, what does Asunander think about all these Annas? Are we going to keep the whole lot under surveillance?'

'It's not been decided yet,' declared Bergman. 'He's in conference with Sylvenius and Gothenburg. I bet they'll send a couple of men over anyway. As well as that profiler I mentioned.'

Inspector Barbarotti checked the time. 'I've got to talk to Grimle in five minutes. Can we spend a bit of time on this after that, go through it all in peace and quiet?'

'We can always try,' said Eva Backman. 'As long as the parents don't take too long. They're already in my office, waiting.'

She got up and seemed to hesitate for a second. Then she left the room.

He talked to Andreas Grimle for half an hour. Once he had finished, he played back the tape straight away to make sure he hadn't missed anything.

He didn't seem to have done. He agreed with Backman that Grimle seemed a pretty likeable young man. And normal. Perhaps the company needed someone like that, too, thought

Barbarotti. If Erik Bergman really was the kind of bastard his sister had claimed.

Grimle gave a rather more positive picture of his dead partner. He did admit they had hardly ever socialized with one another in their spare time; Erik was a bachelor, after all, whereas Andreas Grimle had a wife, a dog and two children under five. 'We are at different stages of our lives. Sorry, *were*.'

The last time he saw Erik alive was the day before he died. They had both been busy at the office in Järnvägsgatan until five o'clock. That was pretty standard. Grimle hadn't noticed anything particular about Erik Bergman, who had not said or done anything to indicate he suspected anybody was out to get him.

Inspector Barbarotti wanted to know what would happen to the company now.

Andreas Grimle said he didn't know. A couple of tax lawyers from Öhrlings PwC had been brought in and were looking into the matter, it might be rather problematic, and there would probably be a court case, Grimle against Erik's parents. But he hoped it would be possible to carry on the business. They'd been moderately successful these last three years.

Shocked?

Of course Grimle was shocked. If there was anything, anything at all, he could do to help the police catch this lunatic, he was prepared to do it.

He had also wondered whether it was sheer chance that it happened to be Erik. The murderer was just standing there, ready to stick his knife into the first person who happened to come by?

Inspector Barbarotti had nodded vaguely and said it was a possibility. The investigation was still in its preliminary stages, and it was too soon to form an opinion on the motive behind the crime.

Did Grimle know whether Erik Bergman had any enemies?

No.

Any competitors? Could the murder be linked to their business dealings in any way?

Not a chance, as far as Andreas Grimle was aware. Of course he had competitors, but there was fair play in their line of work. His partner had fallen foul of some drugged-up lunatic, that was the only conceivable explanation.

Why, Barbarotti had wondered. If Grimle saw Bergman only through the prism of their IT company, how could he be aware of any demons that might lurk in his associate's private life? Oughtn't he to realize his perspective was somewhat limited?

But there was already a twelve-page printout recording yesterday's interview with Grimle, so Barbarotti decided that would do for now.

'Do you recall Erik ever saying anything about anonymous letters?' he asked when they had already shaken hands and Andreas Grimle was about to leave the room.

'Anonymous letters?' asked Grimle, the astonishment written all over his open, honest face. 'No, why on earth should he have done? Why do you ask?'

Inspector Barbarotti did not answer that. He merely urged Grimle to contact the police immediately if he thought of anything he felt to be of even the slightest significance for the investigation.

Grimle promised, said goodbye and wished the police luck in tracking down the killer.

*

The profiler from Gothenburg showed up as Barbarotti was about to ring Backman and suggest a working lunch at the King's Grill.

So it turned into a working lunch with the profiler instead. His name was Curt Lillieskog, and Barbarotti felt they had met on some previous occasion – so did Lillieskog, but neither of them could get to the bottom of when and where it might have been.

Lillieskog was sixty-odd, lean and wiry – and with a lively enthusiasm for his job that made him seem like a teenager. Or gave the impression that he himself had invented the concept of the criminal profile and was now on tour with a mission to sell the idea to others. He enjoys murderers, thought Barbarotti. And he's not ashamed of it.

'Letter writers like this are extremely unusual,' Lillieskog told him as a preamble. 'Or at any rate, those who carry through their intentions. Nice place this, do you often come here for lunch?'

Barbarotti had to admit that he and a colleague or two patronized the King's Grill whenever the police canteen started to pall – and that the traditional home cooking seldom disappointed. They ordered that day's special – breadcrumbed veal patties with mashed potato and lingonberry sauce – and took a seat by the window to set to work on their profiling.

'I think we're dealing with an individual who wants to be acknowledged at any price,' said Lillieskog.

I've heard exactly the same sort of thing a hundred times before, thought Barbarotti. But it could still be right, all the same. 'Expand on that,' he said.

'Gladly,' said Lillieskog. 'It doesn't tell us all that much about our man per se, because it basically holds true for all perpetrators of violence. The vast majority have some underlying and unanswered need for acknowledgement. They have this perception of not having been seen, which often dates back to childhood and is then intensified by various other failings and failures later in life. Put at its simplest, this is what you might call the lynchpin of criminality.'

'I see,' said Gunnar Barbarotti. 'So why write letters?'

'I see two possible alternatives,' said Lillieskog, cutting his veal patty in two with his fork. 'Either it's a signal that he wants to be caught. That deep down he isn't happy about what he's doing, and wants to help the police in their efforts to stop him.'

'Hang on a minute,' said Barbarotti. 'You're assuming he intends to kill a number of people. You think he's serious about this Anna Eriksson, for example?'

'I think it's quite likely,' said Lillieskog. 'He might well have a list of people he's out to get. Three or seven or ten of them, people he has some kind of grievance against. But it could equally well be that he's picking them at random from the phone book. Have you established any link between Erik Bergman and Anna Eriksson yet?'

'Not yet,' said Barbarotti. 'But we've got people working on it. There's no Anna Eriksson in Bergman's immediate circle of acquaintances, I think we can confidently say. Now we're working on friends of friends, as it were, which is a bit more difficult, seeing as . . .'

'Seeing as you don't want to make the letters public,' supplied Lillieskog, with a look that to Barbarotti seemed almost like excitement. 'That's the right call, I'm sure.'

'Sorry,' said Barbarotti. 'You said one alternative was that the victims are chosen more or less at random, and that the murderer is writing letters to me because what he really wants is to be caught. But why write to me in particular? And what's the other alternative? You said you could see two.'

Lillieskog quickly chewed and swallowed, aided by a gulp of lingonberry juice. 'Why he chose you in particular is a hard question to answer. Perhaps he's come into contact with you before . . . a criminal you put away, for example, you'll all need to keep an eye out for that possibility . . . but it might be that he just knows your name. Maybe you were in the papers or on television . . . are you in the phone book?'

Gunnar Barbarotti nodded.

'That could be enough. And it's not necessarily something you are aware of, in fact I think it's likely you aren't. But your other question – what's alternative number two? – well the answer to that, of course, is that we could be dealing with a much more ingenious individual.'

Ingenious individual, thought Gunnar Barbarotti. Sounded as though he was talking about Karlsson on the Roof or some other children's book hero. 'You mean . . . ?' he said.

'I mean that there could be a much more rational reason why he – let's agree for the sake of argument that it's a he – why he's writing these letters. That it's a way of hampering the police in their efforts to catch him.'

He stopped talking and looked at Barbarotti with something suspiciously akin to delight. Barbarotti put down his knife and fork and wiped his mouth with his serviette as he tried to grasp what Lillieskog was talking about.

'Hampering the police?' he said. 'You've lost me now. In what way could our efforts be hampered by his . . . ?'

Lillieskog held up an admonishing finger. 'It's hard to say. And perhaps it isn't succeeding, anyway. All I'm saying is that his *intention* is to mess with you lot. The letters might be obscuring something else. You and your colleagues have to invest a lot of energy in working out why the heck he's writing to tip you off . . . and that energy might be needed elsewhere.'

Gunnar Barbarotti pondered this. He thought it sounded both plausible and utterly absurd.

'It might also be the case that the person he really wanted to murder was this Bergman,' continued Lillieskog enthusiastically. 'And that he wants to divert your attention, so to speak. In all sorts of directions. And if so, we have to admit that he's made a pretty good job of it so far, hrrm.'

'If this is the alternative we're faced with,' said Barbarotti after a few moments' silence, 'it presupposes some planning on the part of the perpetrator. Am I right?'

Lillieskog leant across the table and lowered his voice. 'It presupposes extraordinary planning on the part of the perpetrator,' he clarified. 'And I probably don't need to add that, in that case, we've got something immensely complicated to wrestle with here. *Immensely* complicated.'

'How was he, then?' Eva Backman wanted to know, half an hour later. 'The profiler.'

'A bit barmy,' replied Barbarotti. 'But the worst of it is, I think he had a valid point or two.'

'What do you mean by that?'

'That he had a valid point or two, of course. He said a few things that could possibly be right.'

'Thanks, I get it. Things like what?'

'Like the fact that we might be dealing with a bloke who's got his wits about him. Who . . . well, who's carefully thought through what he's going to do.'

'What he's going to do?' cried Eva Backman. 'He's already knifed a guy to death and written two letters. You make it sound as though this is just the beginning. What grounds do you have for claiming anything like that?'

'Not many,' said Gunnar Barbarotti. 'I hope I'm wrong. What do *you* think?'

Eva Backman shook her head and swore. 'Fuck it, I haven't got time to think one thing or the other when I'm so tied up with interviews and other work the whole time.'

'Ouch,' said Barbarotti.

'I spent all morning talking to his parents and now I've got four of Mr Bergman's bachelor cronies to tackle. If Asunander and dear old Sylvenius decide on surveillance of all the Annas, we can presumably forget all about family life for the next few days.'

'I have no family life,' Barbarotti pointed out. 'But forget that. Aren't some of the Annas more interesting than others?'

Eva Backman shrugged. 'Two of them are under twelve. Let's hope to goodness they're not the most interesting. But that still leaves seventeen . . . if we restrict ourselves to Kymlinge, that is.'

'And if we venture beyond Kymlinge?'

'Well, what do you think?' said Eva Backman.

Bloody hell, thought Gunnar Barbarotti, and retreated to his office. I feel ill, this is so sick.

He had five seconds' peace in his chair. Then Chief Inspector Asunander rang to call him in for a conference.

7

'Astor Nilsson from the Gothenburg police,' indicated Chief Inspector Asunander. 'You and Backman lead on this for now, with Nilsson's help. Clear?'

'Clear,' said Barbarotti.

Asunander was having the usual problem with his false teeth. They slid sideways out of place whenever he spoke, which made him always express himself as concisely as possible. The false teeth themselves were the result of a well-aimed blow with a baseball bat, administered by a drugged-up hooligan a decade earlier. Since that event, the chief inspector preferred to do his job from behind his desk. He never took part in operations, rarely conducted interviews and had a small subsidiary income from devising crosswords for three or four magazines. But he was head of the CID in the Kymlinge police force and he had at least two years to go to retirement.

Barbarotti said hello to Astor Nilsson, a powerfully built man of fifty-five or so with a handshake like a mangle. They were evidently only being allocated one Gothenburg top dog. They each took one of Asunander's visitor chairs. Asunander sat behind his desk and switched off four phones.

'Forensics found zero,' he said. 'No leads. Complex.'

'Witnesses?' asked Barbarotti. 'Anyone see Bergman setting out from home or meet him on the running track?'

'Nothing yet,' said Astor Nilsson, relieving Asunander of the effort of speaking. 'But we may still get something. We've sent people to talk to the neighbours and so on. Oh, and there was a woman who saw him jog past her kitchen window. Just after 6 a.m. She's ninety-two and always wakes early . . . but then we already knew he was out jogging.'

'Only this time he didn't get the whole way round,' said Barbarotti.

'No, he didn't,' said Astor Nilsson.

'I don't interfere in operations,' declared Asunander, glaring irritably at Barbarotti. Evidently he had not been called in to discuss the general progress of their detective work. He exchanged a glance with his Gothenburg colleague and nodded.

'Anna Eriksson,' said Asunander. 'Got to decide.'

Astor Nilsson cleared his throat and took over again. He had clearly been briefed on the issues that were the order of the day, and had already been seated in the room when Barbarotti came in. Perhaps he had been there since this morning.

'We have nineteen prospective victims,' he began. 'We've rung round to them all, first their home number, then their mobile. We got answers from sixteen and—'

'Hang on,' said Barbarotti. 'Who's been doing this? What sort of answers did they get?'

'None,' said Asunander, looking angry.

'Two detectives did the lot,' said Astor Nilsson. 'Borgsen and Killander . . . is that correct?'

'Yes,' said Asunander.

'Borgsen and Killander made the calls, right, but hung up as soon as they got each Anna on the line. Without saying a word, that is. Five answered on their home numbers, the rest on their mobiles . . . they were presumably at work or out enjoying the nice weather.'

He gestured towards the window, where not so much as a single sunbeam penetrated the carefully lowered blinds. 'Some of them could be a long way from here, of course. It was only a preliminary ring round.'

'Excuse me,' interrupted Barbarotti. 'What's our strategy, then? Are we going to warn these women, or . . . ?'

'Decide!' said Asunander.

'That's what we've got to decide,' interpreted Astor Nilsson.

Poor devil, thought Gunnar Barbarotti. Has he been chewing this over with Asunander all morning? 'Yes, I know that,' he said. 'We can hardly start protecting them without telling them first. But you two think that we . . . that we perhaps shouldn't say anything at all?'

There was an ominous clicking from Asunander's teeth, but no words came forth.

'What's your view?' Astor Nilsson asked.

'Hmm,' said Barbarotti. 'Shall we take a vote on it? My view is that we should inform them of the situation right away, naturally.'

'Why?' roared Asunander.

Astor Nilsson gave something that was presumably a sigh of relief. Oh ho, thought Gunnar Barbarotti. I took the right side there, clearly.

'Because,' said Inspector Barbarotti slowly, as he tried to dredge up a sensibly formulated justification. 'Well, there are various reasons, of course . . . the protection aspect is the most obvious, I suppose. It would be good if we could stop him killing anyone else, basically. I seem to remember that's one of the fundamental tasks of the police force . . . protecting citizens. But correct me if I'm wrong.'

'Crrms,' said Asunander, snapping a pencil in two.

'There are other aspects as well,' Barbarotti went on. 'If, say, there's a link between Erik Bergman and Anna Eriksson, maybe Anna Eriksson can provide some details.'

'Exactly,' exclaimed Astor Nilsson.

Asunander growled and muttered something that presumably meant *resources*, and then got to his feet.

'You're responsible,' he said. 'Report to me. Now leave.'

Barbarotti and Astor Nilsson duly left Asunander's office.

'Christ almighty,' said Astor Nilsson once they were out in the corridor. 'I'm already missing home. That was the worst bloody morning I've had since my Leonberger had puppies. Is he always like that?'

'You should see him when he's in a bad mood,' said Barbarotti. 'Shall we go to my office and talk it through? If I've gathered this correctly, we're the lead investigators.'

'Good grief,' said Astor Nilsson, and inserted a wad of *snus* under his top lip.

'That means we'll have to release the victim's name, I assume?' asked Eva Backman. 'Erik Bergman, I mean.'

'Are there other victims?'

'Don't split hairs,' said Backman.

'For there to be any point to this, we must at the very least let all the Annas know his identity,' observed Astor Nilsson. 'Though no doubt word has already got out round the town, that's generally the way. And we'll have to ask them if they're associated with him in any way. Or know who he is, at any rate

. . . and then, well, that'll immediately bring us on to the protection issue, but if I understood correctly, then . . . ?'

'Sorrysen's already got that in hand,' confirmed Eva Backman. 'Just in theory, so far. But of course it's as Asunander says, a job like this can involve vast amounts of work.'

'There is a way round it,' said Astor Nilsson.

'Oh yes?' said Backman.

'Yes, we could always talk to these women without revealing quite everything. It has the advantage of not frightening them out of their wits, too. Just ask them about Erik Bergman, that is . . . without specifying how they fit in. What do you think of that?'

His gaze went from Backman to Barbarotti and back again. Eva Backman studied her shoes. Barbarotti looked out of the window. Five seconds elapsed.

'OK then,' said Barbarotti. 'Why not try that to start with? I suggest in that case that we three handle it all. We'll make initial contact by phone and arrange to meet each of them as soon as possible – face to face – though some of them will be away on holiday, of course.'

'Sixteen of the nineteen are contactable, we already know that,' said Eva Backman. 'So we'll call them in for a chat, then . . . tomorrow, I assume?'

'Yes,' said Barbarotti. 'That's what we'll do. For those in the vicinity, at any rate, but I don't think we need to call anyone home from Majorca or Thailand.'

'And the only thing we're going to ask them is whether they know an Erik Bergman,' said Astor Nilsson. 'Isn't it?'

'Yes,' said Barbarotti. 'Over the phone, only that, but if any of them have something interesting to give us, we'll bring in the Anna in question right away. Then we'll decide how we're going to play it tomorrow. Are we agreed on this?'

Eva Backman nodded. Astor Nilsson nodded.

'Right then,' said Gunnar Barbarotti. 'Here's the list. Nineteen ladies answering to the name of Anna Eriksson. I'll give you six each and take the other seven myself. It's two o'clock, so shall we say we'll reconvene here in two hours and report back?'

'I'll need a room,' said Astor Nilsson. 'Or a phone, at the very least.'

'Come with me,' said Eva Backman. 'It won't be a problem. Half the building is on holiday.'

Once they had left him, it struck Detective Inspector Barbarotti that it was still not twenty-four hours since he had left Visby. It felt like a month.

And somewhere out there was a murderer who was several steps ahead.

It all produced nothing.

That was the sum total.

It was 8 p.m. by the time Barbarotti left police headquarters. Of the sixteen Annas they had got hold of – all of whom had received one call from the police already, though they did not know it – none had any connection to the murdered Erik Bergman. Only two knew who he was, one because her husband worked at a company just next door to Bergman's IT firm in Järnvägsgatan, the other because they had been in the same year at upper-secondary school. Eight of the Annas were at home in Kymlinge and of these, five had heard about the murder. Four of the Annas were elsewhere in Sweden, while four were abroad on holiday.

And that left the three they had not been able to contact. Gustabo syndrome, thought Barbarotti glumly as he cut across Norra Torg. And I've no way of reaching her, either.

A comprehensive dissatisfaction gnawed away at him. What the hell are we doing, he wondered. We're faffing about like clowns without an audience. Of course the rule was to approach cases with an open mind, but this felt like chaos. What was it Backman said this morning? *We're playing into the murderer's hands.*

She had a point there, didn't she? Because if Lillieskog's alternative two was the one that applied – the carefully planning perpetrator – then every action they had taken hitherto must have been exactly what he was expecting. What anyone would have expected. Mustn't it?

A day and a half had gone by since the murder of Erik Bergman. They hadn't picked up the slightest clue. For his part, Barbarotti had spent almost the whole day focused on something else – a crime that had not yet taken place. That was how simple it was to deflect police resources in any direction you chose. He remembered an old post office slogan from yesteryear. *A letter means so much.* Wasn't there an old pop song of that title too?

And he remembered a bank robbery he had read about a few years ago. Germany, if he wasn't mistaken. The perpetrator had sent bomb threats to three different banks in the same town, the police had committed all available resources, and then he had robbed a fourth.

What if a fresh letter arrived tomorrow with a new name? What would they do then?

What if one of the Annas they had talked to began to realize what was at stake?

And the worst scenario of all: what if one of the Annas was actually murdered and word got out that the police had had advance notice of the crime – but failed to take any precautionary measures?

No, thought Gunnar Barbarotti. When we start on our interviews with them tomorrow we've got to show our hand. No matter what it costs.

Maybe they could ring up the security services and ask them to send thirty-eight extra officers? Wasn't that how it worked when they were protecting top politicians and suchlike? Two per person under guard? But there was a difference between a minister and an ordinary Anna Eriksson, of course.

Or why not offer all the Annas the option of being kept under lock and key at the police station? That would definitely be the neatest and cheapest solution.

But it was as this thought came into his mind that he realized it really was time to go home and get a few hours' sleep.

Sufficient unto the day is the evil thereof. Never a truer word spoken, he thought.

8

But it proved impossible to get even a wink of sleep.

It was his usual problem. He couldn't keep his eyes open long enough to read, but as soon as he closed them and tried to sleep, his whole head felt like a hive of bees. When it got to half past twelve, he got up, took a beer from the fridge and sat down at his desk. He stayed there a while in the darkness, looking out of the window towards Kymlinge River. You could see it had been a dry summer. The pale-yellow ovals of the street lights were reflected in the water, but filtered and dulled; the water level was so low that all manner of old junk was sticking up out of the mud. It didn't look pretty. You'd scarcely even be able to drown anybody in that gunk, thought Inspector Barbarotti, taking a drink of his beer.

And of course one had to wonder why a thought like that should come into his mind.

He put on the light and opened a new pad of paper. Might as well try to impose a bit of structure on his thoughts, it was generally one way of quietening down the beehive. He took a pen from the old tea caddy and pondered; then he scribbled down the names of four people:

Erik Bergman

Anna Eriksson

Gunnar Barbarotti

The Murderer

Admittedly the fourth wasn't a real name, he knew that, but that was the point of the exercise. To find new names. He drew a ring round each of the four participants. It didn't help. He put a cross after *The Murderer* and stared at it for thirty seconds, but that didn't help either. He tore out the page, threw it in the bin and started again. He drew a square with one name in each corner instead. He underlined the names and drew in the diagonals. Stared at the result for a while. Tore out the page and tossed that in the bin, too. What crap, he thought.

He started writing questions instead. After ten minutes, he had thought of twenty. He paused and considered. Decided to see if there were any he could answer, chewed his pen and concentrated.

After another ten minutes he was still at zero. Damn, thought Gunnar Barbarotti, this is going nowhere. Twenty questions and not a single answer. You really couldn't say the investigation had progressed particularly far.

Though to be fair, he had only spent one day on it so far. To find the right answers, you first had to ask the crucial questions, that was an old rule and a good one. He briefly considered having a conversation with Our Lord, but found it hard to come up with the right words. It didn't feel right, either. The deal they struck five years ago had specified – if his memory served him correctly, there was no written documentation unfortunately – that he was not allowed to ask for immediate help with cases in progress. Our Lord was not all-powerful and, above all, not a policeman, but after a moment's cogitation Barbarotti found a compromise.

O Lord, he prayed. Send a shaft of light into the befuddled and darkened brain of this poor cop. I'm stuck and I don't know what to do. Throw me a crumb in Your great mercy. It's not really worth points, this one, but never mind. If I can at least feel I'm taking a step in the right direction by the time I go for lunch tomorrow, I'll award You a bonus point, OK? You're already eleven points clear, congratulations.

He listened for an answer but all he could hear was the hacking roar of a motorbike under the chestnuts on the other side of the river. Bloody hooligan, thought Gunnar Barbarotti, he'll wake half the town, somebody ought to ring the police.

Then he drained his beer and stared at the questions again. Five minutes, he thought, I'll give it five more minutes.

Whether it was attributable to some kind of divine guidance was hard to determine, but he gradually started to detect a point of view crystallizing out of the coal mine inside him – or perhaps it was merely his ability to multitask collapsing completely . . . a black hole, yet another sad demonstration that men's minds can only focus on one thing at a time.

But there was something about the Annas . . . and the murderer's potential link with his victims.

Because if – thought Inspector Barbarotti at the same moment as he heard the bell of the St Charles church strike one-thirty in the diluted summer darkness – because if one assumed there really *was* a link between the murderer and his victims and between the victims themselves – and that this wasn't just some madman picking out names from the phone book – then it must be terribly risky for the murderer to give away the name of his intended second victim like this.

Since it was possible that the second victim knew the first – or perhaps knew was pushing it a bit far, Inspector Barbarotti corrected himself as he cautiously padded out to the kitchen to get beer number two, wary and supple as a panther so the thread of his thoughts would not break – but that there was a link, at any rate, and furthermore, that victim number two could conceivably enlighten the police on this matter, and . . .

. . . and ultimately provide some clue about their lowest common denominator, namely the murderer.

Namely the murderer, he repeated silently in his head.

And if this murderer really was one of the unpleasant sort who went in for meticulous planning, as profiler Lillieskog had suggested, then wouldn't it be . . . ?

. . . Well, wouldn't it be bloody odd for him to give the police a chance to talk to Anna Eriksson before he killed her? It certainly would!

It certainly would. Gunnar Barbarotti took a swig of beer and stared out of the window. Was there any flaw in this reasoning? He couldn't see one. So what were the implications for the investigation?

It took him a few seconds to find the answer. Yes, it basically meant they weren't going to get a thing from interviewing the sixteen Annas the next day – no, it wasn't that many, because several were elsewhere, far from Kymlinge, but even so – because . . . ?

. . . because there was every likelihood that the right Anna Eriksson was one of the small group they hadn't been able to contact.

And if the intention really was for her to die, then presumably she didn't have long to live.

Or was even already dead.

He sat there calmly examining this conclusion while finishing his second beer, and gradually realized it was just the kind of conclusion one all too readily reached at this hour. In the middle of the night, alone at a desk with a beer, a waning moon and a sludgy river.

But the realization that his reasoning was correct carried at least as much weight. And then that image of the higher power and the pack of cards reappeared in his mind.

Well what do you know, thought Detective Inspector Barbarotti. A game of patience did go out today, after all. In the end.

The next morning he came across Eva Backman immediately, as they were parking their bikes.

'Something occurred to me last night,' he announced with a certain amount of restraint.

Eva Backman nodded. 'Me too,' she said. 'I'll go first. I think it's one of the three other Annas we ought to concentrate on.'

'What in hell's name?'

'Well, let me explain,' said Backman. 'If it's the case that—'

'Stop right there!' Barbarotti interrupted. 'That's exactly the same conclusion I arrived at. No need to explain. We can call off all these interviews. If anybody needs our protection it's those we didn't find yesterday.'

'No,' said Eva Backman. 'We can't do that. We simply can't ring those poor women a third time. Sorrysen and Killander can talk to them – we'll devise a form with a few questions and it can't do any harm. But not a word about the letters. They mustn't suspect what's at stake.'

Barbarotti thought about this. 'All right.' He said. 'Perhaps that's best. But you and I have got to pick the right one amongst the other three.'

As they were going into the building, she put her hand on his arm for a moment. 'Gunnar,' she said. 'I've got such an awful feeling. I sense . . . I sense we're dealing with someone really repulsive this time.'

He stopped and looked at her. And two things struck him.

One was that he had never heard her say anything like that before.

The other was that she was absolutely right.

'Highly likely,' he said. 'But we're going to solve this, even so.'

By quarter to nine, the number of elusive Annas had shrunk from three to two. Detective Sergeant Molin knocked cautiously on Barbarotti's door and informed him that they had made contact with a certain Anna Eriksson, forty-two, who was on holiday in the Lofoten islands with her husband and children. Mobile coverage was evidently a bit patchy up there, but now she was sitting in a cafe in the main town, Svolvær, and the signal had got through. What was it they wanted?

Molin had not gone into this, saying merely that the police were looking for someone of that name, but as she was clearly not in Kymlinge for the time being, she could not be the person in question.

Presumably they could assume this, asked Molin. That it was another Anna they were looking for? Barbarotti said he thought so, and thanked his colleague. The DS withdrew to the corridor.

That left two.

Anna Eriksson number two was thirty-four and her address was 15 Skolgatan. According to their information, she worked at an advertising agency called Sfinx, but it was closed until early August. She was unmarried and since her flat was just a bedsit of forty square metres, one could assume she lived alone.

'15 Skolgatan is only three minutes away,' observed Eva Backman, who had been brooding in Barbarotti's room for the past half hour. 'I'll pop over and check with the neighbours. Best do it now before they push off to their summer cottages.'

Gunnar Barbarotti nodded and glanced out of the window.

She was right. It was a scorcher out there.

'You do that,' he said. 'But I assume it's a bit too soon for a search warrant?'

'Maybe I'll find her in?' said Eva Backman optimistically. 'Maybe it's just that we've got an out-of-date phone number here. I'll go on to Grimstalundsvägen while I'm about it, OK?'

'You do that,' repeated Barbarotti and started rolling up his shirtsleeves. 'And I'll man the home front in the meantime.'

On this particular morning, the home front turned out to consist of three hours of briefings and reports. Astor Nilsson and profiler Lillieskog sat in on these; they had clearly both stayed over at Kymlinge Hotel. Chief Inspector Asunander was also present in the briefing room most of the time, though he never said anything. He just stood in a corner, sucked on his teeth and monitored proceedings, or so it seemed, a grim, impenetrable expression on his face.

More or less the way you would look at your mother-in-law's funeral, Barbarotti thought at one point.

First up was Kallwrangel, the pathologist. He had been known as Karlsson until about a year ago, and it was a matter of much speculation at police headquarters how the Swedish Patent and Registration Office could have approved his new name. There had even been a piece submitted to the staff magazine under the pseudonym Ballwinckel.

But it wasn't the name issue that was on the agenda this time. Kallwrangel took twenty-five minutes to explain in great detail what everyone largely already knew, namely that thirty-six-year-old Erik Bergman died early on Tuesday morning down by Kymlinge River at a point close to Tillgrens garden centre, as a result of five stab wounds, at least two of which would have been fatal in their own right, and that he had presumably already lost consciousness by the time of the final knife blow. It was not possible to draw any conclusions about the perpetrator on the basis of the wounds on the dead man's body, but it seemed pretty likely that the person in question possessed some degree of physical strength and equally likely that he (or possibly but less plausibly *she*) was right-handed. There had been no signs of a struggle, nor had the murderer left anything behind on the body of the victim that could eventually lead to identification via DNA. The time of the attack was estimated at between 6.40 and 6.50 a.m., the body of course having been discovered at 6.55 a.m.

The latter part of Kallwrangel's presentation was devoted to how the knife had penetrated the various areas of Bergman's body and to a rough approximation of how this knife might look. A single blade, between fifteen and eighteen centimetres long, barely three and a half centimetres wide at its broadest point.

'Like a kitchen knife?' asked Astor Nilsson.

'Like that,' said Kallwrangel, and as nobody had any other questions, he handed over to the head of the forensic team, whose name still *was* Carlsson, though with a 'C'.

Carlsson began by telling them about the murder scene.

The results were very negative, he explained. They had not been able to secure any evidence to provide clues to the identity of the perpetrator; the overgrown bushes growing right beside the crime scene showed signs of having been trampled in a few places, possibly while the murderer had hidden there to wait for his victim, but that was all they could say for now. Nor had they secured any foreign particles from Bergman's clothes – a pair of shorts and a T-shirt bearing the logo of his computer company Informatex – and it could pretty much be assumed that whoever took Erik Bergman's life had not even needed to touch him. Except with the knife blade, that is. Five times.

Then Carlsson moved on to the two letters. They were currently at the National Forensic Centre in Linköping for further analysis, but he still had a few things to say about them. No fingerprints had been secured, either on the envelope or on the letter inside, nor had the letter writer needed to use his own saliva to stick on the stamp, which was one of the modern, self-adhesive kind. Inside the envelope they had found a very small particle that could possibly have been a cat's hair. Or rather, a tiny length of a cat's hair, but hopefully there would be more information about that in the report from Linköping when it came through.

'Cat?' said Gunnar Barbarotti.

'Hrrm, yes,' said Lillieskog. 'It's not unusual for this kind of perpetrator to keep a pet.'

'Thank you,' said Barbarotti. 'Go on.'

Superintendent Carlsson went on. The paper and envelope used by the murderer were of the most common type, at least in Sweden. The pen was probably a Pilot with a nib size of 0.7mm, as they had already guessed. As for where the letter was posted, it was not entirely unlikely to be Gothenburg. In both cases.

'Not entirely unlikely?' queried Astor Nilsson.

'Precisely,' said Carlsson. 'Linköping will make its judgement on that, too.'

'We'll see, then,' said Barbarotti. 'Anything else from your technicians?'

There wasn't. Instead they moved on to what had been gleaned from interviews with Erik Bergman's acquaintances, relatives and neighbours. They had conducted thirty-six interviews, and in order to provide some kind of intelligible overview Inspector Gerald Borgsen, alias Sorrysen, had taken it upon himself to listen to all the recordings and read all the notes. How he had found time for this was a mystery, but Sorrysen had a reputation for being something of a mystery altogether. Quiet, understated, a little reserved and, as his nickname implied, a touch mournful.

It took almost an hour and they possibly had a slightly clearer picture of Erik Bergman by the end. Even his closest circle of friends – three or four other single men with whom he would go drinking – had not found it easy to get close to him. Something of a recluse, they suggested, despite living a fair chunk of his life in the pub. Even when he got drunk, as he occasionally did, he would not open up. To illustrate this, Sorrysen quoted one Rasmus Palmgren, who had known Bergman ever since they started school together. 'You kind of never knew where you were with him. He always gave the impression he'd rather be somewhere else. You could never really tell what he was thinking.' Erik Bergman was not tight-fisted, and if Sorrysen had to hazard a guess, this was the quality that had done most to oil the wheels of his social life.

He always had plenty of money and the drinks were often on him, many informants had told them. As regards possible enemies – the sort who might have decided to stick a knife into him five times or more – no one had any tip-offs to offer them. Erik had never been known for picking quarrels; if it ever came to a scuffle or voices were raised, he preferred to keep out of it. He was not much of a ladies' man either. He wasn't interested in women, this Palmgren had told them, and women weren't interested in him. Was he homosexual? Various of the interviewees had been asked this, but none of them had given a clear-cut answer. On the other hand, they had not completely ruled it out. The conclusion was that Erik Bergman had been as discreet about his sex life – assuming he had one – as he was about everything else.

'The man without qualities?' suggested Astor Nilsson.

'In a way,' said Sorrysen, and Gunnar Barbarotti could have sworn the inspector's face flushed slightly. It was an epithet that could in many respects be applied to him, too. And it was very apparent that he was aware of it.

They had not managed to get hold of the woman Erik Bergman had lived with for a few months ten years ago, Sorrysen told them. Her name was Ulrika Sigridsdotter, and according to some of the interviewees she had moved abroad, soon after she and Erik separated.

Sorrysen took another twenty minutes to conclude his summary, and it was at this stage Gunnar Barbarotti started finding it hard to concentrate.

What if the murderer had simply chosen him at random after all, he thought. After all, Lillieskog saw it as a plausible alternative. What point is there in us trying to analyse the dead man?

If there was no logical link between the murderer and the victim.

If it could just as well have been someone else who got stabbed.

The very thought that the whole thing could be purely arbitrary brought with it a queasy feeling he found extremely uncomfortable. Because that solution contained . . . well, what? An incontrovertible truth about life and its inherent fragility? The fact that you could be snatched away at any time. In the midst of life we are in death, and the distance between being alive and no longer being alive could be measured in millimetres and fractions of a second; you could make prognoses and calculate probabilities to almost a hundred per cent, but when you were lying there in the twilight zone, it was likely to mean that one of your computations had gone awry. Wasn't that so? Even if the number of murder victims in the country stayed fairly constant from year to year, it didn't signify that the individual victim, Erik Bergman for example, was the product of any kind of active principle. Death was the only certainty, yet it always came as a surprise. Almost always, at any rate.

I can't definitely know, for example, that Marianne is alive at this moment, he thought with a sudden, crawling sense of panic – and then it struck him that this was Thursday, the day her children were arriving on Gotland with a mobile phone. At virtually the same second, he realized he didn't know which number to call. Maybe it was one of the teenagers' phones, not Marianne's? Though he would start with her number, of course he would, there was no harm in trying; and he would make sure to keep his phone switched on and be within reach of it all day, so as not to miss her first call. Actually, he felt like popping out of the meeting right now to give it a try, in case they had come over on the early morning ferry. If there was such a thing.

I wonder how my life will look, exactly five years from now? Will I be married to Marianne? And where will I be living, if so? I can't expect her to move to Kymlinge, can I? Though on the other hand, what is there to keep me here, really? Nothing. My children have moved out and I'm as free as a bird to settle wherever in the world I like.

And then – as Sorrysen talked on – his thoughts gathered momentum like a snowball rolling downhill.

Will I even still be a policeman in five years' time? Why not give law another go instead, having certainly been exposed to enough of the reverse side . . . though being a prosecutor doesn't seem that much fun, either. Just look at Dopy Ramundsen or Sylvenius, you'd be hard put to find gloomier individuals, though in fact who says I'll even still be alive, five years from now . . . wasn't that just what I was brooding about, a few minutes ago? Wonder whether I had a little stroke while Carlsson was talking, they can be very slight, and nobody should imagine they're immune just because they haven't turned fifty yet.

When Sorrysen finally rounded off his account by explaining there were still a few important interviews to be done, and all the reports would be available in the usual files, the mental activity in Gunnar Barbarotti's brain was hovering around zero. Or possibly just below; he was having great difficulty keeping his eyes open and the only thing he fully appreciated was that he must be suffering some kind of jetlag after the journey home from Gotland.

Plus the fact that, for now, he was probably not the most efficiently functioning detective in the world.

9

'Something's gone wrong in my head. I can't cope with briefings any more.'

Eva Backman looked at him with a sad smile. 'I agree that you're wrong in the head. But the fact that you can't cope with a three-hour briefing isn't a sign of that.'

'Oh really?' said Barbarotti. 'Well if you say so, inspector. How did you get on with the Annas?'

'I may be able to catch wind of one of them this afternoon,' Backman told him. 'The one in Grimstalundsvägen. Apparently it's possible she's holed up with a secret lover in Värmland. Somewhere near Grums.'

'Hang on, said Barbarotti. 'Wasn't she fifty-six and single? Why would she need a secret . . . ?'

'You're just prejudiced,' said Backman. 'Besides, the secrecy adds a bit of spice, even somebody wrong in the head ought to know that. But in this case it might also be because the lover's married elsewhere.'

'Far away from Grums?'

'Far away from Grums.'

Gunnar Barbarotti leant back in his chair and pondered this. 'Interesting,' he said. 'Just think what interesting lives people lead, who would have thought it . . . at that sort of age, I mean. You do learn things in this job sometimes.'

Inspector Backman sighed.

'If we could possibly concentrate for a minute,' she suggested, 'I ought to have her location confirmed in a couple of hours' time. Perhaps even get to talk to her. But not much luck with the other Anna.'

'Not much luck?'

'Well, none, in fact. I talked to a couple of neighbours – she lives in Skolgatan, one of those middle-class neighbourhoods, they all seem to know each other each quite well round there . . . and to a girlfriend of hers, and that's what's making me nervous.'

'Why?' said Barbarotti, taking out his pen and a pad and starting to make notes. 'Why are you nervous?'

'Because Anna and her friend had semi-arranged to go to Gotland together this Friday – tomorrrow, that is – but she hasn't been in touch all week. Not since last Sunday.'

'Gotland?' said Barbarotti.

'You're not the only one who goes to Gotland in the summer, you know,' Backman informed him patiently. 'Anyway, this friend thought it was odd that she hadn't been able to get through to her. When I asked her how she accounted for it, she said she supposed it was that bloody Conny, of course.'

'Conny?'

'You realize you keep repeating one of the words I've said and putting a question mark at the end of it?'

'No I don't,' said Barbarotti. 'But I'm a bit tired. So who's this Conny?'

'Some guy she's been hanging around with off and on, apparently. Her boyfriend, or whatever you want to call him. They've . . . well, they haven't been getting on very well recently. It was a mystery why Anna would want to be with such an arse, the friend said.'

'I see. And what has Conny the arse got to say about it?''

'Haven't been able to get hold of him,' said Eva Backman with a fresh sigh. 'Name of Conny Härnlind. Runs his own business, heating and air conditioning. The place is closed for the holidays. He's got three phones, and we've left messages on all of them.'

'Is there any link between Härnlind and Bergman?'

'None that I've found yet.'

'OK then,' said Barbarotti. 'All we've got to do is sit here and wait for him to ring, in other words?'

'Yup,' said Backman. 'You don't happen to have any nice board games we could play while we're waiting?'

Once Backman had left him – whether because he didn't keep so much as a pack of cards in his office, or for other reasons – it was no more than a minute before Astor Nilsson came in with a sheet of paper.

'Sorry to disturb you, O esteemed colleague,' he said. 'But there's a bit of new information on the case.'

'Excellent,' said Barbarotti. 'Fire away.'

Astor Nilsson cleared his throat. 'No less than two witnesses independently observed Erik Bergman when he was out on his run that fateful morning.'

'Well there we are,' said Barbarotti.

'One of them was a jogger, who met him at approximately 6.20 a.m., level with the bridge, the other is a jogger who met him by the water tower at 6.25 a.m. Neither of them noticed anything about Bergman to indicate he was about to be murdered.'

'Excess speed reduces power of observation,' said Barbarotti. 'I know that from my own experience. Did they have anything else to say?'

'I'm afraid not. It would have been interesting if they'd seen anybody else out on the track near the murder scene, but they didn't. Neither of them.'

'But they both ran past it?'

'Yes, a quarter of an hour earlier in one case, ten minutes in the other.'

'So the murderer could already have been lurking there?'

'Well if not, he must at least have been on his way,' said Astor Nilsson. 'But our early morning fitness fanatics didn't see a damn thing. Shame, eh?'

'Grab a chair,' said Barbarotti. 'How come you were lent to us? I mean . . . ?'

'They're always lending me out,' explained Astor Nilsson genially, taking a seat. 'That's the way it's been these past two years. I went against my boss in a case, and he can't bear the fact that I was proved right. He can't sack me, of course, but as soon as anyone needs reinforcements within a twenty thousand kilometre radius of Gothenburg, off I go. To be honest, I don't mind. It's good to get out and about.'

'But you're a chief inspector?'

'Yes I am.'

Gunnar Barbarotti studied him. The frustration Astor Nilsson had expressed after yesterday's morning with Asunander seemed to have drained off him. He gave a pretty good-natured impression, sitting there in the visitors' chair with one leg thrown casually over the other and his sockless, sandalled foot wagging up and down. Tanned, thinning hair cropped short, and a body weight of around a hundred kilos. But very far from fat. A harmonious battering ram, Barbarotti decided. A fifty-five year old who had gained a few insights into life.

'What do you really think about this, then?'

Astor Nilsson threw up his hands.

'No bloody idea,' he said. 'But I don't like it. Haven't come across this kind of perpetrator before, in fact. Though I've seen a thing or two in my time.'

Barbarotti nodded. 'And what do you think of the way we're handling this? Are we missing something?'

Astor Nilsson shrugged his powerful shoulders. 'Don't think so. I hate to admit it, but we're just kind of waiting for the second victim. There ought to be a connection between this Bergman and one of the many Annas.'

'You're right,' said Barbarotti. 'And if I understood Inspector Backman correctly, she's homing in on the right one as we speak.'

'The right Anna?'

'Yes. She hasn't been seen for a few days, so one has one's suspicions.'

'Well well,' said Astor Nilsson. 'Efficient work in this place, I must say.'

'Hmm,' said Barbarotti. 'Sometimes, perhaps. But we're far from certain we're on the right track here. It could just as well turn out to be one of the others.'

'Or somebody from the wilds of Sweden or even Kuala Lumpur?'

'Yes, even there. I don't think we've many grounds for feeling optimistic.'

The same could be said five hours later, noted Gunnar Barbarotti as he retrieved his bike from the rack in the police station yard. It was quarter to eight, and a beautiful summer's evening, and no Anna Eriksson from Skolgatan had shown up as the afternoon dragged on. Nor had Conny the air-conditioning arse heeded police requests to get in touch, but that was not the worst of Inspector Barbarotti's worries. He had heard nothing from Gotland.

'You look glum,' observed Eva Backman.

'Life's a bad joke,' said Barbarotti.

'You pedal off home and ring Marianne,' suggested Backman cheerily, 'and you'll soon feel your spirits rise, inspector.'

'Thanks for the tip,' said Gunnar Barbarotti. 'So you're not starting your holiday on Monday, then?'

She shook her head. 'Put it back a week. Ville will have to take the kids to the cottage, and I'll join them next Friday.'

They set off on their bikes, side by side. She didn't sound entirely unhappy with the arrangement, Barbarotti noted with slight surprise, and he was struck by the marked contrast between their respective situations in life. His and Eva Backman's. And yet they were about the same age, both DIs and each had three children.

It was just that his own kids were so far out of reach on this lovely evening. One in London, two in Copenhagen. Which suddenly felt a painfully long distance away. Eva Backman would step inside her nice terraced house in less than ten minutes and see her three. And her husband, of course. Yes, there was the world of difference.

'What's on your mind?' she asked.

'Nothing in particular,' he said. 'This is where I turn off. See you tomorrow.'

'Sleep well, sweet dreams,' said Inspector Backman, and threw him a kiss.

Spot on, he thought. People on their own ought to have a

right to that. A rich dream life, in the absence of anything more substantial.

It was quarter past ten when she rang. Hearing her voice, Gunnar Barbarotti suddenly understood what it must feel like to be saved from drowning at the last second. At the same instant, he felt almost frightened by the wave of emotion that came washing over him; the blood pounded in his temples and his tongue stuck to the roof of his mouth. But as for Marianne, she sounded completely calm and normal.

What's up with me, he thought in dismay. Look at this hand holding the receiver, it's shaking, for God's sake!

Marianne explained that unfortunately the mobile phone her offspring had brought with them was playing up, and that was why it had taken her so long to get in touch.

'So you're in Hagmund and Jolanda's kitchen?' enquired Barbarotti.

'Yes,' confirmed Marianne. 'It's a bit late, I know, but luckily they hadn't gone to bed. How are you?'

'I . . . I miss you,' said Gunnar Barbarotti, and was able to swallow at last.

'Glad to hear it. That's why it's good to be apart occasionally. To learn what missing someone means. Have you caught your letter writer yet?'

'No,' admitted Barbarotti, feeling no inclination whatsoever to talk to Marianne about work. But it was only natural that she should ask, of course. It was the letter writer who had forced him to leave Gustabo ahead of time. That was why they were now at opposite ends of a telephone line instead of skin to skin. 'But we're working on it,' he said. 'How are things with you? Did the kids get there all right?'

She laughed. 'Oh yes. But they were definitely a bit disappointed not to see their detective. You've got it made there, my darling.'

I've deceived them, thought Gunnar Barbarotti. Pulled the wool over their eyes, all three of them. What was it called? Groucho Marx syndrome. That very specific phenomenon of not wanting to join any club that would have you as a member.

'Go on with you,' he said. 'You know what teens are like, they change their views as often as they change their socks.'

They exchanged a dozen comments at about that level of subtlety, then Marianne lowered her voice and said she was in oestrus and a bit tired of sleeping alone in a bed with room for two. Gunnar Barbarotti declared that for his part he was not in oestrus, but was prepared to sleep beside her for the rest of his days – or nights, to be precise – in a bed where there was barely room for a tiny lapdog or something, and at that point Jolanda obviously came into the kitchen for something. He could hear it, even in Kymlinge. Marianne took a deep breath, wished him good night and promised to go into Visby one day very soon and buy a new mobile phone. Without telling the children, obviously, because she didn't want to infringe Gustabo regulations to that extent.

After they had hung up, Gunnar Barbarotti went and sat on the balcony with a beer. Christ, he thought. I didn't realize she meant that much. If I lost her I'd put a bullet through my brain.

He sat there for a while and finished his beer, watching the remains of the sunset, which hung there like a mirage, a smear of palest yellow above Pampas and behind the tower blocks over in Ångermanland. And the jackdaws, that screeching horde, flocking in to roost on the roofs of the town and in the elms in the town park, he watched them too. They were early this year, weren't they? He had always associated the jackdaw invasion with cooler autumn evenings. Late August, September. But of course they, too, must be there the year round, like all other living creatures. *A man without a woman*, was his next thought, but he couldn't remember the rest of it this evening, either . . . *is like a . . . ?*

His beer finished, he finally wrenched himself free of his self-pitying reflections and spared a thought or two for the continuing investigation. The murderer.

The letter-writing murderer. It was the letters that made it all so singular. Made it feel unique, somehow. If the case had consisted merely of their finding a man who had been stabbed to death, they would have swung into action of course, but it would not have carried the same weight. The newspapers still hadn't released the name of the deceased, but he knew they would tomorrow. And that was probably a correct decision.

Perhaps it would also have been correct to tell the public about the letters and release Anna Eriksson's name? Perhaps that way they could have got hold of somebody who knew something?

On the other hand, it was easy to stir up panic. And if there was anything the tabloids liked to do, it was that. Project people's inherent fears, frustrations and anger and direct it at one point, one scapegoat. It used to be ethnic groups, Jews or Gypsies or Communists, but nowadays it was individuals. A government minister, for example. Or an actor with alcohol problems. Or why not an unsuspecting detective inspector in Kymlinge? That was the intrinsic motor of the so-called pack. It had worked for as long as there had been newspapers, and it worked better than ever today, now that vulgarity and smut were the keys in which everything was to be sung.

And now that a TV blonde's new silicon lips were more significant news than genocide in some part of the world that wasn't central Stockholm. Bloody hell, thought Gunnar Barbarotti. Has this country ever been more superficial? Have we ever had a worse tabloid press?

He wondered how aware the murderer was of this. If he was deliberately writing his letters because he knew that it would make things harder for the police in many respects. Particularly the day it came out in the press. Because the fact of the matter is, thought Barbarotti, watching a new swarm of jackdaws make an elegant avian circuit before coming in to land on the ridge of Cathedral School's roof, that two leads aren't always better than one. Especially if one of them has been planted there by the murderer himself with the aim of . . .

Well, the aim of what?

It was a vexing question. Extraordinarily so.

And what lay ahead for Anna Eriksson?

More vexing still.

Same thing again, noted Barbarotti as he came in from the balcony. Rather one vexing question than two.

What was more, they were both pretty scary, and that hardly made things better. He remembered Eva Backman's hand on his arm that morning. The fact that he – Detective Inspector Gunnar Barbarotti of Baldersgatan in Kymlinge – was the addressee of the letters was another disturbing factor, of course.

Because what did it mean? Did it mean that he knew the perpetrator in some way? That the murderer's name – once they got wind of it – would prove familiar? The converse, that the murderer knew who it was he was sending his letters to, seemed pretty obvious, at any rate. Didn't it?

What a total pain, thought Gunnar Barbarotti, checking the time, if only I hadn't taken those letters from the postman that morning – or if he'd come just a minute later – then I would have been snuggling up in bed with Marianne at Gustabo about now. I can scarcely imagine it would have done the investigation any harm.

Rape field, cows, churchyard, broadleaved woodland. Here in Kymlinge there was an acute lack of all those. Well, there was a churchyard of course.

His head full of dismal thoughts such as these, he went to take a shower.

10

'We've located the air-conditioned arse.'

Barbarotti looked up from his reports.

'What?'

It was Friday morning. He had read eight reports, the one in his hand being the ninth. It was the work of a certain DS Wennergren-Olofsson. He had a rather flowery style, seldom making do with three words if he could use twenty. He was also known for being the only officer in the building who took more than ten seconds to sign his name: Claes-Henrik Wennergren-Olofsson.

'Conny Härnlind,' clarified Eva Backman, closing the door behind her. 'The potential boyfriend of Anna Eriksson in Skolgatan.'

'I remember,' said Barbarotti, promptly closing his eyes to escape the sudden flock of names. 'Located, you said?'

'Yes indeed. He's in Thailand, but not with Ms Eriksson. Nor any other woman for that matter – and by that I mean women from Kymlinge and environs. He went out there with a group of other young blokes a week ago, and it's not so hard to guess what they've been up to.'

'Who's prejudiced now?' asked Barbarotti.

'Sorry,' said Backman. 'Well, maybe I was being a bit hasty there, I'm sure they've gone there to discuss philately and ecumenical issues. But be that as it may, Anna's still missing. I spoke to her mum and she doesn't know anything either. They generally ring each other a couple of times a week. She lives in Jönköping. The worrying thing is . . .'

'Yes?'

'The slightly worrying thing is that she evidently told her mum she was going to Gotland, too. Today, that is.'

'And when did she tell her that?'

'Sunday evening. Her mum called three or four times in the week but got no answer, so . . . so I just don't know.'

'Damn,' said Gunnar Barbarotti. 'That doesn't sound good. She's got a mobile, hasn't she?'

'Yes.'

'We'll have to check if she used it at all this past week. I think . . .'

'I just dropped in for a word with Sorrysen. He'll already be in touch with the mobile phone operator, I should imagine.'

'Good,' said Barbarotti. 'Then we'll have the information this afternoon, with any luck. If a single woman doesn't use her mobile phone for four days of her holiday, it means there's something wrong.'

He expected Eva Backman to say something about prejudices – almost hoped she would – but she didn't. Shame, he thought. She realizes where this is probably leading, just like me.

'We'd better be ready with a search warrant, hadn't we?' she suggested instead. 'If we . . . well, if we get that kind of answer from the operator.'

That kind of answer, thought Gunnar Barbarotti once she had left the room. That was one way of putting it, he supposed. A thin layer of linguistic balm applied to the wounds of reality. Though it was far from usual for Backman to talk like that.

Which was also significant, presumably. He remembered again the hand she had laid on his arm.

He sighed and returned to DS Wennergren-Olofsson's deathless prose.

At two o'clock on Friday afternoon, Astor Nilsson and profiler Lillieskog both left Kymlinge police station. Astor Nilsson would be back after the weekend, and Lillieskog would come any day he was summoned.

'I did the follow-up interviews with four of Bergman's acquaintances this morning,' Astor Nilsson told them as they wound up the week over four cups of coffee and four almond tarts, chock-full of preservatives. 'Like we said. And I can promise you on my mother's grave that none of them has the slightest inkling of what lies behind the murder. None of them are saints, of course, but when you scrape away the rubbish, you're left with the facts. Erik Bergman's assassin isn't to be found in his circle of friends. We can stop looking for him there.'

'And then we had a few who were away, didn't we?' said Backman.

'Correct,' said Astor Nilsson. 'I accept that reservation. Though if you're away you can't simultaneously be at home, stabbing people to death.'

'OK,' said Barbarotti. 'Let's suppose you're right. Where *shall* we look, then?'

'I've no answer to that question for the time being,' said Astor Nilsson. 'But I'm going back to Gothenburg and home to Hisingen to think about it over the weekend. If I come up with anything before Monday, I'll let you know.'

'Excellent,' said Eva Backman.

'You know where you can reach me if I can help in any way,' Lillieskog declared in his turn. 'I do wonder about the best-before date of this tart.'

'It's part of a batch from before they started putting dates on,' Backman informed him obligingly. 'Sometime in the sixties. You're both very welcome to bring along a few other treats when you turn up again.'

They shook hands, wishing each other a good weekend, and the party broke up.

'Well then,' said Backman when they were alone. 'That's our expertise gone.'

'Too right,' said Barbarotti. 'Nothing from that mobile operator yet?'

Backman shook her head. 'They promised to email me the lists by three, so we'll just have to be patient until then, anyway. Have you been through all the reports?'

Gunnar Barbarotti shrugged.

'Thirty-eight of the forty-two, anyway.'

'And?'

'Well, it's just as Astor Nilsson says, I'm afraid. There's nothing that seems to lead anywhere. I agree with him that the murderer presumably didn't know Erik Bergman particularly well. Not recently, that is . . . could all go back to something in their past. I mean, these things generally take some time to rise to the surface.'

'Yes, and people do normally have some kind of reason for killing someone. Call me old-fashioned, but . . . ?'

'We can always hope,' said Barbarotti. 'No link to any

Anna Eriksson either, anyway. Things aren't exactly moving forward.'

Eva Backman finished her coffee and bit her lip. 'No, not really,' she said. 'But the murderer must have had some idea of Bergman's habits, mustn't he? He knew he'd be going out for a run that morning. He can't just have gone and crouched in a bush on spec. What does that tell us?'

'That he'd been keeping him under observation for few days, maybe,' suggested Barbarotti. 'Sat in a car and checked out his usual movements, say.'

'And we've asked the neighbours whether they saw a suspicious car in the neighbourhood, I assume?'

Gunnar Barbarotti watched a fly crawl across his bare forearm. 'Haven't seen anything about that kind of sighting in the reports.'

'Great,' said Eva Backman, getting to her feet. 'Just as well to think things through before we take any further steps. I'll come and see you when I hear from the mobile operator.'

'You do that,' said Gunnar Barbarotti.

It took barely more than twenty minutes, in fact, and the result was as unambiguously negative as he and Backman had feared. Anna Eriksson – who lived in Skolgatan in central Kymlinge and was a Telenor customer – had not used her mobile phone since five past eleven on Tuesday morning. In the three days that had passed since then she had received twenty-nine calls but not answered a single one. Six text messages as well, though it was impossible to tell whether they had been read, but she certainly hadn't replied to any of them.

Backman handed the list of calls to Barbarotti. 'Tuesday,

11 a.m.,' she said. 'The first unanswered call is registered as 12.26 p.m. What do you think?

'That's the day Erik Bergman was murdered,' said Barbarotti. 'I got the letter about Anna Eriksson in Wednesday's post. He could . . . he must have posted it sometime on Tuesday . . . maybe in Gothenburg? You don't think he could actually have . . . dealt with them both the same day?'

He stared at Eva Backman, as if he was expecting her to give him a correct answer – but she merely looked at him with empty eyes and a mouth compressed into a line as thin as a razor blade. She sat there, utterly immobile with her shoulders hunched and her hands clasped between her knees, for a good while before she answered.

'How should I know?' she said finally. 'But one thing I *do* know is that it's time to pay a little visit to Skolgatan. We got the warrant from Sylvenius an hour ago.'

Gunnar Barbarotti checked the time. 'Seems a fair way to round off the working week.'

The flat was not large and they found her straight away.

For the first fraction of the first second, Barbarotti felt a perverse kind of triumph. *We were right! It was her! We were on the right track!*

But then he felt nothing but disgust and impotence. Anna Eriksson, thirty-four years of age, single and in the employ of the Sfinx advertising agency in Fabriksgatan, had not gone on a trip to Gotland. Or anywhere else. She was lying under her own bed in her home at 15 Skolgatan, packaged up in two black bin bags, one pulled up from her feet, the other pulled down over her head, and she did not smell good. The sweetish stench coming from her dead body was unmistakeable in the warm, closed-up flat; they could smell it the moment they opened the door, and when Barbarotti knelt beside the immaculately neat linen of the tubular steel bed in the alcove and confirmed the fact – and then straightened up again – he suddenly felt a slight giddiness, resulting not so much from the sight that had met him as from unconsciously having held his breath for over thirty seconds.

'Get that balcony door open,' he instructed Inspector Backman.

Of course it then took nearly an hour before the two plastic sacks were duly removed by the doctor and the crime scene technicians – and a further half hour before the first preliminary identification had been made (with the help of a shocked young couple in the flat opposite) – but Inspector Barbarotti was certainly in no doubt who it was, in the course of those ninety long minutes.

Nor Eva Backman.

Nor was there much doubt about how Anna Eriksson had been killed. Her pale and slightly swollen face was relatively intact, but was framed by an oval of dark, dried blood, smeared across her temples and down both cheeks, and when they carefully turned her round, the trauma to her skull and above her right eye was apparent. Blunt instrument, thought Gunnar Barbarotti automatically, forcing back the queasiness that was welling up inside him. Such as some iron piping. Such as a baseball bat. Such as any fucking thing.

He exchanged looks with Backman and saw she was thinking the same as he was.

The method. The murderer hadn't used the same method.

That was unusual. Perpetrators tended to decide on an MO

and then stick to it. Firearm or knife or bare hands, depending on disposition and taste. But in this case he had swapped. Why, wondered Barbarotti. Or . . . or could they really be certain it was the same murderer?

He was aware that these technicalities bubbling up in his head were doing so to afford him some sort of protection from the grotesque sight of the woman on the floor.

For there had surely seldom been an investigation in which one could be that certain? But the question still had to be asked. Two murderers or one? Rash conclusions were the most dangerous of traps.

Bullshit, he thought, averting his eyes from the victim. Of course it was the same goddamned perpetrator. How likely was it that there were two entirely separate letter writers with identical handwriting? Or one wholly separate letter writer and two different perpetrators? No, forget it.

'How long?' he asked Santesson the pathologist, who was just stretching his back and adjusting his glasses. 'Roughly.'

Santesson glowered at him. 'At least twenty-four hours. Probably longer. I assume you've noticed the smell?'

'Oh yes,' confirmed Barbarotti. 'So it wouldn't be impossible for her to have been lying here since Tuesday, for example?'

'I wouldn't like to say,' said Santesson. 'But nothing's impossible.'

Smart alec, thought Barbarotti, and cast Backman a quizzical glance. Hadn't she seen enough, as he had?

Apparently she had. They left the flat together, and as they emerged onto the pavement they stopped short for a moment in the sunshine, blinking sleepily – as if they needed a few seconds to orientate themselves in reality again. Then Backman remembered where they'd parked the car and gestured to Barbarotti to get a move on.

They had plenty to keep them busy.

Rounding off the week had turned into the start of a long working weekend.

It was quarter past ten when Barbarotti left the police station. He had spent three hours discussing deployments and division of duties – he had talked to the press for an hour. News of the murder in Skolgatan had found its way to the journalists via unknown channels without any police intervention, which was the usual pattern, and the impromptu press conference had been well attended. After a quick consultation they had decided not to reveal the murderer's letter-writing habit; Barbarotti was far from convinced this was the right decision, but if you had doubts it was best to be cautious as a rule. Sorrysen, prosecutor Sylvenius and Astor Nilsson – over the phone from Gothenburg – had all taken the same view, and if they came to a different decision tomorrow, they would be able to broach the matter in a press release scheduled for three in the afternoon.

Throughout all these negotiations, Chief Inspector Asunander had adopted his customary low profile and advisory role, but as no one had sought his advice, he had not been required to strain his false teeth.

When Barbarotti finally got home, he sat on the same chair on the same balcony as the previous evening, and surveyed the lingering traces of the same sunset.

Or a sunset a day older, if you wanted to split hairs, the whole universe having grown a day older, of course, but for his part, Barbarotti felt he had aged a good deal more. About a couple of decades. The jackdaws had already gone to roost, he noted; the shrieks reaching his fourth-floor balcony came instead from young people enjoying the start of the weekend, making the most of the nice weather in parks and outdoor cafes.

He opened a beer of his own, poured it into a glass and downed it in four or five gulps. Almost instantly he felt the extreme tension easing and exhaustion slowly spreading through him.

What is all this, he asked himself.

What sort of lunatic have we got on our hands?

Lazy, sterile questions born of his powerlessness, he knew that. And dangerous. Demonizing the enemy was one of the commonest, and always the cheapest, of mistakes. It was the linchpin in all racism, for instance, all xenophobia. Towards the end of the evening, Asunander had come into his room and hinted that there was a chance of reinforcements; the question was to be decided on Saturday, and Barbarotti realized he would welcome the backup. Generally you were keen to deal with things yourself, locally; if there was one thing people cared about in the police force it was territorial boundaries.

But not with this case, thought Barbarotti. Call in people from Gothenburg and the National CID, that's fine by me. I'll sell my prestige for a pittance.

He was well aware it was the siren voices of fatigue talking, but after three twelve-hour days, which should really have been the last three days of his holiday, he reckoned his feelings had some legitimacy.

He had scarcely had time to think about Marianne all day

and it was only now, at almost eleven o'clock, that he remembered what she had said about going into Visby to buy a phone.

Dear God, he thought. Let her call. One point, OK?

But our Lord was not inclined to improve his ranking that evening, and Detective Inspector Barbarotti – uncomforted, unloved, forgotten, rejected by God and without cleaning his teeth – finally fell asleep some time after midnight.

11

As soon as he got in the car on Saturday morning, he started brooding about parenthood. Perhaps it was a hangover from his reflections on Eva Backman's relationship with her three children and how it compared with his own, but there was more to it than that.

The fact that it could be so different, for example. That people were so bloody different, and that basically anybody at all could become a parent. Anna Eriksson's mother was allegedly in touch with her daughter by phone at least once a week, but she hadn't time to come and identify her body until Sunday. Because she was too busy on Saturday.

On the other hand, she could squeeze in an hour with Inspector Barbarotti, she'd promised that.

He wondered if he'd ever experienced such a thing before. Someone attaching no priority at all to the identification of their murdered child. Or at any rate putting it off because there were more important things to do first.

Though she hadn't sounded particularly odd on the phone, thought Barbarotti. She had cried and given voice to her despair. At a rather unusually high volume, perhaps, but otherwise she had seemed pretty normal. Anna had been something of a favourite daughter, she had explained, and when he asked how many she had, she told him she had five. Plus four sons.

Maybe that was it. If you had nine children, you had to be prepared to lose one. He had not tried to find out how many different fathers were involved, but reading between the lines he was pretty sure it was more than two.

Fewer than nine? I do hope so, thought Gunnar Barbarotti.

As for him, he had had one father and one mother. His father was called Giuseppe Barbarotti, and the only thing he'd ever had from him was his surname; he had never met him and did not know if he was alive or dead. His mother had impressed upon him throughout his childhood that Giuseppe was a handsome bastard, and that it was best to keep away from him. For some reason, he had followed that recommendation. When his mother died twelve years before, he had toyed with the idea of going to Italy to look for his father, but the project had come to nothing. He had been so busy with his own family at the time, with two children and a third on the way, that there somehow hadn't been any scope for delving down into the generations of the family tree.

But now he didn't have that excuse any longer, thought Gunnar Barbarotti. What was stopping him from going to Italy and finding his father? Or his father's grave, if that turned out to be the case.

He knew that for the time being this amounted to no more than a thought he could toy with as he drove along on a sunny Saturday morning – but also that it was a question which might very well stay with him and grow more profound.

He would let time tell, he decided. But it seemed manifestly clear that children were not of equal importance to all parents. And vice versa. He made a mental note to ring Sara that evening, or perhaps on his way home. He had got into the habit of doing that: giving her a call at the weekend, to hear how his darling daughter was getting on in London, amidst the swarming hordes and deadly dangers of the metropolis.

And she was always able to put his mind at rest. She knew that was what the calls were basically all about, and this made him uneasy. Sara could be at death's door but keep it quiet so as not to worry him.

So he had to try to listen between the lines. He wasn't sure how well he had mastered that art; it was now seven weeks since she had left, and so far he had not been able to detect any dark signs. Beyond his suspicion that she worked in a pub, not a boutique as she claimed. She was living in Camden Town, and he planned to go over and see her for the weekend in late August or early September, at which point he would of course get a clearer picture of how things stood.

And then that chilling image of her lying murdered under a bed somewhere ran throught his consciousness, and he gripped the steering wheel harder. He had dreamt precisely that. In his dream it was not Anna Eriksson concealed in those bin bags, but his own daughter.

Life is so damn fragile, thought Gunnar Barbarotti. And so bloody normal until that second when everything shatters.

That's how it is. Like walking across the thinnest of ice, those are the terms. And now his mobile was ringing.

'It works! Good morning, my love.'

Simply hearing her voice was enough to make him almost drive into a German juggernaut in front of him. There's something seriously wrong with my mind these days, he thought. It's as unfocused as a fourteen year old's.

'Hi,' he said. 'Have you . . . ?'

'Yes I have. I'm just coming out of the shop. It's yellow, I got it for virtually nothing because it's an old model.'

For one bemused second he didn't know what she was talking about, but then he realized. 'I don't care what colour it is,' he said. 'But I want the number.'

She gave it to him, twice, and to be on the safe side she promised to text it to him as well, though wouldn't it already be stored in his phone now she'd called? Then she asked him what he was up to. He told her he was on his way to Jönköping to meet the mother of a woman who had just been murdered. It all went quiet at the other end of the line for a few moments and he realized he had been unnecessarily frank.

'The letter writer?' she asked.

'I'm afraid so.'

'Good God,' she said. 'He's killed two, then?'

'Yes, unfortunately,' said Gunnar Barbarotti, as if it was somehow his fault – as a detective and as the recipient of the letters – that Erik Bergman and Anna Eriksson had lost their lives, and he wanted to ask Marianne's forgiveness for it. That was a warped sort of idea, but somehow he felt he ought to have kept the truth to himself.

Though she would have found out about it sooner or later, of course. She read newspapers, presumably, and listened to the radio. Just as well to get it from him.

'It's all a bit much at the moment,' he said. 'I honestly wish I'd never left Gotland.'

'We're going to play throwing the *varpa* on the lawn this afternoon,' she said. 'You'd be welcome to join us . . . sorry, it's dreadful news, of course. Is there anything about it in the papers today?'

'I should think so,' said Barbarotti. 'I haven't actually checked.'

'I'll buy an evening paper,' Marianne declared. 'I want to

keep up with what you're doing, you know. But this investigation, is it . . . I mean, it isn't standard fare for you, is it?'

Why's she asking that? The question flashed into Gunnar Barbarotti's mind. Is it because she can't contemplate living with a man with a job like mine?

'No,' he said. 'It isn't standard fare. I don't think I've ever come across anything like it. Wondering whether to change jobs, in fact.'

He said the last sentence without running the words past his brain first – a shot in the dark to let her know he was not scared of changes, presumably – but when they ended the call ten minutes later, he was aware of them still suspended in his mind. The words, that was. And they had that same irate, bright-red glare as the warning lights on his dashboard. *Fuel within 50km! Top up oil!*

Change job!

I'll have to mull this over in peace and quiet some day, thought Inspector Barbarotti. My life is at a crossroads.

Viveka Hall Eriksson received him in the kitchen of her beautifully situated house in the Bymarken area of Jönköping. Lake Vättern lay like a mirror just a few hundred metres below the generous picture window, and Barbarotti could see that although she had lived a varied sort of life with many different partners, she had clearly not emerged empty-handed from it in financial terms.

And all her children seemed to have flown the nest. Her men, too.

She was sixty-four years old, he had checked that, and was doing her best to look forty-four. It was a few minutes to eleven when they sat down at the table she had laid for coffee, and he guessed she had spent a good part of the morning bringing her appearance to a decent level. She might have fitted in the hairdresser and beauty salon too; her hair was as blonde and beautifully waved as a field of ripe rye, her cheeks were powdered and rouged, her nails freshly polished; she did not look remotely like a woman who has borne nine children.

Nor like a mother who had received news of her daughter's murder the previous day.

'My dear inspector, I didn't sleep a wink all night,' she nonetheless declared in a very loud voice, running a hand over her shiny mauve blouse to make it even smoother and glossier. 'I'm so devastated I don't know what to do with myself. Have you caught him?'

'No,' said Barbarotti. 'I'm afraid not. We don't know who could have done it. That's why I'd appreciate a few words with you.'

'With me?' exclaimed Viveka Hall Eriksson. 'Oh my God, I hope you don't think I know anything about this . . . I don't understand what . . . oh my God?'

She spoke as if addressing someone twenty to thirty metres away; Barbarotti wondered if this was her normal volume or whether it was some kind of acute hysteria manifesting itself, after all. She hadn't really sounded like that on the phone.

'We're just going to have a little chat,' he said, as slowly and understatedly as he could. 'Of course you can't know anything about the background to this tragic event, but we've got to approach this in a thorough way, I'm sure you understand that. We very much want to get our hands on whoever killed Anna.'

'Oh yes,' she said, 'You've got to do that. That bastard mustn't get away with it. She was as good as gold, my Anna, she was.'

'I'm sure she was,' said Barbarotti. 'Now, do you happen to know whether she'd been going out with anybody recently?'

'Going out?' said Viveka Hall Eriksson, as if she did not really understand the meaning of the phrase. 'She didn't have a man, if that's what you mean.'

'Had she been in a relationship which had just ended?'

'God yes, I expect so,' affirmed Viveka Hall Eriksson. 'Men just fell into that girl's lap, I can tell you. They were like leeches, but she kept them in their place, I made sure all my daughters knew how to do that.'

'Conny Härnlind?' ventured Barbarotti, starting to feel slightly desperate. 'Is that a name you're familiar with?'

She gave a snort. 'I don't keep up with their names. But I know Anna could take care of herself, and whoever killed her, it can't have been someone she was with, you've got to understand that. She made sure she had real men. Not these violent types.'

'Erik Bergman?'

'Eh?'

'Is that name familiar?'

'Erik Bergman? No, I never heard that one.'

Barbarotti drank some of his coffee and changed tack.

'The last time you spoke to her was on Sunday, wasn't it?'

'That's right,' said Viveka Hall Eriksson. 'We speak on the phone once a week. About all sorts of bits and bobs. If she wants advice, she gets it, and if she doesn't, I don't give it. That's my way with her, and with the rest of them as well.'

'Do you remember what you talked about?'

'Of course I do. We talked about her going to Gotland, which was meant to be yesterday. I gave her a few tips. I've been to Visby seventeen times in my life, it's a real summer paradise and of course I wanted to share what I'd found out.'

Naturally, thought Barbarotti. Manners and morals have to be passed down. 'Was she going on her own or with a friend?' he asked.

'A girlfriend, but I can't remember her name. Lisbeth or something. Yes, two of them were going. I told her they ought to try for a holiday let over at Gustavsvik, that's the best and cheapest place. Near town and near all the beach life at Snäck, you can't beat it. Have you been to Gotland?'

Barbarotti nodded. 'A couple of times. Yes, it's a beautiful island.'

'Visby's the place to be,' said Viveka Hall Eriksson. 'Otherwise it's all the middle of nowhere and crap. And it has to be summer of course, who'd bloody want to live there all year round?'

'She didn't mention feeling threatened or anything, when you were talking on the phone?' asked Barbarotti.

'Threatened? No, she didn't feel threatened. Why should she?'

Barbarotti sipped his coffee and helped himself to a Singoalla biscuit while he wondered how to make any headway at all. 'Because she was murdered a couple of days later, maybe?' he said. 'You haven't forgotten that?'

'Forgotten?' she cried, her eyes opening very wide. 'How could I forget that my daughter's been murdered? Are you out of your mind? Why don't you go and catch the man who did this instead of sitting here insi . . . insu . . . what's the damn word?'

'Insinuating?' suggested Barbarotti.

'That's it. Don't just sit there inseminating! Catch the man who killed my Anna, that's what we pay our taxes for, inspector.'

'Hrrm,' said Barbarotti. 'That's exactly why I'm here. To see if you've got any little lead that might help us. My colleagues in Kymlinge are busy talking to the people your daughter knew, all those we've been able to get hold of, and—'

'I'll tell you what sort he is, the one you ought to be looking for,' she cut in angrily, the heavy array of bangles on her left wrist clattering against the tabletop. 'You want to look for one of those immigrant types. A foreigner. They can't get women, so then they take them any way they can. It's bound to be some fucking Arab nigger who's done away with my Anna, so just get out there and find him. They're not like us, they don't smell like us and I don't see what they're doing in our country.'

'Oh I think that's going a bit—'

'I shall say what I like,' yelled Viveka Hall Eriksson. 'This is my home.'

When he came out of the house he felt an urge to pick up a stone from the street and hurl it through the kitchen window. He restrained himself and swore at some length through gritted teeth instead.

People like that, he thought. How was it possible to be so vulgar? A sixty-four-year-old mother of nine?

Of course he was used to coming across a bit of everything in his line of work but today – on this sunny morning in high summer – he hadn't been expecting it. Not in this smart house in this kempt and well-heeled neighbourhood.

A mother who had just lost her daughter.

Mindless closet racism, thought Gunnar Barbarotti. Hand

in hand with extreme self-satisfaction and stupidity. Christ, what a woman.

And not so closet, in fact. She'd made no attempt to hide her views, that was one thing she couldn't be accused of.

And she's multiplied her ignorance genes ninefold, he thought grimly as he got into his car. And if all her kids also bred . . .

Well, eightfold, he corrected himself. The way things had turned out. Anna Eriksson of Skolgatan in Kymlinge had not found time, as far as they had ascertained so far, to bring any children into this world, although she was a little over thirty, so . . .

No, I'm on dangerous ground here, he interrupted himself, and turned the key in the ignition. Calm down, inspector. Democracy is the best solution in the long run and not everyone in this land is called Viveka Hall Eriksson.

He decided to postpone his call to Sara until that evening or the next day. He was keeping a lid on his indignation, but it was still lurking there. When he spoke to his daughter, he wanted to be calm and attentive, not agitated and misanthropic.

So he called Inspector Backman's number instead, to ask her how that morning's efforts on the home front had gone.

Backman sounded annoyed.

'It's chaos here,' she said.

'Why's that?' asked Barbarotti.

'Well amongst other things, several pages of coverage in today's paper. Crowds flocking to the murder scenes, apparently. Both of them. A neighbour of Anna Eriksson's claims he saw a man he didn't recognize on the stairs up to her flat on the Tuesday evening, and the joke is, he gave an interview to a journalist before we were able to interview him. And Asunander's going round looking like a beaver with a twisted bowel. He's on about calling in extra people, I assume he means the National CID. We've got a meeting with him and the prosecutor at two. You'll be back by then I suppose?'

Gunnar Barbarotti automatically slowed the car and checked the time. 'I'm not quite sure. I'll join you as soon as I get back . . . Has the pathologist given you a time of death?'

'He says Tuesday afternoon isn't impossible.'

'But it could be Wednesday?'

'Could be Wednesday. Though Tuesday's more likely.'

'Any leads in the flat?'

'We'll know in a week's time. But there ought to be something. He must have killed her in there.'

'Nothing obvious though?'

'If you mean the murder weapon, constable, then no, he appears to have taken it with him.'

'I see,' said Gunnar Barbarotti. 'And this witness, the one who saw a stranger . . . is he reliable?'

'Basically, yes. Though the description he gave us is so vague it fits half the population of Sweden. Only saw him from behind on the stairs. Male individual between twenty-five and fifty, light-coloured shirt, medium-blonde hair . . . and there's absolutely nothing to indicate he's our perpetrator. Though tomorrow's papers will claim there is, you can bet on that.'

'And nobody else has come forward with any sightings?'

'No, but we've still got tons of people to talk to. How was the mother?'

He cast about for a simple way of putting it.

'White trash,' he said. 'In spite of her elegant house.'

'White trash?' said Eva Backman. 'Thought they only existed in America, but that's . . . clearly a misconception. Anyway, I've got a couple of the girlfriends sitting here waiting to give me their thoughts. See you at two, then?'

'If I make it in time,' said Gunnar Barbarotti.

When he got to Kymlinge police station it was already quarter to three, and the meeting with Asunander and prosecutor Sylvenius was over. Inspector Backman chose not to comment on how long it had taken him to drive from Jönköping, and he could see by her look that she would have done the same.

'Looks as though this investigation will be in other hands from tomorrow,' she let drop casually. 'Asunander's in negotiations with National CID and Gothenburg. It'll be good to have a few people with real balls here to tell us what to do.'

'Dead right,' said Barbarotti. 'But Astor Nilsson's already here, isn't he?'

She nodded. 'He's interviewing an interesting sort of guy. Julius Bengtsson. How can anyone be called Julius Bengtsson in this day and age? Sounds like a con man in some old slapstick film.'

'Who is he?'

'Former fiancé of the latest victim. He's got some exciting information to impart, evidently. Do you want to listen in?'

Barbarotti gave a shrug. 'Why not?'

They sat down at the table outside the interview room and the one-way tinted glass, and Backman turned up the sound. Barbarotti observed the two parties sitting opposite one another across the table in the bare room. He was looking at their profiles, Astor Nilsson's left and Julius Bengtsson's right.

Bengtsson was a man of about thirty-five, Barbarotti estimated, with Tintin hair, dyed blonde, and a pointy little beard in the same shade. An orange T-shirt revealing a tattooed snake on his powerful upper arm. A little gold ring in his earlobe. Slightly overweight.

'What do you mean?' asked Astor Nilsson.

'And then she threw all my clothes out in the garden,' said Julius Bengtsson indignantly. 'Had to go out and get 'em without a stitch on. Total basket case that one, if you ask me.'

'I see,' said Astor Nilsson.

'Another time she threw me in the river. We'd had a few beers out Rimminge way, it was summer and we were just ambling home, peaceful like. So I stopped for a leak and then she tackled me and sent me arse over tit into the water. Split her sides laughing as well, bloody cow.'

'How long were you together?' asked Astor Nilsson.

'Oh, ages,' said Julius Bengtsson. 'At least three months, no, more . . . it could even have been six fucking months. But, you know, a bit off and on.'

Astor Nilsson handed him a photograph.

'Do you know who this is?'

Julius took his time, studying the photograph carefully. Then he handed it back.

'Haven't got a clue.'

'Erik Bergman. Does that name say anything to you?'

'Wasn't it him who was knifed this week?'

'Correct. Did you know him?'

'No I fucking didn't.'

'All right. How long is it since you and Anna Eriksson broke up?'

Julius Bengtsson considered the matter.

'Two years maybe . . . two and a half.'

'Did you live together?'

'No way. I avoid that sort of thing like the plague.'

'Oh? And when did you last see her?'

'Last week. Or it could have been the week before that?'

'In what context?'

'Eh?'

'Where?'

'In town. Said hello but the sour bitch just looked away as if I was made of fresh air. She's like that . . . was like that, I guess we should say.'

Gunnar Barbarotti signalled to Eva Backman to turn down the volume, and she did so.

'That'll do me, I reckon,' he said. 'He doesn't exactly seem principal witness material.'

'Hopefully it won't come to that,' said Eva Backman. 'We've got two more former boyfriends lined up, by the way. And a quartet of girlfriends.'

'She's got eight siblings, too,' Barbarotti reminded her. 'Is there really nothing a bit more substantial to go on?'

Eva Backman thought for a moment.

'The friend she was going to Gotland with didn't have much to give us. At least not over the phone. I suppose we'll have to see how she is face to face; she's coming in tomorrow. She only got a day in Visby as it turned out.'

Barbarotti nodded but refrained from comment.

'But actually, I reckon there could be more mileage in that childhood best friend in Torremolinos you talked to yesterday,' Backman went on. 'We'll have to talk to her tomorrow, too . . . she at least seems to know the victim a bit better than the rest do, but we probably ought not to bank on her, either.'

'Anything else?' enquired Barbarotti.

'Not much,' said Backman. 'Sorrysen's at his desk trying to map out Tuesday. What she was doing in the time before her encounter with the murderer and so on. If we can make the assumption that that was when she died. The question is . . . well, the question is how much time he gave us when it came to it, the murderer.'

'What do you mean?'

'Only that you quite possibly only received the letter the day he killed Anna Eriksson. Though it could have been delivered the day before, of course? On the Monday. Or sometime the previous week. You don't happen to remember whether it was on top of the pile of post or anything?'

Barbarotti thought about it. 'It was all more scattered than that. But I'm pretty sure this one didn't have anything on top of it.'

'Could have come on the Tuesday then?'

'It's possible,' said Barbarotti.

'But the first letter came a week in advance. I wonder . . .'

'Yes?'

'I wonder if he dared take the risk of letting several days go by the second time round as well. I mean, giving us a name and a week to investigate . . . it sounds a bit risky, don't you think?'

Barbarotti nodded. 'Maybe he likes risks. I mean, nobody's forcing him to write any letters at all, are they?'

'No, you're right of course,' said Eva Backman, and a look he didn't entirely recognize and couldn't quite identify crossed her face. A shadow of something sombre, he might almost say melancholy. Ominous, he thought.

'And yet he writes them,' she added, as she slowly and with

evident deliberation – as if it were some intricate piece of precision engineering – clasped her hands in front of her on the desk. 'It all seems worrying to me, Gunnar, bloody worrying. Do you think . . . I mean, do you think there'll be more?'

Gunnar Barbarotti was silent for a while, watching her interlaced fingers. 'Don't really know what to think,' he said eventually. 'If I'm honest, I . . .'

'Yes?'

'If I'm honest, I simply don't get any of this.'

'Me neither,' said Eva Backman, putting her shoulders back and appearing to pull herself together. 'Shall we divide up these interviews, then?'

'Suppose we'd better,' said Barbarotti.

THREE

NOTES FROM MOUSTERLIN

1–8 July 2002

I have spent the last few days out walking. Our house is right on the fringes of the Marais de Mousterlin polder, you just turn left out of our blue-painted gate and you're there. Little gravel paths meander their way through lush marshland full of strange plants, birds and pools of stagnant water. I came across one or two other walkers and the occasional dog, but that was all; the curious and distinctive landscape runs all the way along behind the beach from Mousterlin to Beg-Meil; yesterday I also extended my walk beyond the lighthouse and followed the coastal path up to Cap-Coz. It feels good to be alone, I've found myself forgetting from time to time that this is my natural element: being left to walk undisturbed with my own thoughts and ideas. The vigorous growth surrounding me and accompanying my steps feels laden with mystery; eroticism and death are close allies in this torrid, luxuriant jungle. There must be many insects here whose whole lifespan only lasts a day: they are born in the morning, die in the evening and rot away during the night.

I also have to remind myself every now and then where I fit into the wider context: who I am, in the final analysis. This afternoon they came back to me, those thoughts of Anna and her wet hair after the nocturnal swim, and I was obliged to stop in a sun-warmed glade to masturbate away her insistent presence. After that I clambered down to the little beach of Bot Canon and went into the water. I swam round in the bay for a good hour and in the process came to the decision that I would stay on for another four to five days. Until Tuesday or Wednesday of next week. By then I shall have had enough of the present company; I suspect we shall be socializing with the Malmgrens and Gunnar and Anna in some way this weekend, and the prospect attracts me but also nauseates me slightly. I freely admit there's a certain pleasure to be derived from time spent in a group where one does not remotely like any of the other people. Erotic suggestion aside.

I don't know what Erik has been getting up to these past few days. Yesterday and today I left him straight after breakfast. This evening the two of us had *moules marinières* at Le Grand Large, but he said nothing about what he had been doing. I would guess he's been sunbathing on the terrace or down on the beach, he's tanned as brown as a birthmark, and presumably he's spent some of the time with one or more members of the Swedish colony.

In fact I know for certain that he did, because he told me how plans were progressing for the boat trip to des Glénan. Not very far, in actual fact, but Gunnar, or possibly Henrik, has been in touch with an Englishman who apparently lives down here more or less permanently and is willing to rent out his boat for a day.

The idea seems to be for all six of us to go. Erik didn't ask me whether I actually felt like coming along, but maybe that was his point in raising the matter at all. To give me a chance to say I didn't want to – on the spot, there at Le Grand Large

– and as I didn't, the assumption is that I'm joining them and paying my share of the costs. And when I examine my thinking and motivation, I can't really claim to have anything against the arrangement.

Why not?

Why? Why not? These two sterile and perpetual questions that resist answer and constantly plague me. There should be clearer signposts.

A summary of events, some twelve hours afterwards. What has happened has happened and time cannot be put into reverse.

I have showered, slept for four hours, showered again. Erik left the house early this morning and I assume he's in conference with the others over at Gunnar and Anna's. Or at the Malmgrens'. The rain has stopped, it's Monday and the time is eleven thirty.

But back to Sunday morning. Yesterday, twenty-six hours before it all started; it is hard to appreciate that it hasn't been longer than that, but I shall go back to twenty-four hours ago and take it from the beginning; my head is in a whirl and the chronology of it all offers impartiality and a simple memory aid. I am sure no one else is going to record what actually happened, in the proper order, on this most ghastly of days.

The morning is fine and the plan simple: the Englishman with the boat – I never caught his name – lives somewhere in Beg-Meil, and keeps the boat in a small marina on the east side. Gunnar and Henrik are going to fetch it around nine and the rest of us will assemble on the beach a little way beyond the point, just below the Malmgrens' place. Picnic baskets and cool bags, swimming gear, bottles of wine; the women went into Quimper on Saturday and laid in all the supplies. Baguettes protruding from under red and white checked cloths, a gaudy sun umbrella, straw hats, making us look as if we were in a picture. They are in high spirits, talking of tanning oils and untouched sandy beaches. The weather is glorious: a cloudless sky, the temperature probably already up to the twenty-five degree mark. Yes, it's a picture, a Skagen painting in another country and another time, but the same mood. And I can also sense, as clearly as if contemplating one of those rigid old idylls painted in oils, that this is a single, illusory second, set to vanish in the blink of an eye. How can I know this? The sea is calm, a couple of the Glénan islands are faintly visible on the horizon, or at least I assume that is what I can see, though I can't be sure. The beach is still virtually empty of people; there are just a jogger or two, a couple of fishermen. Low tide, but it's on the turn. Erik and I, two women. They belong to two other men, but an outside observer would doubtless assume we were two couples. I remember actually thinking that thought as we stand there waiting for Henrik and Gunnar to bring the boat. I also remember Erik helping Anna with the back strap of her bikini top, which had got twisted.

But before the boat arrives, Troaë shows up.

I wish she had not.

She was in the same red swimsuit as last time, but this morning with a pair of cut-off jeans on top. The same blue summer hat, the same rucksack. But no easel; catching sight of us, she beamed and set off towards us at a gallop, kicking up sand in all directions.

'Mes amis!' she cried. 'Mes amis les Suédois!'

'Bonjour petite!' Katarina Malmgren called back. 'Comment vas-tu ce matin?'

The girl braked to a halt right beside us and was immediately earnest. 'Not so good. I've had an argument with my grandmother.'

'Et pourquoi?' Erik managed to produce. 'Why?'

Troaë launched herself into an animated description of her morning run-in with Grandmother, making faces and doing pantomime; Katarina seemed to understand most of it because she kept laughing at the girl, putting in a comment here and there. We other three tried to follow as best we could: plainly the grandmother had wanted the girl to go into town with her – I assume she meant Quimper – to do some shopping, but Troaë hated shopping. Especially with her grandmother, who took eight hours to buy a cheese and a pair of shoes.

'She called me a *guenon* and said I took after my mother.'

'Guenon?' asked Erik.

'A she-monkey, I think,' said Katarina Malmgren.

Spot on, I thought. A she-monkey is exactly what she is.

The girl had declared her grandmother to be *un chameau*, also some kind of monkey as far as I could tell, so then the grandmother had gone off to town on her own.

'What are all of you doing today?'

Just then, Henrik and Gunnar came into sight. A white plastic craft had rounded the point and was approaching at speed, its engine a piercing roar. I know nothing about boats but nonetheless realized this must be quite an expensive one. I wondered for a moment about this Englishman who was prepared to lend out his boat to a group of strangers without further ado. But perhaps Henrik and Gunnar had been able to demonstrate better boatmanship and nautical sense than I could give them credit for. Katarina explained to Troaë that we were about to go on a trip to the islands.

'Des Glénan!' exclaimed Troaë. 'I love des Glénan! Let me come with you!'

Several seconds passed as the boat came closer, I exchanged a look with Erik but could not ascertain his view, and then the girl slipped her hand into Katarina Malmgren's and pressed herself close to her.

'Please.'

'And Grandmother?' asked Erik. 'What do you think Grandmother will say?'

'She won't care,' Troaë assured them. 'I'm used to getting on with things by myself. She always checks I'm in my bed around midnight, but that's all. Please?'

'All right,' said Katarina Malmgren.

'Je vous aime,' said the girl.

I don't know why she did it. Why Katarina agreed to take the girl on our all-day trip to des Glénan, just like that. She took the decision unilaterally, without asking the rest of us; I'm sure Anna, at least, thought it was a stupid idea, but it struck me that perhaps this was precisely why Katarina said yes. Because she knew that Anna took a totally opposite view, but would find it hard to express that view. I have never entirely understood that intricate sort of game that is played between women, I can only speculate. At any event, the decision was made: young Troaë would come with us in the boat to the islands; none of us offered any objections, not I, nor Erik, nor Anna.

Nor did Henrik or Gunnar, once we had waded out into the water and climbed aboard the *Arcadia*, and the girl kept her excitement and cheeriness in check and did her best to appear grown up and to blend in. She had social skills, that Troaë, I can't take that away from her.

Arcadia was white and plasticky, with a big black engine. There was space for about four people in the cabin, but no one was interested in sitting down there. The women immediately found themselves a spot up on the deck at the front, spread out big red and yellow towels and started sunbathing. Gunnar was instructed to take it gently at the wheel so they were not troubled by strong wind or spray, and the rest of us ranged ourselves along the narrow table in the cockpit. Henrik and I on one side, Erik and Troaë on the other. The girl tucked her hand through Erik's arm and he left it there. We didn't say a lot, it seemed too much of an effort to make ourselves heard above the engine noise, which was insistently loud. I noted that there were seven of us; no one had a life jacket and no one commented on the fact, either.

As we drew closer to des Glénan – which is a cluster of about ten small islands, none of them populated all year round but several of them with additions to accommodate the needs of modern tourism – Gunnar reduced speed, Anna and Katarina climbed down to the rest of us and there was a short discussion about which island to choose. A map was produced and spread out. I did not offer any opinions. They eventually agreed on Ile Brunec, I don't know why, but presumably because it was sat a little apart. It was not one of the five larger islands, spread in a ring round the famous lagoon. Henrik read from the brochure he had with him that there were no houses on Brunec, no restaurant and no facilities.

'Ideal,' said Anna. 'Just white beaches and turquoise sea.'

'Food and wine and warm skin,' Gunnar added.

This proved to be pretty much the case. We went across the lagoon, rounded Île de Saint-Nicolas and dropped anchor on the west side of Brunec in a little channel between sharply pointed cliffs and a beach of ivory sand. We waded ashore in pleasantly warm water about a half metre deep, carrying baskets and bags on our heads. There wasn't a soul to be seen; we had encountered a certain amount of sea traffic on the crossing and there were a dozen or so boats bobbing in the lagoon, but none at Brunec. We seemed to have found an island all of our own with at least 300 metres of sandy beach; the place wasn't very big, maybe two kilometres in circumference with a little row of trees running down the middle. The highest point couldn't have been more than five metres above sea level.

I looked at my watch. It was eleven thirty. I looked at the sky. It was azure blue. The sea was still largely a smooth mirror, the seagulls drifting about in lazy ellipses, and it came home to me that I was at the mercy of these people. For a whole day.

Why did I get myself into this?

I actually thought those thoughts, *Lord of the Flies* fluttered through my head, and that isn't something I've reconstructed after the event.

This was Troaë's second trip to des Glénan, it turned out. The first time, she was here with her mother and father; if I remember rightly, she was four years old at the time.

'But if your grandmother gets home at five o'clock and you're not there, won't she worry?' asked Katarina.

It was a bit late to be asking that question now, but the girl simply laughed and shook her head.

'She just thinks I'm a nuisance,' she said. 'I told you that. For her, the main thing is that I'm still alive when Dad comes to collect me. But it doesn't matter that she's the way she is, I get on better without her.'

'And when is Dad coming?'

She shrugged. 'A few days before school starts, probably. In six weeks or so.'

It occurred to me that Troaë might be a compulsive storyteller. That in actual fact, she lived with her parents in Fouesnant all year round. Or was staying at one of the campsites I had seen near Beg-Meil. That the grandmother did not exist and that we were in for a bollocking for having abducted the girl. But I kept this to myself. I got to my feet and went into the water instead. I swam out from the shore, it really was crystal clear and the sand shelved away steeply after about twenty metres; I regretted not having brought flippers and a snorkel, which would have provided the ideal way of making the time pass. Just floating, watching the deaf, dumb world spread out below the surface. The thought also struck me that more than five years had passed since I got my diving certificate and almost as long since my wife's accident.

When I returned after about half an hour, they had already started organizing lunch. 'Might as well get a couple of bottles of wine inside us while they're still relatively chilled,' Gunnar pointed out. 'I assume the water's too warm to cool them in?'

The question was directed at me. None of the others had been in yet. I shrugged. 'Around twenty, I'd say.'

'I'm thirsty,' said Anna. 'I thought I might take a dip in the nude later, but I need a couple of glasses before I dare.'

I had a feeling she was eyeing me up as she said this, but it might just have been my imagination.

'Anna's got this thing about only bathing naked if she's got company,' said Gunnar. 'Never alone. I wonder why.'

'Get lost, arsehole,' said Anna. She laughed and slapped his backside. Troaë asked what we were talking about and Katarina told her we were admiring the beauty of the island. Then we started lunch. Baguettes and cheese, salads in messy dressings, Bayonne ham, crêpes and avocados. Strawberries, raspberries and cherries; they had gone to a lot of trouble and the cool bag of Alsace wine turned out to contain no less than eight bottles.

In the two and a half hours that followed, we emptied six of them. Troaë claimed she had been brought up on wine and water so she was allowed a couple of glasses too. The usual lugubrious beach conversation developed of course, the more wine the more listless the chat; Gunnar kept on at Troaë to sell us the watercolour, and the girl said she planned to finish it off the next day – if we made sure to be on the beach, she would come and show us the finished work of art. Perhaps she could auction it to us? She had been to various auctions with her father and knew how these things worked. Gunnar and Erik discussed this suggestion for a while with simulated seriousness, but soon lost interest. They changed to the subject of the strange French predilection for bad, sweet breakfasts, and other related subjects. The girl said less and less, fished a book out of her little rucksack and started to read, while I got out *The Confessions of St. Augustine*, which always travels with me. Reading had the effect of drawing some kind of line between the two of us and the rest of the group. A slim but significant boundary. I pondered for a while on the *Lord of the Flies* aspect: a situation like this, in which we were shipwrecked and would be forced to live on the island for months – and how the girl and I would gradually form a kind of enclave, a united front against barbarism, but I soon abandoned the idea as unconvincing and improbable.

Soon after half past two, another boat put in and anchored at the other end of the beach, and a man and woman came ashore and settled themselves on some basic beach chairs.

'There you go,' said Gunnar. 'You've got a decent audience now. Time for your skinny dip, Anna.'

Anna was not slow to take up the challenge. She rose on slightly unsteady feet, removed her bikini and ran into the sea. It might have been an attractive sight, but for the fact that she had drunk too much; she tripped and fell headlong, just a couple of metres from the shore. She swore, picked herself up and turned to the rest of us. 'Come on then, you twats!' she said. 'Chill a bit, why can't you, we're in paradise here!'

Katarina Malmgren hesitated for a second, no more, before throwing off her bikini and galloping after Anna. She was significantly steadier on her feet, ran a good bit further out and launched herself into the water.

Gunnar laughed. Erik laughed and shouted bravo. Henrik and I made no comment. Troaë clapped her hands and cried out something in French that I didn't understand; then she ran into the water after the two naked women.

This time she kept her swimsuit on. I wondered why. Perhaps she realized she couldn't compete with the ample endowments of Anna and Katarina, but I am probably crediting her with more cunning and calculation than she actually possessed.

A minute or two later, the male quartet also went into the water. We all kept our swimming trunks on; for my part, I had good cause to, and I could see that Erik, at any rate, was in the same predicament.

The other couple left the beach around four and at about the same time, Anna and Gunnar announced that they wanted to go on a little expedition of their own. By that time we had polished off the rest of the wine, and it seemed pretty obvious that they were looking for a bit of privacy for a fuck.

'We'll take the boat over to Les Bluinieres,' said Gunnar, waving the map. 'It must be those two we can see over there.' He pointed in the direction of a couple of small islands silhouetted on the western horizon. 'We'll be back in an hour, OK?'

'Go ahead,' said Katarina Malmgren. 'Have fun, ha ha.'

'What are you talking about?' asked Troaë.

'You're too young to understand,' said Katarina, leaving the comments untranslated.

'I wouldn't say that,' put in Erik, thoughtfully watching Gunnar and Anna on their way out to the boat. 'I wouldn't say that.'

'I want to know what you're all talking about,' protested Troaë, crossing her arms. 'It's not fair.'

'You'll get over it with age,' said Erik. 'You've got to learn to have a bit of patience, little girl.'

He said this in Swedish and I don't think Troaë understood that he was addressing her. As for me, I felt as though the wine and sun were starting to addle my brain. I realized the best thing would be to find a shady spot and have a nap. We sat in silence, watching Gunnar and Anna climb aboard the boat. Gunnar got the engine going after a few false starts, and they set off round the cliffs towards Les Bluinieres.

'Not fair,' repeated Troaë once they were out of sight, and it was suddenly far from clear what she was actually referring to. Erik got to his feet. 'Think I'll take a walk round the island,' he said. 'You can come with me, Troaë.'

He said this in flawless French, as far as I could judge, as if he had been formulating it in his head for a while first.

'Oui monsieur!' cried the girl. 'Avec plaisir!' She leapt up and took his hand, and the two of them trotted off into the sun along the water's edge.

I was left there with Henrik and Katarina Malmgren. Katarina had just turned onto her stomach and asked her husband to apply some sun oil to her back. I felt it was high time to put my plan for a nap into practice. I took my towel and withdrew to the shade under the trees. I thought I ought to masturbate before I went to sleep, but I was far too tired and inebriated to make it happen.

I awoke with a headache. And because I was cold.

Possibly also because Henrik Malmgren was standing a metre from me, clearing his throat. 'Are you awake? We've got a problem.'

'Problem?'

'Yes. Gunnar and Anna haven't come back with the boat. It's six thirty.'

I sat up and looked at my watch. I had been asleep for more than two hours. The headache hammered at my temples. I saw that they had shifted our camp a bit further inland, no more than ten or fifteen metres from my sleeping place under the trees. Katarina Malmgren and Troaë were sitting together with their backs to me, Erik a few metres to one side. I shivered, noticing that a cold wind had blown up and dark clouds were covering the sky.

'Haven't come back?' I asked. 'Why not?'

'Don't know,' said Henrik. 'We've rung their mobile several times but they aren't answering.'

'Maybe they didn't bring it today?'

'Maybe not,' said Henrik. 'In any case, something must have happened, and it looks very much as if it's about to rain.'

'Sorry,' I said, heaving myself to my feet. 'Got to get some clothes on.'

'I reckon the temperature's dropped fifteen degrees,' said Henrik.

We went down to the others. I put my trousers on. And a long-sleeved top.

'Have a bit of this, too,' said Erik, passing over a bottle of Calvados. 'The fucking bunnies haven't come back.'

'So I heard,' I said, taking a large swig from the bottle. I looked at the rest of them. Young Troaë was pressed tightly against Katarina Malmgren, who had an arm round her. She looked concerned. 'I think the girl's ill,' she said. I looked at Erik, remembering he had taken her off on a walk before I fell asleep. He averted his gaze and looked out over the sea, towards those islands that we thought must be Les Bluinieres. Their outlines were no longer visible; the light across the water had changed, it was still not dusk but visibility had worsened considerably. Waves half a metre high rode the sea, and you could sense the storm was not far away. I asked whether they had thought about contacting the mainland.

'We wouldn't know where to ring if we did,' said Henrik Malmgren.

I noticed his speech was a little slurred. My headache hammered two heavy-duty nails into my skull. We're all drunk, I thought. We're four pissed Swedes sitting on a desert island without a boat. We've kidnapped a twelve-year-old French girl and we know bugger all about what they got up to on that walk.

'We'll wait another hour,' said Katarina Malmgren. 'There's no reason to kick up a big fuss.'

'I was against them taking the boat,' said Henrik.

'Shut up, Henrik,' said Katarina. 'That's just the sort of comment we don't need at the moment.'

'You're the one who dragged the girl along with us,' said Henrik. 'But I don't suppose you want to hear that either, eh? Nice fix you've got us into.'

Katarina made no reply.

'At least we've got half a litre of Calvados left,' said Erik.

'All I'm saying is that it was a bit bloody irresponsible,' said Henrik, lighting a cigarette with fumbling fingers.

The girl whispered something to Katarina. They stood up. 'She's going to be sick,' Katarina explained accusingly.

'Let her be sick, then,' said Erik.

Katarina and Troaë made their way up to the trees. I turned my head and saw the girl kneel down and retch; at the same moment I felt the first spatter of rain on the back of my hand. Erik passed the bottle to Henrik, who took a deep draught.

We tried to erect a primitive sort of shelter under the trees. Put up towels as shields from the wind and rain, but it was ineffective. Henrik was manifestly drunk and mostly just wandered around cursing to himself. Katarina and Troaë sat together, huddled against each other to keep warm; since throwing up, the girl had scarcely said a word and clearly was not well. Erik and I took it in turns to stand down at the water's edge, spying out pointlessly in the direction of Les Bluinieres. We said very little to one another. At eight o'clock we shared the last drops of the Calvados, though Katarina abstained and the girl did not want any, either, though she was so cold that her teeth were chattering. We started discussing the possibility of making a fire. Henrik scoffed at the idea. 'For fuck's sake, this is the wettest place on earth,' he said. 'And this is the biggest fiasco I've ever been caught up in.'

'Shut up,' said Erik. 'Your childish whining isn't going to help, anyway.'

'I'll gladly shut up,' said Henrik. 'Let me know when you've got the fire going.'

I saw Erik clench his fists and it isn't impossible that they could have come to blows, if Katarina hadn't shouted out at that instant.

'Look! Surely that's a boat?'

All five of us stared out across the waves and were soon able to make out that it really was a boat, and heading our way.

'Is it them?' asked Henrik.

'How should I know,' said Katarina.

'Of course it's them,' said Erik. 'What other idiots would put out in this weather?'

'About bloody time,' said Henrik.

'Would you please be quiet and try to make yourself useful instead?' said Katarina.

'What do you want me to do?' retorted Henrik. 'Rub oil on your back?'

It was indeed Gunnar and Anna in the boat. It breasted the choppy waves on its way towards land and fifteen arduous minutes later we had all managed to get aboard. Erik cut his elbow and the girl sobbed loudly as she clung to the short ladder, trying to fend off the waves.

'There's something wrong with the engine,' said Gunnar. 'It took us two hours to get it started.'

'Hope you enjoyed your trip,' said Henrik.

It was becoming patently obvious that Henrik hadn't the sense to keep quiet; he would soon get what was coming to him. 'You lot go and sit in the cabin,' said Gunnar. 'I'm as freezing as a polar bear's bum, but I might just as well get us home while I'm at it.'

That was a lousy simile, I thought, but I said nothing.

'As long as you don't trust Henrik with anything,' said Katarina.

We squeezed into the dark, cramped cabin, Gunnar turned the boat and revved the engine. You could hear there was something wrong with it; its sound was now a low, dull throb, rather than the piercing drone it had made on the way out. We were breaching the waves sideways on and the boat took the impact hard, forcing us to hunch over slightly and hold on so we didn't hit our heads on the low roof. Even though the more muted engine noise made conversation possible in principle, nobody took advantage of the fact. Up and down, up and down, within a couple of minutes, I was starting to feel queasy; I'd been keeping the lid on my headache for the past hour, but now it returned with renewed intensity. I was wedged between Henrik and Erik. Anna, Katarina and the girl had squeezed in on the other side of the table, to which six pairs of hands were clinging so tightly that the knuckles turned white. Up and down. Up and down. The sound of the motor rose and fell in time with the waves. Every now and then there was a sudden jolt as we slammed down from the crest of a slightly higher wave. My nausea slowly worsened and I started counting my breaths, counting the monotonous throbs of my pulse in my temples. I closed my eyes and wished I really had killed these people that first day in Bénodet. That for once I had actually converted thought into action.

All at once, the engine died. Gunnar dived into the cabin, wet through, his bulk filling the whole opening to the cockpit. 'Sodding thing's stopped again!' he yelled. 'Fuck, fuck, fuck!'

The boat heaved even more. We were rolling from side to side now, up and down, up and down, but as there were six of us in a cabin presumably meant for four, we were wedged there, held in place.

'What the fuck do we do?' said Gunnar. 'My hands are completely numb.'

'How far is it to land?' yelled Anna. There was no external necessity to shout, just an internal one.

'At least half an hour,' said Gunnar. 'But without the engine we won't drift towards land. The wind's from the north west, and assuming we don't capsize, we'll be blown down towards . . . I don't fucking well know. La Rochelle or somewhere?'

'Can't you try getting it started again?' said Anna.

'Don't you think I've tried?' Gunnar snapped. 'I've no sodding feeling left in my fingers. Might be time for someone else to actually do something.'

The boat rolled violently and Gunnar hit his head on the doorpost and let out a series of expletives.

'All right,' said Erik. 'I'll go up and take a look.'

He pushed his way past Gunnar, who wedged himself in to my right and groaned. 'Fucking hell, we haven't even got life jackets. How the hell can you rent out a boat without life jackets?'

'Does Erik know anything about boat engines?' asked Katarina. 'Henrik, oughtn't you. . . ?'

'I'm too drunk,' said Henrik. 'Sorry, but you people who got us into this will just have to sort it out yourselves.'

Anna's balled fist shot out across the table like a piston.

There was a crunch as it hit Henrik somewhere in the face. I thought how impressive it was that she'd managed to land a blow with such precision in the heaving cabin, in the dark.

'What the fuck is . . . ?' cried Henrik. 'You little slut!'

'Calm down for Christ's sake,' roared Gunnar. 'And just buck your ideas up, the bloody lot of you.'

I felt we had reached crunch point. The thin varnish of civilization had worn off these people, normality had evaporated and they had reverted to some crude kind of natural state, while language had mutated from a cement to a weapon. The boat lurched violently and Troaë started to cry.

At least an hour had gone by. We huddled there together in the dark, cramped cabin, tossed about by the agitated, wind-lashed sea. No one said anything, except for the occasional curse; the girls snivelled now and then, Erik and Gunnar took turns at the dead engine, sometimes working together in their attempt to coax it into life. They never asked Henrik or me for help. My headache came and went, and my queasiness basically remained at the same level. I counted my breaths and my pulse, wondering about the silence and why no one really had anything to say to each other in such circumstances. Why none of them made any effort to win back their humanity. Perhaps it was because the situation we were in had gone way beyond their capabilities. It rendered them mute, powerless to act, carnal and afraid. I said nothing myself, either, but then that's my natural strategy. Perhaps they were all thinking we were about to die, perhaps it was isolation in the face of this final moment that each of them was trying to come to terms with. In their own way, as far as they felt capable, and in the cold darkness of fading intoxication.

I had just noticed that Henrik had dozed off to my left, when Katarina Malmgren directed my attention to the girl.

'She's going to be sick,' she said. 'I don't know whether I . . . ?'

'I'll go with her,' I said.

Katarina said something to Troaë and the girl nodded. She gave a faint moan and stretched her hand out to mine across the table. I took it and we clambered up the four steps to the cockpit. The rain was still lashing down, but the waves seemed to have subsided a little, I thought. In the far distance, you could see the lights on the shore and I realized that we were drifting in roughly the right direction after all. Or at any rate, we were not on our way out to sea. As long as we didn't capsize, we would presumably hit land within an hour or two. Or be smashed on some rocks. Erik was clinging to the dead engine. They had removed its black plastic cover to expose its interior, and the thought ran through my mind that probably all they had achieved in doing so was to douse it in damaging saltwater. Troaë started to retch, and I helped her over to the rail and clutched her firmly with my right hand while she leant out over the water to throw up. I realized we had opted for the wrong side: she was vomiting straight into the wind and the mess of phlegm was thrown back over the side at us. She sobbed, and cried out something I didn't understand; it sounded not so much like French as some other language entirely.

Suddenly the boat hit the crest of a wave and we were thrown off balance. I almost fell forwards, overboard, and groped wildly with my free hand for another place to hold on, but found nothing. To avoid dragging Troaë over with me, I let go of her hand, and almost immediately found I could grab a strut of the spray hood. I regained my balance but realized at once that it was the wrong manoeuvre. The girl screamed, flapped her arms in thin air and fell overboard.

I shouted to Erik. I don't know what I shouted, but Erik had seen the whole thing, of course; he shouted something back at me, stood up and stared out over the waves. Troaë came into view in the water, her head and frantically flailing arms, but she was already two or three metres from the boat.

'A rope,' said Erik. 'Throw out a rope.'

I looked round me in panic. There was no rope, no life-buoy. The girl cried out and vanished beneath the surface. Erik swore and shouted something to the others down in the cabin. I picked my way round the spray hood and out onto the deck. The boat was tilting violently from side to side but I hung onto ropes and stays. I scanned the deck desperately for some kind of aid, I didn't know what, while also trying to catch sight of the girl again. After a few seconds she surfaced again, waving her arms and crying out, but this time there were no words, just a stifled, inarticulate sound issuing from her throat. Christ, I thought, she can't even swim! I saw that Gunnar and Katarina had come up to the cockpit and were pointing and yelling.

I hesitated for a moment and then threw myself into the water. I hit my right foot on something hard and sharp, a searing pain ran up through my body and in my first few seconds in the water it was all I could feel. I went under and swallowed cold water, my throat burned, but I pulled myself together and struck out to look for the girl. I could hear Anna and Katarina shouting from the boat, and they were pointing and gesticulating, but I was carried over the crest of a wave and lost contact with them. I caught a brief glimpse of the girl as her head and arms broke the greyish black surface for a split second. Then she was gone. I dived in and tried to see under the water but it made my eyes smart and even when I was able to keep them open for a moment I could make out nothing but my own hands. I rose to the surface again, swallowed more cold water, heard Anna and Katarina and Gunnar yelling more instructions; they had evidently caught sight of the girl somewhere very near me. I swam a few strokes and dived again, trying once more to spy something down in the turbid water, but it was futile. The moment I got my head back above water and could breathe again, I saw Gunnar jump in. We stared at one another. Gunnar swore, and the pain in my foot stabbed me again. Gunnar dived, and I began to feel my strength ebbing away. I had great difficulty simply keeping myself afloat.

I don't know how long we thrashed around in the water. It was probably only a few minutes, but it felt like hours. I had not just given up on the girl's life, but also on my own, when I suddenly heard Gunnar shout: 'I've got her!' He was no more than a metre or two away, and the boat was a little further behind him, just going out of sight over the crest of a wave; I struggled over to Gunnar and his face looked wild and crazed, his mouth wide open and his eyes staring. 'I've got her!' he panted. 'Help me for God's sake!'

He got the girl's head above water but slipped below the surface himself; I couldn't see her eyes or mouth, only her black hair spreading like a huge patch of seaweed over her face. I somehow grabbed hold of her arm and we joined forces to start towing her in the direction of the boat. With every kick of my leg I thought and felt: this is the last one, there's no point, this is the end, I can't do it.

But we did. It must have taken us ten minutes to get her aboard. Everyone was shouting and cursing. Gunnar gouged his cheek on the ladder. Anna fell in but was able to get back up by herself, and all the while the rain lashed down and the waves tossed the boat, and us, like splinters of driftwood, and I can't offer any detailed account of how we actually managed to salvage the lifeless body. That lies beyond the realms of words and reason. Beyond what is conceivable.

Once we had finally heaved her onto the cockpit floor, Katarina knelt down and started CPR. As she alternated blowing into the girl's mouth with pressing her hands on her chest, I remembered that she was a nurse, and none of the others attempted to help; we cowered under the spray hood and silence fell again. A silence that somehow made itself heard above the sounds of the sea and the rain, and after a minute or two we also became aware that the waves were subsiding; the rain that had been drenching us throughout slowed to a whisper on the canvas of the spray hood and it's possible I passed out for a few seconds.

A few minutes later, Katarina Malmgren straightened up. She stared at us, her desperate eyes shifting from one to another while her hands and shoulders shook with exhaustion and the tears ran down her face.

'She's dead,' she said. 'Can't you see she's dead?'

Commentary, August 2007

None. That was exactly how it was.

8–13 AUGUST 2007

12

Detective Inspector Gunnar Barbarotti sat in his car and glared out at the rain.

It was Wednesday evening. The weather had changed in the early afternoon, a bank of cloud having moved in from the south west and released its first heavy drops just after two, and within half an hour the dark skies had parked themselves across the entire firmament, from horizon to horizon. It had been raining non-stop ever since, a persistent and obstinate drizzle, and the temperature had sunk from twenty-five to fifteen degrees centigrade.

It felt rather pleasant, thought Gunnar Barbarotti. He could breathe, as long as he kept the window on the passenger side wound down a few centimetres. Thinking about it, that was the only positive thing he could think of saying about the current situation.

The fact that he could breathe. Over the preceding three days he had felt a shrinking of his power over the investigation, and over his work, and those words he had let slip to Marianne about considering a change of job had come back into his mind with a degree of regularity.

As if his life was somehow hanging in the balance this particular summer, that was his impression.

Hanging in the balance? It sounded a bit defeatist, it really did, but he had the feeling that this was the way he would come to look back on it. The summer of 2007. I took that decision, and that one, and then things turned out the way they did.

He also had a sense that this was how life looked in broader terms, this was its essential structure. Long periods of monotonous routine, for good or ill, and then sudden portals opening up to offer a choice of path. And if you didn't choose in time, the gates closed. Not choosing was a choice in itself.

Or maybe that was just the kind of thought that thrived in the rain.

Well here he was, at any event, watching this house. He had asked for the assignment, voluntarily taken on this rather trivial task, just to get away for a bit. Backman had given him a slightly quizzical and sympathetic look, but said nothing. As usual, she could see straight through him, and he realized he was grateful for it. For the fact that she had that special maternal eye certain women have, the one that renders all pretension pointless.

But maybe I'm just idealizing, he thought. Maybe the fact is that some men are in need of a maternal eye, and that's why we invent one and attribute it to some woman who seems to foster the illusion? Maybe it was the same with Marianne?

And what exactly did he mean by 'some men'?

As for me, I certainly seem to feel the need to focus my thoughts on something other than this epistolary madman, he noted, putting two bits of chewing gum into his mouth to keep himself awake. As soon as he had parked between the neatly pruned lime trees an hour before, he had prayed to Our Lord for nothing to happen, so he could sit there in peace and quiet for a few hours and then drive away after a job well done and enjoy an undisturbed night's sleep. He was convinced he would be able to sleep for twelve hours solid if he only got the chance. Fourteen, even.

One point, Our Lord had enquired. One point, Barbarotti had confirmed.

He had talked to Marianne for ten minutes, and it was really that conversation which was disturbing his peace of mind. In fact, if he were to venture a proper look at the matter, it was this that was keeping him awake. Rather than the chewing gum. She had sounded a bit . . . shut off, that was the fact of the matter; unfocused. He wondered if she'd been having some kind of disagreement with the children.

He hoped that was the case, and that the shutting off was not aimed at him. The strange thing – and just as worrying – was that he, too, had felt rather absent from the conversation. The crazy workload of recent days had done that to him, he thought. Sucked him dry of his most primary functions and needs. Love and tenderness and yearning. Leaving a vacuum, an empty hole.

And filling that hole with dejection and fatigue.

And yet more work.

Gradually, after these perambulations in the slough of self-pity, it was somehow inevitable that his thoughts should find their way back to the case. Just as well, thought Gunnar Barbarotti. It was, after all, the only thing that was really going on in his life.

And had been going on ever since his return to Kymlinge the previous week, in fact. He had worked eight days in a row. And he didn't know any more about the letter-writing murderer than he had done when he disembarked from the Gotland ferry.

Not a single bloody thing. If you worked in a sausage factory for a week, you could presumably take pride in having produced a banger or two, thought Inspector Barbarotti. Whereas you really had to ask yourself whether his seventy- to eighty-hour working week had achieved anything of any value at all. And he wasn't alone. At least ten of his colleagues had worked equally long hours and had equally little to show for it. That was just the way it was.

The murderer, on the other hand, was working alone. Say what you liked about him, he was certainly keeping a policeman or two fully occupied.

Including a few who no longer had the appetite for it.

So there.

Since Monday there had been various changes in the leadership of the investigation, just as Asunander had predicted. Besides Astor Nilsson they were now hosting two gentlemen from the National CID. A Superintendent Jonnerblad and a Chief Inspector Tallin. Gunnar Barbarotti had not yet formed any firm opinion of them, but he assumed they were capable detectives. They hadn't come barging in like a couple of cocky know-it-alls, at any rate, and he had already admitted to himself that the less personal responsibility he had, the happier he would be. So there were currently six of them in what was known as the lead group; apart from the imported officers it comprised him, Eva Backman and Gerald Borgsen, commonly known as Sorrysen on account of his mournful air. Chief Inspector Asunander was part of it too, presumably, but he stayed in the background as usual, sucked his teeth, glowered and waited for his pension. Profiler Lillieskog came and went

– but with nothing new having emerged about the perpetrator in the past few days, he was finding it hard to refine his profile. The fact that the murderer had used a different MO for each murder was unusual, everyone agreed; there seemed to be some sort of general consensus about the psychological make-up of a murderer with a knife – as indeed there was about how a perpetrator who preferred blunt instruments ought to be constructed – but an individual who opted for one method one day and the other the next was very hard to get clear in your mind.

So the general view went. Both murders had had a lot of coverage in a wide range of media, the victims had been named, their photos published, but in consultation with prosecutor Sylvenius, the lead group had decided not to say anything publicly about the murderer's absurd habit of writing letters to the police to warn them beforehand. They might have cause for a rethink later on; it was initially a question of balancing the potential usefulness of so-called Detective Public against the panic that would presumably be unleashed and the criticism they would face when the letters came to general attention at a much later stage.

And so, while they waited for a third letter – and a third victim – they kept their counsel.

But a few hours ago, it had arrived.

The letter, that is – there was no victim so far. Or at any rate, none that they had found. Barbarotti had followed the prescribed procedure and dropped in at home to check the day's post after lunch but, having automatically assumed the murderer would use the same sort of envelope on the potential third occasion, he came close to missing it.

The handwriting was the same, however. Likewise the paper on which the brief message was written; not the commonest in Sweden, but not that uncommon either, and presumably impossible to trace. The postmark was clearer this time, and the letter had evidently been posted in Borås.

The message was shorter than usual.

NUMBER THREE WILL BE HANS ANDERSSON.

There were twenty-nine people by the name of Hans Andersson registered in the urban district of Kymlinge. One of them lived in the house outside which Gunnar Barbarotti was currently sitting in his car on surveillance duty. This was the strategy they had hastily agreed on – for now. All twenty-nine were to be informed that there was a threat scenario involving them, or rather, involving someone called Hans Andersson, and that the police would provide some level of surveillance. In the course of the afternoon, they had been able to contact twenty-seven of the twenty-nine; six were away but had promised to inform the police as soon as they returned.

Of the two men they had failed to contact, one was in either Guatemala or Costa Rica, while the other was believed to be in town but was apparently notoriously hard to pin down. He was a poet and painter, a loner without a telephone, who had announced in the local paper about a month earlier that he didn't want any bloody fuss or gifts on his eighty-fifth birthday.

That was the present state of play. The Hans Andersson whom Barbarotti was currently monitoring lived with his wife and three children at 4 Framstegsgatan, a detached house in the residential district of Norrby. The whole family was at home that evening, and it seemed pretty unlikely to Barbarotti that a murderer would choose to enter such a well-lit house. But if he did, then it would mean they were suddenly dealing with a stupidly reckless individual – or a perpetrator who was doing his best to be caught – and there had been no indication of that hitherto. None at all.

Barbarotti checked the time. It was quarter to nine. Seventy-five minutes until his watch would end. He spat his chewing gum out of the side window and poured a cup of coffee from his Thermos instead.

Who are you? he thought for the hundredth time since reading the letter.

What are the motives behind your evil deeds and why are you writing to me, of all people?

Good questions. But sadly he was nowhere near answering any of them.

Inspector Backman rang just as he was on his way out of Norrby, heading for two hot dogs from the Statoil petrol station by the sports ground.

'There's something I'd like you to take a look at,' she said.

'Now?' queried Gunnar Barbarotti. 'It's nearly half past ten.'

'Now,' said Eva Backman.

'Um . . . I'm a bit hungry. Are you still in the office, then?'

'You guessed it,' said Eva Backman. 'I've got half a pizza left from this afternoon. You can have it; it's here on my desk.'

'Thanks,' said Barbarotti. 'How could I refuse? What is it I'm to look at?'

'A photograph.'

'A photograph?'

'Yes. You'll be here in five minutes, then?'

'What's it of?'

'Eh?'

'What's in the photo?'

'Sorry, I'm a bit tired. Actually, that's what you've got to decide when you get here.'

'All right,' sighed Gunnar Barbarotti. 'I'm on my way. But I don't know what you're talking about. Can you shove the pizza in the microwave for a couple of minutes?'

'It's too far to the microwave,' declared Inspector Backman. 'But I can hang it on the radiator for a while.'

'Thanks,' said Gunnar Barbarotti.

'Well, what do you reckon?'

He stared at the picture. It was a standard colour print, ten by fifteen centimetres. And showed two people sitting on a bench. A man and a woman. Not in sharp focus, and it looked like evening or late afternoon, but there was no sun.

Both were in summer clothes. They were sitting about half a metre apart. The man was in a dark-blue, short-sleeved shirt, pale chinos and sandals, the woman in a thin, beige dress, bare-shouldered. She was barefoot, too, but there was a pair of flip-flops on the ground, beside a reddish-coloured paper carrier bag. The woman was looking unsmilingly into the camera while the man had his head turned to one side and didn't seem aware that he was being photographed.

It took a while to dawn on him, but once it did he was in no doubt at all. The woman in the picture was Anna Eriksson. She had a different hairstyle and colour, but it was definitely her.

'It's Anna Eriksson,' he said.

'We're in agreement there,' said Backman. 'And the man?'

'And the man?' Barbarotti repeated mechanically, and took

a bite of room-temperature pizza. He moved the photograph into the light of the desk lamp and tilted it first one way and then the other, to see if he could make it out more clearly.

'He's pretty fuzzy,' he said. 'What do you want me to say?'

'Look sharp, then it'll seem less fuzzy,' said Eva Backman. 'Here's me treating you to freshly cooked pizza, so you could at least show a bit—'

'Hang on,' said Gunnar Barbarotti. 'I see what you're driving at. You think it might be Erik Bergman?'

Backman said nothing. He held the photo about twenty centimetres from his eyes and focused as hard as he could on the man on the bench. He tried to recall what Erik Bergman had looked like, obliged to rely mainly on his memory of the photograph published in the papers – but he couldn't get the two images to mesh with one another. Backman passed over a copy of *Aftonbladet* with the very photo he was trying to conjure up in his mind. He laid the two pictures alongside each other and compared them. Backman waited in silence.

'Don't know,' said Barbarotti in the end. 'Could be him, of course, but it could just as well be somebody else. Where did you get the picture?'

'One of her photo albums. Göransson and Malm found it down in her basement storage area a couple of hours ago.'

'Her basement storage area?'

'Yep.'

'And why has it taken us this long to go through her storage area?'

Eva Backman sighed. 'She had two. We didn't know.'

'Uh huh?' said Barbarotti. 'And this was all there was?'

'You're wondering if there were any other photos of anyone who could possibly have been Bergman?'

'Yes, I assume that's what I mean,' said Barbarotti, and took another bite of the pizza.

'Unfortunately not,' said Backman. 'Just this. There were only three albums, altogether. There are no other shots in which she's wearing the same outfit as in this photo, either, so presumably someone else took it and gave it to her. With the rest of the photos, it's easy to see which of them come from the same roll of film.'

'I see,' said Barbarotti. 'And what about Erik Bergman's photos? He had some too, I assume?'

'We didn't find any, oddly enough.'

'You didn't? Could mean . . .'

'That the murderer removed his albums, yes. But not everybody takes photos, you know. We'll have to ask his friends about that, but we've only just started thinking along these lines. A lot of people store them digitally these days, as well. On their computers and so on.'

'I know that,' said Barbarotti. 'Oh well, better late than never I suppose. And Hans Andersson? I mean in terms of photos.'

'I know,' sighed Backman. 'We'll have to try getting pictures from the whole lot of them, and see whether any of them turn up in Anna Eriksson's album. And vice versa, possibly.'

'You mean we ought to keep an eye out for Eriksson and Bergman in their albums? Or computers?'

Eva Backman gave a shrug and looked worn out. Barbarotti pondered. 'When?' he asked, looking at the clock. It was five to eleven.

'Jonnerblad and Tallin decided we'd start on it first thing in the morning.'

'Excellent,' said Barbarotti. 'Gives us something to do tomorrow. By the way, do you think it's a coincidence that he's chosen a guy called Hans Andersson?'

'What?'

'I mean the names could scarcely be any commoner. Anna Eriksson and Hans Andersson? Is he just picking them out because he knows it'll be harder for us to identify the right one?'

'Well, we only had five Erik Bergmans.'

'Correct, but at that point we didn't know if it was serious or not.'

Eva Backman nodded. 'Yes, you've got a point there. Well, I suppose there's a chance it's as simple as that . . . and what's more, it could be he hasn't decided which of them he's going to kill. Perhaps he just picks one we're not keeping a very good eye on. In which case . . .'

'In which case,' supplied Barbarotti, 'we're dealing with a complete lunatic. No, I cling to the hope that there's some sort of connection. At least it makes it a bit more comprehensible . . . if there really is some reason behind it.'

He looked at the photograph again. 'Where do you think it's taken?' he asked. 'Something tells me this isn't Sweden.'

'I thought the same thing,' said Eva Backman. 'There's something about this bench and this litter bin. I'm pretty sure it wasn't taken in this country.'

'Great,' said Barbarotti. 'That just leaves us the rest of the planet to investigate.'

Eva Backman crumpled up the pizza box and forced it into the wastepaper basket. 'I bet you a hundred it's Bergman,' she said, pulling her shoulders back. 'Are we on?'

'Suppose so,' said Barbarotti. 'But I doubt we'll ever find out which of us was right.'

'The trouble with you is that you're way too pessimistic,' noted Inspector Backman.

But as she said it, he couldn't detect much optimism in her face, either. Just the same fatigue he felt overwhelmed by himself. 'Can I give you a lift home?' he asked. 'I happen to have the car with me.'

Eva Backman hesitated for a moment.

'All right,' she said. 'I'd more or less decided to crash out here, there's no one at home anyway. But a shower and a proper bed might be nice.'

Three years ago, thought Gunnar Barbarotti, I'd have invited her in for a beer at my place in a situation like this.

But that was three years ago.

13

'We'd better go through all the letter stuff one more time,' said Superintendent Jonnerblad. 'Tallin and I were talking it over yesterday and we're thinking along roughly the same lines.'

They were in the third-floor room that had been put at the disposal of the two National CID detectives. Located next door to Chief Inspector Asunander's office, it was a space that was also intended for high-level meetings – primarily involving Lindweden, the district police commissioner, Asunander and other prominent officials. As far as Barbarotti was aware, it got used at least once a year, when Lindweden invited his fellow Rotarians to a Christmas glögg party. It was done out very smartly: light, delicately grained birchwood, chairs with claret-coloured leather seats, and pictures on the walls. Reproductions, admittedly, just pine forests, storms at sea and that sort of thing, but even so. There was a coffee machine, and a small fridge humming in the corner. A whiteboard, a television set with a DVD player and video.

Superintendent Jonnerblad was in command; there was no formal difference of rank and precedence, but he was at least ten years older than Tallin, had thinner hair and a face that was significantly more lined. Generally forceful, so it seemed natural for him to take charge. Chief Inspector Tallin was somewhat shorter, a slighter figure of roughly Barbarotti's own age. Quiet and thoughtful, one might almost say courteous, in an old-fashioned sort of way. He was vaguely reminiscent of a maths teacher Barbarotti had had in upper secondary, one of those characters who had endeared himself over time, with every sleepy double lesson, every test paper they ran through and every term that passed. They were very agreeable, people like that, thought Gunnar Barbarotti. The sort who weren't perpetually trying to prove something to those around them, were well aware of their own abilities and failings and knew how to keep them in perspective.

Not that there was really anything wrong with Jonnerblad, either, but his style was different. He had kept a fairly low profile at the start, but was gradually taking over more of the decision-making. Not counting Asunander, the lead group consisted of six people – but if we'd been a group of dogs, thought Gunnar Barbarotti, Jonnerblad would have been the one to eat first and to mate with the bitch on heat.

Not that Eva Backman would ever in her life take it into her head to mate with the bitch on heat.

'OK then,' said Astor Nilsson. 'The letters?'

'Hrrm,' said Tallin. 'The letters, yes. We're thinking principally about the fact that they're addressed to you, Barbarotti.'

'That fact hadn't escaped me, either,' said Barbarotti. 'I've thought about it a lot.'

'Excellent,' said Jonnerblad. 'So our murderer chose to communicate with you from the outset. That must be significant, there must be some kind of link between you. I know you've been thinking about it already, but what we want, Tallin and I, is for you to do it in a more systematic way. Take your time. We think it could pay off.'

Barbarotti considered this for a moment.

'What is it you want me to do?' he asked. 'More precisely.'

'Well, it's like this,' said Jonnerblad, a vertical line creasing his forehead. 'We assume the perpetrator has some reason for wanting to kill a number of people. He also wants to taunt the cops. But he doesn't just do that in general terms, he turns to a specific cop. To you, Barbarotti. Why does he do that?'

'Because . . .'

'Because he knows who you are, yes. And if the murderer knows who you are, that ought to mean that you know the murderer, too. There must be some kind of link between you, as I said. It could be as old as the hills, it could be somebody you once stitched up, way back, it could even be someone you punched in the playground in Year 4. But the crucial thing is that he's there. Somewhere in your past, Barbarotti, and what we want, Tallin and I, is for you to sit down and dig him out.'

He sounds like a trailer for a bad Hollywood movie, thought Barbarotti. But that doesn't necessarily mean he's wrong.

'Maybe I should,' he said. 'Private brainstorming, as it were?'

'Something a bit more systematic, we were thinking,' Tallin put in.

'This is what we'll do today,' said Jonnerblad, propping himself on his elbows and leaning across the oval table so Barbarotti could smell his breath. Coffee and eggs, if he wasn't mistaken. A hint of smoked cod roe. 'You're released from the rest of the investigation. You'll be in your office – or you can go home if you prefer – and you'll go through your entire life. Write down the name of every single person you've met, who could conceivably – I say *conceivably* – be capable of coming up with this devilish scheme. You should have at least fifty by the time you've finished. Then you pick out the ten most likely ones and we all look through the lists tomorrow. Concentrate mainly on your police career, of course.'

Well I'll be damned, thought Barbarotti. He's telling me . . . he's actually telling me to go home, lie on my bed and think. In paid work time. For a whole day.

'Not a bad idea,' Barbarotti said, getting quickly to his feet. 'Certainly worth a try. Er . . . I'll be back tomorrow, then?'

'We'll meet here at the same time,' said Tallin.

The Superintendent leant back and looked pleased with himself. 'So that's agreed,' he said.

'Absolutely,' said Barbarotti.

Was he expecting me to object? he thought, once he was out in the corridor. I've overestimated him.

But he simply couldn't lie on his bed and think, not on a day like this. He knew it as soon as he got home. The weather admittedly looked grey and overcast, and there was a possibility of rain showers in the afternoon, but there was no wind and the temperature was around twenty.

The sort of weather made for a long walk, in other words. Smart cop seizes the day; he armed himself with a rolled-up raincoat, a little rucksack, water and fruit, a pen and a notepad, drove out to Kymmensudde and set off on foot along the northern shore of Kymmen. Paths for walkers criss-crossed the forest that extended along the ridge towards Kerran and Rimminge.

If there really was a murderer in his head, as Superintendent Jonnerblad and Chief Inspector Tallin from the National CID clearly believed, then a couple of undisturbed hours spent on a leisurely walk through this peaceful landscape might well be the ideal way of bringing him to light. Mightn't it?

Thus thought Inspector Barbarotti – with the sort of optimism that he didn't normally subscribe to, but felt could usefully serve as a theoretical starting point. To set the tone.

Though in fact he started with a call to Gotland. So he could switch off his phone with a clear conscience afterwards, or anyway, that was the justification he invented.

She sounded a bit mournful. She claimed it was because it was their last day at Gustabo – she and the kids were going home to Skåne the next morning – but he didn't believe her. Not entirely, there was something else, too. First he asked her if it was to do with having to go back to work on Monday, and she admitted that was a factor.

'I've got to leave paradise tomorrow, my holiday ends in three days' time and I'm waiting for my period. None of it's much fun, that's all. I feel . . .'

'How do you feel?'

'Lonely.'

'You've got two children with you and a policeman who loves you, how can you feel lonely?'

'Well that's just it . . .'

'Yes?'

'That policeman.'

'Aha.'

He didn't know what made him say 'aha'. It definitely didn't signal any sudden insight on his part. Just the opposite, in fact; it was more like a dark curtain falling, and for a moment he felt so drained that he had to stop and lean against a tree trunk. A few seconds passed in silence.

'What . . . what's wrong?' he managed to say.

He heard her give a sob.

'I'm forty-two,' she said. 'I've lived on my own for four

years. I don't want it to be like this for another year. I enjoy seeing you when we meet the way we do, but it . . . well, it isn't enough.'

He thought for a second. Possibly a second and a half.

'Then let's get married,' he said.

'If you want, that is,' he added.

She said nothing but he could hear her breathing at the other end of the line. It sounded a little laboured, as if she was out on a walk as well, and sure enough, listening more carefully, he could actually make out the crunch of her footsteps.

'I don't want you saying it because you feel you have to.'

'No, I—'

'I don't want to put pressure on you.'

'You're not.'

'If we move in together and it doesn't work, I shall die. I can't go through all that business again.'

'Bloody hell,' said Gunnar Barbarotti, 'you don't have to tell me. I'm forty-seven; you think I fancy having another four wives to get along with in my old age?'

She gave a laugh. I can make her laugh, he thought. That's not a bad thing.

'You're not serious?'

'Yes I am.'

'You don't sound serious.'

He cleared his throat. 'Do you want to stay in Helsingborg?'

'I . . .'

'Because I don't mind moving down to Skåne.'

She started to cry. I can make her cry, too, thought Gunnar Barbarotti, and felt a stab of panic. But why? Doesn't she want me? Or is she . . . overcome?

'You don't want us to,' he said.

'Yes I do,' said Marianne. 'But I don't know if you really do. I might not be as easy to live with as you imagine. We've only met in the most favourable of settings, and maybe you don't . . .'

'Rubbish,' said Barbarotti. 'I love you. I hate being away from you.'

He heard her blowing her nose. 'All right,' she said. 'But I'll give you a week to cool off, in case you change your mind. Ring me next Wednesday, and if you're still saying the same thing, then there's no way back, OK?'

'OK,' said Gunnar Barbarotti. 'You can start looking out for a bigger flat when you get home.'

Once they had ended the call he turned off the phone. He realized his pulse was hammering like a machine gun. A hundred or a hundred and ten, probably.

Christ almighty, he thought. That's done it.

And now I've got to start fishing up a murderer from my memory. What a day.

He tripped over a root and almost fell into a blackthorn thicket.

He did as Jonnerblad and Tallin said and started at the beginning. He wrote the names one after another on his notepad, and found it a strange occupation, almost a kind of penance, or a final reckoning as if for St Peter at the Last Judgement.

I hurt him, and him, in my journey on this earth. I never got on with him, or him, and perhaps they've had a grudge against me ever since . . . well, ever since we were teenagers. Or students in Lund. Or at police training college. Or at work

. . . That fiddle-playing body builder over in Pampas, that drug pusher, that fascist rapist . . .

Strange indeed, but individuals kept occurring to him, their faces, names and circumstances popping into his mind, one after another. Upper-secondary school alone, that rowdy social science group at Cathedral School, yielded six names – and two teachers as well, not that he could seriously imagine either of them losing their marbles to the extent that they were now writing him letters and indulging in production-line killing. But the method – Jonnerblad and Tallin's method – meant that he initially had to include everybody he felt might have disliked him in any way. Not only those he had overtly clashed with, but also all the others, those individuals for whom he suspected – in certain maximally perverted circumstances – that the possibility could exist.

Leif Barrander, with whom he'd had fights in Year 4.

Henrik Lofting, who had spat in his face in Year 5 because he'd slipped the ball between the boy's legs and humiliated him when they were playing football in PE.

Johan Karlsson, who'd been bullied in Years 7 and 8 and tried to take his revenge on his tormentors (Barbarotti hadn't been one of them, but part of the silent, timid majority) by setting fire to himself. He hadn't managed to kill himself that way, but the scars on his face would never go away.

Oliver Casares, whose girlfriend – Madeleine – he had pinched on a school skiing trip in the mountains. That was what Oliver believed, at any rate, though in fact Madeleine had swapped partners very much of her own accord.

And all the rest. Who would have thought they had that many potential enemies? mused Gunnar Barbarotti. And surely he hadn't been that bloody awful? No worse than anybody else? Had he?

Reaching the old Ulme mill after about an hour, he took a break and counted up his gallery. Thirty-two names. Half a chessboard, and he still had fifteen years as an active police officer to go. He would have no trouble getting up to the fifty that Jonnerblad and Tallin had set him as a target.

He ate an apple and drank half a litre of water. Then he sat there for a while, resting back against the rough wall of the mill and listening to the splash of water; there wasn't much of a flow after a long dry summer, little more than a trickle, but he could still hear it. And then it came back to him, all of a sudden. I'm going to marry Marianne. Good grief.

But he wondered who the week's cooling-off period was really for. Was she buying time for herself, in fact? Would she have some kind of excuse ready and try to stall when he rang next Wednesday?

Considering it in these terms makes the whole thing feel a bit like buying a new car, he thought. Or a flat; he was contemplating a commitment of many years' duration and the seller still wasn't sure if she had really found the right buyer. This was naturally an idea that was both absurd and over-pragmatic, but he persisted in trying to take a sober view.

Visualize them living together. Waking up each morning in the same bed and going off to their respective jobs. Sitting down to dinner with her children. Doing a big shop and inviting people round. Planning holidays together and watching films on TV.

He tried to identify any seeds of doubt. Would they start getting on each other's nerves when it was too late to change their minds? Would she stop loving him after two and a half months? What would Sara say about it? What would Eva Backman say when he told her he was planning to leave her alone with Sorrysen and Asunander and move to Skåne? Were there even any job vacancies with the Helsingborg police?

Wasn't he afraid of taking the step, when it came to the crunch? He hadn't hesitated for a second before he proposed but words were cheap, after all.

Afraid? The hell I am, thought Gunnar Barbarotti. This is the best decision I've made for five and a half years.

He tried to think of any other significant decisions he'd made in the same space of time, but couldn't recall a single one.

Except maybe that holiday to Greece and Thasos.

He looked at his watch and decided to go on a bit further before turning back towards the town. A forest would be the place to live, he thought. Have a dog and spend two hours walking every day. What sort of forests did they have round Helsingborg? Pålsjö forest, wasn't there one called that? It ought to be a beech forest really, that far south. Why not?

He shouldered his rucksack again and turned to a new page in his notebook.

Half an hour later, he was up to fifty-five names. Forty-six men and just nine women. I'm evidently a gentleman after all, noted Gunnar Barbarotti, seeing as I've got hardly any female enemies.

But he was starting to feel he'd had enough of all this cataloguing. What was the point of it? Did Jonnerblad and Tallin really think they were going to find the murderer's name leaping out from amongst all these people he'd jotted down more or less at random on his walk in the forest? He couldn't remember ever having seen this particular method described in all those criminology textbooks he had read, back at the dawn of time. No, it wasn't the *name* that was the most tantalizing thing, thought Barbarotti. It was . . . well, it was the profile, clearly.

What sort of person were they dealing with, to put it at its simplest? What were his motives? Did he even have any? Was there any point trying to understand him in logical, rational terms?

Was there a reason, in short?

The question had been floating to and fro through Barbarotti's head ever since the body of Erik Bergman had been discovered but it dawned on him now, out here in the pleasantly whispering, temperate, well-oxygenated forest, that he had not given himself adequate time to scrutinize the problem properly.

How did it go again? Well, if it was an irrational madman who had killed Bergman and Eriksson, it was hard to speculate. Or rather, that was all one *could* do. Speculate. Guess. Perhaps, deep down, a perpetrator like that really just wanted to get caught, as Lillieskog had suggested, and in that case he would presumably expose himself sooner or later to risks that were too great. Grow bold and reckless and take his game with the police a bit too far. Things would come to a head. They would be able to trap him simply by waiting for him to make his first mistake. And they could only hope he wouldn't kill too many more people in the meantime.

But if he *wasn't* an irrational madman, what then? thought Gunnar Barbarotti just as he reached the birdwatching tower up on the rise at Vreten and stopped to drink the rest of his water. Yes, where would that leave them?

A murderer with good cause for behaving exactly as he was? Who had a plan and fully reasoned motives for killing the individuals he first named in the letters he sent to DI Gunnar Barbarotti of the Kymlinge police? What did such a scenario look like? What on earth was the point of behaving like that?

He sat down on a moss-covered rock and left the question hanging in his mind without attacking it any further – giving the answer the space to develop spontaneously, which was a method that sometimes worked – but the tiny fraction of explanation that finally came to him after eight or ten minutes was the same as ever: to confuse the police as much as possible.

Create problems. Oblige them to put in more resources. Divide their forces and distract them from what was basic and important.

So, thought Gunnar Barbarotti, what is it that's fundamental and crucial here?

If we ignore the letters entirely for now.

There was only one answer.

The link between the victims.

There had to be a link. Assuming the murderer had a reason for his actions, but then that was the basic premise for this line of argument. Somewhere, Erik Bergman and Anna Eriksson's paths must have crossed and that intersection was where the murderer was also to be found.

Presumably also someone called Hans Andersson.

And Barbarotti felt a sudden conviction that if Hans Andersson's name had happened to be, say, Leopold Bernhagen, then there would have been no third letter. Because they would have been able to track down Leopold Bernhagen straight away.

Where had that particular name come from? Bernhagen? It sounded familiar, yet he couldn't place it.

He shook his head. But that's surely exactly what we're working on, he thought. Looking for links between the two victims. We're not going in the wrong direction. We're on the right road.

Though it couldn't be denied that a not insignificant part of the force was also employed in keeping an eye on a bunch of people called Hans Andersson.

And that one part of the force was taking a forest walk and thinking. It seemed pretty absurd when you came to think about it.

Change job? He had suggested as much to Marianne. Why not? If he was going to get married and move to Skåne, he might as well go the whole hog. The summer of change, he thought.

A time of transition. Time to shed his old skin.

He checked his watch again. It was twenty past one, a chillier wind was blowing through the trees and he realized it was about to rain. He got his jacket out of his rucksack and put away his pen and notepad.

But then – the thought struck him just as he was taking a somewhat ungainly leap over Rimminge Beck – but then there was still the question of how employable a forty-seven-year-old former detective really was in the current job market.

I presume I'm not exactly worth my weight in gold, thought Gunnar Barbarotti.

Not in any context.

14

Superintendent Jonnerblad leant so far back in the armchair that it creaked.

'All present and correct,' he declared. 'Glad you could join us, Lillieskog.'

Gunnar Barbarotti looked round the table. The man was right. There were eight people there: Barbarotti himself, Eva Backman and Sorrysen represented the resident force, and Jonnerblad, Tallin and Astor Nilsson the reinforcements.

Chief Inspector Asunander represented himself, or so it appeared; he was not sitting at the table but a little to one side, in some kind of listening pose. Lillieskog also had to be considered part of the reinforcements, thought Barbarotti; to the extent that he represented anything, he could be described as the voice of psychology and science. 'I'll be happy to go first,' Lillieskog said. 'I've got a train at three thirty.'

Jonnerblad nodded. Barbarotti looked at the clock. Just after two o'clock on a Friday afternoon, and it was as plain as a pikestaff that Lillieskog was eager to get home to his nearest and dearest.

Or his goldfish, or whatever his domestic arrangements were.

That's a bit churlish of me, he thought on reflection, and

decided to adopt a different attitude. He'd no call to feel superior; after all, he hadn't even got a goldfish.

'I've been discussing this with a few colleagues,' began Lillieskog. 'The fact of the matter is that we're faced with a rather unusual situation here. A rather unusual . . . perpetrator, we can assume.'

'Unusual?' queried Jonnerblad.

'Just so,' said Lillieskog. 'Unusual, however we look at it. If we imagine sketching out a worst-case scenario, we're probably dealing with an extremely intelligent murderer. One who . . . well, I don't want to overdramatize, but . . . who belongs in the world of literature rather than reality. Or the world of film. A perpetrator who really does have a well-studied plan and carries it out in every particular, without scruples . . . as you all know, that's not exactly common amongst our criminal friends.'

'Frustrated piss-artists who lose their rag and resort to violence,' prompted Astor Nilsson.

'Yes, more or less. That's the usual picture. Or underworld score-settling. But our man isn't like that. Our guarantee of catching him eventually, even so, is that he has a motive; that's the only way we're going to get to him. His aim is to kill a specific number of people . . . and it has to be those particular people, nobody else.'

'It's not inconceivable that it's a random—' Eva Backman started to object, but Lillieskog held up a hand to stop her.

'In my judgement, he does not select his victims randomly. If he does that, then we're talking about an irrational madman. No, this person has a strategy for getting rid of a number of people he feels have done him harm in some way. My guess, and this is generally the way in such cases, would be that he's quite a reserved and defensive individual. Probably a touch handicapped on the social side, but intelligent, judging by everything we know so far. Maybe even extremely so.'

'Psychopath?' asked Astor Nilsson.

'I'm not sure about that,' said Lillieskog. 'Psychopath is a fairly meaningless term. Comes all too readily to hand, but it's seldom really adequate. We can reckon on impaired empathetic ability, but that's true for most perpetrators of violence. He might not even fear being caught. Sees it more as a game, or a contest, between him and the police. And the letter writing presumably gives him a sort of kick. He gets off on it in some way, sees it as self-affirmation. But just to be clear, I don't think we're dealing with a serial killer – this is something else. What worries me, as I say, is that he's a lot smarter than we're used to. He works alone, he knows what he wants to do, and he does it.'

'For specific reasons?' said Tallin.

'For specific reasons,' said Lillieskog. 'My recommendation is that you all start looking for them.'

He leant back and put away his pen in his breast pocket. He had evidently concluded his analysis.

'Any questions for Lillieskog?' asked Jonnerblad.

'One,' said Gunnar Barbarotti. 'How certain are you about this picture of the perpetrator?'

Lilllieskog thought about it for a couple of seconds.

'Eighty–twenty,' he said.

Gunnar Barbarotti nodded. 'And if he falls within the remaining twenty, he's a loony who picks names from the phone book?'

'Or something along those lines,' said Lillieskog.

*

Once profiler Lillieskog had departed, they moved on to the case of Hans Andersson.

'Three days,' observed Jonnerblad. 'It's been at least three days since our murderer sent that letter. We've located all the Hans Anderssons registered in Kymlinge and talked to the whole lot. They're all still alive and none of them have come up with a link to either Anna Eriksson or Erik Bergman.'

'No link at all?' asked Astor Nilsson.

'No significant ones, at any rate,' said Jonnerblad. 'Three or four of them claim to know who Bergman was. One was in the same form at school as Anna Eriksson for two years, but they evidently weren't in the same groups of friends. We've tried to keep it as vague as possible and sworn them to secrecy, which seems to be working so far, but it'll get out eventually of course. Sooner or later we'll have the tabloids snapping at our heels. A murderer writing letters to the police to tell them who he plans to kill is going to be a real scoop. Could well mean shifting fifty thousand extra copies. But we'll deal with that problem when we get to it. Our surveillance of all these Hanses isn't much to boast about, though it's occupying thirty officers round the clock, but even so . . .' He paused for thought, scratching his chin. 'Even so, we have to maintain the protection. Don't you think?'

'Why shouldn't we maintain it?' asked an attentive Sorrysen.

'Because he presumably isn't going to murder any of this lot we've got under surveillance,' said Astor Nilsson. 'He would already have done it if he was going to. In Anna Eriksson's case, he gave us hardly any time at all. Or . . . well, or it could be that it's a Hans Andersson who lives somewhere else.'

'And in that case, he might already be dead,' supplied Tallin.

'There are more than fifteen hundred people in this country called Hans Andersson. And some of them go rather off-grid in the holiday period, so any bad news could take time to emerge. But we've got a nationwide alert out, of course.'

'Naturally,' said Jonnerblad. 'And remember what an outcry there might be if we gave up on the protection. But we can't carry on with it for an unlimited period, of course. It's costing more than policing a high-risk football match.'

'Interesting situation,' said Eva Backman. 'So what shall we do?'

'Suggestions?' said Jonnerblad, looking round the table.

'Stop the surveillance,' said Astor Nilsson. 'But not tell the individuals involved.'

'Give me your reasons,' said Jonnerblad.

'Gladly,' said Astor Nilsson. 'Can I just have a drop of water first?'

Tallin opened a bottle of Loka mineral water and poured him a glass.

'Thanks,' said Astor Nilsson. 'Well, firstly, the pathetic level of surveillance we're providing isn't going to stop any crimes . . . all we're doing is keeping up appearances and that's daft. A sop to public opinion. Secondly, we'll presumably look even more incompetent if the perpetrator strikes and succeeds *despite* our surveillance. And thirdly . . . well, thirdly, as I said, I don't think our good friend the murdering correspondent is going to harm a hair on the head of any Hans we're trying to keep tabs on. Ergo, call the whole thing off.'

'Agreed,' said Eva Backman.

'Agreed,' said Barbarotti.

'Hmm,' said Jonnerblad. 'I think we need to think this through a bit more carefully.'

'Do as you like,' said Astor Nilsson. 'Now can we talk about the bodies we've already got, instead?'

This was permitted.

First, Sorrysen reported on progress in the ongoing interviews with people who had known Erik Bergman. In various capacities. In summary, his opinion was that their picture of Erik Bergman had grown clearer in many ways, but that nothing of vital importance for the case had emerged.

Then Eva Backman gave a similar report on how far they had got with Anna Eriksson's circle of acquaintances. There was a kind of psychological accord between the two victims, Backman stressed; they were both pronounced individualists, and were described by almost all the interviewees as strong if somewhat superficial, and as distinctly self-sufficient characters. Several of the informants had described Anna Eriksson as 'hard' or 'tough', and an old upper-secondary classmate of Erik Bergman's had called his former friend 'cold'.

Sorrysen and Bergman's combined reports took upwards of an hour, information was piled on information, and amongst other things they had established that Anna Eriksson had still been alive at 11.55 a.m. on the Tuesday, when she was seen on her balcony by a reliable witness across the road – and that she had very probably been dead two hours later. Thus within this window – these two hours – the murderer had struck. The technical investigations of the two murder scenes were complete, a number of plastic bags with vastly varying contents had been sent off to the National Forensic Centre in Linköping for analysis, but no results had come back yet, and it was not deemed particularly likely that anything of interest to the investigation would come to light that way. Fingerprints and DNA seemed conspicuous by their absence, and one plausible hypothesis in

Anna Eriksson's case was that he had rung at the door, been admitted, beaten his victim to death with his blunt instrument, put her in plastic bags and stowed her under the bed. As simple as that. The unknown male who had been observed from behind by a witness on the stairs remained shapeless and unidentified, and in a follow-up interview the witness had shown signs of having confused Tuesday with Monday.

As for the letters, a new set of graphologists had carried out fresh analyses. A right-handed man who had written in block letters with his left hand was still their best hunch. The letters having been posted in Gothenburg (the first two) and Borås (the third), he could be assumed to live within a radius of 150–200 kilometres of Kymlinge.

'Brilliant,' commented Astor Nilsson. 'We're dealing with a right-handed man from west Sweden. It can only be a matter of time until we nail him.'

'Hrmm, um, yes,' muttered Superintendent Jonnerblad. 'Our most important task is to keep searching on a broad front. But we're also focusing on looking for links, by checking photo albums amongst other things. So far we haven't really found anything like that, but it would be useful if we did before Hans Andersson turns up dead.'

He cleared his throat again and drank some water. 'And it would be equally useful if Inspector Barbarotti could tell us why he's the one on the receiving end of these letters,' he added.

Gunnar Barbarotti pulled himself more upright in his seat.

'We're entirely in agreement on that point,' he said. 'I've drawn up an inventory of all the skeletons in my cupboard, as requested. You've all seen the list now, and it would be interesting to hear whether there were any names that leapt out at you.'

It all went quiet round the table while they studied the lists of the sixty names he had noted down.

Then they discussed five or six of them for a while – they all had some form of criminal record – after which heads were shaken and the consensus was that the exercise wasn't leading anywhere.

'And none of these say anything extra to you?' asked Superintendent Jonnerblad, looking very tired all of a sudden.

'No,' said Barbarotti. 'Which doesn't mean I'd be entirely surprised if it actually turned out to be one of them. But I wasn't able to pick out ten I'd give low odds.'

'There's a bit too much maths in this for my taste,' declared Astor Nilsson. 'We've got twenty-nine Hanses and now sixty Barbarotti ghosts. Shall we put them all in a random number generator and see which ones stick together, then?'

'Too much sitting thinking behind a desk, too little practical detective work,' Eva Backman put in.

'Detection always needs a specific direction,' Tallin pointed out. 'Or it does once a few days have passed, at any rate.'

'I'm with you on that,' said Eva Backaman. 'I take it back.'

Sorrysen discreetly cleared his throat.

'That photograph,' he said. 'Pardon me, but I got the idea it could have been taken in France.'

The picture of the man and woman on the bench was hastily dug out and scrutinized.

'France?' said Jonnerblad. 'And why is that, exactly?'

'It's something to do with the colour of the litter bin at the end of the bench,' explained Sorrysen. 'That's to say, you can only see part of it, but I assume it's a litter bin. I think I recognize the shade, you see.'

Barbarotti suddenly recalled that painting was a hobby of

Sorrysen's. A few years previously he'd even held a little exhibition in the police canteen. A dozen small, semi-figurative oils and egg temperas, which had met with surprise and appreciation. Barbarotti had been thinking of buying one, but before he could decide, they had all been snapped up. Perhaps Sorrysen had a feeling for colour that none of the others in the group could aspire to?

'The colour of a litter bin?' said Jonnerblad dubiously. 'I don't really know . . .'

'Well I'm damned,' said Astor Nilsson. 'I think you're right. Reminds me of the shade of the shutters on a house I rented once. In Avranches . . . Normandy, that is, for those of you who don't—'

'I don't think we should make too much of this,' interrupted Tallin. 'And what's more, we're far from certain the man on the bench really is Erik Bergman. Aren't we?'

'Of course,' said Sorrysen. 'I just thought it was worth mentioning. It could equally well be southern Italy, but I do realize this isn't a great deal of help.'

'Hrmm, um, yes,' went Superintendent Jonnerblad again, leaning back in his chair. 'France and Italy? I'm afraid we really need to narrow down our field of enquiry a bit rather than widening it out to include the rest of Europe. But thanks for your input anyway. It might prove useful later on.'

'Don't mention it,' said Sorrysen.

Jonnerblad scanned the flagging company around the table. He looked at his watch.

'Time to call it a day, I think,' he said. 'Unfortunately, all we can do is carry on working along the guidelines we've already drawn up. Surveillance of the Hans Anderssons to be maintained at current levels for the whole weekend. Assuming nothing unforeseen happens, we'll reconvene on Monday morning at ten o'clock. Questions?'

Nobody had any. Superintendent Jonnerblad declared the briefing session closed. It was twenty to five on Friday 10 August.

'Your holiday?' Gunnar Barbarotti asked when Eva Backman looked into his room ten minutes later. 'What's happening about that?'

'I'm working till Wednesday,' she said. 'But I'll pop down to the cottage for the weekend as well. Eight hundred kilometres there and back; what we won't do for family harmony, eh? You got any plans?'

Barbarotti shrugged. 'Two-pronged approach,' he said. 'I'll be here, trying to make some inroads. But I'm also planning to find time to decide what I want to do with my life.'

'Good,' said Eva Backman. 'You're right to do that. The latter I mean.'

'OK then,' said Barbarotti. 'See you on Monday. Give my regards to the family.'

'And mine to Marianne,' said Eva Backman.

'I won't be speaking to her until Wednesday,' said Gunnar Barbarotti.

Eva Backman stopped in the doorway. 'Wednesday? Why then?'

'It's this thing,' said Barbarotti.

'This thing?'

'Yes.'

'You're just so bloody obvious sometimes,' said Eva Backman.

15

He slid his index finger into the Bible and opened it.

Found he had landed in St Matthew's Gospel. Chapter 6, verses 22–3.

> The light of the body is the eye: if therefore thine eye be single, thy whole body shall be full of light.
>
> But if thine eye be evil, thy whole body shall be full of darkness. If therefore the light that is in thee be darkness, how great is that darkness!

He read it twice. Oh? he thought. Well yes, that's how it is. Of course it is.

But if this were to be taken as guidance, and that was the whole point after all, the precise nature of the guidance being offered didn't seem entirely straightforward. Did it refer to the case? Or to himself? His general spiritual darkness and blind fumbling along the thorny path of life?

Or to both?

Yes, maybe both, he thought. A single and unclouded eye would be very useful in any circumstances. It would help him see what was actually there to be seen, rather than imagined dangers.

Wouldn't it?

Inspector Barbarotti sighed and closed the Bible. He went into the kitchen and discovered the fridge was empty. Well, it contained some cheese, a tub of spreadable margarine, a litre of milk and four or five other abandoned items, but nothing to amount to a decent dinner. But then, on the other hand, why would anyone want to cook dinner for one person? It was half past six on Saturday night, and too late to ring a good friend and ask whether he or she felt like a bite to eat and a glass of wine. What was more, strictly speaking he only had two friends of the same calibre of loneliness as himself, and to be honest he didn't really fancy an evening of meaningless chat with either of them across a restaurant table.

But sitting alone was worse. People recognized him. *Look, there's DI Barbarotti eating his dinner all alone! Poor guy, his life can't be much fun.*

Christ no, that wasn't an alternative he would consider. But he was hungry. His body's signals were at a stage that could not be ignored. He supposed he'd have to make do with a couple of hot dogs over at the Rocksta Grill; it was a suitably discreet compromise and it had worked before. Maybe he could drop in at the Elk on the way home and see if there were any familiar faces hanging round the bar?

He checked the thermometer outside the kitchen window before he set off. Twenty-four degrees. The heat was back after a couple of days of changeable weather. He didn't even need a sweater. An evening just made for sitting outside in convivial company.

How deep is the darkness in my body? thought Gunnar Barbarotti, and hurried out into town.

And I can't ring Marianne until Wednesday.

*

But he could ring Sara.

The hot dogs from Rocksta and a melancholy beer at the Elk took the time to quarter past eight, and he had scarcely set foot back in his hallway before sensing that he must ring Sara.

Simply must.

He sank down into the deckchair on his balcony and rang the number. He watched the sunset and listened to the jackdaws as he waited to hear her voice from London. After six rings, it went to voicemail. Sara gaily announced – in English and in Swedish – that she was either asleep or in the shower, but would ring back before Christmas as long as the caller left their number. He gave it five minutes before trying again. This time, she answered.

'Hi, it's Dad.'

'Who?'

There was the sound of music and voices in the background.

'It's me,' he said a little louder. 'Your darling father, remember him?'

She laughed. 'Oh, so it's you? Can I ring you back in . . . in half an hour, things are a bit of a mess here at the moment.'

He told her that was fine, but wondered what she meant by 'a bit of a mess' and 'here'. It didn't sound particularly reassuring. Would have been much better if she'd been at home and all he'd been able to hear was the television news or a vacuum cleaner in the background. He'd made out the sound of glass bottles chinking, wherever she was, hadn't he? And smoke, he was sure it must be smoky as hell, though it was hard to get a sense of it over the phone, but if you'd been a detective for twenty years, you just kind of knew.

He went to get the list of sixty names from his briefcase, took the last beer from the fridge and settled back down on the balcony.

Might as well do a bit of work while I'm waiting, he thought. It's what one clings to for security and support. Life is a gravel pit and you're the mechanical shovel.

It took Sara fifty-five minutes to ring; almost a minute per name, in fact, but it didn't help. No matter how hard he stared at them, he couldn't visualize a single one of them as a letter-writing murderer, and no light came on to illuminate his darkness.

'Hi Dad,' said Sara. 'Do you think you could call me back, I haven't got much money left on this card.'

It was the usual procedure. 'How are you?' he asked once the conversation finally got underway.

'Fine,' said Sara. 'Everything's fine. You're not worrying about me, are you?'

'Should I be?' he countered slyly.

'Not in the least,' maintained Sara, and laughed. 'But I know what an old mother hen you are. I'm glad you rang though, because it gives me a chance to tell you I've got a boyfriend.'

'Boyfriend?' queried Gunnar Barbarotti, gripping his beer glass so hard he almost broke it.

'Yes. His name's Richard. He's really nice.'

I don't believe that for a second, thought Barbarotti. He's just trying to lead you on and exploit you, can't you see?

'Richard, eh?' he said. 'Well, well. And what does he do?'

'He's a musician.'

Musician! bellowed a voice inside Gunnar Barbarotti. Sara,

are you out of your mind? Music and drugs and AIDS, the full works, now go home and lock yourself in, and I'll come and fetch you tomorrow!

'Hello, are you still there?'

'Yes . . . I'm still here. Are you quite sure about this . . . I mean, what kind of musician?'

He fired off a quick existential prayer to Our Lord. Say he's a cellist in the London Philharmonic! Three points, God! Anything at all except . . .

'He plays bass in a band that does gigs here in the pub.'

Jesus, thought Gunnar Barbarotti. I knew it. Nose ring and tattoos and three kilos of dirty hair.

'The pub?'

'Dad, I gave up my other job. I only work at the pub now, but it's really nice. Everyone's great and you needn't worry for a single second.'

'You're nineteen, Sara.'

'I know how old I am, Dad. What were *you* doing when you were nineteen?'

'That's exactly what worries me,' he said in a strangled voice, and was rewarded with another laugh.

'You know what, Dad, I do love you.'

'I love you too, Sara. But you've got to look after yourself. It's an entirely different kettle of fish now, compared to when I was young, and it's much worse for a girl. If you'd seen a fraction of what—'

'I know all that, Dad. I'm not a complete idiot. You can trust me and if you met Richard I promise you'd like him.'

I'd interrogate him for fourteen hours without so much as a break for a pee, thought Gunnar Barbarotti. Then I'd banish him to Outer Mongolia.

'Why did you give up the shop job?' he asked. 'I don't think a pub is a suitable working environment for a girl of nineteen.'

'Dad,' said Sara with a patient sigh. 'Just think about it. There are girls of nineteen serving behind the bar in every pub in the whole world. I only work four evenings a week and I earn twice as much as I did in that snotty boutique. I'm doing just fine. I don't smoke, I never have unprotected sex and I don't drink even half as much as you do.'

'All right,' said Gunnar Barbarotti, sensing it was time to throw in the towel. 'I just want everything to be all right where you're concerned, you know that, don't you? How's Malin getting on, by the way?'

Malin was the friend Sara had gone over to London with. They shared a flat up in Camden.

'Oh, Malin's fine too,' Sara assured him. 'But she hasn't got a boyfriend yet.'

'Wise girl,' said Gunnar Barbarotti. 'I'll be over to see you in September, like we said. If I'm still welcome, that is?'

'My heart belongs to Daddy,' said Sara in English, and as this was the best thing she had said in this entire phone call they ended it on a high note, promising to be in touch again in a week.

He lingered on the balcony as the sky slowly faded to evening blue over the rooftops and over the elms along the river. In a year's time, I'll be sitting on another balcony looking out over the Öresund, he suddenly thought. Seeing Helsingör and the Louisiana gallery and so on.

Just imagine that really happening.

Or imagine it *not* happening. Imagine me sitting here on this three-square-metre patch for all the summer nights of the rest of my life. On this particular evening it didn't look bad at all, to be fair, but still. But still?

The worst of it was that he didn't find it particularly hard to paint that picture in his mind's unclouded eye. As time passed, the inertia inside him increased, and it was stupid to try persuading himself he would feel more open to change in five or eight years.

If you're not keen when you're forty-seven, you're not going to be keen when you're fifty-seven, either, he thought. Unless you make a real effort to change things.

But in actual fact, he was keen *now*. As keen as anyone could be. On Wednesday he would ring Marianne and tell her so. Then he could only hope she hadn't fallen prey to doubts. In a way, it was surprising that he had such confidence in her, bearing in mind that they had known each other less than a year and not met each other more than eight or ten times; but maybe the simple explanation was that loneliness was prodding him into action. At my age, he thought, one certainly hasn't got all the time in the world to pick and choose.

To act or to wither away.

Again, it struck him that this sounded crass and pragmatic, really pushing the point, especially as he found it hard to identify any kind of hesitation in his feelings for Marianne. He loved her, he was ready to give up his job and move in with her in Helsingborg, it was as simple as that. Or anywhere else, if she preferred it. Berlin or Fjugesta or any bloody where.

I would have chosen her over everyone else, even if I'd had all the women of the world to choose from, he thought. That's the truth, I'm not lying. Let the sunset be my witness.

*

Then a memory came into his head. One might well wonder why.

A case, about ten years ago. A woman called the station in the middle of the night to tell them she had killed her husband. She gave the address, one of the new blocks of flats down in Pampas. He attended the scene with a female colleague, who later moved to Stockholm, and they verified that it was just as the woman had said. The man was leaning forward over the kitchen table, head resting on his folded arms, and but for the carving knife protruding from between his shoulder blades, you might have thought he was asleep there.

'Why?' Barbarotti asked.

'I didn't know what else to do,' the woman replied. 'He said he was going to leave me. What would have become of me then?'

He regarded her in bewilderment. A somewhat overweight, careworn woman of around fifty-five. 'What's to become of you both now?' he asked.

'I'm going to be taken into custody,' she said. 'But I couldn't have coped with living alone. Not for a single day. And Arne's going into the ground.'

When he interviewed her subsequently, she had stuck to this line as if it went without saying. Nothing that needed to be queried or further explained; her husband had promised to love her and look after her all her life, and when he broke that promise, there was only one logical solution to the problem: sticking a knife in his back. And indeed, the forensic psychiatrist who eventually examined her over a number of days reached the conclusion that she was in full possession of her faculties, and she consequently received a life sentence for murder.

Barbarotti would think back to this case from time to time.

Or rather, it would come sailing into his mind at regular intervals. Like now. And he could do nothing to stop it. It was always accompanied by those questions he couldn't really put into words. And certainly couldn't answer.

Where did her guilt actually lie?

Why did he find it so hard to accept that she had committed a crime at all?

Had he been an autocratic judge in the legal system of some utopian state, he would presumably have acquitted her – against her own will. Because she would never again in her life be in a situation in which she needed to commit such an act to defend . . . well, whatever it was she had defended. He couldn't really get to the nub of it, but then nor did it feel important to put it into words.

The more important thing, he assumed, was the extent to which going round with such notions of crime and punishment in his head was compatible with his own role as a police officer.

The answer eluded him on this beautiful August evening, as it had on every other occasion. When it got to twelve and the jackdaws had fallen silent, he decided to go to bed, but he was scarcely out of his deckchair when his mobile phone rang.

Christ, he thought. Sara. Something's happened to her.

But it was Göran Persson.

For one puzzled second, Barbarotti really did believe it was the former prime minister calling him on some tricky matter of political import – before realizing he was only talking to a namesake.

Göran Persson was a reporter at the tabloid *Expressen* and his reason for ringing was as plain as a pikestaff.

'It's about the two murders in Kymlinge. I've been told the

murderer wrote to you in advance to tell you what he was going to do. What's your comment on that?'

'What?' said Gunnar Barbarotti.

Göran Persson repeated his assertion and his question in exactly the same words.

'I've no comment at all,' declared Barbarotti. 'I don't know what you're talking about. Where did you get that information?'

'Don't you know it's illegal to try to trace a source?' retorted Persson. 'But I suppose I could overlook it. Suffice it to say that I know this information to be true. That you knew Erik Bergman and Anna Eriksson were going to be murdered. We'll be writing about the letters in Monday's edition, and it won't reflect particularly well on the police if you try to deny the facts.'

'I don't believe—'

'I'm in the car on my way down to you right now,' said the reporter. 'Shall we say we'll meet for breakfast at Kymlinge Hotel tomorrow morning? Then we can talk it over in peace and quiet. I reckon it's just as well for us both to play on the same team in this case. The letters are addressed to you personally, as I understand it. Handwritten, in block capitals. Is that right?'

Gunnar Barbarotti thought it over for three seconds.

'What time?' he asked.

'Ten o'clock,' said Persson. 'I've still got two hundred kilometres to go and it's Sunday tomorrow, after all.'

We've got a leak, thought Detective Inspector Barbarotti as he cleaned his teeth and regarded his unusually clouded eyes in the bathroom mirror.

Who?

16

He was reluctant to do it, extremely reluctant, but an hour before his rendezvous with Göran Persson, he called Superintendent Jonnerblad to explain the situation.

'Damn, that's all we need,' said Jonnerblad. 'I think it's best if I see him in your place.'

'That's really not a good idea,' said Barbarotti. 'He seems to know the letters are addressed to me, so I'm the one he wants to talk to.'

Jonnerblad considered this for a moment and switched off a radio.

'All right,' he said. 'But we'll devise a strategy and then you'll stick to it.'

'Happily,' said Barbarotti. 'Do you have anything specific in mind?'

'How much we ought to give away, of course,' said Jonnerblad. 'That's what this is all about.'

'I'm pretty sure he already knows it all,' said Barbarotti. 'Might not be such a bright idea to tangle ourselves up in lies.'

'Who said anything about lies?' demanded Jonnerblad.

'I couldn't say,' said Barbarotti.

'Who the hell let the cat out of the bag?'

'I haven't a clue,' said Barbarotti. 'But quite a few of us are in on the information.'

'Perhaps it was just a question of time,' said Jonnerblad. 'But if you see any of our colleagues strolling round town in an Armani suit, you could tip me a wink.'

'I promise,' said Barbarotti. 'So what about this strategy, then?'

Jonnerblad said nothing but his breathing was heavy. As if he had a fat mistress sitting on his chest or something like that, thought Barbarotti.

Why did these gratuitous thoughts and images keep popping up? They were nearly always disturbing and . . . what was the word . . . counterproductive? They made him lose the thread, you might say. Why the hell should there be a fat whor—?

'Protection measures,' Jonnerblad said at last. 'He'll ask us about our protection measures.'

'We've no need to protect those who've already been murdered,' said Barbarotti. 'I'm not sure he—'

'Hans Andersson,' interrupted Jonnerblad. 'Did he know about Hans Andersson as well?'

'That's what I was about to tell you,' said Barbarotti. 'I couldn't tell. We didn't discuss it.'

'If he doesn't mention him, you needn't either,' decided Jonnerblad.

'And if he does mention him?'

'You make it clear that we've implemented protection measures as fully as circumstances permit.'

'As circumstances permit?'

'Exactly that.'

'Got it,' said Barbarotti. 'Anything else?'

'He presumably wants to keep this bit of news to himself,' said Jonnerblad. 'That gives you a bit of bargaining room.

There's nothing to stop us making this public at a press conference this afternoon.'

'I know,' said Barbarotti. 'I thought about that, too. I don't get why they didn't make a big splash with this today.'

'And what's your conclusion?' asked Jonnerblad. 'Having thought about it?'

'That he must have received the tip-off just before he rang me. It was past midnight, so they simply wouldn't have had time to put it in any sooner.'

'Very possibly,' said Jonnerblad. 'But why is he getting in touch with us at all?'

'Good question,' said Barbarotti. 'Because he didn't believe it, maybe?'

'They don't usually let that get in their way,' said Jonnerblad. 'But you could be right in this case. So you didn't get the impression it took the chat with you to convince him, then?'

'Well . . .' said Barbarotti.

'Were you sober?'

Inspector Barbarotti didn't reply.

'Call me as soon as you're through with him,' summarized Jonnerblad. 'Employ a police officer's common sense, this isn't your first time, is it? And if you happen to winkle the name of his source out of him, that's fine by me.'

'I doubt I'll be able to,' said Barbarotti. 'Journalists generally take good care of their moles.'

'I bet they bloody do,' muttered Jonnerblad, and with that, the strategic planning call was over.

Göran Persson didn't exactly look at ease at Kymlinge Hotel. In Gunnar Barbarotti's estimation, he would probably have preferred a dining room in New York or Rome, but they were where they were. The reporter had evidently finished his breakfast; he had got through more china than the average family of six, and mangled remains of meat, cheese and fish, flakes of Danish pastry and crumbs of egg were strewn all over the table, while the morning paper had ended up as a drift of crumpled pages on the floor.

Looks like a burnt-out reality TV star, Barbarotti thought grimly. On the way downhill. Three days' growth of beard, hair still spiky from the shower, and a black T-shirt under a fringed-leather waistcoat. Fortyish, give or take five either way.

Though maybe it's not as bad as it looks, he thought as he sat down opposite the reporter. Maybe his main job is infiltrating motorbike gangs. Investigative journalism and all that, and we shouldn't judge a book by its cover. Glad I'm not prejudiced about these things.

'Hi there,' said Persson. 'You're Barbarotti?'

Barbarotti admitted that this was correct. Persson tucked a pouch of *snus* under his lip.

'We're going with a four-page feature,' he said. 'Two double-page spreads. It's a bloody fascinating story, this one.'

'You reckon?' said Barbarotti.

'We really want to include those letters. Exactly the way they look, that is. It's bound to help you lot catch the bugger.'

'I'm not so sure we want to release them,' said Gunnar Barbarotti.

'Of course you fucking do,' said Göran Persson. 'Don't suppose you want us to write a load of shite about the force, eh? There's a photographer due any minute now, thought you could take us round to the police station afterwards. You want anything to eat or drink?'

Gunnar Barbarotti nodded. He went over to the buffet and

furnished himself with a cup of coffee and a fistful of hard little biscuits. He tried to steel himself against pouring the coffee into the reporter's hair and felt a pang of regret at not having left Jonnerblad to deal with the whole caboodle.

But let himself be bossed around? The hell he would.

'All right,' he said, once he was back in his seat, 'I'll have to discuss it with my colleagues. But if I might just point something out, I think you've got the wrong ends of various sticks, which isn't exactly unusual in your line of work. Can you tell me a bit about how you received the tip-off? I haven't looked through your paper for fourteen years and don't intend to do so tomorrow, either.'

Göran Persson looked at him for a long time, one corner of his mouth giving a slight twitch. The corner of his *snus* peeped out. Then he pulled himself up straighter in his chair and cleared his throat.

Then he recited, from memory, the murderer's communications. Slowly and emphatically, word for word. Including the third, the one about Hans Andersson.

'Which stick is it you think I've got the wrong end of?' he added.

Blast, thought Barbarotti. What kind of cretin would . . . ? Hang on a minute, could it be . . . ?

But at that instant a photoflash went off, and it was to take him more than twenty-four hours to get back to this particular train of thought.

'Nisse Lundman,' said the photographer. 'Thought I'd take a few shots while you two were talking, if that's OK?'

'It's OK,' said Göran Persson, winking at Barbarotti. 'So, why is this psychopath writing specifically to you?'

'Psychopath?' said Barbarotti.

'Don't split hairs,' said Persson.

'I don't know,' said Barbarotti.

'Are you sure about that? Or are you just trying to keep information from me?'

Inspector Barbarotti did not reply. He ate a couple of biscuits and looked out of the window. The photographer took a couple of pictures.

'All right,' said Göran Persson. 'But the police didn't release any of this to the public. The warning letters. I'm going to talk to a couple of the victims' relatives later today. We'll see what they've got to say about that.'

'Yes, I suppose we will,' said Barbarotti.

'And this third man, Hans Andersson . . . you haven't found him yet?'

'No,' said Barbarotti. 'But I promise I'll ring you as soon as we do, so you can get on with tormenting his friends and family, too.'

'Let's not be so petty,' said the reporter, showing his *snus* again. 'Shall we take a little trip to the police station now?'

'I need to make a call first,' said Barbarotti.

'I'll take a leak while you do it,' announced Göran Persson. 'God-awful coffee in this place.'

Jonnerblad answered after half a ring. Barbarotti described the state of play in half a minute.

'Damn,' said Jonnerblad.

'You could say that,' said Barbarotti. 'What should we do, then?'

'Do we have any choice?' asked Jonnerblad.

'I don't think so,' said Barbarotti.

Jonnerblad went quiet at the other end of the line for a few moments.

'All right then,' he said. 'If you come with him to the police station, I'll take over. I can be there in fifteen minutes.'

'Right, we'll do that,' said Gunnar Barbarotti. 'I'll try not to hack his ears off in the meantime.'

'Is it that bad?' asked Jonnerblad.

'You'll see,' said Barbarotti.

It was ten past eleven when Inspector Barbarotti delivered *Expressen* reporter Göran Persson to Superintendent Jonnerblad on the third floor of police HQ. Chief Inspector Tallin was also on hand, so it was deemed unnecessary for Barbarotti to stay.

Barbarotti was grateful for it. He hurried out of the building, got in his car and set off home. But the reporter was still nagging away like an inflamed tooth in his skull, and he thought that if it really were Our Lord's intention that the day of rest be used for recovery and recreation, this particular Sunday had got off to a bad start.

And that if Our Lord meant people to read newspapers, he would have to have a serious talk to Him about that, next time he had Him on the line.

Turning into Baldersgatan, he also realized he didn't want to go home. Purely objectively speaking, it was a glorious summer's day; why should he sit in his doleful little flat, the frustration gnawing at him as he waited for death? He had no reason to. There must be more meaningful recreation to engage in. Significantly more meaningful.

Thus thought Inspector Barbarotti as his car took him slowly past facades the shade of pale urine to his own peeling apartment block, and before he reached the traffic lights at Drottninggatan, Axel Wallman's name had floated to the surface of his mind.

He took out his mobile and rang the number.

Axel Wallman had taken early retirement and lived in an old summer cottage on the northern shore of Lake Kymmen.

The role of pensioner was still relatively new to him. Thirty years before, he and Gunnar Barbarotti had been at upper-secondary school together; Wallman performed better than anyone else in the school when they took their university matriculation – top grades in all subjects, apart from PE, where he made do with the lowest score – and a brilliant academic career was predicted for him. Socially, however, he was a loner: round-shouldered, stand-offish, difficult. Barbarotti hadn't had a great deal to do with him at school, despite them being in the same form in all three years – but he had got to know him when they were studying at Lund.

He probably wouldn't have got close to him there, either, had it not been for their living arrangements. For three years they had shared a basic two-roomed flat in Prennegatan. Barbarotti was studying law, Wallman, linguistics. And a whole series of languages. Latin and Greek, of course, then some of the Slav languages, and ending up in the realms of Finnish. Or Finno-Ugric, to be more accurate. His doctoral thesis was a comparative study of external local locative cases in the Vepsian, Cheremis and Votyak languages, a volume which Barbarotti still had in his bookcase, the pages cut but the contents unread.

Though by that point, of course, he had left jurisprudence behind him. He had graduated from police training college and become a detective. Wallman presumably wasn't easy to work with, Barbarotti could see that; cut out for research maybe, but certainly not for teaching. And things had changed in the ivory towers of academe; they used to have a considerable function as a cover and a kind of sheltered workshop for brilliant if introverted minds, but in Sweden towards the end of the 1980s, teaching was expected as well.

Especially in the case of languages, which were viewed as constituting some kind of means of communication between human beings.

This was where Wallman had run into a brick wall. True, he did get a lectureship at the University of Copenhagen, but was then transferred to similar ones in Umeå, Uppsala and Åbo Academy in Turku. This whole sideways career was also punctuated by extended periods of sick leave and – if Barbarotti had understood it correctly – ongoing disputes with colleagues and students, plus the odd scandal or two. Wallman had been off his radar for the whole of this period, roughly 1985–2000, and when they ran into each other by sheer chance a few weeks after the millennium, the former genius had already been winnowed out of the academic machine and thrown on the rubbish heap.

As he put it himself.

But – to use his own words again – it served those petty ink-shitters right. 'I have a fluent command of twenty-one languages, but now only Saarikoski and the birds will get to hear them.'

Saarikoski was Wallman's dog, a placid, seventy-kilo Leonberger and, according to its owner, an incarnation of the Finnish poet himself. As for the birds, he met them when he and Saarikoski were out for walks together through the forest round the lake. Or when he was just sitting on the dilapidated verandah overlooking the shore, drinking beer.

Or writing something, though it was hard to tell what. Since they had resumed contact – in some sense this went hand in hand with Barbarotti's own career as a divorcee, of course – they had met roughly once a year; no more than four or five times in all, and there was still a great deal about Axel Wallman that remained unexplained.

He didn't answer the first time Barbarotti called, but then he never did. The second time, he picked up the receiver. He didn't say anything, and that was another of his rules; if it was somebody wanting something, it was up to the person in question to make the first chess move. Introduce themselves, for example.

Gunnar Barbarotti did just that.

'Barbarotti here. I'm thinking of paying you a visit. I've had a hell of a morning and I could do with spending an afternoon in brainy company.'

'I'll ask Saarikoski if he's free,' growled Axel Wallman.

He evidently was. Wallman said his detective friend was welcome as long as he didn't cause too much bother and brought a bag of supplies along. Barbarotti promised to see to it and to be there within the hour.

The patch of land round Axel Wallman's summer cottage bore a striking resemblance to Wallman's own face. Overgrown and irregular; beard stubble and stinging nettles; piles of old junk and neglected pimples; a bloody plaster possibly indicating an attempt to shave at some point in the last month and piles of planks under tarpaulins, possibly indicating someone had planned to carry out repairs sometime in the past decade.

Though presumably not Wallman himself. His hair was grey, thinning and shoulder length, his clothing comprised a dirty, lime-green T-shirt, a shabby pair of dungarees and black shoes with no socks. It struck Barbarotti that a reasonably observant witness would be more likely to assess his age as a good sixty rather than the not yet fifty that was actually the case.

And if there really were such a thing as an academic rubbish heap, as Wallman claimed, he undeniably appeared to belong in such a place.

This one, for example. But there was still just about a lake view, observed Gunnar Barbarotti, even if the undergrowth of nettles, alder, aspen and birch had shot up by half a metre since last year.

Just like last year, Axel Wallman was sitting on a plastic chair on the verandah. The table beside him was cluttered with all sorts of stuff: books, old newspapers, pens, pads of paper, tobacco, matches, a paraffin lamp and some empty beer cans. He didn't get up as Barbarotti came into his line of sight, but he did look up, and Saarikoski, lying in the shade at his feet, went so far as to thump his tail twice.

'Hello Axel,' said Barbarotti. 'Thanks for letting me come and see you.'

'There's a ghost stalking through history,' replied Axel Wallman. 'Her name is Femina.'

'Never a truer word spoken,' said Barbarotti, setting the supermarket bags down on the verandah floor. One contained beer, the other pasta and the ingredients for a Bolognese sauce.

'I'm forty-eight and a virgin,' said Axel Wallman. 'Does that interest you?'

'No,' said Barbarotti. 'I can't honestly say it does.'

'It doesn't bother Saarikoski either,' said Axel Wallman gloomily, starting to roll a cigarette with nicotine-stained fingers. 'But then he was castrated even before I got him. What have you got to tell me about the current state of things, and is it beer you've got in that bag?'

Gunnar Barbarotti moved a few items of clothing off another plastic chair and sat down. He passed a can of beer to his host and opened one himself. Looking out over the lake, he thought that when Axel Wallman died in his chair one day, nobody would discover the fact; nature would continue to devour both him and the house; Saarikoski would probably just lie there, draw his last breath at his owner's feet, and be buried in the same fashion.

Overgrown and consigned to oblivion. Maybe not such a bad way to go, when all was said and done.

But it was not to discuss the brevity and vanity of life that he was here. He didn't think so, at any rate; the precise reason still escaped him. His old comrade in misfortune had popped into his head and he had simply felt the urge to see him; there was no need for more complicated motivation than that. Not on a gorgeous August Sunday like this one.

They supped their beer and sat in silence for half a minute.

'What do you make of a murderer who sends letters to the police telling them who he plans to kill?' said Gunnar Barbarotti eventually.

There was no need to let Axel Wallman steer the course of the conversation. If he did, they would soon end up in some incomprehensible labyrinth or other. Strindberg's French verb forms or encrypted codes in the Second World War.

'Is that the current state of things?' asked Axel Wallman. 'Murderers writing letters?'

'For the moment,' said Barbarotti.

'And he murders them as well? Doesn't just write letters?'

'He murders them as well.'

'I've never had a lot of time for the current state of things,' said Axel Wallman, lighting up his rustic cigarette. 'Is it a male or a female?'

'Male, I think,' said Barbarotti.

'Good,' said Axel Wallman. 'I'm not very good with females, as I may have mentioned. I find them essentially incomprehensible. But if you let me look at what the murderer wrote, I'm prepared to have a go at linguistic analysis.'

'I haven't brought them with me,' admitted Gunnar Barbarotti.

'Haven't brought them with you? What the hell are you doing here then, wasting my precious time?'

'Bringing you beer and food,' Barbarotti pointed out. 'And anyway, I know them off by heart.'

'You never could learn things off by heart,' muttered Axel Wallman. 'But fire away if you like.'

Inspector Barbarotti drank some more of his beer, considered for a moment and recited from memory the three messages the murderer had sent him. Axel Wallman sat quietly, scratching his beard.

'Again.'

Barbarotti wasn't sure whether it was strictly necessary for the analysis or whether Wallman was just trying to catch him out on memory function. He cleared his throat and repeated what he had said. Once he had finished, Wallman sat back and looked pleased with himself.

'In my judgement, we're dealing here with a thirty-eight-year-old Smålander,' he said, and gulped some beer.

'What?' said Gunnar Barbarotti.

'A thirty-eight-year-old Smålander,' repeated Axel Wallman, and belched. 'Are you going deaf, too?'

'A thirty-eight-year-old Smålander. How the hell can you claim that?'

'Not claim,' said Axel Wallman. 'I'm not claiming anything. But the only hypothesis one can possibly propose on linguistic grounds is the one I just gave you. What sort of people is he murdering?'

'Oh, a mixture,' said Barbarotti. 'But what's it based on then, your analysis?'

'The expression "this next time",' said Axel Wallman. 'Admittedly its use is spreading, but it was originally southern Swedish, though not from Skåne.'

'You're pulling my leg,' said Barbarotti.

'Not impossible,' said Wallman. 'I'm sure fingerprints are generally a more reliable method than attention to modern Swedish-language usage when it comes to fighting crime. But it could also be that the murderer's pulling *your* leg. He could be a Norrlander trying to sound like a Smålander.'

'Hmm,' said Gunnar Barbarotti. 'And age thirty-eight, what are you basing that on?'

'The median man in this country is probably thirty-nine,' said Axel Wallman. 'I subtracted a year because perpetrators of violent crime are usually a little younger than the average. It's to do with the testosterone.'

He stubbed out his cigarette and started to giggle. Gunnar Barbarotti leant back and studied him. Axel Wallman seldom laughed in Barbarotti's presence, but on the rare occasions when he did, he resembled nothing so much as a young teenage girl, her merriment leaking out in intermittent gusts through slightly flaring nostrils. Bearing in mind Wallman's appearance and general profile, this created a rather curious impression. He's crazy, thought Gunnar Barbarotti. So am I, for that matter. Why am I sitting here drivelling on about the investigation to Axel Wallman? Didn't I come here to get away from work? Definitely time to change the subject.

'Here's to you, Axel,' he said, raising his beer can. 'That's enough of my problems. What are you keeping busy with at the moment?'

Axel Wallman took a gulp of his beer and allowed himself a belch. He started to roll another cigarette and appeared to be thinking. 'A Hallander,' he said. 'He could be from Halland, too. What did you say?'

'What are you keeping busy with?'

'Keeping busy?' said Axel Wallman. 'I don't know if that's quite how I'd express the process, but I've been translating a few of Barin's poems. Do you want to hear?'

Barbarotti kicked off his shoes and nodded. 'Why not?'

Axel Wallman picked up a spiral-bound pad, flicked to and fro in it for a while, hawked noisily and spat a gob of phlegm over the verandah rail. 'This one here,' he said, suddenly looking like a little boy about to tell a riddle at a kids' party, 'it's not too bad, this one here, in fact I'm damned if it isn't better than the original. I suppose I'll have to make it worse in a few places, you have to be sure to do justice to the flaws when you translate, and not everybody accepts that rule, but I do . . . well, it isn't anything I expect you to have the capacity to understand, but I'd still like—'

'Just read it, Axel,' said Barbarotti. 'Cut out the damn preliminaries and analysis, I'm all ears.'

'All right, you cretin,' said Axel Wallman. 'Listen up now, because this is great poetry.'

He took another gulp of beer, scratched Saarikoski under the chin and began:

'My beloved, you are the fat child that fell over in the mud when the war came,

you are the impression the warrior's foot left on the floor beside the blonde plait of the thirteen-year-old girl,

you are the salt in the salt-cellar the girl's mother had in her cardigan pocket the day she was thrown into the mass grave on the far side of the ridge,

that place where nobody goes any more – but you are not the water purling in the brook near there

and not the bird singing at twilight

nor the sweet shade in the grove of green.

Thus it is, my beloved, nor could not be arranged in any other way.'

He nodded reflectively a couple of times and closed his pad. Gunnar Barbarotti drained his beer and shut his eyes. A fly buzzed through the air and landed on his wrist. Why am I here? he wondered again. How is it that I have ended up in this particular company on this particular Sunday in my forty-eighth year?

This question struck him as both a touch frightening and highly pertinent, and he sat there contemplating it for a while without finding any pithy answers. Then Axel Wallman spoke up and said how stimulated he felt by reading such a bloody good poem to his old mate, and asked to read a few dozen more.

So he did, and that was how they passed the afternoon. Axel Wallman read his translations of Mihail Barin's late poems, which were by turns seemingly simple and darkly convoluted.They drank more beer, cooked a dinner of pasta with Bolognese sauce, took a dip in the lake, and as evening came, Gunnar Barbarotti realized that he had too high a concentration of alcohol in his blood to be in a fit state to drive himself home and would consequently have to stay the night.

This met with no objection. At eleven, Axel Wallman announced that he had now completed his allotted share of this godforsaken Sunday, read out a short and fiery appeal for poetic freedom, unfortunately incomprehensible because it was in Hungarian, took Saarikoski with him and retired to bed. Barbarotti set up his solitary camp on the leather sofa with the aid of a blanket and a cushion smelling pungently of mould and ingrained tobacco smoke. That question from Ecclesiastes came back into his mind – *but how can one be warm alone?* – and he lay there trying to come up with an appropriate prayer to the currently extant God.

But the right words eluded him, and he eventually fell asleep with a feeling of being very far away.

From Marianne, from his children, from a murderer who was trying to talk to him, for reasons he couldn't fathom – and many miles away from himself.

17

That black Monday started with a couple of heavy downpours and a brisk wind from the south west. Gunnar Barbarotti left Axel Wallman's cottage just after eight with a feeling of autumn in his breast, and he had not driven more than a couple of kilometres when the windscreen wiper blade on the driver's side came loose. It went whirling off like an abortive afterthought and within seconds was swallowed up by the long grass edging the ditch at the side of the road. He stopped at the Statoil petrol station in Kerranshede and bought a new one, which with some difficulty he eventually managed to fit. While he was at it he bought a coffee and a copy of *Expressen*, despite his vow to Göran Persson; then he sat in the car, rain pelting down on all sides, and read through what the star reporter had to say about the murders of Erik Bergman and Anna Eriksson.

And about the letters.

And about police shortcomings.

And yes, four pages – two double-page spreads – had been given over to 'The murder mystery of the decade' and 'The letter murderer of Kymlinge', and to be on the safe side, the word 'EXTRA' was printed in white on black at the top of every page, so no reader could be misled into underestimating the importance of the story.

There were plenty of pictures: a small one of lead investigator Jonnerblad; another, double the size, of Inspector Barbarotti – looking rather like a patient waiting to be called in to the doctor to have his constipation diagnosed; an aerial photo of Kymlinge with the two crime scenes helpfully marked with white crosses; and a couple of faked pictures of the letters – all three of them. The murderer's texts were reproduced in full, but the captions were at least honest enough to admit that these were not photographs of the originals, the police having refused to release them because it might detrimentally affect the investigation. *Expressen* was, as always, an organ working in the service of truth and enlightenment. In addition, the top of page eight featured a picture of two middle-aged women with shopping bags. They had nothing to do with the murders; on the contrary, claimed the short text alongside, they represented the ordinary, decent citizen, and in answer to the reporter's direct question about whether they were scared, both of them agreed that they most certainly were. They scarcely dared to go out. Their answer to the follow-up question about the extent of their confidence in the police was something along the lines of it being time for the powers of law and order to show what they could do.

In the longest piece of text, the murderer was described as an unusually cunning psychopath, and there were quotations from Jonnerblad, prosecutor Sylvenius and Barbarotti, too. Barbarotti did not recognize a single word of what he had supposedly said, and he found it hard to believe that Jonnerblad had honestly – on his honour as a police officer – promised to catch the perpetrator within a few days, a week at the most.

But the worst thing – the very worst thing of all – was the

headline plastered above his own face in that constipated waiting room:

IMPLICATED?

Implicated? Thought Gunnar Barbarotti. What the hell is he insinuating? If I write a letter to the Pope's mother it hardly means she's *implicated* in anything, does it?

He gulped down his coffee and threw down the newspaper with an indignant backhand. A moment later, Asunander rang. He sounded like a stone crusher with a hangover.

'I'm on my way,' Barbarotti assured him. 'Be there in twenty minutes.'

'Krrn . . . sss,' said the Chief Inspector, and for the rest of the drive to Kymlinge, Gunnar Barbarotti was left wondering what he had been trying to say.

'Who,' said Chief Inspector Asunander, 'in the hottest circle of Hell . . . has been selling info to a bloody . . . hack?'

This was a sensationally long and coherent sentence by Asunander's standards, and it was followed by an equally eloquent silence round the table. Barbarotti was aware that the same thought must be going through the mind of every one of the dozen assembled there. Even the detective sergeants most directly involved in the case had been summoned to the meeting.

One of us? Could it be one of us?

Or perhaps the thought was in fact only going through eleven of those minds? Because if it really was one of the twelve who had taken the chance of earning a bit of cash by leaking to the press, well, wouldn't an entirely different thought occur to that person in these hostile, icy seconds? *Can they tell from the way I look?* For example – or maybe *Ha ha, you lot haven't got a hope of exposing me, you petrified mud stirrers!*

Though Barbarotti was sure the latter was the kind of thing that would only pop into his own poor head. I'm still out of kilter today, he thought hastily, just as Jonnerblad punctured the silence.

'Apart from those of us around the table, there are about ten possible names we could choose from,' he said.

Asunander growled something unintelligible.

'That's the current situation,' Jonnerblad went on. 'And unfortunately that's the way things are these days. That applies to the whole country, not just Kymlinge. The police force leaks like a sieve and I'd like to issue a warning to everybody here – and by all means pass it on. If this happens again, if information carries on getting out to the press, information we haven't agreed in advance to release, then I shall bring in a man from Stockholm to carry out an internal investigation. He's called Superintendent Wickman, and people have been known to hang themselves after having to talk to him for a few days.'

He paused. As if by agreement, Tallin took over. 'We're going to hold a press conference at two o'clock this afternoon,' he declared. 'Other than what is said there, in future only Superintendent Jonnerblad and I will talk to the press. You're all likely to get calls from journalists. Refer them to Jonnerblad and me. Cite technical investigative reasons.'

'Anybody here not understood that?' asked Jonnerblad.

Since the question was somewhat ambiguously phrased, heads were shaken and nodded with equal vigour, roughly the same proportion of each, and Gunnar Barbarotti suddenly recalled how it used to feel when he played in a boys' football team and they got a dressing-down from the captain at half-time after falling comfortably 0–4 behind. Boys will always be boys, he thought, with a glance at Eva Backman, the only woman in the room. Can't be fun having to spend one's time with this bunch of neo-pubertal males, day in and day out, he thought. Not much fun at all.

And back home she had four more men, of course, his train of thought continued. A unihockey-playing husband and three teenage unihockey-playing sons. When they weren't away on holiday, that was. Which must at any event mean that she . . .

'Barbarotti,' said Jonnerblad, breaking into this gender analysis, 'It's your role in particular that's going to be a bit problematic in view of today's *Expressen*.'

'Why's that?' queried Barbarotti.

'They're not going to leave you alone, that's what I mean.'

'No problem,' said Barbarotti. 'I'll switch off my phone and go to a hotel.'

'Not a good idea,' said Astor Nilsson. 'Remember you've got to go home and check the post every day.'

'Perhaps it's time to make a deal with the Post Office,' suggested Tallin.

'Post Office?' said Astor Nilsson. 'Does it still exist? I thought—'

But Tallin didn't care what Astor Nilsson thought about the Post Office. 'If the murderer carries on writing letters,' he clarified, 'we might be able to get our hands on the correspondence twelve hours earlier. Though of course that would mean we create even more potential for leaks . . .'

'We can reckon on a few hoax letter writers too,' Eve Backman put in. 'Don't you think?'

'Probably,' muttered Jonnerblad, and it was at that moment Inspector Barbarotti realized who *Expressen*'s source must be. He waited for a few other comments to go to and fro across the table while he weighed up his idea, and of course it was possible to raise any number of well-founded objections, but in some potent whorl of his unstructured brain, he knew he was right. That simply had to be it.

'Excuse me,' he said. 'It's just struck me who must have given that information to the paper.'

'What?' said Jonnerblad.

'The hell do you mean?' said Asunander.

'It's simple,' said Barbarotti. 'And casts no aspersions on anybody here. It's the murderer himself, of course.'

'What?' repeated Superintendent Jonnerblad.

'How can you . . . ?' said Eva Backman.

'I don't follow,' said Chief Inspector Tallin.

'It's the murderer himself who contacted the press,' Gunnar Barbarotti said slowly, with the curious inner satisfaction that a blind chicken must feel when she finally locates a grain of corn.

For ten seconds, nobody said a word. Chief Inspector Tallin raised his right hand and lowered it again. Jonnerblad clicked his biro and Asunander his false teeth.

'That's not possible,' came a cautious protest from a ruddy-faced trainee by the name of Olsén.

'Oh yes it is,' said Astor Nilsson. 'Barbarotti's right, of course he damn well is! It's obvious, don't you get it?'

After fifteen minutes' fairly febrile discussion, it seemed that a narrow majority of those present actually did.

Get it, that was.

They agreed that it could very well be just as Inspector Barbarotti suggested.

That it was the murderer himself who had contacted *Expressen*.

Who had blown apart the secrecy which until now had shrouded the letters and their messages about who was next in line to lose their lives. That for some reason it was not in his interests for the police to sit on the information. That he wanted the media on board as well, not just the occupants of Kymlinge police HQ.

'Oh my God, that's it,' said Inspector Backman. 'Congratulations, Gunnar.'

'You bet. He wants maximum attention on all this,' Astor Nilsson summed up. 'The police, the press, the whole shebang.'

Eva Backman nodded. Barbarotti nodded. Chief Inspector Tallin nodded cautiously, after a glance at Jonnerblad. It was an astonishing conclusion in many respects, but none the less logical for that.

If one sided with the small majority who believed it, at any rate.

The sense of it in actual fact being this self-willed, cold-blooded perpetrator who was choreographing the whole investigation began to seem inescapable.

Barbarotti spent the rest of the morning on the phone in his office. He set up meetings with people who were linked to Erik Bergman and Anna Eriksson in one way or another, but had not yet been formally interviewed, and when it got to 12.15 he went home – following his orders – to check that day's post.

More than half the mat in the hall was covered in mail, but he still saw it straight away.

A long thin envelope in a light shade of blue, just like the last time. His name and address handwritten in slightly clumsy, angular capitals, in the same way as on the three previous occasions. The postal district, Kymlinge, underlined once.

A stamp from the same boat-themed set as before.

Gunnar Barbarotti considered for a moment, then put on a pair of thin gloves, slit open the envelope with a kitchen knife, unfolded the sheet of paper and read the message:

CALL OFF PROTECTION OF HANS ANDERSSON. HE CAN GO ON LIVING. THINK I'LL KILL HENRIK AND KATARINA MALMGREN INSTEAD. DON'T SUPPOSE A MAN LIKE YOU IS GOING TO STOP ME?

He read it through twice, trying to fight down a feeling of unreality. A sense of none of this being real, of the whole thing amounting to some piece of absurd criminal theatre, throbbed in his temples with dreamlike intensity.

Henrik and Katarina Malmgren?

Two names? Was he going to kill two people this time? Barbarotti put the letter back in the envelope. Wondered why he had opened it; he had promised Jonnerblad that he would immediately hand over all future communication intact, in a sealed bag.

He had broken this promise after no more than a couple of seconds' hesitation. It was . . . it must be something to do with that boys' football team. That feeling of being left in the hands of some great and only modestly gifted team leader. Gunnar Barbarotti was not that keen on people telling him what to do, and this had always been the case. So that was presumably the simple explanation for him still being a DI rather than a chief inspector . . . if the truth were told. That, plus his lack of real ambition of course; but either way, there was going to be one hell of a stink, just because he'd opened the letter and read its contents before handing it over to His Lordship.

So what, thought Barbarotti, hunting out a plastic bag and dropping the light blue envelope into it. I'll be changing jobs and moving to Helsingborg anyway, and what's more, I open my post myself. That's a basic human right.

He took off the gloves and secured the bag with a rubber band. Then he rang Jonnerblad's mobile number.

'I'm just having my lunch,' Jonnerblad informed him. 'Can't it wait?'

'Not the way I see it,' said Barbarotti.

'Oh?'

'I've just received another letter. He claims not to give a damn about Hans Andersson. It's Henrik and Katarina Malmgren he's after now.'

'You opened it?' said Jonnerblad.

'Correct,' said Barbarotti. 'It was addressed to me.'

'Shit,' said Jonnerblad, then chewed and swallowed.

Gunnar Barbarotti waited. Carrot, he reckoned. Whole or sliced, not grated.

'Two people, then?'

'Exactly right,' confirmed Barbarotti. 'And they're both called Malmgren.'

'Well get yourself over here, for Christ's sake,' said Jonnerblad. 'My office in ten minutes.'

'Understood,' said Inspector Barbarotti.

But Jonnerblad did not end the call. 'Actually,' he added, 'to be on the safe side, don't say anything about this letter just yet . . . to anybody else, I mean. Let me and Tallin look at it first.'

'I thought we concluded it was the murderer who tipped off *Expressen*?'

'It very likely was,' said Jonnerblad. 'But just initially? Stupid to take risks, and there's the press conference at two, you know. I presume you agree we shouldn't make this one public, at any rate?'

Gunnar Barbarotti thought about it.

'It could well be that Persson's already been informed,' he said.

'Well there's a thought,' sighed Superintendent Jonnerblad. 'But I shall be interviewing Persson in any case, right after the conference. OK, see you in a few minutes then?'

'I'm already on my way,' Inspector Barbarotti assured him.

18

In the event, a quintet of them gathered in the briefing room to absorb the murderer's latest chess move. Besides Barbarotti, Tallin and Jonnerblad, Astor Nilsson and Eva Backman were also in attendance, and Gunnar Barbarotti assumed the lead investigator had had time to rethink in the few minutes that had passed since their phone conversation.

Rethink and realize that in present circumstances, thinking power was probably more important than secrecy. They scrutinized the text of the letter in dogged silence; Astor Nilsson was the first to make a comment.

'Fiendish,' he said.

'What do you mean by that?' asked Tallin.

'I mean diabolically deliberate,' said Astor Nilsson. 'He's forcing us to dance to his tune like . . . well, like fleas in a goddamned flea circus.'

'Expand on that,' said Jonnerblad, as he started rubbing at a stain on his shirtfront that had evidently found its way there over lunch.

'Happy to,' said Astor Nilsson. 'Firstly, what do we do about Hans Andersson? What if we stop the surveillance and then he murders one of the Hans Anderssons anyway? What if he spills the beans to *Expressen*? Where does that leave us?'

'In a corner,' said Eva Backman.

'Exactly. The murderer told the cops to skip the surveillance and those stupid idiots believed him! I don't think it takes much imagination to—'

'Thanks, that'll do,' said Jonnerblad. 'We'll keep up the surveillance, at least to start with. Naturally. But our top priority at the moment has to be identifying . . . what were their names? Henrik and Katarina Malmgren?'

'Correct,' said Barbarotti.

'So there are two of them and they presumably belong together in some way. Could be a married couple or a brother and sister, and with that kind of link it ought not to be too hard to find them. Hopefully there'll only be the one pair by that name, eh?'

'If we're lucky,' said Astor Nilsson. 'Malmgren must be a bit less common than Andersson, at any rate.'

Jonnerblad checked the time. 'The press conference starts in five minutes,' he said. 'Tallin and I will take care of that, and you can watch on internal TV if you like. But by the time we're through, an hour from now, I want those Malmgrens identified. Is that clear?'

'Clear as a bell,' said Eva Backman. 'I'll go down and see Sorrysen, and we'll get this fixed. No problem.'

'Sorrysen?' queried Tallin. 'I thought his name was Borgsen?'

'What's in a name?' said Barbarotti.

'All right,' said Jonnerblad, rising to his feet. 'We'll reconvene here at quarter past three. Make sure you tell the other group members too. All those who're available, that is. Questions?'

'One,' said Gunnar Barbarotti. 'If any of the journalists seem to know about this new letter, how will you handle it?'

Jonnerblad considered this for a moment. 'We'll play it right down,' he said.

'Low profile,' confirmed Tallin.

'Best of luck,' said Barbarotti.

'It's going to be a bit tricky interviewing that Göran Persson,' predicted Astor Nilsson. 'Whatever happens.'

'Why's that?' asked Tallin.

'Because every single word will instantly find its way into print. There'll be no easy way of keeping him quiet, and trying to make him reveal his source isn't exactly going to be a hit . . . as my grandchildren say.'

Has he got grandchildren? Barbarotti found himself thinking in confusion. And old enough to be talking about hits?

'I am aware of that particular problem,' Jonnerblad replied irritably. 'And I've no great respect for the tabloid press. But the idea of them deliberately shielding a murderer just to sell some extra copies, well, I hope they draw the line there.'

Once the door had closed behind the two officers from the National CID, Astor Nilsson cleared his throat, looking from Barbarotti to Backman and then back again. 'I've got an admission to make,' he said. 'I might almost say I'm finding this interesting. I must just have a perverted mind.'

'Interesting?' said Eva Backman. 'You men never cease to amaze me. I enjoy a bit of murder, that's why I joined the police! Just remember not to tell *Expressen*, that's all, or it might be misconstrued.'

Astor Nilsson nodded and managed to look a bit embarrassed for a moment. Inspector Backman gestured to Barbarotti to come with her and they went down two floors to enlist the help of Inspector Borgsen, alias Sorrysen, and his well-documented computer skills.

*

It took less than twenty minutes to locate Henrik and Katarina Malmgren.

Or at any rate, their preliminary judgement was that they had found the right people. Admittedly there were some fifty Henrik Malmgrens and sixty Katarina Malmgrens in the country, and presumably some of these were related to one another in various ways – but there was only one married couple with the right names, and for some reason all three detectives believed it stunningly likely that these were the two individuals the murderer had in mind.

'Why?' said Gunnar Barbarotti. 'Why am I so sure it's them?'

'I don't know,' said Eva Backman. 'But I feel the same. After all, we've really only got three possible constellations to choose between: siblings, parent–child and husband–wife. Haven't we?'

'Well I suppose they could be cousins, too,' Sorrysen pointed out. 'Or aunt and nephew or I don't know what. They needn't even be related.'

'Now you're just being difficult,' said Eva Backman.

'Sorry,' said Sorrysen. 'My vote's on the married couple. Or at any rate, we ought to look at them first of all.' He donned his minimalist glasses and studied the list he had just printed out. 'Especially as there happens to be neither a Henrik nor a Katarina Malmgren in Kymlinge.'

'We'll focus on them for starters,' said Barbarotti. 'Then we can broaden it out if necessary. So, what's their address?'

Eva Backman took the list and read aloud. 'Henrik and Katarina Malmgren. Number 24 Berberisstigen, in Gothenburg. I've an idea it's out in Mölndal – Ville's sister lives somewhere round that way. Pretty fashionable – upper middle class, anyway.'

Barbarotti looked over her shoulder. 'They've got three

phone numbers,' he said. 'Landline and two mobiles. What do we do?'

Sorrysen checked the time. 'We've got a good half hour before the end of the press conference,' he said.

'No point wasting time,' said Barbarotti.

'Dereliction of duty to just twiddle our thumbs,' said Backman.

'Pass me that phone, Gerald,' said Barbarotti.

He drew three blanks. He listened to three different recordings – Mr Malmgren twice, his wife once – and was politely asked to leave messages or try one of the other numbers, and when he ended the third call and observed his colleagues' grim faces, he felt the cold shiver of confirmation creeping down his spine.

It's them. It has to be them.

But the voice of calm deliberation sounded in his head at the same time. *Don't jump to conclusions.* It was twenty to three in the afternoon. A Monday. If Henrik and Katarina Malmgren were at work, say, wherever that happened to be, it was only to be expected that neither of them answered their phones. Half past seven in the evening would be another matter. He could see that Backman and Sorrysen were hoping to leave the next decision to him, but he suddenly felt uncertain. Was it right just to leave a message and ask the unknown couple to contact the police in Kymlinge?

It only took him a few seconds to understand where that uncertainty emanated from; it wasn't the possibility of Superintendent Jonnerblad's criticisms and rebukes that was preying on his mind, but something to do with the murderer.

With the simple fact, to be more precise, that this was

exactly the step they might be expected to take. The most obvious course of action. Barbarotti felt with a sudden flare of anger; he had no desire to play into their opponent's hands any more. Better to do something unexpected for once, but the only question was what.

'He could be bluffing this time, too,' said Eva Backman, as if she had been thinking along the same lines. 'Maybe he only ever intended to kill the first two and now he's just stringing us along.'

'But why?' said Sorrysen.

Eva Backman shrugged. 'Don't know. I don't think there's any point hunting for motives in this case, anyway.'

'I thought that was exactly what we were going to do?' objected Barbarotti. 'Have you forgotten what Lillieskog said?'

'Not forgotten,' said Backman. 'I'm just a bit suspicious of certain kinds of expert, that's all. And just a bit sceptical that I'm really going to get away on my holiday on Wednesday.'

'Where the latter's concerned, I'm afraid you could be right,' said Sorrysen, starting to straighten the piles of paper on his desk. 'Looks like we've got quite a lot of work ahead of us. It would be really handy if we could find some link between this couple and our two victims, it would make things easier.'

'Certainly would,' agreed Eva Backman with a look at the clock. 'OK, so what do we do? More thumb twiddling until the press conference is over?'

Inspector Barbarotti shook his head and felt in his jacket pocket. 'Can I have a bit of quiet,' he said. 'I'll give them my mobile number. It can't hurt, I won't say I'm a police officer, but if they call back at least it means they're still alive. I'm tired of not being allowed to make any decisions.'

'Nobody's said you mustn't,' said Inspector Backman. 'Off you go.'

Barbarotti nodded, rang the three phone numbers again and left three more or less identical and deliberately non-specific messages. He pocketed his mobile and regarded his colleagues.

'Shall we take a bet on it?' he said.

'On what?' asked Eva Backman.

'On a house in Berberisstigen in Mölndal coming on the market this autumn.'

Inspector Gerald Borgsen pointed out that, practically speaking, it was autumn already, but neither he nor Backman accepted the challenge.

By the time Gunnar Barbarotti left the building around half past seven on Monday evening, his mobile had rung thirteen times since three o'clock. In every single case it was some journalist digging for the truth and eager to ask an urgent, pertinent question, but he politely declined on each of the thirteen occasions.

There was no word from Henrik or Katarina Malmgren, however, and when he paused for thought, he could not remember ever having felt so frustrated. With the possible exception of when Helena announced she was leaving him, six years before.

But at work? Never. The whole investigation felt like a brain hijack; at various points in that disconsolate afternoon, Bo Bergman's poem 'The Marionettes' had come to mind, which was clearly no coincidence. The murderer pulled the strings and his police puppets pirouetted in comic obedience; he fed them a name or two and they immediately set about taking the steps anybody could have expected them to take. The murderer above all. The puppet master.

But *why*? Was there any point to his behaviour beyond messing them about? Was the letter writing part of a plan, a bigger pattern that Barbarotti and the rest of them could not see?

He had asked himself these questions a thousand times this past week, and they remained as rhetorically unanswered as ever.

The press conference had gone well, Jonnerblad and Tallin assured them, almost with one voice, which was no more than Barbarotti had expected. The views of the assembled media – an audience of more than eighty, apparently – would doubtless be there for all to see in the next day's papers, or to be imbibed from the TV and radio news that night.

Or online. None of the journalists present had asked any questions about Henrik or Katarina, so at least their fears that the murderer was communicating with the police and the press more or less simultaneously had proved unfounded. This time, at any rate.

Whether it really was the murderer who had fed information to Göran Persson was a question that remained far from resolved. Six hours after the insight had struck with such clarity, Gunnar Barbarotti was no longer quite so inclined to believe it as he had been at the time.

And there lay the nub of his frustration, he thought once he had turned down from Grevgatan and was cycling along the riverside. A clutter of question marks, catching on each other as casually and randomly as bent metal coat hangers in the bottom of a musty wardrobe. (Again he wondered where all those images came from.) Were the married couple in Berberisstigen in Mölndal really the people referred to in the murderer's latest letter, for example? And if so, was he actually planning to kill them? Hans Andersson – whichever of them had been the actual one, if any – was evidently to be let off the hook. Why? Had that been the intention all along or had something happened along the way to make the murderer change his mind?

And above all: where were the Malmgrens? Despite an intense afternoon's work, with the willing assistance of half a dozen colleagues in the Gothenburg police, they had found neither hide nor hair of them. On the other hand, they each still had a fortnight of their annual leave left – he from the University of Gothenburg, she from Sahlgrenska hospital – so the chances of them being on their travels somewhere in the big wide world, their mobiles left in the desk drawer at home, were judged by the entire team to be fairly high. More and more people seemed to favour that kind of escape nowadays, for whatever reason.

The other alternative, namely that they weren't answering because they were already dead, met with a variety of assessments in the group, but since none of their hypotheses were built on anything but pure speculation and guesswork, it made little difference. Further phone calls with family and friends were scheduled for that evening and the following day, so they would presumably have a clearer picture sooner or later. Barbarotti himself had spoken on the phone to a half-sister of Katarina Malmgren's, and she had told him it wasn't unusual for the couple to go off the radar from time to time. A week or a few days, a kind of lifestyle choice, or so she gathered. Some modern idea. She thought they generally told someone in advance by email or phone, though she had very little contact with them herself. There was a seven-year age difference between her and Katarina and they weren't exactly on the same wavelength.

Barbarotti did not enquire any more deeply on that score, but thanked her and said he would be back in touch. Then he called the next person on his list and learnt even less. And then the next. The team – including its temporary reinforcements in Gothenburg – had spoken to a total of a hundred people in four hours, many of them so loosely linked to the Malmgrens that it had felt like looking for snowballs in a desert – to quote Astor Nilsson – and the sum of their combined efforts was that by 7 p.m. they were in possession of a huge jumble of information of no use whatsoever.

And anything that might conceivably be of use – in the most optimistic scenario – would effectively be hidden by all the dross. This phenomenon was of course nothing new in the context of any investigation, but it felt particularly conspicuous in the Malmgren case.

And perhaps they hadn't even identified the right people. Perhaps it was a Katarina Malmgren in Lycksele and a Henrik Malmgren in Stockholm who would, in the not too distant future, shuffle off this mortal coil. Or had already done so. Christ Almighty, thought Gunnar Barbarotti, what puppets we are.

Don't suppose a man like you is going to stop me?

That was what today's epistle had said. Addressing him personally, not the police in general. The letter writer was still opting to communicate directly with him, Detective Inspector Gunnar Barbarotti, and nobody else. Why?

Why, why? Could it really be that there was some kind of personal connection between him and the murderer after all, as Jonnerblad had suggested? He had added eight names to his existing list of potentially suspicious acquaintances from the past, but this had failed to ring any bells and the method felt more pointless the more he thought about it.

And what was the intention this time? The letter writer's intention?

He and Backman both tended to think – as possibly the others in the group did, too, but Backman was the one he had mainly discussed it with – that in reality, the deed had already been done. If the Malmgrens were going to be murdered, it would have happened by now. But if they were located alive, that probably meant they were in with a good chance of staying that way. With the two earlier murders, definitely in the second case and possibly in the first as well, the tip-off letters had arrived far too late for the police to have any chance of reacting, and in the case of Hans Andersson there was still no victim at all. It seemed scarcely likely that the murderer would attempt to kill two people who were under strict police surveillance – and if he did it anyway, it would prove either that he was stark staring mad or that he wanted to be caught. If not both.

And in that case, they would soon have him under lock and key and be able to wind up the investigation.

But the Malmgrens had not been located alive, that was the problem. Maybe their dead bodies were already awaiting discovery? Maybe the murderer was safe and sound elsewhere, waiting to read the news in the morning papers?

Maybe that was what turned him on and made him do it, thought Barbarotti with an air of resignation, turning up Hagendalsvägen. Could it be as banal as that?

At any event, the geographical perspective appeared to have widened; there was neither a Katarina nor a Henrik

Malmgren registered in Kymlinge. It was hard to speculate what that might signify, and all the harder when one had just spent ten solid hours speculating. For a moment, Barbarotti caught himself wishing he could exchange his life for Axel Wallman's.

The academic rubbish heap? Perhaps there was an equivalent rubbish heap for superannuated policemen? Yes, he realized, there almost certainly was something like that. The only question was whether he had attained sufficient maturity to qualify for it.

It didn't bloody well matter, anyway, because the day after tomorrow he was going to ring Marianne, and the direction of his life would be decided forever.

Thus thought Inspector Barbarotti, employing a restrained amount of violence to force his bike between two child-sized saddles in the bicycle rack in the yard.

He unlocked the door of his flat, went into the hall and was suddenly aware of feeling hungry – despite the ten or so cups of coffee he'd consumed that afternoon, along with probably twice that number of Singoalla biscuits. He took a rapid inventory of the contents of fridge and larder and decided to do his signature dish: spaghetti with pesto, capers, olives and flakes of parmesan cheese. A glass of red wine, if he had a bottle in the flat, and a slice or two of fresh pear – he had just finished all his preparations when there was a ring at the door.

For a few seconds he debated whether to bother answering, and afterwards – when what happened next had already happened – he wondered why on earth he hadn't had the sense to listen to his first, well-founded impulse.

*

It was Göran Persson, with a photographer in a red baseball cap.

'Glad to find you in,' said Göran Persson, and the photographer's flash went off.

'I haven't got time,' said Gunnar Barbarotti. 'Excuse me.'

He tried to shut the door but the reporter had planted his solid, size-ten foot right across the threshold. 'Just thought we ought to have a little chat,' he said. 'A friendly word. People are interested in this case, you know.'

'Get your foot out of my door,' said Gunnar Barbarotti. 'I have no comment to make.'

The photographer took another picture.

'No comment?' said Göran Persson. 'Oh come on, I'm sure you have. How about this: we sit down at your kitchen table and exchange a few thoughts for ten minutes. Then I write up the conversation and you can either approve it, or not.'

'Not,' said Barbarotti.

'You want the police to come across as bloody-minded and dictatorial?'

'Bloody mi— What the hell are you raving on about? We're in the middle of a murder enquiry here, and you're doing us no favours by running around the place and writing a load of sensationalist crap. Your newspaper is a disgrace to the free word.'

Anger was growing inside him like a cloud of smoke.

'Hang on, could you just repeat that?' said the reporter, fishing a pen and notepad out of his jacket pocket. The camera flashes continued.

'For the last time,' said Barbarotti. 'I've no intention of talking to you. Move your bloody foot or I'll punch you in the face.'

Göran Persson grinned. 'Now now, constable, I think you need to think a bit more about what you're saying. Let us in and stop being so stubborn. I've talked to that boss of yours . . . Jonnerblatt or whatever the fuck he's called, for over an hour. I'm a bit tired of self-important cops.'

Gunnar Barbarotti gritted his teeth and closed his eyes for a second. Then he clenched his fists and thrust them against the journalist's chest with all his strength, sending him toppling out onto the landing. Then he closed the door and locked it.

He went back to the kitchen with another camera flash slowly fading from his retina – and with the sound of a crash as something fell downstairs slowly dying away in his eardrums.

Stupid, he thought. I didn't handle that very professionally.

Then he sat down to his dinner.

FOUR

NOTES FROM MOUSTERLIN

7–8 July 2002

'Can't you see she's dead?'

Katarina Malmgren repeated what she had said and after that I don't think anybody uttered a word for a full minute or more. We all sat or stood there, packed into the cockpit, young Troaë slumped lifeless at our feet, listened to the rain easing off and felt the waves growing gentler beneath us. The wind was also dying down, as the darkness intensified and seemed to enclose us more fully; sea, sky, coast, they were all the same grey-black impenetrable shade, and the only thing that stood out was a number of little points of light inland, no more than five pinpricks in the blackness, and it was impossible to gauge how far away they were. Perhaps no more than a kilometre, perhaps considerably further. Way over to the left, to what must still have been our west, I discovered a light that came and went, and guessed it must be the lighthouse at Beg-Meil. If so, we had drifted a long way east, which seemed to fit with the wind direction. In retrospect, I just don't know how I was in any state to make those observations, those meaningless assessments; my body felt totally numb, my head was throbbing dully, and I felt an intermittent stab of pain from my injured foot. This is rock bottom, I remember thinking. Absolute rock bottom.

The first person to say anything was Anna.

'Dead? She can't be dead?'

Henrik, who had been the least active during the rescue efforts, gave a snort. 'Look at her,' he said. 'If she's not dead, what do you think she is, then?'

But his voice sounded a good deal more pitiful than the words themselves.

'Be quiet Henrik,' said Katarina. 'Oh my God, what shall we do?'

'What shall we do?' Gunnar repeated stupidly. 'How the hell could this happen?'

Anna turned to me. 'You bloody idiot, it was you who let go of her so she fell overboard.'

'I lost hold,' I said. 'I'm sorry.'

'Sorry?' said Henrik. 'Oh, so you're sorry, are you?'

'What do you want me to say?' I asked.

Katarina Malmgren started to cry. Loudly, in a demonstrative sort of way.

'I don't see why you're howling,' said Erik. 'You're the one who brought her on this fucking trip.'

'I didn't,' said Katarina.

'He's right,' said Anna. 'It was you who dragged her along. So what are you going to do now? What are you going to do now, eh?'

There was something panicky yet almost triumphant in Anna's voice, a combination I hadn't heard before. 'I nearly drowned too, you know!' she cried. 'But nobody cares about that, of course.'

I recalled that she had in fact fallen in the water in all the chaos, and that she might well be right in what she was saying. Or had had a real scare, at any rate. None of us had bothered about her, we'd all been focused on the girl. Everyone went quiet for a few seconds.

'The storm seems to have died down,' said Gunnar. 'We're probably drifting towards land. Come on, pull yourselves together, let's go down to the cabin and discuss what the hell we're going to do.'

So we did. We left the dead girl up in the cockpit and all six of us squeezed into the benches down in the pitch-black cabin. Katarina asked whether at least one of us ought to stay and keep watch over the body, but no one took any notice of the suggestion.

'Why isn't there any light?' complained Anna. 'Why the hell isn't there any light on this bloody boat?'

'Calm down Anna,' said Gunnar. 'Try to behave as if you're a grown up for once in your life.'

'Grown up?' shrieked Anna. 'You've got a cheek to talk about grown up, you perverse pile of shit.'

I don't know what Anna was referring to, but maybe Gunnar did, because he gave her a clip round the ear. I don't think the blow really landed home, she probably had time to put up a hand to fend him off, but the gesture in itself was sufficient to shut her up.

'So, what do we do?' said Henrik.

He sounded scared, I noticed. A sort of nervous, slightly muted fear that he wasn't able to hide.

'Good question,' said Erik.

'The first thing we've got to do is calm down,' said Gunnar.

'It doesn't help anybody, shouting and yelling and blaming each other.'

'Oh my God, the girl's dead, don't you understand?' said Katarina for the third or fourth time, as if she were the one finding it hardest to take in. As if she had to keep reminding herself of it. 'Why didn't you pull her out?'

'What do you mean?' I said. 'Don't you think we tried?'

'I don't know,' said Katarina Malmgren.

'There were two of us trying,' I pointed out, 'and four just standing there shouting.'

'Only one let her fall overboard,' Henrik added, and I don't know what he was driving at by saying it.

'Good God, are we just going to leave the girl lying up there?' said Katarina, her voice scarcely holding. You could hear that panic had her in its grip, and that talking and questioning were very likely her only way of holding it in check.

Gunnar raised his voice. 'For Christ's sake, stop behaving like this!' he shouted. 'Don't you see there's nothing to be gained by blaming each other? We're all in the same boat, you know.'

Erik gave a laugh. 'Bravo,' he said. 'The same boat, fucking clever of you to notice that.'

Gunnar ignored him. 'We've got to decide together what we're going to do,' he declared. 'We've all got to agree to be in on this, whatever we decide.'

'What are you talking about?' said Katarina. 'What do you mean, going to do?'

'He always goes on like that,' said Anna. 'I told you he was perverse, didn't I?'

Henrik cleared his throat. 'Let me remind you we have a

dead girl on board,' he said. 'I agree with Gunnar, we've got to decide.'

He sounded as though he had summoned up a bit of courage, or was trying to do so, at least.

'Thanks,' said Gunnar.

'I don't understand what we're meant to discuss,' said Katarina. 'There's nothing *to* discuss, is there?'

'I think there is,' said Gunnar. 'And I think some of you realize that, too.'

'We've got to . . .' said Katarina, 'got to try to reach land, and when we get there we've got to find help, of course.'

'Help with what?' said Henrik.

'That's obvious, isn't it? With . . . well, with . . .' said Katarina, but clearly couldn't find any way of finishing her sentence.

Everyone went quiet for a long time. I remember that extremely clearly, and I think it was only then that they all, to the best of their abilities, really tried to understand the situation we had ended up in. Tried to rise above the usual trivial level of their consciousness and actually display the sort of maturity that the moment and the circumstances required.

But Anna was the first one to open her mouth.

'Jesus Christ,' she said. 'We took a twelve-year-old girl out to sea without permission and let her drown. If anyone had asked me at the outset, we'd never even have—'

Erik interrupted her. 'We need to cover up.'

'What?' said Katarina. 'Cover up? What do you mean?'

'We need to get rid of her somehow,' said Erik.

'Are you out of your mind?'

'Far from it,' said Erik. 'We've got to get rid of the girl and hush the whole thing up, that's the best solution.'

'That's the worst thing I've ever—' began Katarina, but Gunnar broke in.

'Can you go on, Erik?' he said.

'Sure,' said Erik. 'What would we gain by dragging her dead body off to the police? How would we explain ourselves? What would they think?'

'Correct,' said Gunnar, and I suddenly recalled that he was some kind of teacher in daily life. Right now he was behaving pretty much as if he was in a classroom, listening to his pupils report back on their group work. Erik went on.

'We've acted like idiots and now here we are with a drowned girl. If we want to carry on acting like idiots, we'll go to the police, that's what I think. But if we want to be a bit more sensible, we'll make sure we dispose of the body smoothly.'

'I feel sick,' said Katarina.

'Smoothly?' asked Henrik. 'If we do that, how's it going to look if they find us out later on?'

'Why should they find us out?' asked Gunnar.

'Because . . . because somebody saw us, let's say,' said Katarina. 'With the girl. She'll be reported missing and there'll be a search.'

'Of course she'll be reported missing,' said Gunnar. 'But nobody actually knows she came with us today.'

'What?' said Anna. 'What the hell are you saying?'

He repeated what he had said, slowly and pedagogically. 'All I'm saying is that there's no one who knows Troaë came out to the islands with us today.'

'Surely there must be?' said Anna.

'Well, who then?' asked Gunnar. 'When you all climbed into the boat, the beach was empty, wasn't it?'

'I don't know,' said Anna. 'Well, maybe it was, actually. But they must have seen her at that restaurant, at any rate. When we were all eating together.'

'That was a week ago,' said Erik. 'We've no need to deny being with the girl that time. All we've got to deny is meeting her today.'

'But was there really no one else there when we set off this morning?' asked Katarina. 'Are you all sure about that?'

I considered the matter. Presumably the others were doing the same. Trying to remember back to how things looked as we stood on the beach, waiting for Henrik and Gunnar to turn up with the boat. As we waded out into the water. As we clambered aboard. Had there been any people nearby? I didn't think so. A fisherman or two, the odd walker perhaps, all of them some distance away, but I couldn't remember seeing anyone in the immediate vicinity.

'I don't think so,' said Anna. 'I really don't think anyone can have seen us.'

'No,' admitted Katarina, and her voice was different all of a sudden. Sort of mild and compliant. 'No, I'm sure there wasn't anybody near enough to notice the girl.'

'Well then,' said Erik. 'There you are.'

'But what about that couple?' Anna said. 'The ones who put in at the island for a while.'

'The girl was lying down with her book the whole time they were on the island,' said Gunnar. 'I'm completely certain of it. They were at least one hundred and fifty metres away. All they saw were a few inoffensive Swedes on holiday. They certainly couldn't have counted us and they didn't stay more than an hour.'

Erik cleared his throat. 'There are no witnesses,' he concluded. 'We were out at des Glénan today. There were six of us, the whole time. We met a girl a few days ago, who said her name was Troaë, or something like that. Since then we've seen no sign of her.'

Katarina started to say something but broke off. Another silence descended. I could feel Henrik shivering to my right. My headache throbbed against the top and sides of my skull and the boat gave a violent lurch; for the last half hour, since we got the girl out of the water, it had been more of a gentle bobbing, but now the sea was making its presence felt again.

'Erik's right,' Gunnar said finally. 'There are no witnesses. What do you say?'

I had remained more or less passive throughout this conference, and said nothing now, either. The thought of what might potentially have happened on that walk Erik took with the girl round the island came into my head, but I kept it to myself. Merely registered that it chimed in pretty well with Erik's unexpectedly active role in the discussion. A twelve year old who was not only dead but had recently been sexually assaulted was naturally something one would be wary of handing over to the police. I wondered whether it would come to a vote in the end, but it was increasingly clear that this would scarcely be necessary.

'I agree,' said Henrik. 'Going to the police at this stage would be senseless stupidity.'

'All right,' said Gunnar. 'What do the ladies say?'

This was a democratic invitation to the two women to voice their opinions. I wondered whether it was a conscious decision to save me until last, or if it just happened that way. Neither Anna nor Katarina seemed to want to go first, anyway – maybe neither wanted to be the first to concur with the proposal of getting the body out of the way and setting off down the road of lies and denial. Be that as it may, for a few seconds I had a mental image of the pair of them wrestling with some kind of empathy and female remorse at the prospect of such an option, but when Katarina spoke up, I realized this had been a misjudgement on my part.

'I suppose you're right,' she said. 'I'm not going to object. It would be a total disaster for us all if this got out . . . and we've still got two weeks' holiday ahead of us, Henrik and I.' She paused briefly for thought. 'Of course it's terrible that this awful accident happened, but whatever we do, we can't give the girl her life back.'

'I think the same,' said Anna. 'Can't we try to get that bloody engine going and get ashore now?'

'How, then?' said Gunnar half an hour later. 'And where?'

Cigarettes had been smoked. A bath towel had been draped over Troaë. Anna had peed over the side.

Other things had happened too. Working together, Erik and Henrik had tried to get the engine going again, but without success. Katarina had found a torch that died after about a minute, and there had been a lot of discussion of whether we should simply dump the girl's body overboard, but the collective opinion in the end was that this would not be a good idea. There was every chance of her floating ashore and being found the next day, at which point a police investigation would immediately be launched, a development that could easily lead to things taking the wrong turn. Better for the girl to be treated as missing, much better. For a few minutes we considered the possibility of fixing weights to her body, so she would stay safely down in the depths, but we simply couldn't find any suitable objects on board the *Arcadia* – and even if we had, it would have been risky, of course, as the owner could well have spotted that some of his equipment was missing.

So Gunnar's questions were justified.

'How?' said Erik. 'I don't know. But I suppose burying her somewhere would be the best thing.'

'With our bare hands?' said Anna. 'Great idea.'

'But surely there must be a spade at one of our houses?' said Katarina.

'Assuming we come ashore anywhere near the houses,' said Anna.

'Are there any alternatives?' asked Gunnar.

'What?' said Anna.

'To burying her,' said Gunnar. 'If we're definitely getting rid of the body.'

'Well we can't fucking chop her up,' said Anna. 'Or burn her. You'll have to bury her, that's pretty obvious.'

'Who's "you"?' queried Erik.

'Well I'm not doing it,' said Anna.

'Nor me,' said Katarina.

'You'll have to muck in together,' said Anna. 'You guys who didn't save her.'

'Hang on a minute,' said Henrik.

'Eh?' said Anna. 'Are you on the phone?'

'Be quiet, Anna!' said Gunnar. 'I don't want to give you another slap.'

'You perverse fucker,' said Anna.

'What I wanted to say is that I have a suggestion,' said Henrik.

'Let's hear it,' said Gunnar.

Henrik cleared his throat in a slightly ostentatious way. 'It's just that I think it's unnecessary for all of us to risk getting caught. Better for one person to do it on their own.'

A few seconds passed in silence. 'I don't really know . . .' began Erik, but then evidently changed his mind.

'And I think it's pretty obvious which of us it ought to be,' Henrik went on. He had acquired a new sort of authority in the past few minutes. As he gradually sobered up, presumably. 'Pretty obvious,' he repeated.

'I get what you mean,' Katarina put in. They were operating as husband and wife again, and it only took a slight hint for them to understand each other. Henrik turned to me.

'You were the one who messed it all up,' he said. 'You were the one who made the girl drown. Weren't you? I think it's your goddamned duty to see that we get through this. There are no two ways about it.'

I looked around me. Tried to detect the others' expressions in the dark cabin now that my eyes had adjusted somewhat to the lack of light, but it was impossible to make out any details. I could hear their breathing, feel the oppressive presence of their bodies, the smell of stale alcohol emanating from their pores, but I couldn't read their thoughts with my own eyes. And none of them was saying anything. Nobody uttered a single word after Henrik made his proposal. Ten to fifteen seconds passed, the boat was barely rocking and I wondered if we might possibly be very close to land, in a bay or inlet perhaps, it almost felt that way. I thought of Dr L and all the money I still had in my travel kitty.

'OK,' I said. 'I assume I've no choice.'

When we were only a hundred metres or so offshore – as far as one could judge, we were coming into a curving little bay with just a few lights showing – Gunnar unexpectedly got the engine started. This earned him some acclamation, but the girl's body, now wrapped in two bath towels, naturally muted the elation. Erik and Henrik asked me if I felt like going ashore to bury her somewhere on this unfamiliar stretch of coastline, but I instantly rejected the idea. I told them I needed a spade and would prefer to find a place somewhere in the wetlands between Mousterlin and Beg-Meil. Henrik said he thought that was a wise decision and offered me a cigarette; I'm not a habitual smoker, but I accepted because I recognized it as some kind of gesture of reconciliation and acknowledgement. By this time it was almost half past eleven, and we slowly made our way along the coast, never more than fifty to a hundred metres from land in case the engine gave up again. And so as not to lose our sense of direction, of course. After about fifteen minutes, having rounded a couple of points, the last of which must have been Cap-Coz, we saw the lighthouse in Beg-Meil. We passed it just as the moon broke through the clouds for the first time, giving those of us who happened to be up in the cockpit – Katarina, Gunnar and I – a chance to see each other's faces for a brief moment. But none of us felt inclined to make much use of the opportunity, lowering our eyes, and within a few seconds the moon was behind dark clouds again.

A short while later we came round the point at Mousterlin; the beach to the west lay in complete darkness, and we all helped to lug the bags, carriers and empty bottles ashore. Last of all, Gunnar and Henrik heaved the dead Troaë over the side, and I slowly towed the floating body the remaining thirty metres to land. Gunnar and Henrik waved goodbye and turned east to return the boat to the marina in Beg-Meil. I have no idea whether they were also intending to rouse the owner in the middle of the night and tell him about the engine problems. Perhaps they had arranged to hand over the key the next day.

Up on the beach, the rest of us gathered for a moment around the body. The darkness was intense, and felt almost like a piece of clothing against the skin; the wind had died down entirely and there was no moon to be seen. The only light came from a couple of pinpricks between the trees a bit further east; I calculated it must be the hotel just inland from the sea at Pointe de Mousterlin.

'What are you planning to do?' asked Katarina Malmgren.

I answered that my idea was to hide her in the dunes temporarily while I made my way back to Erik's house for a spade.

'You could borrow one from us, I suppose,' offered Katarina. 'But I don't know if there is one and it might be foolish to get us involved.'

'Very foolish,' I said.

Erik said nothing. Anna said nothing.

'Right then,' I said, hoisting the girl into my arms. She wasn't heavy – somewhere between forty and forty-five kilos at a guess – and although my injured foot was still rather troublesome, I was able to carry her without too much difficulty.

'I'll go on ahead,' said Erik after another short silence.

Katarina asked Anna if she wanted to come to their house and wait for Gunnar there. Anna hesitated for a moment, but then said yes.

Yet still the three of them lingered there indecisively. I

shifted my hold on the girl so she was hanging over my right shoulder. 'Don't worry,' I said. 'I'll take care of this now.'

At that they nodded and left me alone with Troaë.

An extraordinary walk and some extraordinary hours lay ahead of me. I started to feel as though I was performing some kind of ancient ritual. There were no witnesses, only the night, the earth, the heavens and eternity; despite what I had told the others, I carried the girl almost all the way to our house; the risk of simply not being able to find her again if I hid her somewhere in the dunes seemed too great, and I did not want to expose us to that sort of unforced error. When I say us, I don't mean me and the other Swedes, but me and the girl; I had not gone many steps with her over my shoulder before I started to feel a strong sense of affinity with her. I was alive, she was dead, yet in some way she still represented youth, a youth that by force of unfortunate circumstances had experienced something I had never come close to. She had crossed the boundary, the ultimate boundary, and perhaps her soul was already somewhere else; perhaps in actual fact it was keeping a watchful eye on us, as we slowly and cautiously picked our way through the marshy terrain. From all around us came the unobtrusive sound of the discreet processes of decay and birth. Bubbling, whirring, gurgling, croaking and pattering. I was entirely taken up by my task; I soon began to feel as though I was fulfilling some kind of duty, a deep, imperative duty of which no one else in the group could have any conception, and I also felt a bitter gratitude that I was the one entrusted with the privilege of arranging the girl's burial, I truly did. But at the same time, madness was lurking, creeping behind us on the lightest of feet through the living darkness, and in front of us and all around;

none of this frightened me in any way, but it was a reality, a possible outcome of this walk, I realized that. The possibility that the girl and I might simply lie down and let ourselves be persuaded by this all-consuming, vigorous growth, and that I would accompany her on her final journey; we were in the polder itself now, pungent smells of stagnant water and impenetrable foliage surrounded us on all sides and I thought that maybe, maybe it would be a sort of loving act to just sink with her into the warm, muddy water and yield to forces so much stronger and more primordial than our own.

But I didn't stop. It didn't happen after all, and instead I continued my stately progress, step by step and breath by breath; my walks of recent days had taught me to find my way, more or less, around the network of little paths, and within a time that I afterwards estimated to be something under an hour I had reached the place where two paths crossed, and from which Erik's house was just about visible. He had switched on an outside light at the corner of the house but otherwise all was in darkness. I carefully lowered the dead girl into a sort of sitting position, propped against a tree trunk about twenty metres from the house. I went through the gate, found my way to the tool shed in the darkest corner of the garden and opened the door.

I didn't even need to put a light on, because I almost instantly came across a spade propped against the wall, and returned past the silent house to where I had left the girl.

I had already decided where her grave was to be, and it took me twenty to twenty-five minutes to get there. It was an open area that I had previously tried to walk through, but the bogginess of the ground had forced me to turn back. This time I stepped carefully from one firm tussock to the next. It wasn't easy in the dark, with the girl hanging over my shoulder, but the moon showed itself again for a second, a waning moon, big and pale, and that helped me get my bearings. I picked my way through the waist-high grass to about ten metres from the path and then stopped, laying down the body before thrusting the spade experimentally into the bog.

It was as easy to dig as I had imagined and – to cut a long and painful story a little shorter – I soon had the girl in the ground. The remarkable thing was that I scarcely even needed to shovel any soil into the grave on top of her; it was as if the ground sucked her body down, the wet, fragrant earth enveloping her as if in an embrace, and in some strange way I understood that this was where she belonged. Here and nowhere else.

I went back up to the path. Checking the time, I saw it was twenty past two. I suddenly felt overwhelming fatigue descend on me and, as an owl hooted just a few metres away from me, I had no idea where I would find the energy to get back to the house.

But I somehow managed that, too. Erik must have been awake at some point after I took the spade from the tool shed, because the outside light had been switched off. I put the spade back in its place and had a shower, standing under the steady stream of water for a long time in an attempt to wash away every trace and every memory of that terrible day, and by the time I finally got to bed it was almost 4 a.m.

Then I slept for four hours, showered again and started writing.

No sign of Erik, he must have gone out first thing in the morning. I'm sure he's conferring with the others. It's Monday, two in the afternoon, and I feel a strong impulse to go back and find the place where I buried the girl, but I realize I have to restrain myself.

I feel other impulses, too, telling me to pack my things and get away from here, but I feel paralysed by exhaustion.

My foot is quite painful, too, it's swollen now and a dark half-moon has appeared on the outside of the ankle; I'm sure it's nothing serious, but a few days' rest is too tempting an option for me to pass up.

Naturally it could well be important for me to know what plans they've been hatching during their conference, too. I lie down in one of the loungers on the terrace under the sun-shade and wait for Erik.

I feel as though I am a different person from the one I was twenty-four hours ago.

Commentary, August 2007

Yet it isn't the case. When we shed our skin and become another person, that's all that happens. The shedding of skin. What's inside it, our core and our true identity, we always carry with us.

We can't escape it, any more than I can escape those days and what happened. Those people stayed inside me like ticks, sucking the blood and the reason out of me, and what is now happening is of course nothing other than a logical consequence. Actions have consequences, and sooner or later everyone must take his or her rightful responsibility, just as I am shouldering my responsibility by carrying out these bloody but inescapable deeds I am now engaged in.

As the years have passed, the girl has occasionally recurred in my dreams, often bringing me out in a cold sweat as I experience anguished flashbacks of those minutes in the waves – and that nocturnal walk through the marshes, one of us living and the other dead – but since I finally made up my mind, the character of the dreams has changed. All at once there is light, and a very clear element of reconciliation; when I encountered the girl in my bedroom the other morning in the soft light of dawn, we were on a long stretch of beach, perhaps that one between Mousterlin and Bénodet, though I can't be sure; we recognized one another from a long way off, and I could see even from that distance that she was wearing not only her rucksack with the easel sticking out, but also her characteristic, slightly crooked smile, and as we met we only stopped for a brief moment, exchanged a few encouraging phrases, and she brushed my cheek in a light, even fleeting movement before we each continued walking in opposite directions.

She never put it into words, but I could see in her face that she was grateful to me for having finally started taking on those people. I could see she was on her way into womanhood.

Cause and effect, then, and once I have finished my work, everyone will realize it was all about that, and nothing else.

Sometimes I dream about Dr L as well, always the same short sequence, and every time I wake up and remember it, I feel my need for solace momentarily satisfied. He is seated behind his big, dark desk, I enter the room, he looks up from the papers he has been reading, pushes his glasses up onto his forehead and nods to me in that thoughtful way of his.

I understand, he says. There's no need to sit down and explain, just carry on.

Carry on.

14–16 AUGUST 2007

19

In his dream, he was jostling for space with some fat angels.

A sort of semi-organized queue had formed; he was at the foot of a winding staircase, surmounted some fifty metres above by a gate in a crumbling limestone wall. That was where they were all to enter. Some of the angels looked more familiar than others, and amongst those he identified first was his ex-wife Helena, whom he glimpsed a few steps above him. It seemed a little odd to him that she had been given such elevated status. In the twenty-five years he had known her she had never been an angel, far from it, but just beside her he could see the Digerman brothers, a couple of old lags he had put away a few years ago for armed robbery and other violent crimes, so maybe moral conduct was not a top priority here after all – and at that moment he caught sight of Axel Wallman and Superintendent Jonnerblad. They stood there, arms around each other's winged shoulders, apparently deep in conversation on some vital issue. How best to advance through the crowd, perhaps; it was just a matter of getting up the stairs and in through the gate, as far as Barbarotti could see, and before he knew it he had gone swishing past the lot of them and was at the head of the queue.

St Peter was waiting there, who else? He should have realized, of course, but he was completely floored by the simple question he was asked by the white-bearded and, he had to admit it, slightly cross-eyed gatekeeper.

'Give me three good deeds you have accomplished during your time on Earth.'

Only three, he thought happily, but then he started to tie himself in knots. His brain short-circuited, his tongue was tied, his armpits leaked sweat; he gaped like a goldfish a few times, and St Peter raised a quizzical eyebrow.

I loved my children, he thought, especially my daughter – but this felt a bit ponderous, and for good reason. Surely everyone loved their children, even mass murderers and madmen? He clearly needed something with a bit more oomph. But what . . . what on earth had he actually achieved? Could he produce any nuggets of gold that were soiled neither by self-interest nor . . . nor the dulling gloss of everyday banality?

Could he say that he had caught a few evildoers but let twice as many get away? It really wasn't much to boast about. He sensed that St Peter had pretty unimpeded access to what was going on inside him, too, so there was no use offering anything he himself felt dubious about.

'Well?' said St Peter. 'It says here that you are forty-seven years old. You ought to have been able to achieve something in that time.'

'It's just that I wasn't really prepared,' explained Barbarotti. 'For standing here quite so soon, I mean.'

He became aware of the angels behind him starting to grumble about how long he was taking in the doorway, and he was also struck by how odd it was that they should already be kitted out in wings and white shifts, if they still hadn't slipped through the pearly gates. Or had this lot just popped back outside for a bit of fun? Back down to Earth on some pretext or another? Had they already got the official seal of approval? They were fat, at any rate, some of them really bloated in shape; he identified a certain Conny, known as Tall Conny, who used to work behind the bar at the Elk with drooping eyelids and an unlit cigar stub in the corner of his mouth, and he had most definitely undergone a total physical transformation. He appeared to be about a metre sixty tall and to weigh 130 kilos.

St Peter glared at Barbarotti before entering a mark in the big ledger he had open on a table in front of him and waving his hand irritably.

'Off with you,' he said. 'I'll let you have a few more years. But I don't want you giving me this sort of bother next time you come. I'll send you to Hell if you do.'

Barbarotti nodded his gratitude and St Peter took up a little hammer and tapped a bell, the sort you used to find on reception desks at old-fashioned hotels, and then the whole scene dissolved like mist.

But the sound of the bell lingered and the dream swirled rapidly up to the arid surface of reality. He was lying in his bed, rolled up in his bottom sheet and his quilt, and that persistent sound was naturally not coming from some ancient porter's lodge but from a mobile phone lying beside him on the bedside table, and before he really registered what he was doing, he answered it.

It was Helena.

For one moment he thought that he was still in the dream. For his ex-wife to feature both there and in real life – within such a short space of time – seemed pretty unlikely; but there was a genuine quality of vinegar and sandpaper in her voice that dispelled almost all of his doubts. This was the real her.

'Gittan rang,' she said. 'She's been reading *Expressen*. What the hell have you been up to?'

Gittan was an old friend of theirs, or rather, since the divorce, of his wife's. She lived in Huddinge and preferred reptiles to men.

'Eh?' said Gunnar Barbarotti. 'What time is it?'

'Quarter to eight, but that's irrelevant. It says in *Expressen* that you assaulted a journalist.'

'What?'

'You heard.'

'Of course I did, but what are you saying?' Barbarotti grumbled as he disentangled himself from the quilt. Quarter to eight? Hadn't he set his alarm for quarter to seven?

'Gittan saw the headline on the newsstands on her way to work. The evening papers come out early in this part of the world, and I want to know how I'm supposed to explain this to the kids?'

'Oh, I see.'

Appreciation of the nature of the information that had been imparted to him seeped inexorably into his system, like the poison after a snake bite, and it came home to him that St Peter had committed a grave error in sending him back down to Earth.

'I'll call you later,' he said. 'I haven't assaulted anybody, and you can tell Lars and Martin that from me.'

He got to his feet and went to hide in the shower.

The next call came at eight minutes past eight. It was Inspector Backman.

'The shit's going to hit the fan,' she said. 'I just wanted to warn you if you hadn't heard.'

'Thanks, I'd heard,' said Barbarotti.

'An official complaint has been lodged, accusing you of assault.'

'I suspected as much. We'll have to talk later.'

He had no sooner hung up than *Aftonbladet*, the main evening paper, rang. They wondered if he had any comment. He told them he hadn't, except that he hadn't yet read what their highly esteemed competitor's pages had said about him, and he most definitely hadn't assaulted anybody.

Then he got dressed, and after that he rang Superintendent Jonnerblad.

'You're off the case until further notice,' Jonnerblad informed him. He sounded as though he was biting down on an iron bar.

'Thanks,' said Barbarotti. 'Anything else?'

'Don't come into work today. And stay away from the press. Is that clear?'

'Crystal clear,' said Barbarotti.

'You're gagged,' said Jonnerblad.

'Understood,' said Barbarotti, and rang off.

He switched on the coffee machine and started spreading butter on a couple of slices of bread, and then Swedish Television rang to suggest he come to the royal capital and grace the sofa of the morning news programme the next day. Barbarotti said he was sorry but he was unable to do so because it could be detrimental to ongoing investigations, and hung up. He had barely sat down at the kitchen table when TV4 rang. They wondered whether he would like to be a guest on their evening sofa; he informed them politely but firmly that he was unfortunately already fully booked and thanked them for their interest.

He gulped a mouthful of coffee, took a bite of bread, and received a call from the radio programme *After Three*. Before the woman had time to introduce herself, Barbarotti said he was in the middle of an important interrogation and hadn't time to talk.

Then he switched off all the phones, finished his breakfast and read the local morning paper. There wasn't a word about any police assault.

Marianne, he thought. Marianne would be exposed to *Expressen* today, as well.

He reactivated his channels of communication with the outside world just after ten; he had enjoyed a long bath, forty-five minutes to the strains of Bach cello suites, sent up a three-point prayer of existence to Our Lord, and missed twelve calls to his landline.

Fourteen to his mobile, and six messages to each of them.

I'm in clover here, thought Inspector Barbarotti. No doubt about that.

Or in the eye of the storm, or however one cares to put it.

Off the case until further notice?

That had never happened to him before.

An official complaint? That *had* happened before. It happened to everyone, but it was normally a matter of some familiar perpetrator losing his rag and wanting to get his own back. The official investigations were always shut down, it was all part of the game, really, both the complaints and the shuttings down. Which was a shame – because now and then a police officer actually did overstep the mark, everybody knew that.

He still hadn't dared venture out to buy a copy of the evening paper; he wasn't sure what time they usually got to Kymlinge and the thought of returning home empty-handed was far from appealing. Better to wait another half hour, he decided. Maybe think about some kind of disguise, as well?

Still no call from Marianne. He wondered why that could be. It was the only thing that mattered to him, really. This was the uncomfortable truth that had started to dawn on him; he didn't care what the rest of the world thought, or cared very little, at any rate, but the way Marianne reacted was vital to him. In the original sense of the word – crucial to his existence.

He took this problem and both his phones and went to sit out on the balcony.

So why hadn't she been in touch? Either it was simply that no one had alerted her to the scandal of the day, or . . . or she had already read it and chosen to remain silent.

He couldn't countenance the latter. Jesus Christ, no way, thought Gunnar Barbarotti. There was no way the act of pushing that bloody hack Persson out of his front door could have such a devastating impact on his private life. Things simply hadn't the right to develop in this sort of way – he had already had a word with Our Lord about it while lying in the bath with Bach, and Our Lord had been of the same opinion.

He listened to his messages. Two were from Jonnerblad, one on each phone, and two from Inspector Backman; five were from assorted journalists and the other three from good friends who seemed to be acquainted with that day's edition of *Expressen*, to judge by their tone.

Both Jonnerblad and Backman asked him to contact the police, and he had no problem deciding which channel he would choose when he did so. No problem at all.

Eva Backman's private mobile. She rarely switched it off, and this time was no exception – she replied after three rings and asked him to wait. He assumed she wanted to go somewhere private before she spoke to him, and when she came back on the line he realized why she, of all the cops in the world, was the one he would hand-pick if he were forced to spend a year on a desert island with a colleague. If we didn't have six kids with other people we could have got married, he thought suddenly. It wasn't exactly a new idea, but it had been lying fallow for a while. It had no prospect of survival.

'How are things?' she asked. 'I'm a bit worried about you.'

'I'm fine,' said Gunnar Barbarotti, as a call came in on his landline. He checked the display to make sure it wasn't Marianne and left it to ring. 'But I haven't read the paper yet. What does it actually say?'

'It's utter rubbish,' said Backman. 'Ridiculous to splash it across the newsstands like that. What really happened?'

'That bugger tried to force his way in here last night. I pushed him out onto the landing.'

'Thought as much. It says in the paper that you knocked him to the floor and threw him down the stairs. He did himself some damage too, evidently. Jonnerblad's holding another little press conference at the moment, but he wants a word with you afterwards.'

'So I gather.'

'Good.'

'And I'm off the case?'

'Until further notice, as I understand it. And it's just as well for you to lie low, I reckon. The atmosphere's a bit overheated here.'

'Really?' said Barbarotti. 'How's the investigation going?'

'You know what, I think we might be starting to make progress,' declared Eva Backman, and he could hear that she was trying hard to sound optimistic.

'Progress?' he said.

'Yes. We've discovered that that couple, Henrik and Katarina Malmgren, were going on holiday to Denmark, and Sorrysen has just reported that they took the late evening ferry to Fredrikshavn . . . on Sunday, if I've got that right. But something isn't entirely clear, so I think he's on the phone to the ferry company as we speak.'

'Aha?' said Barbarotti. 'What is it that's not entirely clear?'

'I don't know yet. I can ring and tell you once I've had a word with Sorrysen. But we've had the analyses of the first three letters. Linköping tells us there are no fingerprints, and no saliva either . . . our friend the murderer seems to have been pretty scrupulous, but then we knew that already.'

'Yes, I had a feeling they wouldn't find anything,' agreed Barbarotti. 'Well, tell Jonnerblad he can ring me on my mobile if he wants anything. I think I'll switch it on for five minutes on the hour and half hour, there's a bit too much shit in circulation for me to keep it on the whole time.'

'I can understand that,' said Eva Backman. 'If it doesn't sound way too soft of me, I actually feel a bit sorry for you.'

'It sounds way too soft of you,' said Barbarotti.

'Yeah, I suppose so,' said Eva Backman, and gave a laugh. 'But then you're forgetting I'm a woman. We've got that, you know, empathetic streak that you blokes are lacking.'

'Empa . . . ? What did you say it was called?'

'Doesn't matter. Anyway, I thought I'd drop round on the way home from work today. Brainstorming with the gang here doesn't really work for me . . . If you don't mind, that is?'

'You'll be welcome,' said Gunnar Barbarotti. 'I'll treat you to a beer on the balcony. What's happening about your holiday?'

'Seems to have been postponed for a few more days,' said Eva Backman. 'And Ville's threatening to come back from the cottage. The boys have started moaning about his cooking, apparently.'

'Police officers shouldn't be allowed holidays at all,' said Barbarotti. 'It just messes up routine procedure. But that's all the time I can spare you right now. I need to get out and buy an evening paper, and then I'm going to lie down on the sofa and relax for a couple of hours.'

'I take back what I said about feeling sorry for you,' said Eva Backman, and rang off.

It was even worse than he had expected.

And he had expected quite a lot. He sank down at the kitchen table, spread the paper out in front of him and realized, rather to his surprise, that he felt sick.

He was all over the front page. Half of it was taken up with a headline in inch-high letters.

EXPRESSEN REPORTER KNOCKED OUT COLD BY THE POLICE

The other half comprised a large, grainy picture, which that flash-happy photographer had seemingly managed to take at the exact moment he shoved Göran Persson in the chest. It didn't look pretty; the detail that had come out in sharpest focus was Barbarotti's facial expression, reminiscent of a ruthless karate king delivering the fatal blow to his defenceless opponent.

And that goddamned reporter did indeed look as if he was falling helplessly backwards.

But knocked out cold? By a pair of fists to the chest?

He turned to page eight, where the truth about this new case of police brutality was exposed, and related in all its atrocious detail. With purely peaceful intentions, experienced and respected crime reporter Göran Persson had tried to obtain a comment from police officer Gunnar Barbarotti at his flat in central Kymlinge – on the grounds that the perpetrator of the two murders recently committed in the town had sent letters to this particular officer, as reported in detail in Monday's paper. Without any provocation, Barbarotti had at that point attacked the poor defenceless journalist, punching him violently, and had then thrown him down a steep staircase, knocking him out and breaking two bones in his body.

In his body? thought Barbarotti. Well, where the heck else would they be?

Shocked and injured, Göran Persson had left the scene with the help of the paper's photographer and spent the night in Kymlinge hospital. The incident had been reported to the police and the whole affair naturally put a severe damper and hindrance on the investigation currently being undertaken – with no sign of progress to date – by the Kymlinge police, with reinforcements from Gothenburg and the National CID as they hunted for the letter-writing murderer, now assumed to have two lives on his conscience.

Damper and hindrance, thought Barbarotti. Perhaps he had

bumped his head after all? Unusually, the article was unattributed. Maybe someone at the paper had realized it would look like wearing too many hats if Göran Persson put his name to the piece.

The officer leading the case, Detective Superintendent Jonnerblad, had not been available late on Monday night when *Expressen* tried to contact him for a comment on Inspector Barbarotti's reckless attack on free speech and its representatives. In a hastily conducted opinion poll of people in and around Kymlinge, as many as 66 per cent said they had little or no confidence in the police force's ability to get to grips with the rise in criminality. Over the summer, for example, not a single one of the twenty-two reported house-burglary cases in the district had been solved. There were good grounds for asking what the police force was doing with its time.

On page five there were more pictures of combatants Persson and Barbarotti. He had no idea where they had come by the photograph of him, which gave him the dishevelled appearance of someone who had just emerged from a ditch where he had slept off a drinking bout. He had dark shadows under his eyes and looked rather like the late Christer Pettersson, suspect in the Olof Palme assassination case. The reporter, for his part, had a split lip, a bruise under one eye and a bloodstained bandage round his head, and roughly resembled an emphysema patient who had just been run over by a steamroller.

There's no end to this, thought Detective Inspector Barbarotti. If I see that devil again I shall give him a proper thrashing.

And it struck him that thoughts like this were utterly typical of perpetrators of violent crime across the board.

*

He slid his finger into the Bible.

The same place. It was remarkable. How unlikely was that? But perhaps he had left it lying open at that page for a while, last time? He seemed to remember there was a card trick that worked like that. And old books nearly always fell open at the most frequently read pages if you left it to chance, didn't they? Or an index finger.

Matthew, then.

Matthew. Chapter 6, verse 23.

> But if thine eye be evil, thy whole body shall be full of darkness. If therefore the light that is in thee be darkness, how great is that darkness!

He looked at the surrounding verses and saw that there were crucial matters under discussion. Our Lord and God and Mammon were all there – but still, he thought, *my eye is evil*? What did that signify? What lesson was he expected to draw from it?

The fact that things felt pretty dark at the moment hardly needed pointing out by a higher power.

He closed the Bible with a sigh and switched on his mobile.

Four new voicemail messages, but above all, a text from Marianne. Finally, he thought, his fingers fumbling over the keys. My life's turning a corner.

She asked him to give her time.

Or that was how you could describe it if you wanted to see it positively. Given what she had read in today's *Expressen*, she needed to consider things, she wrote. *I've read it, need to think*. It would be wrong to make any hasty decisions. But he was welcome to ring.

That was all. He wandered round the flat in restless indecision for fifteen minutes, until he plucked up courage. She didn't answer. He wandered round for ten more. Tried again, and this time she was there.

'You mustn't believe everything you read in the papers,' he said. 'That's not how it happened.'

He knew how unconvincing he must sound. Like when a notorious addict tries to justify beating his wife for the umpteenth time. *It wasn't my fault.* She took her time replying, but he at least had the presence of mind not to offer any more lousy excuses in the ominous seconds of silence.

'Yes, I'd really like to know what happened,' she said finally. 'Of course. But there are the children to think about, too. Them above all, in fact. They've read the paper and they're finding it a bit hard to take in that it's you. I don't know what to tell them.'

He swallowed. The children? A couple of hours ago, Helena had said almost the same thing.

'I see,' he said. 'Here's what happened: that reporter tried to barge into my flat. I bundled him out of the door, that was all.'

'That was all?'

'Yes.'

Silence. He could feel a clenched hand twisting in his stomach.

'You don't believe me?'

'Gunnar, please, I don't know what to think.'

'You prefer to believe what they write in *Expressen*?'

'No, of course not. I'm only saying that . . . that it's hard to get the children to understand something like this.'

'Yes, I get it. And what about . . . us?'

She hesitated again. Dark seconds went sailing by on the way to no-man's-land. Or a graveyard. Or an inferno. Where were all those images coming from, he wondered. These images and rootless thoughts again.

'I don't know about us,' she said in the end. 'You'll have to give me a bit more time.'

'Are you saying this just because of what they printed in *Expressen* today?'

'No . . .'

'I'd be grateful for an honest answer, Marianne. I proposed to you last week, remember. You promised me an answer this Wednesday. Today's Tuesday.'

'I know what day it is.'

'Good. So I'll ring you tomorrow as we agreed.'

'If you ring me tomorrow, the answer's going to be no. You've no right to pressurize me like this.'

'OK, I won't ring then. Do you want to give me a new date or should I consider this a closed chapter?'

'Why are you putting pressure on me, Gunnar? I can't make a decision right now, why do you find that so odd?'

He checked himself and thought about it – and at the same time felt a slight pride in having been able to do it. Check himself. I've grown up a bit, he thought. If this had been in the Helena years, I'd have slammed the phone down at this point.

'Sorry, I've had a bad day today,' he said. 'I've been served up to the whole of Sweden as a hooligan. An official complaint's been lodged against me, I've got the sack and the woman I love doesn't want me.'

'You got the sack?'

'Suspended from work, anyway.'

'But surely they can't . . . ?'

'Oh yes they can. And it's only natural, considering the situation. Isn't it?'

Her breathing at the other end of the line sounded distressed. Amazing that one can detect distress just from a breath, he thought. Amazing that it's audible on the phone. For some reason he found this comforting.

'Gunnar,' she said, 'how about this? Ring me on Saturday, and we'll see. I'll talk this through with Johan and Jenny, I've got to do that . . . can you bear to wait until then?'

'I think so,' said Gunnar Barbarotti. 'I might need a bit of time to sort out one thing and another, myself.'

'Saturday, then?'

'Saturday.'

He felt a bit better after the call than he had done before he rang her. Or so he tried to convince himself. He switched off the phone without listening to the other messages.

How do I feel inside, he wondered. Darkness or light? Graveyard or inferno?

He crumpled *Expressen* into a ball and rammed it into the bin, then went to sit on the balcony with a crossword instead.

20

Inspector Backman turned up around 6.30, bringing with her three big red files.

'Thought you could probably do with a bit of stimulation,' she said.

'Thanks,' said Barbarotti.

'Save you having to go to the park and feed the pigeons.'

'Quite so.'

'If you read through them tonight, I could collect them on my way to work tomorrow morning. This is basically everything we've got in the case to date. You know most of it already, of course.'

'Have Jonnerblad and Asunander approved this?'

'I didn't ask them,' said Eva Backman.

'Smart,' said Barbarotti. 'Let's go and sit on the balcony. You've got time for a beer?'

'Always,' said Backman. 'My menfolk haven't carried out their threat to come home – yet. And it's a nice evening.'

'They seem to be getting ready for a crayfish party in the garden next door,' said Barbarotti. 'Perhaps we can pinch a bit of their atmosphere.'

Inspector Backman smiled.

'Perfect,' she said, sinking into one of the chairs. 'You've really thought of everything.'

'One does what one can,' said Barbarotti. He went to the kitchen and returned with two beers and two tall glasses. This balcony may be small, but it was definitely built for two, he thought involuntarily.

'But in return, I want a thorough update,' he said. 'A proper oral report, all nice and clear, before I start my reading. You don't happen to have solved the case between you in the course of today?'

'Not exactly,' Backman admitted. 'But things don't look promising for the couple from Gothenburg, I'm afraid.'

Barbarotti poured the drinks, and they raised their glasses to each other and each took a deep draught.

'Oh yes?' said Barbarotti. 'Not promising?'

'Not at all,' said Backman, lounging back in her chair. 'Mmm, it makes a bloody nice change to work on a balcony instead of inside a police station. I'm sure a lot of cases would benefit from this sort of approach.'

'We can make this a permanent thing,' suggested Barbarotti. 'For as long as I'm suspended, at any rate. If you come round and brief me every evening, you'll get a beer for your trouble.'

'Why not?' smiled Eva Backman.

'Not at all promising?' Barbarotti prompted her.

She cleared her throat and her expression grew grave. 'Yes, it's starting to look that way. Everything points to Henrik and Katarina Malmgren having taken the late evening ferry from Gothenburg to Fredrikshavn on Sunday, and there are strong indications that they didn't disembark on the Danish side.'

'Strong indications . . .' queried Gunnar Barbarotti. 'Could you spell them out, please?'

'The fact that their car was left on the car deck, for example,' said Eva Backman. 'Well, that's the only one, in fact, but it weighs pretty heavily, as I said. Don't you think?'

'They didn't drive the car off the ferry?'

'You've got it. An Audi, packed with holiday stuff, was left standing on the deck. Now of course it's possible they decided to abandon the car and all their luggage and just walked off the ferry, but no one in the team has come up with any plausible explanation for them doing that. Maybe you can, though?'

Gunnar Barbarotti frowned. 'You mean they could have been murdered on the ferry? And . . . ?'

'And thrown in the sea, yes. That's one theory. Another is that they were murdered and stuffed into some other vehicle . . . and buried later in some bog in Denmark. Or somewhere on the continent, free choice of location.'

'Crossing borders with dead bodies in the boot? Sounds a bit much.'

'There are no borders in Europe any longer,' said Backman. 'But sure, I agree with you. It seems more likely they were dumped overboard under cover of darkness.'

'Christ Almighty,' said Gunnar Barbarotti. 'Do you really believe that?'

'Well, what conclusions do you draw yourself?' asked Eva Backman.

'I'm not sure,' said Barbarotti.

'Two people drive onto a car ferry in their car. When everyone else has disembarked and the boat's empty, four hours later, the car's still sitting there. Ergo?'

Barbarotti said nothing. For a while he just sat there contemplating the three red case files on the table. He waved away a wasp that was trying to sneak a look.

'And the link with the other victims?'

'We've scarcely had time to start on that yet. There are no obvious connections, at any rate. Henrik Malmgren's a senior lecturer in philosophy at the University of Gothenburg. His wife Katarina's a nurse anaesthetist at Gothenburg's Sahlgrenska hospital. Thirty-seven and thirty-four years of age respectively, no children and neither of them feature in our records.'

'I know all that,' said Barbarotti. 'Has anyone searched their place yet?'

She looked at her watch. 'They've just started. Tallin, Jonnerblad and Astor Nilsson are there. The prosecutor took a while to authorize it, but the car's been seized, too. It's a primary line of enquiry, to quote the National CID.'

'Primary line of enquiry? We're looking for victims. I thought that a primary line of enquiry was to do with finding the perpetrator?'

'So did I,' said Eva Backman, taking a drink of beer. 'Not that we local cops have much to boast of either. He did stand up for you to the press, by the way, Superintendent Jonnerblad, and I get the feeling your reputation's going to be somewhat restored in tomorrow's *Aftonbladet*.'

'So I heard,' said Barbarotti with a nod.

'Heard?'

'I spoke to Jonnerblad a couple of hours ago. But who reads that sort of official correction?'

'Not many people,' said Backman.

'No, that's just it. I've helped them put a face on police violence, in this town at any event, and there'll be no shaking it off for a few years, I'm sure of that. He's not letting me back into the group, either, Jonnerblad. He thinks it wouldn't be tactical at this stage.'

Eva Backman nodded.

'Not until *Expressen* withdraws its official complaint to the police . . . a provocation to the public's sense of justice, he said it would be.'

'There is another reason for keeping you on the out of things, you know,' said Eva Backman.

'Oh yes? And what's that?'

'You're the one the murderer writes to. There is a slight conflict of interests there.'

'So if he wrote to police HQ, we'd all have to stand aside from the case?'

'Well . . .'

'We'd have to hire in some cops from Estonia?'

Eva Backman gave a laugh. 'Maybe. No, I suppose it's mainly the other thing that's making them keep you out of it. You had rather too much exposure today, just as you say, and people need time to forget. A few days, at the very least.'

'But that shouldn't exclude me from sitting in my office and investigating on the case.'

'Of course not. But it's much nicer here, like I said.'

'OK,' sighed Barbarotti. 'You want another beer?'

Eva Backman shook her head. 'Thought I might fit in a run, and two beers in my system would be a bit too much.'

Barbarotti nodded and rapped the pile of folders with his knuckles. 'You get going,' he said. 'I'll devote the evening to looking through the material. I'll let you have my comments first thing tomorrow, if you drop by.'

Inspector Backman got to her feet just as the partygoers down in the next-door garden struck up a well-loved drinking song. 'Ah, there you go,' she said, glancing over the balcony rail. 'One day you and I are gonna get to a party too, just you wait and see.'

'One can always hope,' said Gunnar Barbarotti. 'What's happened about your holiday, by the way?'

'Postponed until further notice,' explained Inspector Backman. 'What did you expect?'

About three hours and a dozen drinking songs later, he had read through the contents of all three folders. Darkness had descended and an August moon, marbled in yellow and blood red, had sailed up over the uneven copper roofs of Cathedral School. All the jackdaws had fallen silent and the only screeching came from the drunken partygoers down below. He was still out on the balcony; an evening chill had crept over him, but a woolly cardigan and a blanket over his knees had kept it at bay.

It really was a strange case. He basically knew that even before he started wading through all the case material, but he could not help being struck by it again. In all likelihood, one of the strangest he had ever experienced.

And terrifying. Particularly when you tried to visualize the perpetrator himself. To paint a picture of such a person.

If Henrik and Katarina Malmgren really had been murdered, too, the man now had four lives on his conscience. That alone – the number of victims – made him kind of unique. There weren't many murderers in the country with four dead bodies to their names, Barbarotti knew that. Most of those currently serving their sentences at Hall, Österåker or Kumla prisons had only one, and just a few had two or three. When you had killed four people, you were undeniably playing in the highest league.

Or the lowest, depending on the standards by which one measured.

And the fact that he had tipped off the police by letter in all four cases must make him extremely unusual in an international context, too, Barbarotti thought. Lillieskog had claimed not to know of any other case in which advance warning had been given in this way – that was why he had been unsure about the profiling. All profiling was built on experience, and if there was no experience, well, then you were building on a quagmire. So much for that sort of precision.

The reams of papers in the folders included a statement from an eminent criminologist, asserting that 'for once it could be a case of a murderer with some potency to his grey matter, which was why the police force currently found itself stuck in such a tight corner'. Barbarotti was aware of feeling inclined to agree with this somewhat rough and ready hypothesis.

A smart devil, in short. Possibly without a criminal record. Possibly with an unshakeable determination to implement his plan and avoid getting caught. Just as Lillieskog had claimed, in fact.

Not random killings. Not a serial killer, despite the large number of victims. Once he had killed those he intended to kill, it would be over. The only question was: how many were there on his list? And above all: what was the connection between the individuals on that list?

There were hundreds of other questions, of course. Would they be able to stop him before he had finished, for example? Before he had murdered all those he was planning to murder? Would they be able to stop him at all?

And Hans Andersson? What did the murderer mean by – to use his own words – 'Hans Andersson can go on living'? Had there ever been an intended victim by that name or was it just a bluff? A smokescreen deployed in the midst of the battle, for some reason?

And were Henrik and Katarina Malmgren really dead? In the folders, there were pictures of both of them: a man with a thin face and thinning hair, spectacles and an expression for which Barbarotti could find no better word than 'ordinary' – while Katarina was dark and had a livelier look to her, attractive in that powerful, slightly Mediterranean way. And there was a Kymlinge connection, too. She had evidently lived in the town for five years as a teenager, at the end of the eighties, out in Kymlingevik. And of course that was another important question: what role did Kymlinge play in all this? Did the killer have the same local links as three of his victims?

In short, was he here in town? Did he just head off somewhere else to post his letters? And to kill Mr and Mrs Malmgren, perhaps?

And if one were to assume they were actually dead, how had he achieved it? If it was as Backman said, then on top of everything else he must be a singularly cold-blooded individual, thought Barbarotti. Killing a man and his wife aboard a boat and then simply heaving their bodies over the side – without attracting attention – could not be at all straightforward.

And why choose that particular method?

As usual, Gunnar Barbarotti was well aware that all these small but significant questions, prone to – how had he put it the other day? – catching on each other as randomly as bent metal coat hangers in a dark wardrobe? . . . that these questions basically all belonged under one heading: *Why?*

Why were these murders being committed? What was the reason . . . because presumably there *was* a reason? A nub, a pivot, which would make the whole thing comprehensible, once they finally gained sufficient insight. That was what it was all about. Comprehending. Understanding as much as they could and leaving it at that.

When Gunnar Barbarotti was going through school in the liberal seventies he had been taught that it was more important to ask the right questions than to know the right answers. He had often wished his school years could have coincided with some other decade.

As he listened to one of the crayfish party guests perform 'Knockin' on Heaven's Door' – accompanying himself on the guitar with a pretty peculiar set of chords – his mind turned to the letters and the question of timing. Was the murderer genuinely giving the police a chance? Or was it rather a case of the messages about the intended victims always arriving too late to offer any prospect of saving lives? Not even a theoretical possibility of doing so? Barbarotti watched a pigeon come in to land on the balcony rail of the flat next door as he reversed through his memory. The most recent letter had arrived in Monday's post; if the Malmgrens really had been murdered, the crime – crimes – had in all probability been committed on the Sunday night or in the small hours of Monday. OK then, the murderer had in all likelihood posted the letter before he set to work, but he must have known that by the time the police had it in their hands, he would already have carried out his plan.

And what was more, he must have been absolutely certain he was going to succeed.

Was there any chance of intercepting the items of mail any earlier? They had discussed getting the Post Office involved – but taken no action. How would it work, in practice? Would all the postmen and postwomen in west Sweden who sorted the mail for their own rounds have to be alerted to the name of the addressee and the envelope type currently in favour, and be instructed, if they suspected anything was brewing, to contact the Kymlinge police? Or *their local police authorities*, as police appeals on the radio always said? No, thought Gunnar Barbarotti, that just didn't sound workable. It seemed to be playing into the murderer's hands even more.

He always expressed himself in the future tense – said that he was going to kill this person or that – but by the time the matter came to Barbarotti's attention it had already descended through the tenses to the . . . what was it called . . . preterite? It had already happened. Too late to do anything about it.

Perhaps there was a linguistic aspect to it all that would appeal to Axel Wallman.

He sighed and listened distractedly to the muted applause, thankfully announcing that the tipsy troubadour had finished knocking at those pearly gates. Barbarotti, remembering that morning's dream, assumed he had not been admitted.

He tucked the folders under his arm and came in from the balcony. It was after eleven and if nothing else, thought Gunnar Barbarotti, I've been spared thinking about Marianne and my inner darkness for a few hours. That's always something.

Work is the only effective way of counteracting anxiety, he had read somewhere. Perhaps that was right. And if you had been sacked – albeit temporarily – there was surely nothing to stop you indulging in a bit of private detection?

Especially if you happened to be the only one in direct contact – albeit rather one-directionally – with the murderer.

Suspended? Gagged? Well, thought Inspector Barbarotti,

why don't I just get a late deal on a package to the Med and stop giving a shit about all this?

Another good question.

21

On Wednesday morning he woke early, aware of having slept only patchily. There was a dull thrum in his head and a prickly feeling all over his body. As soon as he took the local paper out of his letterbox, he realized there would be no need to go down to the convenience store to read about himself. Monday evening's contretemps between the powers of law and order and the representative of free speech had not gone unremarked by Kymlinge's voice in the world. It was front-page news, with further reports inside.

But unlike *Expressen*, the paper chose to publish neither names nor pictures of the parties involved; it only said that a reporter from an evening paper had got into a dispute with a police officer, resulting in an official complaint. It was not even spelt out who had complained about whom, and Gunnar Barbarotti thought what a shame it was that the local paper had only about a tenth as many readers as that muckraking rag from the capital. Not counting *GT*, though that was more or less identical to *Expressen*.

But the local paper hadn't stinted on its coverage of the murders themselves, or the letter writing, though there was nothing he had not already read in Backman's red files, and he was aware of feeling rather grateful for this fact. The newspapers knew nothing more than the police, at any rate.

What's up with me? he thought. Surely that's not anything to be grateful for? Have I so little confidence in the lead investigators since they lost their ace that I expect to glean more from the papers than the formal case material? Do I belong with the 66 per cent now?

I must be losing my grip.

Backman turned up to collect her files just after eight, and promised to keep him updated on the day's developments.

'And if you come round for a while this evening I'll give you something to eat, too,' offered Barbarotti. 'Not just beer and a whiff of crayfish.'

Eva Backman thought about this for a moment before she accepted. With the proviso, she said, that the situation down in the summer cottage in Blekinge didn't take such an alarming turn that Ville arrived home with the kids. You never knew, and it also depended a bit on the weather, which was looking rather grey at present. Though of course there was a difference between Kymlinge and coastal Kristianopel.

'So did these give you any ideas?' she wanted to know as he handed over the case files.

Barbarotti shook his head. 'No,' he said. 'They didn't. Nothing immediate, anyway.'

'Pity,' said Eva Backman.

'Though it's all churning round at the back of my mind, and I'm pretty sure there's going to be a breakthrough once we combine Mr and Mrs Malmgren with the two previous victims. As long as you lot make a proper search of the place, you'll find the connection this afternoon.'

'You lot?' said Eva Backman.

'You lot,' said Gunnar Barbarotti.

She gave him a worried glance. 'And if we don't?'

'If you don't,' said Barbarotti, massaging his throbbing temples with his knuckles, 'it can only mean one thing.'

'That there's no connection?'

'Exactly. It can be difficult to identify where two people's lives intersect, but if you add in a third and a fourth, the common denominator will surface pretty quickly. Or it should do, with halfway competent investigators at the helm.'

'So you'd have me believe we're not playing on the strongest of teams?'

Gunnar Barbarotti forced a crooked smile. 'Now there you go with your unihockey metaphors and stuff I know nothing about, Mrs Backman.'

'Bullshit,' said Eva Backman. 'Anyway, we'll just have to see who turns out to be right. I'll keep in touch, like I said.'

'I'm grateful for that,' said Barbarotti.

She left, he washed up the breakfast things, and after that he was suddenly at a loss as to how to make the minutes and hours go by.

There's a time for sitting waiting, he thought, but today I feel as if I've got ants crawling all over me, body and soul. Please God, let there be a bit of action now, so I'm spared this idle pacing round my three-room flat like a broody female polar bear. Two points, OK?

Our Lord gave a sigh and slung a gust of wind and a few stray spatters of rain at the kitchen window but, having heard far worse things in the course of the centuries, he decided not to pass comment on the supplicant's terrible imagery. After all, a person couldn't help having gone to school in the seventies.

As previously discussed.

*

Instead, Our Lord began angling for his points an hour and a half later. Not unexpectedly, he had to recruit Inspector Backman to help him.

'Bad news is good news,' she began cryptically. 'Just you listen to this.'

'I'm listening,' Barbarotti assured her. 'Fire away.'

'Firstly,' said Backman, 'we've found Katarina Malmgren.'

'Ouch,' said Barbarotti.

'Yes. Or to be more accurate, a Danish fisherman did, early this morning, not far from Skagen. He was taking his boat out and was only about fifty metres offshore when he came across the body of a woman, floating in the water.'

'How do you know it's her?'

'There's been no formal identification yet, but plenty points to it being her.'

'Such as?'

'Such as various ID items in the breast pocket of her jacket; plastic cards are pretty water-resistant. She's being transported back to Gothenburg at the moment. That sister, I think you talked to her, didn't you, she's on her way down from Karlstad to identify her.'

'That's right,' Gunnar Barbarotti recalled. 'I did actually talk to a sister of Mrs Malmgren's before I was dismissed . . . half-sister, if I remember rightly. What about the husband, you haven't found him yet?'

'Correct. He's still missing. Probably floating about in some other bit of the sea. Or he's got caught in a net or propeller, in which case it might take a while.'

'I see,' said Barbarotti. 'And the cause of death, how about that? What did Katarina Malmgren die of?'

'Strangled, with some kind of ligature. The marks on her neck leave us in no doubt'

'Strangled? He . . . so that means he's changed method again?'

'It seems so, yes,' said Backman. 'It's too early to say anything about time of death, of course, but the Danish pathologist says she probably died some time on Sunday night. Looks to have been in the water about forty-eight hours when Trulsemanden found her.

'Trulsemanden?'

'Our fisherman, that's his name. He's seventy-eight.'

'Hang on . . . isn't it the system now . . . don't they have to have complete passenger lists on ferries these days? Since the *Estonia* disaster?'

'In principle, yes,' said Eva Backman. 'But unfortunately they don't require ID.'

'Meaning?'

'Meaning you can book a ticket in the name of Jöns Jönsson, and when you pick it up, all you have to do is say that's your name. You'll get your boarding documents even if you're actually called Lars Larsson.'

'OK,' sighed Barbarotti. 'Which in turn means we won't happen to find the murderer's name in the passenger lists?'

'Precisely right, I'm afraid,' said Eva Backman. 'We got our hopes up on that score for about ten minutes, too.'

'Though I suppose one could go through the lists anyway . . . how many names would it be?'

'Just over fifteen hundred people,' said Eva Backman. 'We'll be doing it, of course, but it's one heck of a job.'

Gunnar Barbarotti thought for a moment. 'And the search

warrant?' he asked. 'Did you find anything of interest at the Malmgrens'?'

'We don't know yet,' admitted Eva Backman. 'But we've got four cardboard boxes that we're about to go through. They had six desk drawers each, plus at least ten photo albums. And we've got both computers.'

'I assume you know what you're looking for?'

'We're looking for all sorts of things. But above all, anything that can link the Malmgrens to Anna Eriksson or Erik Bergman.'

'Or both.'

'Or both. We're also working flat-out on the mobile phone data. And if the same number comes up on either of the Malmgrens' phones as on Eriksson's or Bergman's, we'll investigate further. Happy now, inspector?'

Gunnar Barbarotti considered this.

'I've nothing to add for the time being,' he said. 'Is there anything particular you'd like for dinner?'

'It's been a while since I had lobster,' Inspector Backman reminded herself aloud.

There was a well-stocked fishmonger's in Skolgatan in Kymlinge; Barbarotti shopped there from time to time and when the Polish owner, a former ski jumper named Dobrowolski, said he couldn't particularly recommend the lobster he had on offer that day – especially if it was being cooked for a woman – the detective inspector allowed himself to be talked into buying scallops and langoustines instead. He was presented with eight other ingredients to boot, and even the name of a white wine that was an indispensable complement to the dish in question, and as a result he had to take a detour via the off-licence on his way home, as well.

It felt very odd to be out buying one luxury item after another on a mid-week morning, and it was with a distinct touch of guilt that he put away his purchases in the fridge and cupboard when he got home. Quite apart from anything else, the coming meal was of course one he should have been serving to Marianne, not Inspector Backman, but it was as it was, thought Gunnar Barbarotti. The letter writer had struck for the third – and in all probability the fourth – time, and with a cold-bloodedness which, as far as Barbarotti could currently judge, one could only describe as breathtaking.

How did it go, again? He – if, at least for the sake of argument, they could assume the murderer wasn't a woman? – had boarded a Stena Lines ferry from Gothenburg to Fredrikshavn. It had departed on time at 23.55 on Sunday evening, Inspector Backman had informed him – and at some point on the roughly three-hour crossing to Denmark, he had killed Henrik and Katarina Malmgren, exactly as promised, and dumped them overboard. How did anyone go about something like that, wondered Barbarotti. *However did they do it?*

Katarina Malmgren had been strangled with a noose. That was no easy way to kill a person, especially not on a boat rammed with passengers and potential witnesses. He must have had a pretty thorough plan. Known exactly what he was going to do, and, suspected Gunnar Barbarotti, something more besides. He must . . . he must have known the Malmgrens.

Mustn't he? In order to kill them, he would surely have had to separate them first, and why should a married couple allow themselves to be separated by a stranger on a ferry in the middle of the night? It would have taken a good deal of ingenuity to achieve. Sleeping pills in their cocktails or something even more artful and manipulative.

Though of course there was no guarantee he had used the same MO on Henrik Malmgren. He could have shot him first, for instance, and then taken his time tackling the wife. It wasn't impossible . . . and yet, thought Barbarotti, there was still a lot of food for thought in the notion of them recognizing each other. The murders had, in all likelihood, been committed somewhere on the open deck, and why would anyone go out on deck with a stranger in the middle of the night? If they were travelling with their other half, that is. The thought persisted.

First him, then her. Or the other way round.

Both at the same time?

No, that simply didn't seem possible.

Though the fact that they were acquainted, the murderer and his victims, wasn't news to anybody. They had already decided that there must be some kind of motive behind it all, hadn't they? That the targets were not merely chosen at random.

As he reached this point in his deliberations, Gunnar Barbarotti heard rustling sounds from out in the hall. The day's post had arrived, and five minutes later he wasn't sure whether he had really had a premonition or was just imagining it.

But one thing was in no doubt: Our Lord had two well-earned points in the bag.

Gloves on again, and the envelope propped against the fruit bowl on the kitchen table.

Pale blue, a long thin rectangle, just like numbers three and four.

His name and address written in those same clumsy capitals. The stamp from the same archipelago set, a stylized sailing boat against a blue sea and sky.

He tried to work out how many days had passed since he held the first letter in his hand, that morning when he took it from the postman out on the stairs, on his way to Gotland and Marianne. Twenty-two, he counted. Only just over three weeks, in fact. Four letters so far, four murders. If you included Henrik Malmgren, that was, and surely you had to?

And now number five. A fifth person was waiting to be killed – or already had been killed, realistically speaking. The murderer's cool calculation was already well documented, thought Barbarotti, but the idea that the unopened envelope might contain the name of a person who was still alive – and in some way linked to the other victims – was hard to swallow. Very hard.

Unopened, yes. *Neither slit open nor read.* What should he do?

Yes, what should he do?

And here, thought Detective Inspector Barbarotti, here we have the crux of the matter. No two ways about it. *What should he do?* With a view to his future career – and his promotion prospects in the CID – it was extremely clear what he should do. Call Superintendent Jonnerblad on the spot and ask them to come and get the letter. Since his removal from the case he had been given no new instructions on how to deal with any further letters, not explicitly, but it would be tricky to claim he had opened it in good faith. Both Jonnerblad and Tallin would be bloody furious if he did that again. They would interpret it as him blithely going his own way. Every constable knew that, and they would never let him back into the team.

He stared at the envelope on the kitchen table. Suddenly,

Birgit Cullberg came into his head. He wondered what on earth she thought she was doing there, he felt no connection either to her or to modern dance of any kind – but then it dawned on him. A few years ago, he had happened to see an interview with the ageing dance legend on TV. The young interviewer had asked her one of those so-called clever questions that require some careful manoeuvring, she had reflected on her answer for quite a while, presumably hoping to improvise a response on some delicate cultural-political issue and avoid saying the wrong thing.

Finally, her face split into a wide smile and she delivered the most sublime of answers:

'You know what, I don't give a damn.'

That's the way to tackle it, thought Gunnar Barbarotti. *I don't give a damn!* Thank you, Birgit Cullberg. I shall blame you when they start on at me.

He pulled the gloves on again, got a kitchen knife and slit open the envelope. I'm changing job anyway, he thought for the umpteenth time since his return from Gotland and Gustabo. I'm going to be a gravedigger or the like, somewhere round Helsingborg.

DON'T KNOW IF YOU'VE FOUND THE MALMGRENS YET. ONLY ONE TO GO NOW, GUNNAR. THANKS FOR YOUR INVOLVEMENT.

He sat staring at it for a good five minutes. Reread it. Counted the words. Eighteen. Read it again, striving to understand, but there was . . . there was some malfunction of his own perception; or of his ability to understand written Swedish, perhaps? What did the message mean? What was the information being conveyed by these eighteen words?

In actual fact.

Only one to go now, Gunnar. There was a comma between the words 'now' and 'Gunnar'. What did that indicate in terms of meaning?

Was there one last victim, whose name was Gunnar?

Or was the 'Gunnar' a direct address to him, Gunnar Barbarotti? From the murderer?

Or . . . and it was probably this astonishing potential interpretation that had knocked his perception and linguistic comprehension off-kilter . . . did it mean . . . ?

Thanks for your involvement?

Everything went black in front of Inspector Barbarotti's eyes; the kitchen seemed to lurch, he hung onto the edge of the table, and the sensation that slowly spread through him was like the ice forming on a lake on a dark, cold November night.

An indeterminate amount of time passed – perhaps ten minutes, perhaps more – before he was able to get to his feet and stagger over to the phone.

22

'Sorry, what did you just say?'

He repeated what he had said without changing a word.

'*Another* one?'

'Mmm.'

'And you opened it?'

'Mmm.'

'Are you out of your mind?'

'. . .'

'I asked if you were out of your mind.'

He cleared his throat and tried to summon a rational word or two, but none came.

'It just happened.'

'It just happened?'

'Yes.'

'What the hell are you saying? Who am I even talking to here?'

'Hmm.'

'Oh my God, what's the matter with you?'

'I . . . I had a stroke. You can tell Jonnerblad that.'

She was saying nothing. His eye fell on his left hand, which was resting on the dark-stained kitchen table, and for a moment he felt as though it belonged to someone else. How could one tell?

'OK then, I'll tell him that. You got a letter, then you had a stroke. Is that what you want me to say?'

'Mmm.'

'Gunnar, you . . . you're not serious, are you? And what does the letter say this time? Try to get a grip. Have you been drinking?'

'No I bloody haven't.'

'Good. You sound like yourself at last. You know what, I think I'll come round and pick up that letter personally.'

'Thanks.'

'I'll be with you in fifteen minutes.'

'Thanks.'

'You can borrow my gloves. I don't suppose you brought any of your own?'

'Gunnar, what on earth's happened?'

'I don't know. I imagine I . . . I had some kind of mental collapse.'

'Mental collapse? Why?'

'No idea. I don't normally. It felt as if . . .'

'Yes?'

'As if I just froze to the spot.'

'Froze to the spot? Where were you?'

'Here, at the kitchen table. I must have been stuck here for a quarter of an hour before I managed to call you. Couldn't move.'

'And now? Do you feel any better?'

'Yes. I'm starting to thaw out.'

'You look pretty ropey, I have to say.'

'Thanks.'

'You ought to go to the doctor. It could . . . it could be something neurological.'

'I don't think so. Here, read the letter.'

Detective Inspector Eva Backman regarded him critically for a few more seconds, then did as he had said. She read the short text, frowned, shot him a glance across the table and read it again.

'Gunnar?' she said. 'He writes Gunnar, nothing else.'

'Mmm.'

'And that he's going to be the last one?'

'Mmm.'

'Or maybe he's talking directly to you. It could be that as well.'

Gunnar Barbarotti nodded. Inspector Backman sat in silence for a few moments and then something appeared to occur to her. She took a deep breath and clasped her hands in front of her on the table. She leant a little closer to him.

'Is he going to kill someone else, a person called Gunnar? Or is he going to kill someone else, called we don't know what?'

'I don't know.'

'Or . . . ?'

He gave a start. 'What?'

She shot him a quick glance, furtive almost, then turned her attention to the letter and studied it carefully again.

'No,' she said. 'Let's discount that possibility. I think . . .'

'What do you think?'

'I think he's going to kill someone else and it's someone called Gunnar. Or rather, he's probably already done it.'

He drummed the fingers of his left hand gently on the table, and she gave him that motherly, womanly look again.

What possibility is she talking about, he wondered. What's up with me? I feel as if I'm in an aquarium.

'You agree with that interpretation?'

'Of course.'

She leant closer still. He was aware of the scent of newly washed hair.

'Gunnar, did your . . . that thing you described happening to you . . . has it got some connection with this letter? It happened when you were reading it, didn't you say?'

He nodded.

'You don't look quite normal.'

'I never have. It's hereditary.'

'I don't mean it like that. But you're as white as a sheet, and yesterday you had a tan.'

'Oh?' said Gunnar Barbarotti.

'Have you got a plastic bag?'

He took one out of the kitchen drawer and she dropped the letter in it. Peeled off the gloves and sealed the bag.

'How do you feel now?'

He shrugged. 'A bit better? But kind of muffled, somehow.'

'Can you follow my finger with your eyes?'

She moved it from right to left in front of his face. 'No, without turning you head.'

He obliged without protest but she made no comment on how he had performed in the test. What's she up to? he thought. Does she suspect it really was a stroke?

But then his own opinion on the matter was also shrouded in darkness. She merely sat there for a while, scrutinizing him across the kitchen table. Then she seemed to come to a decision and got to her feet.

'Gunnar, I'm going to contact Olltman. You stay at home, and I'll ring you in an hour, OK?'

He took his time answering. Olltman, he thought. Yes, maybe that's the right thing. Why not?

He hadn't seen Olltman for a long time. Not since he and Eva Backman had helped Kristoffersson, a colleague of theirs, to her consulting rooms early one spring morning four or five years ago – after Kristoffersson had spent ten hours staring down the barrel of a hunting rifle out in a summer cabin near Kvarntorpa. It had ended with another fellow officer, Nyman, shooting the rifle owner and blowing half his brains out. Some of them had landed in Kristoffersson's lap, Barbarotti remembered.

Olltman was good. Everybody knew she was good. Even though they rarely talked about her.

He nodded, but realized he would never have agreed but for the fact that Olltman was a woman. Under any circumstances. He wondered why.

23

Her consulting rooms were on Badhusgatan, opposite the tennis courts, and he arrived twenty minutes early. He sat there with an old *National Geographic* in his hands while he waited. It was all about killer whales; he knew nothing more about killer whales by the time Olltman emerged and shook him by the hand a quarter of an hour later than he had done when he got there.

'Good to see you, Gunnar,' she said, showing him into a room with a colour scheme of green and desert sand. 'I think we've met a couple of times before.'

'Once, anyway,' said Barbarotti. 'But it was a few years ago now.'

She nodded, and they each took a seat in one of the stylish and ergonomic Bruno Mathsson armchairs. On the diminutive table between them stood a bowl of grapes and a clock.

Tell me why you're here.'

'I'm here because my colleague Eva Backman sent me.'

'Sent you?'

'Thought I ought to come.'

'But you didn't object to her suggestion?'

He thought about it.

'No.'

'Good. Can you tell me how you're feeling?'

'I think . . . I think I might be a bit depressed.'

'Depressed?'

'Yes.'

'How does that manifest itself?'

'I don't feel good.'

'I understand. I'm going to ask you a series of questions, the same as I ask everybody who comes to see me. It's to help me get a picture as quickly as I can of how you're feeling. You may not think all the questions are relevant, but it would be good if you could still answer them as honestly as you can. Is that all right for you?'

'Yes.'

'So you're feeling depressed?'

'I . . . I think so.'

'How long has it been like this?'

'Not that long. A few weeks, I suppose.'

'Are you eating properly?'

'Er . . . yes.'

'Breakfast, lunch and dinner?'

'Usually.'

'Alcohol? How much do you drink?'

'Not all that much.'

'All right. And how's your concentration?'

'Conecentration? I don't quite get . . .'

'Have you noticed yourself finding it hard to focus properly? Hard to make decisions?'

He pondered. 'Well yes, I have, actually. I'm not as sharp as usual.'

'Has this got worse recently?'

'I think so.'

'OK. Any problems sleeping?'

'Not as such. Though . . .'

'Yes?'

'Though I did sleep badly last night.'

She wrote something on her pad and he couldn't suppress a yawn.

'Has anything happened lately that you can link to your not feeling so good?'

He nodded. 'Yes, a thing or two. Maybe you read the papers?'

She allowed herself a brief smile. 'Yes, but not *Expressen*.'

'But you've been informed?'

'Yes. And you connect this reporter incident with not feeling good?'

He gave a shrug. 'He didn't make me feel any better, that's for sure. And besides . . .'

'Yes?'

'I didn't hit him, I just gave him a little push to get him out of the door.'

'And the headlines turned that into assault?'

'Yes.'

'You must have lost your temper with him, even so. Do you feel that's been happening more readily of late?'

'I don't think so. I consider losing one's temper with the tabloid press to be a healthy sign.'

'Why is that?'

'Because things are as they are.'

'How do you mean?'

He thought briefly and then found the words.

'They're infantilizing the whole population. Them and the reality TV shows. We'll have nothing but morons in this country within twenty years.'

She gave another smile and he assumed she was with him on that point.

'What's more, they set themselves up as prosecutors, judges and whippers-in, all in one big jumble.'

'I can agree with a fair bit of that,' said Olltman. 'But something more acute happened today, didn't it?'

'Yes.'

'And what was that?'

He cleared his throat and shifted in his chair. 'I don't know what happened. It all just went, kind of . . . black. And then I couldn't move. It's hard for me to describe.'

'Where were you?'

'At home. I was sitting at my kitchen table.'

'Having breakfast?'

'No . . . no, I'd just read a letter.'

'A letter?'

'Yes. You're bound by professional confidentiality?'

'Of course.'

'To everyone and in all contexts?'

'Yes.'

'Are you familiar with these murders that have been committed in Kymlinge recently?'

'Roughly speaking, yes.'

'Are you aware, too, that the murderer writes letters saying who he intends to kill?'

'So I understand.'

'I received another one of those letters this morning. I think that was what triggered . . . whatever it was that happened.'

'I see. You received a letter telling you to expect another murder?'

'Yes.'

'Anything else?'

'Yes. We've just had two other victims confirmed, from Gothenburg. We have four people dead . . . plus this fifth one in my letter today. That's a lot.'

She nodded thoughtfully, stroking her cheek with one finger. He found himself wondering what sort of age she was. Between fifty-five and sixty, presumably, but because she was so slenderly built, she could pass for considerably younger. At least from a slight distance.

And she *was* at a slight distance, sitting a metre and a half from him. He could see he had rattled her. Of course, he wasn't a standard patient, he realized that; here he sat, rabbiting on about five dead bodies as if it was the most normal thing in the world, and they weren't figments of his imagination, either. This was real, it was actual. And yet . . . and yet it wasn't about those dead people, he thought, just at that moment, it was actually about him. Temporarily suspended Detective Inspector Gunnar Barbarotti. He somehow felt he had to keep reminding himself of this at regular intervals.

'Can you tell me in a bit more detail how it felt when this happened, at the kitchen table?'

He went through it again for her. He didn't feel he was finding the right words, but she listened and nodded as if she understood, some of it at least. Or maybe she was just trying to encourage him?

'What did the letter say? You needn't give me chapter and verse of course, but was it different from those you'd read before? You've had . . . how many is it now?'

'Five in all. This was the fifth. Yes, it was a bit different.'

'In what way?'

'For one thing, he said it was the last letter, and there was only one more person left to murder . . . and for another, it felt as if he was addressing me more directly than before.'

'I don't really understand what you mean.'

'Sorry. It was just that for a moment I got the impression it was my turn next.'

'That he intended to kill you?'

'Yes, though I'm sure that isn't the case. And it wasn't obvious at the time, either. But it just came washing over me, and . . . well, then my colleague indicated the possibility. Or at least I thought that's what she was doing.'

'That all seems a bit unclear.'

'And so it is, but nonetheless, that was the thought that brought on my paralysis.'

'Paralysis? Do you think that's a good expression for the way you felt?'

He thought about it.

'Yes, that feels pretty right to me.'

More nodding, as if she was discreetly rewarding him for giving several right answers in a row.

'Are you finding it painful to talk about this?'

'Not particularly. I . . . I have confidence in you.'

'Thank you. But there is one other thing I've got to ask you . . . to go back to your feelings of depression. Have you ever felt so depressed that you've considered taking your own life?'

'No,' said Barbarotti.

'Now or previously?'

'No, I don't think it would ever occur to me.'

'You've never had any thought of that kind?'

'No.'

'Let's look at your situation more generally. Are there other factors that you think might be playing some role in your feeling down? Things that have happened in your life recently?'

He took a long time to answer, but she didn't rush him. She just sat there calmly, not moving, leaning back in her armchair, her right leg crossed over her left, waiting patiently. He thought that was a quality he admired, patience. Maybe because he didn't possess very much of it himself.

'Hrrm, yes,' he said finally. 'There are a few things, when I come to think about it. Though I don't normally think about it.'

She gave another of her fleeting smiles.

'No, we don't always think about things,' she said. 'But perhaps it's time now. Can you tell me what's been having a negative impact on you recently?'

'My daughter, for one,' he said.

'And what about your daughter?'

'She's left home. She's nineteen, finished upper secondary last summer, and now she lives in London and has got together with some shaggy musician.'

'A shaggy musician?'

'I don't know, I've never seen him.'

'But you're worried about it?'

'Yes.'

'Very worried?'

'Worried as hell. I've been divorced for nearly six years. Sara's been living with me since my wife and I separated, and I miss her. I've got two sons as well, but they live in Denmark with their mother and her new guy.'

'So you have a closer relationship with Sara than with your sons?'

'Yes.'

'How long is Sara staying in London?'

He gave a shrug. 'Who can say? I mean I know she's left home, I get that, but I'm worried about her. I suppose she's going to come back to study at some stage, this is one of those gap years they like to give themselves these days. It's nothing out of the ordinary, I realize all parents go through this.'

'Have you been over to see her?'

'Planning to go in September.'

'Good. My son pushed off to Geneva after he finished upper secondary. I was worried too, but once I'd seen him in his new surroundings, it passed.'

'It's worse with girls.'

'I can see that. But I think it would be good for you to see her in her new habitat. Are there any other things worrying you?'

He ate three grapes before answering her.

'I've proposed to this woman, but I'm scared she's going to say no.'

'Ah? Have you known her long?'

'About a year.'

'And you want to marry her?'

'Why else would I have proposed?'

'OK. And she lives here in Kymlinge?'

'Helsingborg. She lives in Helsingborg.'

'I see. And when did you propose?'

'A week ago. She was meant to be giving me her answer today, but now an official complaint's been lodged against me for punching a reporter from *Expressen*, she's put it off until Saturday.

Dr Olltman looked surprised, then she changed legs.

Crossed the left over the right instead, and appeared to be considering.

'Are there any other negative elements in your life?'

'The fight with the reporter wasn't good. People think I'm a police bully.'

'Mhmm?'

'I've been suspended from work.'

'You're not working on the case any more?'

'No.'

'More? Is there anything more?'

'I don't know if I really want to be a police officer any more. I . . . I'm sitting there on my own in my bloody flat, feeling like a pig on tarmac.'

She gave a laugh. 'A pig on tarmac, I haven't heard that one before.'

'Nor me, it just came to me. Though I've no real idea whether pigs are unhappy on tarmac or not. I know hardly anything about pigs.'

'That makes two of us.'

He could see she was finding it hard not to burst out laughing, but then she took a deep breath and assumed a serious expression. She quietly watched him with her intensely blue eyes. Interesting that it's possible still to have such blue eyes at that age, he thought. They look more as though they belong in the skull of an eighteen year old.

'So if I can just summarize for a moment,' she said, stretching a little in her seat, 'a variety of things have exercised a negative influence on your life in recent months. Your daughter's left home. You feel lonely and aren't happy with your job. You've found a new woman, but you're not sure whether she really wants to live with you. You're receiving strange letters from a murderer. You've been reported to the police for hitting a reporter and you've been suspended from work. Have I got that more or less right?'

He toyed with adding that he kept wondering about the meaning of life, but decided to leave it. 'Yes, I suppose that's right, by and large,' he said.

She smiled and the blue in her eyes seemed to spill over a little. 'Do you find it so surprising that you're not feeling good . . . in the circumstances?'

He considered this. 'No, you're probably right. But it would still be nice if something could be done about it.'

'We can always try. If you were to weigh up all these things, which one would you say was worst?'

'Marianne,' he said instantly. 'Or Sara . . . though Sara's sort of out of my reach.'

'She's got to be allowed to live her own life?'

'I assume so.'

'But Marianne is the woman you've proposed to?'

'Yes.'

'And she's going to give you her answer on Saturday?'

'I hope so.'

'What's the worst thing that could happen?'

'Her saying no, of course.'

Dr Olltman folded her hands. 'But if she says yes, then you could live with all the rest?'

'Yes . . . ?'

'The murderer's letters and the *Expressen* reporter and the unsatisfactory work situation . . .'

'Yes, in that case I could live with them.'

'Good,' said Dr Olltman. 'I think I understand the way things are for you. If I signed you off sick for two weeks and we met for another session on Friday, how would that sound to you? Same time?'

'No medication?'

'We'll wait and see after Saturday. But I want you to take this form home with you and fill it in this evening or tomorrow. It's a sort of scale for estimating how you feel. It'll take ten to fifteen minutes but it's important that you sit down quietly somewhere and take it seriously. Then we can look at the results together on Friday, if that's all right with you?'

She handed over a stapled sheaf of paper. He took it, rolled it into a tube and put it in his jacket pocket.

'And I want you to ring me at once if you feel it's all too much for you. Or if you find yourself suffering from those acute symptoms again. My mobile number is on the last page of the form. How are you feeling now?'

'Like a pig in a muddy puddle.'

She laughed again. At least I've put her in a good mood, thought Inspector Barbarotti.

'One more thing,' she said when they were already back in the waiting room. 'If you've a good friend you could go and stay with for the next few days, I really would recommend it.'

'I'll think about it.'

'See you on Friday, then.'

'Yeah, see you.'

They shook hands and parted.

24

By the time he got back home it was already three thirty. His mobile had been switched off for almost three hours, but when he put it back on there was only one message. No irate lead investigators. No journalists. My five minutes of fame, thought Barbarotti.

The message was from Eva Backman and she said he was welcome to ring if he felt like it. He made some coffee and took his cup out onto the balcony before he called her.

'How are you?' she wanted to know.

Judging the time was not right for another pig metaphor, Barbarotti said he was OK, considering.

'I'm afraid I won't be able to come this evening after all,' she said.

'Are Ville and the kids on their way home?'

'No. Jonnerblad insists we work overtime. Until nine, probably later.'

'It doesn't matter. I couldn't find your lobster, anyway. Does this mean you're getting somewhere, then?'

'Can I ring you back in half an hour, I've got somebody to interview in five seconds' time.'

Barbarotti told her that was fine, went to get his half-finished crossword and drank the rest of his coffee. He was aware of still not really feeling at ease in his own head, and by the end of ten minutes, he hadn't solved a single clue.

He also felt a slight sense of irritation creeping over him. Why was he staring at a crossword like some prematurely retired archivist? Why wasn't he at police HQ interviewing suspects, too? How much longer were they going to exclude him from the investigation?

He was aware that he probably already had the answer to this last question, Dr Olltman having signed him off sick for a fortnight. Had they cooked it up between them, she and Jonnerblad? No, he didn't really think a crude conspiracy like that seemed very likely. But who knew how things would look in two weeks' time? What with one thing and another.

Best take one day at a time, one minute even; that's how life ticks by, after all, in seconds and minutes, even if it isn't something one thinks of very often. Because we don't usually have time for fundamental reflections like that. But the swallow drawing a line in the sky is actually doing it right now, not yesterday or tomorrow.

Though just now . . . just now, the swallow had disappeared, he noted a little ruefully . . . and what mattered was Eva Backman getting to the end of her interview, picking up the phone and making sure he was kept in the loop.

Everything else was unnecessary waiting, and everything has its time.

'What did Jonnerblad say about the letter?'

'You mean the fact that it'd been opened?'

'Yes.'

'Not much. I explained the situation.'

'Explained the situation?'

'Yes.'

She left it at that and after brief consideration, he did too. There were presumably more pressing matters to discuss.

'Well?' he said. 'Are you going to update me or not?'

For a split second, he got the feeling that she was about to say no. That she was about to obey some kind of order and say she was sorry, but . . . but Barbarotti's temporary suspension and sick leave meant he wasn't allowed access to any case information.

But Eva Backman was not that kind of officer. 'Yes, things are moving,' she said. 'We've come up with a find or two.'

'Such as?'

'Such as some snaps of the Malmgrens. They're pretty interesting, actually.'

'Yes?'

'Well, to be exact, there are seven photos that seem relevant – they were in one of their albums. You want to hear?'

'You damn well bet I do.'

'OK then. Our current thinking is that they were taken in summer 2002, but we're not entirely sure. Typical holiday snaps, you could say, about twenty of them, all from the same holiday, but it's these seven that are of interest.'

'Why's that?'

'Because the others are just scenery. Henrik Malmgren standing against a backdrop of blue sea, on his own, Katarina Malmgren sitting on a big boulder, on her own . . . you know the sort of thing.'

'I don't want to know why the rest aren't of any interest. I want to know why those seven *are*.'

'You sound almost your old self,' observed Eva Backman. 'Well, these seven shots include other people. And unless we're barking up completely the wrong tree, we think we've been able to identify two of them. Are you following?'

Gunnar Barbarotti nodded, which of course Eva Backman could scarcely have seen over the phone.

'We're talking about Anna Eriksson and Erik Bergman.'

'What? Anna and . . . ? I mean, both of them?'

'Yessir. Anna Eriksson and Erik Bergman. And the Malmgrens. We have all four victims in the same photograph. What do you reckon to that?'

'Well I'll be—'

'No swearing. Your prognostication was spot on – we found the link today. These four people clearly spent time together when they were on holiday some years ago . . . and probably only then, because neither Mr Bergman nor Ms Eriksson are in any of the other albums.'

'I see. And what did you say about the year in question?'

'We're guessing 2002, seeing as it says '2002 – 02' on the spine of the album. And going by seasons and so on. If they stuck their snaps in chronologically, this must have been summer 2002. We think, in fact we're pretty sure, that the pictures were taken in France.'

'France? Wasn't that Sorrysen's theory?'

Eva Backman paused for a drink of something. 'Yes, it was. Gerald's got a feather in his cap today. And that other photo he deduced that from, the one we thought might have been Erik Bergman and Anna Eriksson on a bench, seems to have come from the same roll of film. Perhaps the Malmgrens sent it to her.'

She went quiet and he could hear her leafing through some papers.

'Four victims on a holiday trip,' he said. 'Well I'll be damned. OK then, how are you taking this forward?'

'It's a bit complicated,' Backman explained. 'It isn't just that quartet on the seven photos. There are a few other people, too.'

'Other people?'

'Yes. And we can't really tell if they're members of the gang, so to speak. But we're starting to have some idea . . . the pictures were taken on three separate occasions. At a restaurant, a boules pitch in a park – that's another reason we've fixed on France – and a cliff overlooking the sea. Could be a lake, but it must be a pretty big one if so, and it doesn't seem particularly likely, bearing in mind that the sea is in quite a few of the other shots—'

'These other people,' Barbarotti interrupted, 'what can you tell me about them?'

'I'm coming to that,' said Inspector Backman. 'That's the really interesting bit. Could any of them be the murderer? Is there anybody amongst them . . . ?'

' . . . called Gunnar?' supplied Barbarotti.

'It's hard to tell from a photograph whether somebody's called Gunnar,' Backman pointed out patiently. 'But we think we've found a way into the problem. There's one man who crops up in four of the shots, and in one of them he's got his arm round Anna Eriksson. So it could be that . . .'

'Anna Eriksson,' said Barbarotti. 'Good, I'm with you. So you're busy re-interviewing everyone who knew her?'

'We've just made a start,' said Eva Backman. 'The unfortunate truth is that people don't turn up at the police station simply because you think of them. But Astor Nilsson and I have just been talking to a girl, Linda Johansson, I don't know if you remember her . . . anyway, she claims Anna Eriksson was with some guy for a while, a few years back, and that he could be the one in the photos.'

'Uh huh? And?'

'She thinks his name is Gunnar, but she can't recall the surname.'

Gunnar Barbarotti digested this information.

'Not Barbarotti, at any rate?'

'No, this one looks a good ten years younger than you. A bit like Zlatan, actually.'

'Definitely not me then,' said Inspector Barbarotti. 'But it's pretty bloody vital for us to find him.'

'Thanks for the tip,' said Eva Backman. 'Well, that's all I've got for you for the moment. And I need to get back to work. Sure you got on OK at Olltman's?'

'It all went fine,' Barbarotti assured her again. 'She said it was important to my recovery for you to keep me informed like this.'

'I don't believe you.'

'That was how I interpreted what she said, at any rate,' said Barbarotti. 'Back to the grindstone you go, and ring me as soon as you get stuck.'

'Kiss me,' said Eva Backman.

'There's somebody else,' said Barbarotti.

It took an hour and three quarters to prepare the langoustines and scallops according to Dobrowolski's instructions – and barely ten minutes to consume them.

When one was eating alone, anyway. The wine, on the other hand, lasted rather longer; once he had put everything into the dishwasher he took the bottle and the glass onto the balcony; the weather had been grey all day, with intermittent showers, but now, with the time approaching nine, the western sky suddenly laid on a magnificent sunset. He decided to refrain from ringing Backman again to ask how things were going, although his fingers itched to do it. So he solemnly and unhurriedly drank up the whole bottle of wine instead. He found himself wishing he hadn't given up smoking twelve years before; a cigarette or two would have fitted the bill perfectly, with his balcony bathed in apocalyptic light under purple-coloured clouds, illuminated from beneath by a sun no longer visible above the horizon. You almost expected a ladder to be lowered from Heaven, thought Barbarotti – and a host of chubby cherubs arrayed in gold to appear with harps and assorted other blissful attributes. What was that over-the-top painting tradition . . . the Düsseldorf School, wasn't it?

Rather pleased with this excursion into art history, he turned his thoughts to darker topics.

Very much darker – black expressionism, you might say. Four people had been killed. Four people who had met on a holiday in France in . . . what had Backman said . . . 2002?

And this, this holiday, was supposedly the background to them being robbed of their lives, five years later? Murdered one after another by a perpetrator who also amused himself by sending letters to a detective inspector in Kymlinge to announce the names of those he was going to kill?

Why?

He sipped his wine. This particular *why* had not diminished in size in the light of the link that had now emerged, Barbarotti felt. Not in the slightest.

But there were now various new questions to ask, questions of a different nature.

How had they met, for example? These four and their murderer. Had they all left Sweden together? Or only happened across each other once they were down in France?

Could it have been some kind of package holiday?

He pondered. The package holiday idea did not seem far-fetched, and in that case there must be quite a few other people in possession of information about this quartet doomed to die five years later.

Say it had been a coach trip; Barbarotti on his part would never have chosen that method for seeing the world, but he knew some people favoured it. Not just for going to the theatre in Stockholm or on a glassworks tour of Småland. You could go to Rome and Lisbon. Lake Garda and Amsterdam and Lord knows where else.

Fifty people in a coach. Ten or fifteen days in mainland Europe. Something happens and somebody decides to take the law into their own hands.

Five years later. Why on earth? thought Gunnar Barbarotti, swallowing a mouthful of wine. And incidentally, why keep referring to a quartet when it now seemed to be a quintet? There was no doubt that this Gunnar – who had mercifully turned out not to be himself – was an obvious candidate for the death list. Which could mean there were six people caught up in this whole tangle. Five victims and a perpetrator.

Or even more? Perhaps not – the letter writer had maintained Gunnar would be the last to die, so hopefully he would stop at five. Bad enough, definitely bad enough.

But what about Hans Andersson? Extremely unclear, thought Barbarotti. For there to be someone else involved, someone the murderer initially intended to kill but then decided to let go . . . well, that would be a very odd strategy indeed. If this Hans Andersson really were part of the French gang, wouldn't that mean – if nothing else – he would be able to identify the murderer? Always assuming he existed at all.

Wouldn't it? thought Barbarotti, and at that moment a vast cloud of jackdaws came sweeping in over the balcony and made him lose his thread. Should have a pen and paper, he thought. Should try to be a bit more systematic.

Should put my poor head to something else entirely, he thought once the jackdaws had swept off out of sight. I am no longer part of this investigation.

He drank yet more wine and checked the time. Twenty past nine. Maybe Backman would have finished for the day by now? Maybe he could give her a ring after all?

But he decided not to. He went inside instead and found the evaluation sheet Olltman had given him. Came back out to the summer evening and the last glass of wine.

One question, he thought, one question they had to find an answer to, and soon.

Who this Gunnar was. Because there were most certainly indicators that things didn't look very good for him.

Then he leant back in his chair and looked at the first page of the form.

Department of Clinical Neuroscience, Psychiatry Section, Karolinska Medical University, it said at the top.

I've become a case study for medical science, thought Gunnar Barbarotti, getting out his pen. Mum would have been proud of me.

But as he sat there trying to diagnose his supposed soul – broken down into such concepts as zest for life, feelings of anxiety, mood, ability to concentrate and emotional commitment – the apocalyptic sky darkened to a shade that reminded him of coagulated blood, a cold gust of wind blew in over the balcony rail and that morning's moment with the murderer's letter at the kitchen table came creeping back into his mind.

Thanks for your involvement?

Gunnar?

He suddenly realized he had gone cold all over.

25

On his way out to Axel Wallman's on Thursday morning, he stopped for provisions at the ICA Basunen supermarket in Kymlingevik and caught sight of the headlines:

NEXT VICTIM'S NAME IS GUNNAR
POLICE POWERLESS TO ACT

said one.

GUNNAR
YOU'RE A DEAD MAN

declared the other.

Well look at that, thought Barbarotti. He's roped them both in this time. Wants to be in the limelight for his finale, evidently.

He realized he had forgotten to ask Inspector Backman how the interview with Göran Persson had gone. Whether the latter had doggedly persevered in his refusal to reveal his source, or whether it was simply that he didn't know. It seemed reasonable to assume that the latter was the case. The infantilization wing of the press had a lot to answer for, but supporting murderers was presumably a bit much even for them.

Though of course it would still be useful to know how the perpetrator was contacting them. Was he doing it by letter, as he was with the police, or did he use some other method for the fourth estate, as the mass media was called in democracies with slightly wider scope than Sweden's.

Barbarotti made a mental note to raise the matter with Backman when she gave him her next briefing. If things turned out as he hoped, she would come out to Wallman's cottage that evening – he hadn't spoken to her, only texted and received a sort of promise in reply, but of course you could never be sure. The unihockey gang might arrive home or Jonnerblad might insist on another evening shift; both of these seemed on the cards. But anyway, he could ring her tomorrow and ask.

He didn't buy any of them, not *Aftonbladet*, nor *GT* nor *Expressen*. The hell I will, he thought. Not another krona into keeping that scandal factory going.

Then he bought food and beer, enough for Inspector Backman as well, if she plucked up the courage. While he was in the store, two separate reporters called to propose an extended interview so he could give his view of things – one of them made noises about financial remuneration – but he declined as the usual matter of course. He realized he would be rising in the charts again as a result of Dead Man Gunnar.

In the twenty minutes it took him to drive out to Wallman's, the phone rang another three times, but he didn't bother to answer it. Merely checked it wasn't Inspector Backman or Marianne trying to contact him, and it wasn't.

Axel Wallman hadn't altered appreciably over the last four days. Under his dungarees he now sported an orange T-shirt, but that was about all.

'What are you doing here?' he wanted to know.

'I rang, didn't I?' said Barbarotti. 'You said you'd be happy to see me.'

'I remember that,' said Axel Wallman.

'Well of course you do, it was only two hours ago.'

'Don't interrupt. I said I'd be happy to see you, but that presumably doesn't rule out my asking you what you're doing here? Correct me if I'm wrong, Saarikoski?'

The dog thumped its tail twice. 'He says I'm right,' interpreted Wallman. 'So, what brings you here? We can have a beer while we get to the bottom of this.'

They opened a beer each and sat down on the plastic chairs. Barbarotti remembered that one of Dr Olltman's questions had been whether he consumed much alcohol, and he raised the can to his lips with a slight feeling of guilt. It was only quarter past eleven in the morning, distinctly on the early side for a drink.

But things were as they were. 'It's been rather heavy going,' he said, 'these past few days.'

'Serves you right,' said Wallman. 'And your murderer's still on the loose, I gather?'

Barbarotti nodded.

'Oughtn't you to be out looking for him instead of lazing around here, drinking beer?'

'I'm suspended,' said Barbarotti.

'That's a concept I'm familiar with,' said Wallman. 'Back when I was still working, I was often suspended. It's nothing to mope over.'

'Thanks,' said Barbarotti. 'And I'm not moping. But I don't feel that great. I've been to see a psychiatrist. You're familiar with those too, I expect?'

'Seen quite a few,' confirmed Axel Wallman. 'The trouble with them is they're incurable, the whole lot. I made one perfect diagnosis after another, but it made no damn difference. And they didn't pay my bills, either.'

'Life isn't easy,' said Barbarotti.

'So you've come to me and Saarikoski for some peace of mind?' said Axel Wallman, scratching his armpits. 'On your doctor's advice . . . well, that could mean he's a wise man after all. On the rubbish heap, we're all the same. Small and insignificant, I grant you, but all the same.'

'It's a woman,' said Barbarotti. 'My doctor, that is.'

'Yikes,' said Wallman. 'Did I tell you I was a virgin?'

'You did mention it, yes.'

'Nothing's changed on that front since Sunday.'

Barbarotti reflected for a moment.

'I think I'll go for a walk,' he said. 'I could do with a bit of exercise. There's a track along by the lake in that direction, isn't there?'

'Well there was yesterday, at any rate,' said Wallman. 'Though we've decided to skip our walk today, Saarikoski and I. So you'll have to manage by yourself.'

'I'll do my best,' said Gunnar Barbarotti.

After about half an hour, when he had gone a good way round the edge of the lake and worked up a bit of a sweat, his phone buzzed in his pocket. An incoming text message. Just another reporter trying to winkle out the truth, thought Barbarotti, but he stopped and checked the message anyway.

Thinking of you. Marianne.

Marianne, thought Inspector Barbarotti. She's thinking of me. Wow, thank you God!

He sank down onto a rock on the shore of the lake. A sudden feeling of fatigue swept over him. It wasn't at all like what he had felt at the kitchen table, but put him more in mind of . . . of champagne? It was all over in three seconds, however. *Thinking of you.* Imagine three words carrying such weight. A flock of Canada geese – carrying quite a bit of weight themselves – were sitting there sunning themselves just a few metres from him, but his presence didn't seem to bother them. The least of these my brethren, thought Barbarotti. Got to answer, this is crunch time. A few well chosen words and my soul is safely in port.

It took him a good while to compose his message. Finally he keyed it in with trembling fingers.

As I am of you. Gunnar.

He was content with the result of his deliberations. No big words; little words expressing big thoughts are better than the other way round, his Swedish teacher had always tried to impress on them in class. (Understatement is more effective than hyperbole in virtually all phases of life, remember that everybody!) He took the opportunity of sending a grateful thought in her direction now.

Then he stayed on his rock for a while, pondering the remarkable choreography of existence, pondering that form he had completed on his balcony the night before, and the bumpy road he had travelled to his present position in life's system of coordinates, and Marianne – and whether there would be another incoming buzz.

But there wasn't. Oh well, thought Gunnar Barbarotti, I'm happy enough with what I've got. I've put that bit of distance between myself and the valley of the shadow of death, and one can't ask too much. He got to his feet and set off back to Axel Wallman's shack.

Inspector Backman called at around five to tell him she hoped to show up in a couple of hours' time. Barbarotti instantly started firing off his battery of accumulated questions, but she interrupted him and said he would just have to wait until they met face to face. There was quite a lot to tell him, the day had been far from wasted as far as the investigation went, but how was he doing himself? And was she really going to have to make the acquaintance of that weirdo Wallman?

'Yes, he's part of the package,' admitted Barbarotti. 'For today, at any rate. I'm spending the night here, but you needn't. Fresh air and invigorating forest walks, these are the leaves from which I shall weave my cure.'

'Poetic.'

'Yes, but a quotation, unfortunately. But be that as it may, I can't think of anything better . . . though actually, my brain's been in touch, and tells me it could do with something to get its teeth into.'

'I can supply plenty of that,' promised Eva Backman. 'And you haven't had any more attacks?'

'Not even a whisker of one,' said Barbarotti.

'Welcome to Paradise Scrapheap, lovely lady,' said Axel Wallman, making the effort when she finally put in an appearance just after seven thirty. 'I prefer women police officers, just as I prefer women priests.'

Barbarotti had prepared her for Axel Wallman, as far as he possibly could.

'Thank you,' was her simple reply. 'Is dinner ready then, as I was promised?'

'But of course,' said Barbarotti.

'You're married, I suppose?' said Wallman.

'Big beefy husband and three kids,' said Backman.

'I'm single myself,' said Wallman.

'I guessed that,' said Backman.

'How the hell could you guess that?'

'My feminine intuition.'

'That's what terrifies me,' said Wallman. 'You women, you have this way of seeing straight through a person. You're a mystery to me. How does it feel, being so mysterious?'

They spent about an hour eating and chatting, including a rendition of a couple of fairly short poems by their host, and then he and Saarikoski withdrew, leaving the two DIs in peace on the verandah. Backman produced a file from her briefcase, and this time it was blue.

'First of all, congratulations,' she said.

'What for?' asked Barbarotti.

'You're no longer suspected of a crime. *Expressen* withdrew its complaint. In principle, you can come back to work first thing tomorrow.'

'Good,' said Barbarotti. 'Though as I understand it, I'm signed off sick. What's all this about the press and their sources? I saw the newsstands on my way out here.'

'They told us the way it happened,' said Backman. '*Expressen* and *Aftonbladet*, both of them. He sent *them* letters, too.'

'Handwritten, left-handed?'

'No, these weren't, actually. They'd been printed out on a

standard printer. They were sent to a named reporter at each paper, Göran Persson and Henning Clausson respectively. But they apparently can't be traced back. In this latest instance, identical copies were sent to each paper, about half an A4 page . . . have you read what they wrote?'

Gunnar Barbarotti shook his head.

'Well, forget it. I think I can safely say we've found the relevant Gunnar though, and that's the main thing. We've been talking to friends and acquaintances of Anna Eriksson all day, and they confirm she had a relationship with a guy called Gunnar Öhrnberg.'

'Öhrnberg?'

'Yes. They were together for most of 2002, evidently. They never lived under the same roof, but were considered a couple even so . . . from March to sometime just before Christmas, it seems. He lived in Borås at the time, and she was here in Kymlinge. And they went to France together that summer, somewhere in Brittany. She sent cards to a couple of her friends, and one of them's postmarked Quimper.'

'Excellent,' said Barbarotti.

'Yes, and our witnesses in Gothenburg claim the Malmgrens were somewhere in Brittany too, that summer . . . five years ago, that is.'

'Brittany,' said Gunnar Barbarotti. 'Have you been there?'

'No,' said Eva Backman. 'Have you?'

He nodded. 'I have, actually. Impressive scenery, quite wild, amazing cliffs . . . seafood paradise. Hydrangeas everywhere, with enormous blooms that look like cauliflowers. We were there once, before the boys were born, early nineties, just Helena, Sara and me . . . go on.'

Eva Backman leafed through her file. 'There were a couple

of pictures of Gunnar Öhrnberg in Anna Eriksson's album, too, but we didn't know then . . . including a nude shot.'

'You said you'd found him.'

'Depends what you mean by found. We know most of what there is to know about him: he's thirty-seven and lives in Hallsberg these days, works as a teacher at an upper secondary called Avenue School, history and social studies. Term started on Monday, well just for the staff . . . but I'm afraid he didn't turn up.'

'Didn't turn up?' repeated Barbarotti.

'No, he didn't. And in fact, it seems nobody's seen him for the past week.'

'You mean . . . ?'

She stared out into the darkness for a few moments before answering him.

'It seems there are grounds for suspicion, yes. He's got no family. He'd been away travelling during the summer holidays, apparently. Particularly the west coast. He's a diving instructor too, based at a place called Kungshamn. But he came home to Hallsberg at the start of August, we know that for sure. A couple of us are going up there tomorrow to check over his flat . . . Jonnerblad said you could tag along if you felt like it.'

'Who's going?'

'Me and Astor Nilsson. Some forensics officers from the Örebro force are meeting us up there.'

Barbarotti thought about it for two seconds.

'OK,' he said. 'I've got a date with my psychiatrist, but I'll cancel it.'

'I'd be very glad personally to have you along.'

'Thanks,' said Barbarotti. 'You're a great cop. If a bit soft . . . anything else?'

She gave a laugh. 'Well, there's been a lot of discussion about whether the Gothenburg force should take over the investigation, or thc whole thing should be passed to the National CID. But as we've already got people from both of those helping us out, Sylvenius decided we're going to carry on as we are. Though we've had to rely on more help from Gothenburg with the Malmgrens, of course.'

'Excellent. You can't change the line-up mid-match. What about the husband, by the way, has he surfaced anywhere?'

'Mine?'

'No, not yours. Henrik Malmgren, I mean.'

'Ah. No, he hasn't surfaced. Neither has mine, as a matter of fact.'

'I see. And those photos, I assume you've got them with you?'

Eva Backman took a pile of papers out of the folder. 'They're not the originals, you'll have to make do with scanned copies. But they're just as sharp.'

She spread them out on the table. Barbarotti leant forward and started studying them.

There were seven of them, as she'd said. Seven holiday snaps, a bit amateurish, a couple of them slightly out of focus. Format ten by fifteen centimetres. Unless anyone had accidentally shrunk or enlarged them in the scanning process.

Three of them – and the focus of these was relatively sharp – showed the outdoor seating area of a restaurant. In the middle of the day, judging by the light. People round a table, others in the background. A climbing plant in flower against a wall. Without a moment's hesitation he identified four of the individuals. They were the four victims: Erik Bergman, Anna Eriksson, Henrik and Katarina Malmgren.

'Which one's Gunnar Öhrnberg? Him?'

He pointed to a physically fit-looking man in his thirties, with dark hair and a prominent nose. He remembered what she had said about Zlatan Ibrahimović. She nodded.

He checked the other pictures. Gunnar Öhrnberg featured in four of them in total, but there was only one in which the entire quintet appeared, and that was one of the restaurant pictures. It was also the only one in which Katarina and Henrik Malmgren could be seen together.

'It was their camera . . . wasn't it? The Malmgrens', I mean.'

Eva Backman shrugged her shoulders. 'We think so.'

'There's a sixth person here, a guy in the restaurant and boules pitch shots.'

Backman nodded and checked her watch. 'The sixth man, yeah.'

Gunnar Barbarotti raised a quizzical eyebrow.

'That's what we're calling him. Know what, Gunnar, I've been staring at these photos all day. If we're driving up to Hallsberg tomorrow, I could do with a good night's kip. I'll leave you to pore over them and draw your own conclusions in peace and quiet. Then we can discuss them in the car tomorrow. Is that OK for you?'

'Yep,' said Barbarotti. 'What time are we leaving?'

'Eight o'clock from police HQ. Are you really going to sleep here tonight? I mean . . . *here*?'

'It'll be fine,' said Barbarotti. 'I shared a flat with this lout for three years. I'll be there at eight sharp tomorrow morning.'

Eva Backman studied him for a few seconds with a deep frown, then she got to her feet and went off into the darkness. He heard her start the car, saw the cones of light from her headlights briefly rake the trees as she backed round, and thirty seconds later, silence again reigned supreme over Paradise Scrapheap.

26

He decided it wouldn't hurt to be a bit more systematic. He got a pen and a notepad from the briefcase he had with him and numbered the seven photos. The restaurant pictures ended up as 4 and 5, the cliffs 6 and 7.

Thoroughness is a virtue, he thought. Picture by picture, there's a murderer hidden here somewhere.

Picture 1

Setting: Restaurant, outside tables. Small group of people round a table. Wall with climbing plant. Plates of food, wine bottles and glasses on the table.

Time: Day.

People: Erik Bergman, Anna Eriksson, Gunnar Öhrnberg, Henrik Malmgren, Katarina Malmgren.

Taken by: Unclear. Could be the Sixth Man?

Comments: Some other restaurant patrons visible in the background, plus half a waiter in black and white. Everyone round the table looking into the camera except Anna Eriksson who seems to be staring at something above the photographer's head. All smiling like you do when you know a picture's being taken, looking a bit strained. Empty chair on the right of the table nearest the camera, could be the photographer's?

Picture 2

Setting: The same restaurant. Time: A bit later. Coffee cups on the table.

People: Erik Bergman, Anna Eriksson, Gunnar Öhrnberg, all sitting along the left-hand side of the table, same positions as in Picture 1.

Taken by: Henrik or Katarina Malmgren. Or the Sixth Man. The picture is taken from their side of the table.

Comments: They are unaware of being photographed. Erik Bergman is looking to the right at something outside the shot. Gunnar Öhrnberg is lighting a cigarette for Anna Eriksson. The hand and half the lower arm of someone else, probably male, visible in the bottom right-hand corner. An unknown woman is standing behind Erik Bergman, leaning forward slightly, but is presumably not a member of the group.

Picture 3

Setting: The same.

Time: Roughly as in picture 2.

People: Henrik Malmgren, the Sixth Man, Gunnar Öhrnberg.

Taken by: Katarina Malmgren?

Comments: Picture taken sideways, from the end of the table.

None of the subjects seem aware of being photographed. Gunnar Öhrnberg is not on the same side of the table as the two other men, and looks to be leaning forward to say something to the Sixth Man.

Barbarotti took a break and stared out into the darkness. He tried to remember the title of a film he had once seen, a thriller – the whole thing revolved round identifying individuals in some old photos in order to find a murderer – but its name escaped him. He couldn't remember much else about the film, either, except that it involved enlarged, grainy pictures, faces of unfamiliar but significant people who stayed in the observer's mind. The enigmatic quality in the identity of a face, the strange process of something living being captured, forever a fixed point in the flow of time. It must have been at least twenty years since he saw the film, black and white if he remembered rightly, it could even have been a really old one.

He pushed these reflections aside and bent to his work again. His eyes homed in on the unknown figure, the sixth guest at the table. Picture 3 was undoubtedly the shot in which he could be seen best. A tall man of about thirty, quite tanned. A white, short-sleeved shirt, sunglasses pushed to the top of his head. Short hair, browny blonde, and a thin face with a few distinctive features: wide mouth, longish nose, regularly shaped jaw.

He looks, thought Inspector Barbarotti, he looks like just about anybody.

Anybody at all. He picked up his pen and his classification list again.

Picture 4

Setting: *A park.*

Time: *Early evening.*

People: *There are at least twenty people in the shot, most at some distance. A group of men playing boules, two elderly ladies chatting on a park bench, a shaggy dog nosing a tree trunk. In the foreground, 4–5m from the camera, Henrik Malmgren, Anna Eriksson and Erik Bergman are standing. Anna Eriksson is licking an ice cream. Henrik Malmgren is taking a drag on his cigarette.*

Taken by: *Katarina Malmgren?*

Comments: *On the left of the picture, the corner of a small building and the edge of a striped awning, which could be an ice-cream kiosk. The three group members could be waiting for the others to buy their ice creams. The picture is slightly out of focus.*

Picture 5

Setting: *The same park.*

Time: *Same time or soon afterwards.*

People: *Erik Bergman, Anna Eriksson, Gunnar Öhrnberg, Henrik Malmgren, the Sixth Man. They are in a row, watching the game of boules. Several boules players and a few other people are also in the shot.*

Taken by: *Katarina Malmgren?*

Comments: *This picture is not quite in focus either. Gunnar Öhrnberg's arm is round Anna Eriksson. There's a degree of uniformity about the men. All are wearing pale-coloured, short-sleeved shirts, knee-length shorts and sandals without socks. Fairly tanned, all in their thirties. Henrik Malmgren maybe stands out slightly, a bit shorter than the other three and the only one with glasses. Anna Eriksson is still holding an ice cream.*

Picture 6

Setting: Cliffs, a flat rock overlooking the sea.

Time: Day.

People: Anna Eriksson, Erik Bergman, Katarina Malmgren, all three in swimwear, sitting with their backs against the cliff and sunbathing.

Taken by: Henrik Malmgren?

Comments: Typical holiday photo. All have their eyes closed against the bright sun. They are sitting on straw mats, and towels and bags are visible at the bottom of the picture. The sea and horizon are in the background on the left-hand side. Erik Bergman and Anna Eriksson are wearing sunglasses, Katarina Malmgren has an open paperback in her hand.

Picture 7

Setting: The same as picture 6 but taken from further back.

Time: Day.

People: Erik Bergman, Anna Eriksson, Gunnar Öhrnberg, Katarina Malmgren. A few people are bathing in the sea. A sailing boat further out.

> Taken by: *Henrik Malmgren?*
>
> Comments: *Another typical holiday photo. There is sand at the foot of the rocks. The four are eating, and Anna Eriksson is looking at the camera, waving – her hand is blurred. Both women are in bikinis, different shades of red.*

And that was it. Gunnar Barbarotti put down his pen and ran his eyes over all seven photographs. He waved away a mosquito, who was late to the feast. What am I doing? he thought. Is it possible to glean anything from this? What happened to these people?

Justifiable questions, without a doubt. Especially the last one. He leant back and shut his eyes. He ruminated.

Behind every crime there was a story, and the trick was to lay it bare. That was the basic aim of virtually all detective work: exposing the preconditions. And *backwards*, always a backward movement, searching, feeling one's way towards the crucial period of time.

So in this case, unless all indications were mistaken: five people on a holiday trip to Brittany. In the summer of 2002 . . . it must be that summer, mustn't it? He had forgotten to ask Backman if the date had been confirmed. Two couples, it seemed: Henrik and Katarina Malmgren from Gothenburg, Anna Eriksson from Kymlinge and Gunnar Öhrnberg from Borås. And a fifth person: Erik Bergman from Kymlinge.

Plus a sixth? Who was that man? Gunnar Barbarotti opened his eyes. He leant over the photos and scrutinized them again. Number six was at the restaurant and at the boules park. But he wasn't in the photos on the cliffs. What did that signify?

Drivel, thought Gunnar Barbarotti, it doesn't signify anything in particular. Perhaps he'd just gone for swim at that point; pictures 6 and 7 could well have been taken only a few minutes apart.

It was hard, he thought as he ran his eyes over the photos on the table and then raised them to the dark lake and the strip of forest outlined against the slightly lighter sky on the far shore, it was hard to ask any kind of sensible question at all. That was just a fact. He had been away from the investigation for three days, and there must be lots of factors of which he was unaware.

Where? for example. Where in Brittany were these pictures taken? If friends and acquaintances of the Malmgrens knew they had gone on that holiday – isn't that what Backman had told him? – well then, surely the investigators had also been able to get more details? Loads of details. How had they travelled? By car or on some kind of package? What were the dates of their stay? Was there conceivably any link between the Malmgrens and Gunnar Öhrnberg? That question must surely have been pursued as far as was possible by now.

And as the link between the murders should presumably have been established by now, hopefully they would also have started on a fresh round of interviews with the friends and acquaintances of the first two victims.

And – again hopefully – they would have found out a useful thing or two.

This is daft, thought Gunnar Barbarotti. It's pointless indulging in this armchair speculation. I'm too many steps behind. Better to draw a line under it for tonight and get a proper update on the way to Hallsberg tomorrow.

He collected up the photographs and his notes, stuffing the

lot of them into his briefcase as he glanced at the time. Five past eleven – high time indeed.

He set the alarm on his mobile for half past six. Why not allow himself an early swim, as for once he happened to have a lake only twenty metres away?

And especially in view of the state of the guest bedding at Paradise Scrapheap. He found it hard to imagine Axel Wallman had bothered to change it since his last visit.

So that was how it would have to be: late to bed, early to rise.

And as for that murderer, wasn't it about time they brought him in?

FIVE

NOTES FROM MOUSTERLIN

8–9 July 2002

I fell asleep there in my lounger on the terrace, and was woken by Erik when he got home a couple of hours later.

'How's things?' he wanted to know.

I didn't really get what he was driving at. Was he just asking how I felt, or was he wondering if I intended to leave soon? Or perhaps he was alluding to how I had got on the previous night. I assumed the last of these, but chose to answer the first.

'Fine,' I said. 'A bit tired but OK otherwise.'

He stood there regarding me with a look on his face I hadn't seen from him before. As if he was only now realizing I was a more complex person than he had taken me to be. But then he's not used to trying to get inside other people's skins. Erik's very self-contained, and as he looked at me now, grinding his jaw as his eyes darted around, he gave the impression of being about to lose control of something – something he didn't normally feel a need to control, but had now found in his hands.

'They're standing us dinner tonight,' he said finally. 'Over at Thalamot in Beg-Meil. So we can discuss everything. So it all went to plan last night then?'

'Yes,' I replied. 'It went to plan.'

He sat down at the table. I got up from the lounger and looked at my watch. It was half past four. 'I'll go and have a shower,' I said. 'What time are we supposed to be there?'

'Eight o'clock,' said Erik. 'So we ought to leave here around half seven, I suppose.'

'Sounds good,' I said. 'And what exactly are we going to discuss?'

He looked at me in some confusion. 'Well isn't it obvious?' he said. 'We can't put all this behind us, just like that.'

'Oh, I see,' I said.

He said nothing for a while, and then lit a cigarette.

'What kind of person are you?' he said.

'I'm like everybody else, I think,' I replied. 'I don't understand what you mean.'

He took a few drags. 'Right,' he said. 'Well, I guess you'd know that best yourself. We'll say half past seven then, shall we?'

'Fine by me,' I said.

Le Thalamot was empty apart from a table of Germans having langoustines and mussels. The tourist season still hasn't really got going, even though we're into July; I assume it will look rather different here in a couple of weeks' time. On the beach, along the paths through the polders, in the restaurants and crêperies.

And at the campsites. But by then I shall be far away. I don't know exactly where – but south of here, at any event, I shall head south. I've had a feeling for a while now that I'd like to die by the Mediterranean, perhaps the Middle East, or why not Cairo or Alexandria? There's something about those latitudes that strikes a chord with me, though I'm not sure quite how it resonates or what it expresses, but then there's no need for us to understand everything. The important things are the route and our feelings, not the destination and the purpose.

The quartet had already arrived and was waiting for us at a long table at the back of the restaurant, by an open window that looked out over a garden, at a safe distance from the German party. I noted that all four of them had dressed up a bit for the occasion; the two ladies were wearing dresses I hadn't seen before, Anna's pale green and Katarina's red, and the gents were in freshly pressed short-sleeved cotton shirts. They had ordered a drink each and were taking cautious sips as Erik and I came in, and Gunnar and Henrik got to their feet when they saw us.

'Nice to see you both,' said Gunnar. 'Have a seat. Do you want a drink?'

Considering it was less than twenty-four hours since we had been cursing each other over the dead body of a girl, this all sounded excessively formal, and I realized different choreography applied tonight. Choreography that had been worked out and noted down in the course of the day's consultations, wherever they had taken place. I felt an ironic smile start to twitch inside me.

'Sure,' said Erik. 'Gin and tonic for me.'

I said a glass of white wine would do for me and we sat down. Erik between Anna and Henrik, and me between the two women. This, too, seemed to have been calculated in advance, though I couldn't quite see what was intended by it.

Once Erik and I had our drinks, we raised our glasses to each other. I couldn't see a smile on any of the others' faces, it was more a passing moment of solemn solidarity and community. Then we devoted a long time to ordering from the menu, with Katarina transmitting our words to the waiter as usual, and as we waited for the food to arrive we chatted about French wines, French cheeses, the days and months to avoid when eating seafood; the whole thing, I thought, was a replay – though duller, less slick and hopeful – of the conversation that had taken place at that first lunch in the old port in Bénodet. Ten days ago, if I was not much mistaken.

We also drank a good deal less wine, and ordered fish and meat instead of seafood, and it was only when we reached the dessert that Gunnar finally came to the point.

'We want to thank you,' he said, turning to me. 'Thank you for taking on such a very unpleasant task and completing it.'

He paused. I had no comment.

'That is, I assume you completed it in a satisfactory manner?'

I waited a few seconds. I could feel all their eyes on me. 'You want to know if I buried the girl properly?' I asked.

Gunnar and Henrik both looked round uneasily and it struck me that it was pretty unwise of them to have this discussion in a public place if they were so worried about outsiders hearing it.

'It's OK,' said Erik. 'Nobody here understands Swedish.'

'Do you want to know where?' I asked.

'No, no,' Gunnar hastened to say. 'Of course you needn't tell us that. But it feels important to us to know that everything went as planned.'

Planned? I thought.

'And that there's nothing we ought to know about,' Katarina chimed in.

I wondered what it was they really wanted. Were they just after some kind of general reassurance to make them feel safe, or was there more to it than that? But if so, I really had no conception of what it might be.

'It all went the way I'd imagined it,' I said. 'You can carry on drinking your wine in peace.'

'That's not what I mean,' said Gunnar. 'I just mean it's important for us to know this is over and done with now.'

'It is,' I said. 'All over and done with.'

'We've also got to be sure we're all singing from the same hymn sheet if the police turn up after all,' said Henrik. 'I mean to say, we're going to be down here for a couple more weeks, and . . .'

'How long are you staying?' Katarina asked me, attempting a smile.

'I'm leaving the day after tomorrow,' I said.

'On Wednesday,' said Gunnar. 'Excellent. But anyway, it's vital that we all deny categorically taking the girl out to the islands with us. Or seeing her that day at all, in fact. She spent a few hours with us one afternoon the previous week, but that was it. And that's all we need to remember.'

'How did you get on with the boat?' I asked.

'There were no problems about the boat,' said Henrik.

'Glad to hear it,' I said. 'Well, one girl more or less doesn't make much difference, I guess.'

I felt Anna give a start, sitting close beside me as she was, and I expected her to say something. But Gunnar raised a warning finger and gave her a look. It was enough, and she held her tongue. Anna had said very little all evening, in fact. The same went for Erik. It was Gunnar, Henrik and Katarina who did the talking, and presumably that was no coincidence.

It was only quarter to ten when we finished at the restaurant. Gunnar and Henrik shared the bill and we walked home along the bridleway between the polder and the steep bank down to the beach. Erik and I turned off to our place without any further ado and had a glass of Calvados on the terrace before we turned in, but we didn't seem to have much to talk about.

'Wednesday, then?' he said.

'Yes,' I said. 'I'll be heading off in the morning.'

'Probably just as well,' he said.

'Right,' I said.

He gave a brief laugh. 'The girl's name,' he said.

'Yes?'

'Henrik came up with what it meant.'

'What it meant?'

'Well, what it stood for, at any rate. If you spell it out and take each letter. T-R-O-A-Ë . . . in English, can you work it out?'

I thought about it for a bit, then shook my head.

'The Root of all Evil,' said Erik. 'Good, eh?'

'The root of all evil?' I said. 'It sounds like something that *might* have a sequel after all. This whole saga, that is.'

I don't really know what I meant when I said it, and Erik didn't respond. He just stubbed out his cigarette and gave me another of those appraising looks.

Then we wished each other good night and went to bed.

On Tuesday morning I went to the boulangerie and bought a copy of *Ouest France*. I glanced through the paper from the first page to the last. Despite my poor French, I could plainly see there wasn't a word in it about any missing girl.

It was lovely weather and I was sure Erik had already set off for the beach. Heading for Bénodet I assumed, now that he knew nude sunbathing was allowed there, something which clearly appeals to him. I decided to stay at the house, do my packing and write a few more pages.

Sum up my impressions. The first thing that strikes me is that how much is ruled by chance – or by mechanisms beyond our control, at least. When Erik picked me up from that petrol station on the edge of Lille, I'd been trying to hitch a lift for exactly fifty-five minutes; I remember that very clearly, because I'd set myself a limit of an hour before I went back into the cafe. If he'd turned up two minutes later, we would never have met at all. I would have been picked up by some other vehicle and deposited in some other place entirely.

Would Troaë still have been alive, in that case? It would be easy to answer yes to that question, but I think that would be a simplification of the truth. There is no human means of determining this, of course; she could have turned up that morning anyway, and she could have gone out to des Glénan with the Swedes. The same sequence of events could have unfolded, and one thing is for certain: the weather would have been the same, the rain would have blown in, the engine would probably have broken down – but would the girl have started feeling sick on the way home, would the boat have crested the same treacherous wave, and would someone have let go of her hand? I have no way of solving this riddle but the thoughts and questions will not leave me alone. What is the extent of my participation in the events and processes of this world? Are there a variety of alternatives – and other conceivable actors – on the way to a given goal?

Maybe Henrik Malmgren would be able to guide me through all this, I can see these are problems that properly belong within philosophy. The archetypal mother of all scientific disciplines, but I have no intention of asking Henrik Malmgren's advice. I assume I won't ever see any of them again apart from the various superficial exchanges I shall have with Erik before I leave tomorrow. Amongst other things, I must make sure I'm not in debt; I reckon we're all square on what we've spent on food, and I also paid my share of the trip to des Glénan. I don't think I owe him any money. In other respects, I think it best for me to view this stay in Finistère as a parenthesis, something that, in a sense, never happened. Everybody has to be allowed periods like that in their lives, the intention simply can't be for us to be held to account for every last thing, for every unfortunate circumstance and every second that happens to veer off course.

If I can just get away from here, I will do my best to forget these two weeks. I will erase that walk with the girl in my arms from my mind, the intensity of her presence, her remarkable lightness; I have heard so much about the weight of dead bodies, but this was not at all the case with Troaë. I will repress those ghastly minutes in the water and I will never try to recall the way the ground and the earth enclosed her in their embrace. I will keep these notes of course, but that does not mean I will come back to them and reread them; it is enough for me to be aware that they exist, and if anyone happens to need them in the future, they are still here.

Perhaps I should devote a few lines to the individuals who have peopled my existence this past fortnight, but I have no urge to. I cannot overcome my reluctance and if they had the slightest idea – any of them – how much I despise them, it would undoubtedly come as a major surprise. My inside is not written on my outside, for better or worse, and that has always been the case. I remember Dr L and I discussed this state of affairs in some detail, and he felt initially that it was an element of, and a factor in, the pathology of my illness, but I think in the end we agreed it was a question of a legitimate characteristic. Revealing one's soul in one's face is not necessarily a sign of a good state of health, and it certainly isn't anything to aspire to if it doesn't happen naturally.

I spent the morning cleaning my room and getting all my packing done. I took a walk inland for about an hour and a half, and as I passed the boulangerie I picked up an evening paper. No word of a missing girl in there, either. When I got back to the house, Erik still wasn't back, and I presumed he had joined up with the other Swedes, perhaps not wanting to spend any more time in my company. In fact, on reflection, I guess that is the case, and probably applies to all five of them. They are biding their time until I leave, so they can calmly go back to their trivial beach life and forget what happened. I briefly toy with the idea of doing as they want and going on my way this evening. But there's no bus to Quimper until first thing tomorrow, and hitchhiking on the road from Mousterlin and Fouesnant is not a tempting prospect. I could draw undue attention to myself, too, which is the last thing we need at the moment.

Erik comes home as I am sitting on the terrace writing these lines. He asks if I want to go for dinner at Le Grand Large, they've had some fresh mussels in. I say I've still got a last bit of packing to finish and I'll make do with a sandwich. Erik showers, puts on a change of clothes and heads off again. It's half past seven by the time I set down my pen and go to the fridge.

*

I stand at the stove, frying a couple of eggs. I'm trying to follow the news bulletin pouring out of the transistor radio on the window ledge. My French has improved a bit in the time I've been here and I can understand most of what is said. The water has come to the boil in the kettle and just as it switches itself off I hear a cough from the terrace. I rest the spatula in the pan and take it off the gas. I wipe my hands on a tea towel and go outside.

An elderly woman is standing under the sun umbrella. She is dressed in black and looks almost like a Greek widow; though the draped fabric is less voluminous, her hair is raven black, doubtless dyed, and she is wearing a wide-brimmed straw hat, blood red. She is frail and small, no more than 160 cm, but there is strength in her face. It is exotic somehow, with dark eyes, a sharp nose and a firmly set jaw. She looks at me, peering slightly; perhaps she is a little short-sighted.

'Troaë!' she says.

'Oui?' I say.

'Troaë? What have you done with Troaë?'

She speaks a strange French with extravagantly rolled 'r's. I try to say I don't understand what she is talking about.

'Petite Troaë. I am her grandmother. I know she is with you and the others. But now it is time for her to come home.'

I throw my hands wide to signal that I still have no idea what she wants. Out of the corner of my eye, I catch sight of the big adjustable spanner lying on one of the plastic chairs. Erik left it there after he tried to fix up the rusty old bike he found in the tool shed. That was four or five days ago and he had no luck with it. He put the bike back but forgot the spanner. I remember us talking about it; it happens to be a Swedish make, a Bahco, and I even remember the model number, 08072. I look at the woman for a moment. Her eyes are no more than thin slits, her face looks like a cat's and she has both hands clenched into fists at her sides. She evidently thinks herself invincible, I know the type.

'Troaë?' I say as I take a step to the left and grab hold of the spanner. 'There must be some mistake.' I flounder for a second or two as I try to recall the word 'mistake' – *erreur* – but then it comes to me.

'It is not a mistake,' she says. 'She has been talking about you people for several days now and when she left home on Sunday she told me she was going to find you and spend the day with you.'

I do not hesitate. I swing the spanner in a wide arc and hit her with full force from the side, above her left ear. Her hat flies off and she slumps to the terrace floor like a hunter's prey felled by a bullet.

Commentary, August 2007

Words mean so little, actions so much more. And yet we surround ourselves with words, words, words. The really important points in a human life are few and can be spaced far apart. Years, even decades apart. When one day we come to sum it all up, we become vividly aware of this; how little it weighs, all that we have said and written, and how heavy those really decisive actions seem. It's not the words for which we will have to answer, and I don't really grasp why we're forever seeking their protection. Why do we not dare to find repose in silence and in our thoughts? In the hours and moments when we don't attach proper weight and importance to our actions, we devastate our lives, and that is nothing new, but everything would undeniably look different if we took more time for stillness and reflection.

My killing programme is going to plan. I still have work left to do, but I am in no doubt that I will be able to complete my task. The fact that they rejected a financial solution only goes to show the conceit of those people. My demands were by no means unreasonable. I assume they conferred and came to a collective decision to refuse, and in a way I am glad about this alternative outcome. Money offers nothing more than temporary solutions, short-term half-measures, such are the terms and conditions.

These past few nights I have dreamt of the girl's grandmother, that fragile and expressive little woman with the demanding eyes and those poisonous words that sealed her fate. She comes to me in my dream in the form of a bat, symbolism I do not really understand, flying in through the dark, open rectangle of a window and alighting on my knee or my arm, then sitting watching me with piercing yellow eyes; she says nothing, but just perches there with her diminutive head tilted first to the right, then to the left, and after a while she flies off again with a characteristic whoosh. I always wake up at that exact moment and the strange thing is that I find myself filled with a sort of joy, or at the very least gratification.

Of all human actions, killing is the most conclusive.

17–19 AUGUST 2007

27

'You look sprightly,' said Inspector Backman as they got into the car.

'I swam five hundred metres this morning,' admitted Barbarotti. 'Did you?'

'Of course he's bloody sprightly,' said Astor Nilsson. 'He's been on holiday for three days. While the rest of us have been working our arses off.'

'Who's driving?' said Eva Backman.

'Me,' said Astor Nilsson. 'I can find my way to Hallsberg. I knew a woman there once.'

'Really?' said Barbarotti.

'Yep,' said Astor Nilsson. 'A dark and mysterious beauty from the rolling plains around Viby. In other circumstances, we would have married each other.'

'Maybe you should take the chance of looking her up,' suggested Backman. 'You never know.'

'Don't think so,' said Astor Nilsson. 'If I'm not much mistaken, I'll find her in the cemetery.'

'We'd better leave it then,' said Backman. 'We're going to be busy enough as it is.'

'Certainly are,' sighed Astor Nilsson, turning out onto Norra Kungsvägen. 'This case has already made me a worse person.'

*

'In fact, to be honest, it's giving me sleepless nights,' he observed ten minutes later, once they had made their way out of the town and Eva Backman had issued various instructions to her children over her mobile phone. 'Do you think we're going to find a body up there?'

Eva Backman shrugged. 'I wouldn't like to say what we'll find. But there's a lot to point to Gunnar Öhrnberg being dead, wouldn't you say?'

'Wonder what the MO's going to be this time,' said Astor Nilsson. 'What do you reckon to poisoning, he hasn't tried that yet, has he?'

'We don't know how Henrik Malmgren died,' Eva Backman reminded him. 'And he hasn't shot anybody yet, I seem to recall.'

'Excuse me,' said Gunnar Barbarotti, who had volunteered for the back seat. 'I wonder if you'd mind giving me a short update? Now I've been taken back into the fold again and am expected to make myself slightly useful.'

'I shall teach you all I know,' said Astor Nilsson, grinning at him in the rear-view mirror. 'You didn't land one on that reporter, did you?'

'No,' said Barbarotti, 'I didn't.'

'Shame,' said Astor Nilsson. 'But maybe just as well for you. So where would you like us to start? I could do with somebody with a sense of order to impose a bit of structure on all this for me.'

'Thanks,' said Eva Backman. 'I get your snide implications. And there was me thinking we could see a bit of light at the end of the tunnel.'

'Woman,' said Astor Nilsson. 'Enlighten us.'

'I'll give it a go,' said Eva Backman. She took a deep breath, adjusting the back of her seat into a slightly more upright position. 'You have to admit, gents, that we do know quite a lot, when it comes to it. We know, for example, that this is all in some way connected with events that occurred in Brittany in the summer of 2002 . . .'

'We *know*?' queried Astor Nilsson.

'OK,' said Backman. 'Perhaps *know* isn't quite the right word, but we're *pretty convinced* that's the case, at any rate. We've found a single factor that links all four victims, and that's the fact that they were all in the same place for a number of weeks – we don't know exactly how long – that summer. Do you two think we should doubt whether we're on the right track?'

'I've tried to doubt it,' said Astor Nilsson. 'All night long. But it's hard to believe that we're not onto something here. Though there's also the fact of it being the only thing we've got.'

'What do you mean?' asked Backman.

Astor Nilsson wagged a pedagogical finger.

'We've found just one link. A single one. Of course we damn well take that as our starting point. All I'm saying is that if there were other links, it would be a different matter.'

'Of course,' Barbarotti agreed from the back seat. 'But if there are other connections, presumably they ought to come to light? In the course of our investigations.'

'They should have done that already,' said Backman. 'At any rate, I reckon we can consider the France solution credible for now, unless anything crops up to argue against it. Don't you think?'

'Agreed,' said Astor Nilsson. 'Let's assume Brittany 2002. But what the hell happened there?'

They all fell silent for a few seconds.

'We still don't know exactly where, either?' Backman said eventually, turning her head to the back seat. 'We've found various maps and brochures at the Malmgrens' and we think they were staying somewhere on the south coast, in Finistère. But they could have travelled round a fair bit, and . . . well, it's not clear, as I say.'

'And the others?' asked Barbarotti.

'We haven't found anything very useful at the others' places, but we're busy looking into travel agents and so on. Unfortunately, five years is plenty of time for things to disappear.'

'My hair disappeared in three,' said Astor Nilsson.

'The photographs,' said Barbarotti.

'Yes,' said Backman. 'To be honest, they're the only evidence we've got. Something occurred to me last night. What do you think about the time aspect? The pictures were taken over a period of time, but how long was it?'

'What?' said Astor Nilsson.

'Well, what I mean is,' said Backman, 'could this be a case of a single day, that is . . . well, could it be that they only met up for the one day?'

Barbarotti considered this as he extracted the photos from his briefcase. 'No,' he said. 'I think it must have been at least two different days. They change clothes and so on. Could even have been three. But I get why you're bringing it up.'

'So do I,' said Astor Nilsson. 'Did they just find themselves together on one particular day, or did they socialize over a slightly longer period? It's pretty clear they didn't know each other beforehand, isn't it? We haven't got anything to point to it, at any rate.'

'Correct,' said Backman. 'Their meeting up wasn't planned.

But something must have happened, or at any event, that's what we can surmise. In the course of those days, something happened that . . . well, that led to all five of them losing their lives five years later. Assuming Dead Man Gunnar really is dead.'

'Exactly,' said Astor Nilsson, and yawned. 'I concluded that's what we're assuming, as well. And if I'm not mistaken, that's also why we're in this car on our way to Hallsberg.'

They lapsed into silence again. Barbarotti subjected the photos to another round of scrutiny.

'The Sixth Man?' he said. 'What do you think?'

'That's just it,' said Astor Nilsson.

'What is?' asked Barbarotti.

'It's him,' said Eva Backman. 'What I mean is, I think he's our man.'

Barbarotti scratched the back of his neck, looking out of the car window as they passed a group of brown and white cows. 'What do you mean when you say that's just it?' he asked Astor Nilsson.

Astor Nilsson let go of the steering wheel for an instant and threw his hands wide in frustration. 'Only that it's so bloody obvious,' he said. 'And I don't like things that are too obvious. But yes, I agree it must be him. Shame he looks like everybody else.'

Barbarotti nodded. 'Yes, you're right. And he's a bit out of focus, as well. Plus it was five years ago. Has a decision been made on what we're going to do with this?'

'Jonnerblad's in two minds,' said Backman. 'Sylvenius and Asunander, too. Things have a way of going wrong whenever we start publishing photos of suspected murderers.'

'There's no need to say anything about a murderer,' said Barbarotti.

'Oh?' said Astor Nilsson.

'They can say the police urgently want to make contact with the man in the photograph. Or with anyone who can provide any information about him.'

Astor Nilsson grunted. 'But they're bound to say in the paper that he's the murderer anyway, you know that. Or to leave the reader in little doubt, at least. I thought you'd learnt a thing or two about the workings of the newspaper world?'

Barbarotti sighed and stuffed the pictures back in his briefcase. 'So what the hell are we going to do then?'

'Oh, we'll publish them all right,' said Astor Nilsson. 'We've just got to let a couple of days go by, so those gentlemen can give their reservations a decent airing.'

'I see,' said Barbarotti. 'And yes, I'm sure you're right.'

'Unless anything unforeseen crops up to solve the case before then,' said Backman. 'In the metropolis of Hallsberg, for example.'

'For example,' said Astor Nilsson.

'So, Hans Andersson, then?' asked Gunnar Barbarotti after another short pause. 'I assume you've discussed the possibility of that being his name?'

'The man in the photo or the murderer?' said Backman with a quick smile.

'That's just it,' said Astor Nilsson.

'There you go again,' said Backman.

'I'm well aware of that,' said Astor Nilsson. 'But that *is* just it. If there's one thing that gets on my nerves more than anything else in this saga, it's fucking Hans Andersson. If there were any kind of logic to all this mess, he ought by rights to be dead. Whoever he is. And if in fact . . .'

He stopped short.

'You mean you're hoping for another body?' said Eva Backman, passing round the Lakeröl pastilles. 'Don't you think we've enough of them as it is?'

'No,' said Astor Nilsson, tossing four pastilles into his mouth. 'You interrupted me. What I was going to say was that if . . . *if* the Sixth Man turns out to be called Hans Andersson, say, then presumably he and the murderer *aren't* one and the same. In that case we haven't got the perpetrator in the frame at all, and this sixth guy is just some poor Hansie who happened to be . . . on the margins, and because he was only on the margins, and what's more, can't identify the murderer, he emerged unscathed.'

Barbarotti and Backman mulled this over for a while.

'In that case,' said Backman, 'In that case it would be bloody interesting to get in touch with him.'

'Damn right,' said Astor Nilsson. 'But I don't think the guy in the picture *is* called Hans Andersson.

'Why not?' said Eva Backman.

'I don't really know,' said Astor Nilsson. 'If we were playing Cluedo, or whatever the damn thing's called, he'd be bound to be called Hans Andersson, but as far as I know we're not playing Cluedo.'

'We're in agreement there,' said Gunnar Barbarotti. 'I've also reached the conclusion that it's not Cluedo we're playing here.'

*

They were somewhere near Götene when it started to rain. And Inspector Backman's mobile rang. She answered it, said 'Yes' five times, 'No' twice, and then rang off.

'The Örebro police,' she said. 'They'll be in place at eleven. An inspector called Ström and two forensic technicians.'

'Good,' said Astor Nilsson. 'So all we need is a dead body and it'll all go swimmingly to plan.'

'How much do we know about this Gunnar Öhrnberg's movements?' asked Barbarotti. 'He's been off the radar for a while, I gather?'

'Ten days,' Backman confirmed. 'Though nobody realized until Monday, when the teachers were due back to prepare for the start of term. And I don't suppose anybody thought he was missing then, either, but when we called and they started checking round, it turned out nobody'd seen him since the Tuesday of the previous week . . . so yes, that makes it ten days today, in fact.'

'And he's single?'

'It's a bit hard to be gone for a week without being missed if you're married,' said Astor Nilsson with a wry smile in the rear-view mirror.

'Yeah, presumably,' admitted Barbarotti. 'Who have you talked to?'

'Only one person, in actual fact,' said Backman. 'But she seems pretty competent. Director of Studies at the school. She mounted her own little investigation when she saw the way the wind was blowing, and I think we can depend on her.'

'No other links between Öhrnberg and the other victims? Apart from Brittany, that is?'

'No,' said Backman. 'But he was an item with Anna Eriksson, remember. They were together for most of 2002, if our witnesses are to be believed. Not much of a relationship apparently, according to several of them. Gunnar could be quite domineering, they never moved in together and no one was particularly surprised when it ended. But we have to bear in mind that these were all accounts from *Anna's* friends and acquaintances.'

'He worked at a school in Borås back then, didn't he?'

'Yes, but only for three terms. And none of his colleagues there who we've been able to locate can remember Anna Eriksson.'

'Maybe he didn't take her to staff parties?'

'No, I don't suppose he did.'

They passed Hova and the rain stopped.

'I have this dream,' said Astor Nilsson.

'Do you?' said Eva Backman. 'I thought you weren't sleeping?'

'It's a daydream,' Astor Nilsson explained patiently. 'Anyway, in it he's alive, this teacher Mr Öhrnberg, and we can sit down for a four-hour chat with him this afternoon and get to the bottom of everything.'

'I'm with you on that one,' said Barbarotti. 'What time is it? I forgot to take my watch off when I went for my swim this morning and it's stopped.'

'Twenty past nine,' said Astor Nilsson. 'We'll be at Hallsberg half an hour early. What do you say, shall we stop for a coffee and see what *Expressen*'s writing about us today?'

'Just a coffee for me,' said Gunnar Barbarotti.

'The satnav's not working,' observed Astor Nilsson once they had turned off the E20 and were coming into the once-important railway hub. 'But if I remember rightly, there's only one street.'

This turned out to be not quite the truth. Admittedly the high street ran through the whole place, alongside the railway tracks, but there was another road parallel to it, and various others intersecting it. Astor Nilsson pulled up outside Stig's Bookshop, went in and was immediately taken under the wing of an enthusiastic, moustachioed gentleman of around sixty. At five past eleven they parked outside a smallish block of flats at 4 Tulpangatan. A tall man with a shaven head came hurrying over to meet them.

'Ström. How was the journey?'

They shook hands and introduced themselves. Astor Nilsson assured them the journey had been a piece of cake. Inspector Ström waved a hand towards two younger men who were just getting out of a blue Volvo. 'I brought two forensic technicians, as we arranged. Just in case. Jönsson and Fjärnemyr.'

They shook hands with the new arrivals as well. Jönsson had half his right index finger missing, Barbarotti noticed, but it was clearly no barrier to his work as a crime scene technician.

'The caretaker's already been in and unlocked the door,' Fjärnemyr informed them. 'We can go straight in.'

Ström took the lead as they went up the stairs. It was a three-storey block with a typical sixties layout, but it all looked very spruce and had presumably had a facelift quite recently. Two flats on each landing, and Öhrnberg's was on the top floor. Inspector Ström stopped outside the door and waited for the rest of them.

'I hope you don't mind,' said Eva Backman, 'but I think I'd like to go in first. No point us all tramping in together.'

Barbarotti saw Ström wince. Aha, he thought. An old-school type. He could scarcely be above forty, but it evidently threw him to have the only woman in the group of six taking command.

'Not at all,' he said, holding the door open.

Eva Backman took a big step over the drift of post and newspapers on the hall floor. She opened doors to the right and left, and straight ahead of her, and went round the flat for a good minute before returning to the others.

'Nix,' she said. 'No body, no nothing. The slightly off smell is just the bin bag in the kitchen. He hasn't been home for over a week and the weather's been warm.'

'What do you want to do?' said Inspector Ström, his eyes moving from Astor Nilsson to Barbarotti and back again. To make a point presumably, whether consciously or not.

'How about this?' said Astor Nilsson. 'You leave us to get on with things here for a couple of hours and we'll see what we find. No need for us all to get in each other's way. If you're back here with the caretaker –' he looked at his watch, then at Ström – 'shall we say one thirty? Then we can show you what we're taking with us and close up the flat. OK?'

Inspector Ström nodded. Technicians Jönsson and Fjärnemyr nodded.

'Right then,' said Barbarotti. 'Bye for now.'

Gunnar Öhrnberg had been – or possibly still was – quite an orderly and methodical man, that was one of their conclusions after they had spent an hour and a half going through his flat. All the rooms were clean and neat. He had well-stocked bookshelves, with books mainly from his own subject areas – history, social studies and civics – but also a fair bit of fiction. The desk in his study had a computer and multifunction printer and every last detail was meticulously arranged. Shelves of folders and box files, all carefully labelled. Though one had to bear in mind, Barbarotti thought, that term hadn't yet started.

And perhaps it never would start again for Gunnar Öhrnberg, but it was too early to be certain on that score. Far too early. After all, he could just have shoved off on some last-minute holiday deal and forgotten he was due at work. Or got lost when he was out hiking in the fells. Or . . . well, what? Barbarotti asked himself as he closed the door of the impeccably stocked linen cupboard. Been kidnapped? Had a stroke when he was out picking mushrooms in the forest and lost his memory?

There were some framed photographs lined up on an oak sideboard in the living room. Six unfamiliar faces, of which two were elderly – his parents, at a guess – and two were children. A boy and a girl, both of them dark-haired. And a bridal couple; the man looked a bit like Gunnar Öhrnberg, so Barbarotti thought it was probably his brother, and that the two children were his niece and nephew. In a cupboard in the sideboard he found no less than ten bottles of whisky, all single malts, seven of them open. Something of a connoisseur, it seemed. There was a humidor with six cigars in it as well.

But no photo albums anywhere. And no obvious gaps in the bookshelf where they might have been, either.

'Another one who doesn't seem to have been a photographer,' said Eva Backman. 'No sign of a camera anywhere.'

'We can have a go with his computer,' said Astor Nilsson. 'There could be pictures on there. And goodness knows what else besides.'

'Handwritten address book, at any rate,' said Barbarotti. 'Anna Eriksson's in there, but none of the others.'

'Is Hans Andersson in it?' asked Astor Nilsson.

Barbarotti shook his head. 'I'm afraid not. But let's take it with us anyway.'

'Of course,' said Astor Nilsson, pulling up the blinds on the balcony door.

The TV set and the sound system were both Bang & Olufsen. The CDs, probably about a hundred of them, were kept in modern storage towers – lots of jazz but plenty of rubbish too, Astor Nilsson noted – while the DVDs that they found behind yet another door of the roomy oak sideboard were no more than thirty in number. About half of those were porn.

'Once a bachelor always a bachelor,' said Astor Nilsson.

'Are you saying that from experience?' asked Eva Backman.

'Unfortunately not,' said Astor Nilsson. 'Only wish I could get a bit turned on by that crap, but it doesn't work.'

'Sorry,' said Backman. 'I didn't mean to snoop into your private life.'

'Don't worry about it,' said Astor Nilsson. 'I'm an open book, me. Anyhow, he seems to be a well-organized devil, this schoolmaster of ours. He should have taken the bin bag out, but maybe he didn't twig that he was going to be murdered.'

'No one can keep tabs on everything,' said Barbarotti. 'But he wasn't murdered here at home, at any rate. I think we can allow ourselves that conclusion.'

'It would be good to know that he *was* murdered before we start talking about where he *wasn't*,' said Eva Backman.

'That sounded complicated,' said Astor Nilsson. 'But can

we say we're done here now? We need to talk to a few people as well, after all.'

'The basement storage area,' said Barbarotti. 'Shall we go down and take a look? While we've got the key.'

Backman nodded. 'Yes, you do that. Meanwhile, we'll start lugging out what we want to take away. We'll wait for Ström and Co. downstairs. It might be a good idea to grab a bite of lunch too, don't you think?'

'Absolutely vital,' said Astor Nilsson. 'When I'm hungry I'm the worst police officer in the whole of Sweden. I just don't hear what people say.'

'What's that?' said Barbarotti, making Backman smile.

28

'You didn't find anything I assume?' asked Astor Nilsson. 'In the basement, that is.'

Barbarotti shook his head. 'Loads of diving equipment. And skis. And cross-country skis. Walking boots and rucksacks, so he was quite sporty, it seems, didn't just lounge about drinking whisky and smoking cigars.'

'I don't like you talking about him in the past tense,' said Eva Backman. 'I know it sounds silly, but it makes me uncomfortable.'

'You're doing the same,' said Barbarotti.

'I know,' said Eva Backman. 'I don't like that, either.'

'There's a Chinese,' said Astor Nilsson. 'Will that do, my Lord and Lady?'

'That'll do,' said Barbarotti. 'We can be sure of quick service, if nothing else.'

And so it proved. Gunnar Barbarotti even had time to pop into a jeweller's and get himself a new wristwatch. It only cost 249 kronor but the shop assistant promised him in an impenetrable Närke accent that it was made to last forever.

'No rubbish just 'cause it's cheap. You'll be wearin' that 'un for your funeral.'

Barbarotti paid and thanked him. There was a police station

in Västra Storgatan in Hallsberg, but he had arranged to meet Tomas Wallin in the railway station cafe. An interrogation room rarely proved more than an interrogation room.

Tomas Wallin looked tanned and healthy, but he opened the conversation by saying how terribly worried he was.

'Something must have happened to him. Gunnar would never just stay away like that.'

Barbarotti shot him a glance. A shortish, heavily built man, somewhere between thirty-five and forty. Sandy, close-cropped hair and honest blue eyes.

'I'm going to record this,' said Barbarotti, switching on the tape recorder. 'So we don't miss anything important.'

'Oh. Er, OK,' said Tomas Wallin, and gulped some water.

'So your name is Tomas Wallin and you're a good friend of Gunnar Öhrnberg's. Can you say your full address and telephone number?'

Wallin did so.

'Örebro, then?'

'Yes.'

'All right. Can you tell me how long you've known Gunnar Öhrnberg?'

'Seventeen or eighteen years. We met on military service up in Arvidsjaur.'

'Lapland Ranger regiment?'

'That's right.'

'And you've stayed in touch ever since?'

'On and off. Mostly these past few years, actually, since Gunnar moved to Hallsberg.'

'But you've been living in Örebro the whole time?'

Wallin shook his head. 'For about ten years. Born and raised in Gävle, then I lived up in Umeå for a while.'

'What line of work are you in?'

'I'm a dentist.'

Barbarotti swallowed his surprise. If he'd had to guess it would have been gym manager or something of the kind. He found it hard to connect Tomas Wallin's stocky figure with the nimble dexterity of a dentist.

'So you see each other a fair bit?' he said.

'Yes,' said Wallin. 'We've got similar hobbies, as well.'

'And what are they?' asked Barbarotti.

'Well, diving is the main one. We're both instructors. We sometimes work a week or two at a diving centre down near Kungshamn. We've been on a few foreign trips too, of course. The Red Sea, the Philippines, that sort of thing. And we go hiking in the mountains.'

'Every year?'

'For the last three years we have.'

Gunnar Barbarotti considered this. '2002,' he said. 'Do you remember what happened in 2002?'

'You mean did we go hiking?'

'Yes.'

Tomas Wallin thought for a few seconds. 'No, not that year. We went a couple of times in the early nineties . . . and then in more recent summers. As I say.'

'But not this year?'

'We're thinking of four days in September.'

Optimist, thought Barbarotti. 'And the diving job?'

'How often, you mean?'

'Yes please. And which years, if you can recall.'

Wallin thought a bit more. 'Well, we were there this July, of course. And last year and the one bef—'

'2002?'

'Yes, we were there in 2002 as well. I think we only missed one year in the noughties, and that was 2001.'

'What time of the summer do you usually go there?'

'It's always the last week in July,' Wallin replied at once. 'Sometimes the first week in August too.'

Barbarotti felt a sudden little quiver of anticipation. 'I see,' he said. 'We'll talk a bit more about this summer in a minute, but first I'd like us to concentrate on summer 2002. Do you think you can remember back that far?'

Tomas Wallin shrugged. 'If you mean the diving week, I'm not sure. Was there something unusual about 2002, then?'

'That's what I wanted to ask *you*,' said Barbarotti. 'Gunnar was in a relationship with a woman called Anna Eriksson. They went to France together that summer, just before he met up with you at the diving centre.'

Tomas Wallin frowned. 'I don't remember any Anna. Though you're right about him being in France. It was Brittany, I think; he brought back a bottle of Calvados and I pointed out to him that they make Calvados in Normandy, not Brittany . . . but anyway, we had a glass or two after a night dive, I remember that.'

'Excellent,' said Barbarotti. 'Did the two of you talk about what he'd been up to in Brittany?'

Wallin made a 'Search me' gesture with his hands.

'I expect so. But I can't remember anything particular.'

'People he'd met, that sort of thing?'

'No.'

'Can I ask you to take your time and have a good hard think about this. It could be important.'

Tomas Wallin drank some more of his water. He sat there

for a while saying nothing, looking out of the window. 'Why could it be important?' he asked.

'I'm afraid I can't tell you that at the moment,' said Barbarotti.

'It isn't anything to do with . . . ?'

'With what?'

'With these murders down your way. Dead Man Gunnar and all that . . . I mean, a person can't help putting two and two together even if they're not a detective.'

Gunnar Barbarotti nodded. 'I can understand you doing that,' he said. 'But I'm sure you realize there are things I can't talk to you about.'

'Of course,' said Tomas Wallin. 'Sorry, it's just that I'm so worried about Gunnar.'

I'll have to ask him if he's married, thought Barbarotti. Hope he won't take it the wrong way.

'And you, have you got family?'

'Wife and two daughters,' said Tomas Wallin. 'The youngest has just turned one.'

Good, thought Gunnar Barbarotti. Just healthy male friendship, then.

I'm as stuffed with prejudice as usual, was his next thought. And maybe envious, too, because I haven't got a friend like Tomas Wallin?

He checked the tape recorder and focused again. Gave Wallin his card. 'In case anything else occurs to you about 2002,' he said. 'You can call me direct if you do. The slightest thing, if it's about France or this Anna.'

Wallin nodded and put the card in his wallet.

'Right then,' said Barbarotti. 'Let's go over to the present, so to speak. When did you last see Gunnar Öhrnberg?'

'Two weeks ago,' Wallin replied at once. 'The Saturday before last. He came over to our place in town and we had a bite to eat. He stayed the night and went home on the Sunday morning.'

Gunnar Barbarotti looked in his diary. 'That would have been Saturday the fourth of August?'

'Correct,' said Tomas Wallin. 'We got back from Scorpius the Monday before, and that was when we invited him.'

'We?' said Barbarotti. 'Scorpius?'

'Emma and me. She's my wife. I took the whole family to Scorpius this time. That's the diving centre I told you about – it's on a little island between Kungshamn and Smögen. My wife took Advanced.'

Gunnar Barbarotti presumed this was some kind of diving certificate, but he didn't bother to enquire. 'OK,' he said. 'Did you notice anything special about Gunnar? On the diving week or when he was at your place on the Saturday?'

'Not a thing. He was just the same as usual.'

'Are you sure?'

'Yes.'

'He wasn't worried about anything?'

'No.'

'He didn't seem jittery?'

'No, no.'

'And, thinking back, you don't feel he might have been hiding anything from you? Having known him for so long, you ought to be able to tell that kind of thing.'

He was prepared for another emphatic denial, but in fact Tomas Wallin hesitated for a moment, and scratched his neck nervously. They were small signs, but Barbarotti could tell something was coming.

'We-ell,' he said. 'I don't suppose it's got any bearing on this, but I think he was seeing some new woman.'

'Some new woman?' said Barbarotti, hardly able to conceal his disappointment. 'He hadn't been in a relationship before that, then?'

Wallin shook his head and assumed an expression that was presumably intended to excuse his friend. 'No, it was somehow never the real thing where Gunnar and women were concerned. Confirmed bachelor and all that. Since he moved up to Hallsberg I'm pretty sure there hasn't been anyone. He didn't say anything about it, at any rate.'

'But you didn't ask him?'

'My wife did. When he was at ours. He sort of avoided the question and Emma reckons that's because he was trying to keep it secret. Because she's a married woman . . . well, she's good at seeing that kind of thing, my wife.'

Yes, thought Barbarotti. And she's not the only woman in the world with that ability.

'But you haven't seen Gunnar since the morning of the fifth?'

'No.'

'Spoken to him on the phone?'

'Once,' said Tomas Wallin. 'On Monday.'

'What was the call about?'

'Nothing, really. He rang to thank us for inviting him round . . . oh hang on, he said he might be going fishing with a colleague of his for a couple of days.'

'Some fellow member of staff?'

'That was how I understood it.'

'Did he mention a name?'

'No, I'm pretty sure he didn't.'

Gunnar Barbarotti glanced out of the window and saw an X 2000 express pulling in at platform one. Well at least they still stop here, he thought. A few of them, at any rate.

'When did you realize Gunnar was missing?' he asked.

'On Tuesday. The school rang to ask me if I'd seen him.'

'So they know at the school that you're good friends?'

Tomas Wallin shrugged. 'Apparently so.'

'And you've no idea where he might have gone?'

'None at all. It seems completely incomprehensible to my wife and me.'

Barbarotti pondered. 'I think that's it for now,' he said. 'Can I ring you if anything else crops up that I need to ask?'

'Of course,' exclaimed Tomas Wallin. 'There's nothing I want more than . . .'

He couldn't find the right words to go on. Perhaps because there weren't any, thought Barbarotti grimly, switching off the tape.

'And you'll get in touch if you think of anything else?'

'Of course,' repeated Wallin, starting to get up.

'Especially that summer . . . 2002.'

'Understood,' said Tomas Wallin, and they parted.

They were in the car again.

Eva Backman had reported back on her chat with the single mother who lived next to Gunnar Öhrnberg in Tulpangatan. A lot of people on their own these days, Backman observed. Two in this group alone, Astor Nilsson added.

The woman's name was Gunnel Pekkari. She was thirty-five, divorced and lived with her five-year-old daughter and cat. She was quite a looker, Inspector Backman said by way of introduction, at least by today's standards: big breasts, doe eyes and newly enhanced lips. Backman thought it wasn't impossible that she'd had a fling with Öhrnberg. Or that they'd been to bed together a few times, at any rate. What with them living wall to wall with each other like that, it would have been a practical arrangement.

But there had been nothing like that of late, unfortunately. Gunnel Pekkari had had nothing to tell her. Oh, except one small detail: she had met her neighbour on the stairs around seven on Tuesday evening, the seventh, that was, and she could swear he was alive at the time. But he'd been in a hurry and they'd just exchanged a quick greeting, he on his way out, she coming in.

Incidentally, she thought Gunnar Öhrnberg was good-looking, carried himself well, but maybe had a slightly big nose; as for his inner qualities, she had had no opinion to offer.

'Great,' said Astor Nilsson. 'He was alive on the evening of the seventh, anyway. At least we know that.'

Then he told them about his visit to Ms Manner-Lind, Director of Studies at Avenue School. Since Tuesday, when she had begun to suspect something was amiss, she really had been doing her best to track down Gunnar Öhrnberg. It quite often happened that one teacher or other missed the first planning day, she said – but not two, they generally didn't dare, and particularly not a teacher of Öhrnberg's calibre.

Not that he wouldn't dare, but because he was who he was. Hardly ever off sick and a rock in all weathers. Popular with pupils, colleagues and parents alike. And with the school management. If they ever needed a stand-in, he always volunteered. Overtime? No problem. Someone to supervise a school trip? Öhrnberg immediately stepped forward.

So Ms Manner-Lind had had a word with various people.

With Josefsson and Pärman, with whom she knew Öhrnberg sometimes socialized out of school. With Rosander, who had been due to go char fishing on Lake Vättern with Gunnar Öhrnberg, but they had had to cancel because Rosander's wife was admitted for a hip operation. With Öhrnberg's brother in Östersund and with his parents in Kramfors.

And yes, most certainly with his friend Wallin in Örebro, but nobody had any information, nor could they offer even the slightest clue to where the missing teacher might have gone.

So in the end, she had contacted the police.

'I had an uncomfortable feeling after we rang off,' said Astor Nilsson.

'Did you?' said Barbarotti, who had opted for the back seat for the homeward leg, too. 'What sort of feeling?'

'Well,' said Astor Nilsson. 'If not even Ms Manner-Lind manages to winkle you out, there's a pretty good chance you're lying dead somewhere.'

'I think most of this points us towards—' began Barbarotti, but he was interrupted by the ringtone of Backman's mobile.

She answered. She said 'Yes' a few times, then looked out of the window and said 'Laxå, I think,' then she swore, nodded, and alternated uncertainly between affirmative and negative answers for a while. She rounded off with a 'Yes, of course' and ended the call.

'What the heck was all that?' said Astor Nilsson.

'It was Jonnerblad,' said Backman. 'Turn in at this petrol station. We've got to go back.'

'Why?' asked Barbarotti.

'Because they've found the body of a man in a field of wheat outside Kumla. There are various indications that it's Gunnar Öhrnberg.'

'What did I say?' said Astor Nilsson.

'A field of wheat?' queried Barbarotti.

Backman nodded. 'The farmer found him when he was out on the combine harvester. He's a bit mangled, apparently.'

29

Gunnar Öhrnberg certainly was a bit mangled.

That was putting it mildly. The field of wheat in question was in a place called Örsta. On a dirt track leading from a slightly wider tarmac road, there was a row of parked cars. Four police cars, four others, plus a number of people, a motorbike and an eagerly barking dog. Thirty metres into the field, a green combine harvester stood at rest, with another bunch of people around it. The sun had just set when Barbarotti, Backman and Astor Nilsson arrived. The town of Kumla was silhouetted to the west, with the cemetery and church in the foreground, and behind it a settlement clambering up a ridge, outlined against an orange-tinted evening sky. Barbarotti automatically scanned the scene for anything that could be the wall of Kumla prison, but his gaze alighted instead on a lovely old water tower with a beautifully rounded shape.

'I wonder why Ström didn't ring us direct,' he said once they were out of the car. 'Seems a bit unnecessary to go via Jonnerblad.'

'You know what,' said Astor Nilsson, 'I almost get the feeling he doesn't like us, that inspector.'

'That's odd,' said Eva Backman.

They were escorted out into the field by a Chief Inspector

Schwerin, and when they were finally confronted with what remained of schoolteacher Gunnar Öhrnberg, Barbarotti felt for one critical moment that he was about to throw up. But the two hot dogs and mash he had bolted down before they left Hallsberg stopped halfway and decided to stay in his stomach.

The farmer's name was Mattsson and he hadn't really been able to stop his huge combine in time. Hence the mangling. In the olden days they talked about the grim reaper, thought Gunnar Barbarotti; maybe this was emblematic of the modern age. Death with his harvesting machine.

'Yes, it's a bit of a mess,' said Chief Inspector Schwerin. 'But there's a bullet hole in his head, too. He was as dead as a doornail when the farmer mowed him down.'

'Bullet hole?' said Astor Nilsson.

'Oh yes,' said Inspector Ström, who had joined them. 'Right through his skull. Entry point left temple, exit point right temple.'

Eva Backman checked her watch. 'It's half past eight,' she said. 'What time did he . . . was he found?'

'About quarter to six,' said Schwerin. 'Mattsson was in shock. Had his mobile with him but wasn't able to make a call. It was his wife who rang, at ten past six.'

'Eleven minutes past six,' clarified Ström.

'Ström, could you go and see how Bengtsson and Linder are getting on?' said Schwerin.

Inspector Ström nodded and left them. Gunnar Barbarotti surveyed the macabre scene. About half the field was still unharvested. The farmer had been working inwards from the edge, and the combine was stranded like some huge prehistoric animal that had suddenly run out of stamina. On a rectangle the size of a football pitch, the wheat still waved in the mild autumn breeze. It was waist high and ripe for harvest. The police had cordoned off a small area with blue and white plastic tape; a team of pathologists and assorted technicians and photographers were crawling around the combine harvester and Öhrnberg's mangled body, and there were more people gathered outside the tape barrier, a good thirty of them.

'Who are all these people?' asked Gunnar Barbarotti.

Chief Inspector Schwerin gave a shrug of his shoulders. 'Word got round. Neighbours and other interested parties. The newspapers are here as well. This sort of thing doesn't often happen in our neck of the woods.'

'Have you asked them to move on?'

'Oh yes. But most of them were already here when we arrived. We have right of public access in our country, after all, and a free press.'

Barbarotti looked at the chief inspector. An undemonstrative little man in his sixties. He seemed to be taking the whole thing very serenely, and maybe that was the right approach, when all was said and done. He didn't feel particularly inclined to start trying to shoo the spectators off home. No doubt they had already trampled over any potential clues in the fertile soil of Närke.

'Have you found a bullet?' asked Astor Nilsson.

'No, but we're looking. Though I don't think we're going to find one.'

'Why's that?'

Schwerin smiled gently. 'Because he was presumably shot elsewhere. It's hard to imagine the perpetrator bringing the victim with him, taking a walk into the middle of a wheat field and doing the deed there. Much easier to visualize him being shot somewhere else and then dumped here.'

Barbarotti mulled this over. He's right, he thought. Of course that's what happened. 'And your people are sure it's Öhrnberg?' he asked. He was far from convinced himself. The head was in such a bad state that it could basically have been anybody.

'We're pretty sure,' said Schwerin. 'He had his wallet and ID on him.'

Barbarotti nodded.

'Can they give us an estimate of how long he's been lying here?' asked Astor Nilsson.

'The pathologist reckons at least a week,' said Schwerin. 'Well, I expect this one's going to land on your desk. Might be a good idea for us to send the body to Gothenburg?'

'Yes, do that,' said Astor Nilsson. 'But make sure you collect up all the bits first.'

Backman's mobile rang. She withdrew a few steps. Coming back a minute later, she said 'Jonnerblad. Yes, he wants him sent to Gothenburg. And he also wants *us* to stay on here tomorrow . . .'

She nodded to the chief inspector. 'So we can gather slightly more of the bigger picture to take back with us, as it were.'

A gathered picture and a gathered body, thought Barbarotti. Schwerin gave another of his benign smiles. 'I'd planned to play golf tomorrow,' he said. 'But it'll keep. I'm not actually that keen on golf, it's mainly my wife, in fact . . . still, I suppose there'll be one or two interviews to get through, and so on?'

'One or two,' confirmed Astor Nilsson. 'How about the farmer, is he up to talking to us?'

'You can always try,' said Schwerin, pointing across the field. 'He's over there. Ran over a deer last year, but I imagine this was a whole lot worse.'

'Smart thinking,' said Eva Backman, 'leaving him in a field of wheat.'

'How do you mean?' asked Barbarotti.

The two of them were waiting together for Astor Nilsson to finish talking to Mattsson the farmer as the August sky turned dusky blue on its way to black. Barbarotti was chewing on a grain of wheat.

'Well, if he wants somewhere to hide him where he can be sure he'll be found eventually. He's got a guaranteed hiding place until harvest time.'

Barbarotti took another grain of wheat from the ear and popped it into his mouth. 'You're right. But wouldn't you leave tracks when you went out into the field?'

'Not very visible ones,' said Backman. 'If you take things gently, I think most of it pops up again fairly quickly. Like after rain. I can't help thinking that was a pretty smart move.'

'Yes it was,' said Barbarotti. 'And we've got various other things pointing to our man being just that, haven't we? Pretty smart.'

Eva Backman nodded and looked out over the darkening field. 'Five people, can you take it in? He's killed five people in one summer and we haven't done a damn thing to stop him. He sends us letters and tips us off, and the papers too. What are we getting paid for, when the chips are down?'

'I know,' said Barbarotti. 'But we'll get him. And I don't think those tip-offs were worth having.'

'Oh?' said Eva Backman, blowing her nose. 'Would you bloody believe it, I think I'm getting hay fever now, too. Can't cope with traipsing around newly harvested fields.'

'There's no end to all these torments,' said Barbarotti. 'Anyway, I think Öhrnberg must have been killed long before I got that letter about Dead Man Gunnar. The tip-offs aren't even coming in the right order. The Malmgrens caught the ferry on Sunday, but he shot Öhrnberg several days before that, didn't he?'

Eva Backman thought about this. 'You're right,' she said. 'I've drawn up a timeline for all this, it's in my office. We'll have to check it out when we get back.'

Barbarotti's mobile rang.

It was a journalist from *Aftonbladet*. A young woman, and she'd heard they had found another body in a field of rye outside Karlskoga.

'Wheat,' said Barbarotti. 'And Kumla. But I don't know anything about a body.'

He cut her off. Got to get this mobile number changed asap, he reminded himself.

Chief Inspector Schwerin had recommended the venerable Stora Hotellet in Örebro and they had taken his advice. They each bought a beer in reception and sat at a table in the dining room, looking out over the Svartån river and the castle. Dinner service had ended and they were alone in the large room, where only half the lights were still on.

'There you have the second most beautiful castle in Sweden,' said Astor Nilsson, gesturing out of the window.

Barbarotti and Backman looked at the old stone castle as they sipped their beer.

'Which is the most beautiful, then?' asked Barbarotti.

'Kalmar,' said Astor Nilsson.

'You get about a bit, don't you?' said Backman.

'I told you,' said Astor Nilsson. 'My boss would send me to Paris if it meant he could avoid seeing me. OK, shall we sum up this pile of crap?'

'We can try,' said Barbarotti. 'Shall I?'

'Fire away,' said Eva Backman.

'Thank you. So Gunnar Öhrnberg was shot through the head with a large-bore gun. Something like a Pinchmann or a Berenger. Most likely on Wednesday of last week. Most likely somewhere in Närke. Well that's about it, I think.'

'Not quite,' said Astor Nilsson. 'Then manhandled into some kind of vehicle, the boot of a car for example. Driven off to a wheat field in the lovely but godforsaken location of Örsta, just outside the former shoemaking town of Kumla. Dragged into the middle of said field to be harvested in due course by farmer Henrik Mattsson. Clever idea to put him in the middle of a field of crops, by the way.'

'Clever?' said Barbarotti.

'We've already discussed that,' said Eva Backman.

'Right then,' said Astor Nilsson. 'Do you know what we're going to find in tomorrow's papers about one thing and another?'

'I had a word with Schwerin about that,' said Barbarotti. 'We can expect masses of coverage, especially in *Nerikes Allehanda*. We're making a public appeal for information in there. Any suspicious vehicles seen in the Örsta area, and so on. And in the vicinity of Tulpangatan in Hallsberg, too. Yes, the lines to our colleagues are going to be busy, I think. There are a couple of hotlines for anyone with information, I gather. We'll just have to see what comes in.'

'Good,' said Eva Backman. 'The whole country must have read about the case by now. It's about time someone owned up to having seen something, too.'

'Wishful thinking,' said Astor Nilsson. 'But if you shoot your victim in the forest at three o'clock in the morning and dump him in a field an hour later, it's not all that likely there'll be many witnesses.'

'Bloody pessimist,' said Eva Backman. 'Well, I suggest we drink up and get to bed.'

Gunnar Barbarotti looked at his watch. It had stopped.

Just as he emerged from the shower on Saturday morning, Marianne rang.

'Where are you?' was her opening question, the same one asked in every single phone call nowadays. In the global era immediately preceding Armageddon, he had read in some reactionary opinion piece recently. Now that people had turned into a rootless swarm of locusts flying aimlessly about the world.

'Örebro,' he conceded. 'I'm looking out over the second most beautiful castle in Sweden.'

'I know,' she said. 'I've seen it. But Kalmar's actually even better.'

Is that some kind of universally acknowledged truth then, wondered Barbarotti in surprise. 'Yes, I think so too,' he said.

'What are you doing there?"

'Haven't you read the papers?'

'No.'

'Good. Don't. I love you.'

In some peculiar way he had managed to suppress the fact that it was Saturday. *That* Saturday. I'm clearly losing it, thought Barbarotti. How could I have forgotten? I've got a goldfish brain, not a human one.

But he recalled the situation as soon as he was reminded of it. At least that was something.

'Do you want to marry me?' he asked.

She laughed. He awarded Our Lord a point out of sheer delight. For there was something in her laugh that told him . . . what exactly?

Well, that it was all going to turn out right in the end. Quite simply, he could hear it in her voice. It was going to be him and Marianne, come rain, come sleet or snow, or however the damn thing went. Suddenly it was as if all hesitation had blown away over the edge of the world, and he could not fathom why he had ever doubted.

This insight, crystal clear, came to him within a second. As her brief laugh was still caressing him down the phone.

'I'd like to see you, at any rate,' she said. 'I was wondering about next weekend. How are you fixed?'

'I'm free,' he said. 'For you, I'm always free.'

'And the letter murderer?'

'I shall have solved the case by next weekend,' Barbarotti promised. 'Do you want me to come down to you?'

'No,' she said. 'I thought I'd come and see you, this time. If that's all right? The children are going to be with their dad in Gothenburg, so I can drop them off and pick them up on the way.'

'It's a deal,' said Barbarotti. 'We'll have lobster – I've got a good recipe. Friday evening, then?'

'Friday evening. Gunnar?'

'Yes?'

'Oh, and I think I love you. I forgot to mention that.'

He was still smiling as he made his way down to the breakfast buffet.

'Are you drunk or have you solved the case? asked Eva Backman.

'Neither, unfortunately,' said Barbarotti.

'He's probably been out swimming again,' suggested Astor Nilsson, nodding out towards the Svartån. He himself looked as though he had spent the whole night trying to mate with a reluctant she-bear. 'Jesus, I didn't get a wink of sleep all night. This case is going to do for me.'

'Right, let's get three cups of black coffee and bite the bullet,' said Eva Backman. 'Here comes Schwerin, by the way.'

The chief inspector looked as bland and relaxed as he had in the farmer's field the day before. 'I thought I could just talk things through with you before we go to the police station,' he explained. 'Before it all kicks off, so to speak. Don't you think we've got a lovely castle?'

'Sweden's second loveliest,' said Barbarotti. 'Yes, it wouldn't be a bad idea for us to go over things.'

'Have you seen *Nerikes Allehanda*?' asked Schwerin, passing over one of his copies of the paper.

Barbarotti looked at the front page. DEATH'S HARVEST, it said, in letters three centimetres high, above a picture of the stranded, flash-lit combine harvester and a group of dark figures in the background. It looked ominously suggestive, more like a film poster than anything else, thought Barbarotti.

'Christ Almighty,' said Eva Backman. 'Do they give his name and everything?'

'No,' said Schwerin. 'His parents are coming to identify him this morning. They live in Kramfors. We've taken him to ÖUH, and we'll be sending him on to Gothenburg as agreed.'

'ÖUH?' queried Backman.

'Örebro University Hospital,' said Schwerin.

'Right then,' said Astor Nilsson. 'Let's have this breakfast.'

They went to the table where the three of them had sat for their evening beer. There was much silent leafing through a couple of copies of *Nerikes Allehanda*, which provided an eloquent account of the macabre discovery in the field outside Kumla – and also made the link with the earlier high-profile murders in west Sweden. After a few minutes, Chief Inspector Schwerin cleared his throat tentatively.

'So if I might ask, are you actively pursuing anyone, that is to say, how far have you actually got with the investigation?'

Astor Nilsson stopped chewing and momentarily went cross-eyed.

'Things are gradually moving forward,' said Eva Backman.

'The reason I'm asking is the press conference,' clarified Schwerin. 'It's at three o'clock. We're expecting a lot of people, and it would be good if you could join us.'

'Of course,' said Barbarotti. 'DI Backman and I can cover that while Chief Inspector Nilsson here takes his afternoon nap.'

Astor Nilsson grinned and carried on chewing.

'What's the schedule for the day apart from that?' asked Backman.

Schwerin took out a black notebook. 'Four officers will tackle the neighbours in Hallsberg,' he said. 'That's already underway, in fact, and the idea is for us to have a preliminary report from them in time for the press conference. We've a general meeting at two. By then we should have been able to speak to farmers round Örsta . . . maybe you could . . . ?'

'Absolutely,' said Astor Nilsson. 'We'll drive round the farms and make some enquiries.'

'Good. And I daresay we'll get various nuggets of information coming in on the public hotline, which we'll have to assess and act on. I shall try to keep an overview of that with Ström, who you've already met, and another DI. Well that's how I planned it, anyway, but perhaps you've got your own ideas?'

'That sounds great,' said Barbarotti.

'Brilliant,' said Astor Nilsson.

Backman's mobile rang. It was Jonnerblad, asking whether he and Tallin should come up to Örebro. Backman said there was no need, and promised to keep him informed of developments as the day progressed.

'It would probably be just as well to have a word with Mr Mattsson, too,' said Barbarotti. 'Ask him if he noticed any part of his crop looking at all trampled . . . if we can establish the route the murderer took across the field, it isn't entirely impossible that we'll find a footprint or two. Öhrnberg must have weighed a good seventy-five kilos, surely?'

'That means the murderer isn't some frail little woman,' said Astor Nilsson. 'But I guess we knew that already?'

'There were loads of people trampling about out there last night,' said Backman. 'But of course we ought not to pass up the chance.'

'Can we take a forensic technician with us to Örsta?' asked Barbarotti.

'By all means,' said Schwerin. 'Anything else?'

'We'll have to see what turns up as we go along,' said Astor Nilsson. 'But briefing at police HQ at two o'clock, right?'

'Two o'clock,' confirmed Schwerin.

'There doesn't happen to be a jeweller's anywhere near this hotel, does there?' asked Gunnar Barbarotti. 'I need to buy a watch.'

'Just across the street,' said Schwerin. 'But I'm pretty sure they don't open until ten.'

'That's all right,' said Barbarotti. 'It can wait.'

30

Chief Inspector Schwerin opened the meeting by asking whether any of those present had read Finnish writer Mika Waltari's *Sinuhe the Egyptian*.

They hadn't. Schwerin then told them that the book was largely about an Egyptian brain surgeon living more than a thousand years before Christ – and about how people viewed things at that time. Brain operations, for example; if all the correct procedures had been undertaken and everything had gone as it should, the operation was considered a success. Even if the patient died. The chief inspector was inclined to draw a parallel with that morning and afternoon's police operations: everything had gone according to plan and everyone had done their best, but unfortunately it didn't help – there had been no sign of any murderer.

Interesting comparison, thought Gunnar Barbarotti, exchanging glances with Eva Backman, who looked half amused, half uneasy, he thought.

Though of course it was too early for any evaluation and all the reports were strictly preliminary, Schwerin was at pains to stress. They had spoken to fifty-two people in all, a complete pack of cards, thirty in Hallsberg – mainly neighbours and colleagues of Öhrnberg's – and seventeen in and around Örsta, outside Kumla, plus a handful of acquaintances in

Örebro. They had all declared themselves shocked, to varying degrees. None of them – at least as far as initial assessments indicated – had anything substantive and relevant to contribute. The person who had last seen the murder victim alive, apart from the perpetrator, was apparently a woman who worked in the convenience store fifty metres from Öhrnberg's flat in Tulpangatan. He had been in to buy yogurt, fruit juice and bread just before half past nine on Tuesday evening.

Tuesday, 7 August, reflected Barbarotti. A week before he got the letter. Thanks very much, he thought again.

The special police hotline had so far (the time was 13.50) received a stream of calls amounting to about a hundred. They were a very mixed bag. Four of the callers had been asked in for interviews but only one of these had so far taken place, and it did not seem to have yielded anything of value. But it had been recorded and a transcript would be made in the course of the afternoon.

Barbarotti noticed that Astor Nilsson had dozed off. He was sitting to Barbarotti's immediate right, leaning back with his arms folded and his chin down. He had put on dark glasses, too, so it might just go undetected. Barbarotti hoped he would keep his head upright and not start snoring. The room was full of ambitious young police officers and a member of the investigation team falling asleep wouldn't look good at all.

When Schwerin opened the floor for questions after about half an hour, there was only one. A spindly probationer shyly asked whether the body had been formally identified yet.

'Apologies,' said the chief inspector. 'I forgot to mention that detail. Yes, our man is undoubtedly Gunnar Öhrnberg.'

So now we know, thought Gunnar Barbarotti, giving Astor Nilsson a nudge in the side.

When it came to the crunch, they realized it might be best to let slightly fewer people handle the press conference. Say two. Say Chief Inspector Schwerin and Inspector Backman.

Barbarotti stood with his back pressed to the wall at the very rear of the packed room, and as he observed his two colleagues sitting up front at a table festooned with microphones, he could see it had been the right choice. The calm chief inspector to inspire confidence. And sharp, quick-witted Backman.

An older man, a slightly younger woman, it wasn't a new recipe.

The number of journalists whose bosses had responded to the invitation was around fifty. They were sweating. Three video cameras were whirring. The venue looked as if it had been designed for about thirty people, and if it had any kind of ventilation system, it was clearly not in working order. The temperature was hovering around the thirty-degree mark; it was all tailor-made for encouraging people to get out of the place as soon as possible. Barbarotti wondered to himself whether the mild-mannered chief inspector really was that fiendish. It somehow wouldn't surprise him.

The questions were innumerable. About Öhrnberg. About the other murders. About progress on the investigation.

'Are we dealing with a serial killer?' asked a dark-haired man from TV4.

'No,' said Eva Backman. 'We have reason to believe he's finished killing now. It was these five individuals he was after, and unfortunately he succeeded in his intention.'

'How do you know there won't be more?'

'We have indications that point in that direction.'

'What indications are those?'

'We can't go into that at the moment, I'm afraid.'

'Is it because he's said as much in his letters?'

'Amongst other things.'

And so on. Barbarotti looked round but couldn't spot his old antagonist from *Expressen* anywhere. He realized, of course, that *that question* was bound to come up sooner or later. And so it did: after about fifteen minutes, a tall man got to his feet and introduced himself as Petersson from *Agenda*.

'There was a police assault on a reporter at the start of the week. What's your comment on that?'

'None at all,' said Eva Backman. 'When the main conference is over, the police officer in question will take questions on that, if there are any.'

She had persuaded him that he ought to. Not that it had been all that hard; he knew sticking your head in the sand didn't work where reporters were concerned. The very phrase 'No comment' signalled guilt and shame from a mile away. But he felt a slight sense of unease as he took his seat at the microphones, forty-five sweat-drenched minutes later.

'So it was you?' came the opening question from a dark-haired woman in her fifties.

'Who what?' said Gunnar Barbarotti.

'Who knocked down Persson from *Expressen*?

'No,' said Barbarotti. 'I didn't knock him down.'

'Well an official complaint was made that you had,' noted a beefy type in the first row.

'*Expressen* withdrew its complaint after less than twenty-four hours,' Barbarotti reminded him.

'Can you tell us what happened?' asked a voice with a Finnish accent from towards the back of the room.

'Gladly,' said Barbarotti. 'It was nine o'clock at night. I was just sitting down for something to eat after working a twelve-hour shift. Then Persson turned up and tried to force his way into my flat.'

'How did he do that?' somebody asked.

'He rang on the doorbell. I opened my door. He wanted to come in and ask me questions. I said I hadn't got time, and he had already questioned various other officers earlier in the day. I had given him a long interview myself, the day before.'

'So you threw him out by force?'

'No. He was blocking me from closing the door. I got tired of him in the end. Pushed him out onto the landing and locked the door.'

'But he fell down the stairs?' the first questioner came back.

'I've no idea how he managed that,' said Barbarotti. 'But maybe nothing's beyond *Expressen*.'

A few people laughed.

'Do you think you acted correctly?'

'Presumably not,' said Barbarotti. 'But I chose the lesser of two evils. Naturally it was not my intention that he should hurt himself.'

'What was the other evil?'

Gunnar Barbarotti thought for a moment.

'I know most of you are serious working journalists,' he said. 'I hope your esprit de corps doesn't prevent you from applying some common sense to your take on this. Methods like Göran Persson's only harm the reputation of the press in this country.'

'Is *Expressen* represented in this room?' somebody asked.

'Yes,' replied a fair-haired woman of around thirty.

'Can you provide a comment on why your paper lodged an official complaint and then withdrew it?'

'No,' said the woman. 'I'm afraid not. I was asked to step in today. I think Göran Persson's on leave, actually.'

'Checkmate,' rumbled a deep male voice. 'Now I say to hell with this, let's get some fresh air.'

The proposal met with unanimous approval. Gunnar Barbarotti downed half a bottle of mineral water and gave a sigh of relief.

At five that afternoon they headed south-west once more. Astor Nilsson commandeered the back seat and was asleep before they passed the Kumla turn-off. Eva Backman was driving. Barbarotti had got out the seven photographs from Brittany and was staring at them again. Or at three of them, anyway. He was trying to squint at the Sixth Man and get a slightly clearer idea of what he looked like. It was no good. The fuzziness of his face in all three shots persisted.

'People can never learn to use the focus properly,' he said.

'And what do you say to our own focus?' asked Eva Backman.

'Not the sharpest,' admitted Barbarotti. 'What's Jonnerblad decided about releasing these for publication?'

They had been in contact with Kymlinge half a dozen times during the day. They had given an account of their conversations with various farmers around Kumla, of the futile search for footprints in Dead Man's Field (it was only logical for Dead Man Gunnar to end his days in a field named after him, as the headline writers at *Nerikes Allehanda* had quickly appreciated) and the rest of their investigations around Närke.

They had been supplied with at least one new detail from Jonnerblad in return: that the records showed the same unidentified mobile number had called both Anna Eriksson and Gunnar Öhrnberg. A pay-as-you-go phone, untraceable, and it appeared to have been used only twice. But the dates were interesting. The call to Anna Eriksson was made on Tuesday 31 July. At 10.36. Presumably the day of her death. The call to Öhrnberg was made almost exactly a week later: Tuesday 7 August, at 13.25. Both calls had lasted about a minute. Had the killer rung to make an appointment?

The assumption did not seem entirely unreasonable. Why else get a pay-as-you-go card and only use it twice? Jonnerblad had wanted to know. Unless you were up to no good?

But untraceable, that was the thing.

'Sorry, what did you say?' said Backman.

'I asked if Jonnerblad and Tallin had finished their dithering yet,' said Barbarotti. 'If it wasn't time to give this face to the media now?' He tapped his pen irritably on the photographs.

'I think he said Monday,' said Backman. 'So in the papers on Tuesday, in that case. Well, I suppose that's the route we've got to go down?'

'Do you think that's wrong?'

'I don't know what I think,' said Eva Backman, 'But I know what's going to happen when we do it. And I'm starting to feel a bit tired, you know. I think I might have to punch a journalist soon, to get a few days off.'

'I'm not sure that's the best way to go about it,' said Barbarotti.

Astor Nilsson swore in his sleep on the back seat. 'Fucking baker,' it sounded like.

'What's his problem with bakers?' asked Barbarotti.

'No idea,' said Backman. 'But he can fall out with absolutely anybody, if he chooses to.'

Barbarotti's mobile rang. He looked at the display. 'Sorrysen,' he said. 'Right, prepare yourself for news of a breakthrough.'

Breakthrough was a bit of an exaggeration.

One small step in the right direction was nearer the mark.

'We've found the holiday home the Malmgrens were renting.'

'Good,' said Barbarotti. 'And where is it?'

'Finistère. Twenty kilometres or so from Quimper,' said Sorrysen. 'If you know where that is.'

'I think so,' said Barbarotti. 'More or less.'

'A hamlet called Mousterlin,' said Sorrysen. 'The nearest slightly larger place is Foosnong, or however it's pronounced.'

Barbarotti thought it sounded like a sneeze. 'How's that spelt?' he asked.

'F-o-u-e-s-n-a-n-t,' said Sorrysen.

'Got you,' said Barbarotti. 'How did you find out?'

'Some bloke rang us,' said Sorrysen. 'He runs an agency in Gothenburg that rents out houses in France. Mainly Brittany, it seems. He's been away on holiday himself this August, but when he got home and saw the papers he checked his computer. And found the Malmgrens. They rented that house in Mousterlin for three weeks in June and July 2002.'

Barbarotti digested this. 'What else did he have to say?'

'Not much,' said Sorrysen. 'But we haven't interviewed him formally yet. He only rang us two hours ago, so he's coming in tomorrow.'

'And it was only Henrik and Katarina Malmgren who stayed there? Not any of the others?'

'We don't know. And this agent doesn't know either. He's going to try to find out from the owner of the house down there. It's a six-bed property, though, so it's not impossible.'

'Just imagine if they had,' said Barbarotti after he had thanked Sorrysen and passed the news on to Backman. 'If the whole gang was staying under the same roof.'

Eva Backman thought about it.

'Why on earth would they do that?' she said. 'I mean, they didn't even know each other, I thought we'd established that?'

'Maybe the Malmgrens went in for a bit of sub-letting?' suggested Barbarotti. 'On the Internet or something, people can do that, can't they?'

'Would you want to share a cottage with four strangers on your summer holiday?' said Backman. 'I'd rather stay at home.'

'I wouldn't do it,' said Barbarotti. 'And nor would you. But you never know. Maybe they needed a cheap holiday?'

'He was a senior lecturer and she was an anaesthetic nurse.'

'Fair enough,' said Barbarotti. 'You win. They didn't all stay in the same house.'

'No need to be down in the mouth about it,' said Eva Backman. 'All we've got to do is wait for some other agents to get back from holiday and read the papers. Don't you think?'

'Waiting is one thing we're good at,' said Barbarotti, gathering up the photos on his lap and putting them away. 'What are you doing tomorrow?'

'Spending it with my nearest and dearest,' she said. 'The whole circus is coming home today. And not before time – rumour has it the school term starts on Monday.'

Barbarotti felt a sudden pang in his heart. Start of term? Why couldn't Sara have been born a year later? Then he, too, would have had a start of term to anticipate.

Must ring her tonight, he thought. I bet she's been wondering why she never hears from me.

Or maybe it would be better to wait until tomorrow? When all was said and done. Sunday morning; this was Saturday night, and he didn't feel at all like listening to that smoky chink of bottles all over again. Not remotely.

Perhaps he'd be better off devoting a bit of time to Our Lord this evening? Surely He was the one sitting on his throne of clouds and wondering why he never heard from that nice detective inspector from Kymlinge these days?

Yes, that was definitely the way it was.

31

But in the end, neither of these happened.

Neither the chat to Sara, nor the chat to Our Lord. By the time Eva Backman dropped him outside the entrance of the flats in Baldersgatan – having first seen Astor Nilsson onto the Gothenburg train – it was twenty past eight. He was as hungry as a wolf and realized there was precious little in the fridge for him to get his teeth into.

A few scraps of cheese and ham, an egg or two and a dubious half litre of milk, if he remembered rightly. Not worth even going up to check.

So he took a stroll to the Rocksta Grill, bought his usual two frankfurters with mash and pickled-gherkin mayonnaise and, since he had his briefcase to lug about with him, sat down on a nearby bench in the park round the fire station while he devoured his supper.

And as he did so, the investigation naturally started running riot inside his head. Or carried on doing so, to be more accurate. It was as persistent as a cracked rib or a bad toothache.

All those victims. All those letters.

All the fruitless interviews and all the sprawling effort expended. France? What had Sorrysen said that place was called? Mosterline? He decided to look it up in an atlas as soon as he got home.

And what was the significance of the killer having rung two of the victims but not the rest? If that really was the case. Or had he used other untraceable numbers for the Malmgrens and Erik Bergman? If he needed to contact them before he killed them.

And yesterday evening's grotesque scene out in the middle of the field wasn't easy to put out of his mind, either. Had the perpetrator envisaged it all when he positioned his victim's body? Had he had a mental image of it looking more or less like that? Did he actually *want* the body to be semi-massacred by a combine harvester? On a lovely warm August evening with the moon in the last quarter? Was there some meaning to it all? And if so – what sort of pervert were they dealing with here, for goodness' sake?

Inspector Barbarotti took a bite of frankfurter, focused his mind and pushed the questions away. Here I am on a park bench for my Saturday night dinner, he thought. Frankfurters and mash from a kiosk. That's what I've achieved in my forty-seven-year-old life.

Oh well, it was another beautiful evening and the food wasn't bad. Then his thoughts turned to Marianne, thoughts that seemed to flow in automatically as soon as he cleared some space. They flew into his dazed brain like a dove of peace and love from an entirely foreign continent. A whole flock of doves, to be more accurate. They wheeled within him, filling every last cranny. Strange image, but that was the way with his mental capacities nowadays. He shook his head to get rid of the birds. Once we're actually married, he thought instead, I won't have to eat frankfurters on a park bench again for the rest of my life.

Because that's what will happen, surely? It'll be her and me?

Perhaps this is actually the last time? As the thought struck him, he swallowed down his doubts and his last bit of sausage simultaneously. The very last time?

He scraped his cardboard tray clean of mash and mayonnaise, too, crumpled it up and jammed it in the litter bin. He realized the meal had left him thirsty, and decided on a beer at the Elk before heading home.

Seeing as he was already out and about.

The one beer turned into three.

There were reasons for that. Two of his old schoolfriends, Sigurd Sollén and Victor Emanuelsson, had both found themselves single again and were having a night on the town. As the saying went. Spying Barbarotti, they insisted he join them to chew over the faults of their old teachers for a while. He would be able to remind them of any they had happened to forget.

A good hour went by, and Sigurd Sollén started to get a bit carried away and wanted them to talk about the murder mystery of the decade instead. He had a few tips and ideas that he'd happily share. But a few questions, as well.

Barbarotti downed his last mouthful of beer for the evening and assured Sollén and Emanuelsson that they would get every last detail served up to them in the second volume of his memoirs – *Looking Back: A Copper's Life* – which was scheduled to appear in time for the Gothenburg Book Fair in 2023.

Or thereabouts.

'Hark at you, inshpector,' slurred Sollén. 'Gone and got all shuck up, eh?'

'Shuck up?' said Emanuelsson.

'I shaid shtuck up,' said Sollén.

'Are you tight, you old bastard?' said Emanuelsson in surprise, but by then, Gunnar Barbarotti had already left the table.

When he came in through the door of his flat, the time had advanced to ten to eleven, though Inspector Barbarotti was in blissful ignorance of the fact because he still – for some reason – had the defective watch of eternity from Hallsberg strapped to his wrist.

But he registered that he hadn't been at home since Friday morning – which strictly speaking was only the previous day, when he hastily changed his clothes ready for the trip up to Närke with Backman and Astor Nilsson.

He also registered that he was still wearing those very clothes and was pretty well suited to a park bench at the moment. It couldn't be denied.

But Friday's post was there on the hall floor and he decided to take a look before going for a shower.

Three bills, some kind of reward voucher from Statoil and a bulky brown A4 envelope, that was all. He left the brown envelope till last.

His name and address were written in angular, slightly uneven capitals. Black ink. There was a collection of foreign stamps running almost all the way along the top edge. It took him a few minutes to make out where it had come from.

Cairo.

Cairo? thought Gunnar Barbarotti. What the hell was this? He remembered Egypt had cropped up at some point earlier in the day, but couldn't remember the context. The date on the postmark was clearly legible. 14.08.07.

Four days ago. He got out the bread knife, sat down at the kitchen table and sliced open the envelope.

He pulled out a sheaf of closely written sheets of paper. Computer printout, single spaced. Sixty to seventy pages, he reckoned, but they weren't numbered.

His eyes went to the top of the first page.

'Notes from Mousterlin', it read.

'What in Christ's name? thought Inspector Barbarotti.

The kitchen clock, which wasn't defective, was showing ten past three by the time he finally stepped into the shower.

SIX

Notes from Mousterlin

8–9 July 2002

'You did what?' yelled Erik.

'I killed her,' I told him again. 'She's over there by the tool shed if you want to see her.'

Erik stares at me. His mouth opens and closes. Tiny twitches on his face and neck show me how agitated he is.

'I thought it advisable,' I say. 'What else could I have done?'

'You're not . . .'

He turns his back on me, takes two steps and thinks the better of it. Spins round and tries to see across to the tool shed, but it's too dark. It's impossible to make out if there's really a body lying there.

'Why?' he said. 'Why in God's name?'

I talk him through the chain of events all over again. As I do, he sinks onto a chair and slumps forward with his elbows on his knees and his head in his hands. 'What the fuck shall we do?' he groans when I've finished. 'Can't you see what you've done?'

'What I've done?' I say. 'She knew, man. It was the only thing I could do. What other way out was there?'

He stares at me again. Then he sees the spanner lying there on the white tiles of the terrace.

'With that?' he asks.

I nod. 'Bahco 08072,' I say. 'It was the only thing to hand.'

We both look at it for a few seconds. There's a bit of semi-dried blood round the spanner head, and a couple of dark patches on the terrace. I didn't bother to clean up after myself, just moved the body. Erik gets out his mobile phone.

'I'm calling the others,' he says. 'Fucking hell, I thought this was all sorted.'

'So did I,' I say. 'But do get the others to come, I expect that's best.'

He looks at me as it's ringing, and for the first time I think I detect fear in his eyes.

Less than half an hour later, all four of them are there. It's twenty to eleven at night, but still not properly dark. This area is renowned for its evening light, and we don't need a torch as we stand round in a semicircle surveying the dead woman by the tool shed wall. We can see her very clearly. Now that she's no longer alive, she looks even smaller, and I doubt she weighs much more than her granddaughter. The air isn't at all cold but I notice both women in our party are shivering.

'Jesus Christ,' says Gunnar. 'What the hell have you done?'

'Done?' I say. 'I thought we'd agreed to obliterate all traces of the girl's death?'

Anna whispers something to Katarina, I can't hear what. Henrik's puffing frantically on a cigarette and finding it hard to keep still. He's shifting restlessly, muttering incoherently.

'You killed her,' says Gunnar.

'Yes,' I say. 'I killed her.'

'Murdered,' says Katarina.

'Christ all fucking mighty,' says Henrik.

'Yesterday you were thanking me for taking on an unpleasant task,' I remind them. 'What do you think would have happened if this woman had gone to the police?'

'What did she say?' asks Gunnar. 'Why did she come here in the first place?'

'I thought I'd already explained that,' says Erik.

'We'd like to hear it from the murderer's own mouth,' says Gunnar.

'Can't we go and sit on the terrace?' Anna suggests. 'I don't want to stand here any longer, it's making me feel sick.'

We go over and sit down round the table. Erik lights two patio lanterns and brings out a bottle of red wine. 'I expect you'd all like a glass?' he says.

Nobody refuses, and he gets the glasses and pours the wine. I notice there are more bats this evening than usual, whirring through the diluted darkness. They appear and vanish, appear and vanish, quicker than thoughts.

'Well?' says Gunnar. 'Please be so good as to give us a thorough explanation. Before we go to the police and report you.'

'I don't think you'll be going to the police,' I say.

'Don't be so sure,' says Henrik, and takes a nervous sip of wine.

'OK,' I say. 'But if I hadn't killed her, we'd all have been at the police station by now. I thought we had an agreement?'

'We had an agreement to keep quiet about what happened on Sunday,' says Gunnar. 'Not to kill an old woman.'

'Murder,' says Katarina.

'Good God, so you killed her, just like that?' asks Anna. There's a touch of hysteria in her voice.

'I've never done anything like this before,' I say. 'I've never buried a drowned girl and I don't go around killing old ladies with spanners. I simply don't get what it is you're accusing me of?'

It all goes quiet round the table. Henrik and Anna light fresh cigarettes. Erik's put on sunglasses for some reason, even though it's eleven at night. I can see that Gunnar and Henrik are thinking hard. I can tell that both of them, separately, are starting to see the point in what I've said. And done. Against their own wills, they're realizing that they, too, are in a bind – they don't want to admit that my actions are the consequence of what we previously agreed on. To stay silent about what happened on the boat trip to des Glénan. The fact that the girl Troaë drowned, and it was in deciding to hush it up that we committed ourselves to this course. The responsibility isn't just mine, it is theirs too, and I can see the bitter truth of it slowly seeping into their mildly intoxicated brains even as they cast about for words to process and resist it with.

'You're out of your bloody mind,' says Anna.

'Be quiet, Anna,' says Gunnar. 'We've got to think out some way of dealing with this.'

'Dealing with?' says Anna. 'What the hell do you mean, dealing with?'

'The Root of All Evil,' says Erik and gives a sudden bark of laughter. 'I wouldn't be fucking surprised if they knew just what they were doing when they christened her.'

I can hear that Erik is getting drunk. Henrik stubs out his cigarette and turns to me. 'I would maintain that you have misread the situation,' he said, and blew the last of his cigarette smoke into my face, intentionally or unintentionally. 'Pretty drastically, what's more.'

'Oh yes?' I say. 'And in what way have I misread it?'

'The following,' says Henrik, and I can see he's getting a bit excited at the prospect of an argument, just as if this were some kind of academic dispute. 'You claim we are all equally responsible, but that isn't the case, of course. In actual fact . . . well, in actual fact the blame is entirely yours, and we have decided to keep quiet so as not to dump you in it. It was you who let the girl fall out of the boat and drown, it was you who buried her instead of going to the police and telling them what had happened, it was you who murdered her grandmother. Don't you see that if we tell the whole story now, you alone will bear the full responsibility. We are the ones who are protecting *you*, and we are not indebted or obliged to you in any way.'

'Exactly,' said Katarina.

I think for a moment. I look round the table. 'OK then,' I say. 'If that's the way you see it, let's go to the police right now.'

Henrik had been looking pretty pleased with himself after his exposition, but now his mask dropped. 'You're crazy,' he says. 'I really do believe you're fucking crazy.'

'That's what I've been saying,' Anna points out.

None of the others seem to have any objections to this analysis. Katarina shakes her head and looks out into the darkness. 'What a lot of bats this evening,' she says. 'I wonder why?'

'Maybe they're harbingers of death,' I say.

Gunnar frowns and stares at me intently. It's only Erik, behind his dark glasses, whose look I can't read. Henrik leans across the table towards me again. As if all this were between him and me.

'What is it you want?' he says.

'Sorry?'

'To go to the police? Is that what you want?'

'Not necessarily,' I say.

'What do you mean?'

'I'm prepared to stick by a collective decision,' I say. 'Like last time. But I won't accept the role of scapegoat.'

Henrik leans back in his chair. He exchanges a glance with Gunnar. 'Have you got any suggestions?' he asks.

I shake my head.

'He's out of his mind,' says Anna. 'Christ, can't you see he's out of his mind?'

Gunnar stands up. He takes Anna with him and they move away. Not towards the tool shed but in the other direction. Over to the dustbin and the apple tree. Erik asks if he should open another bottle of wine, and Henrik says he might as well. Entirely involuntarily, I find myself thinking about Anna's face as it looked after the nude swimming session that first evening. I don't know why that image should have embedded itself in my consciousness with such sharp claws. It keeps flashing up before my eyes.

Maybe, I think, it's because I know that if I'd taken her by the hand at that moment, she would have come with me like a shot for sex on the beach. I think Gunnar must be a terrible lover.

Gunnar and Anna come back to the table. 'We've got to decide what to do,' says Gunnar.

'Good idea,' says Erik. 'We can't have her lying there when Monsieur Masson comes to cut the grass tomorrow morning.'

Gunnar ignores this comment. 'So have you got another bottle of wine or not?'

Erik goes to get one. Anna takes a seat beside Katarina and lights a cigarette. I can see she's been ordered to keep quiet from now on. Katarina and Henrik are whispering to each other but I can't pick up what they're saying. And they don't intend me to, either.

'Would you like me to give you all a minute on your own?' I ask. 'If you happen to want another conference.'

'There's no need,' says Gunnar. 'I've got a proposal.'

'Good,' says Katarina.

'My idea is this,' says Gunnar, trying to fix me with a look. 'We're prepared to keep quiet again, if you get rid of the body. We won't go to the police, and if they seek any of us out for any reason, we don't know anything. About the girl, or about her grandmother. You're leaving tomorrow morning, and there's no need for us ever to see each other again.'

He pauses and exchanges looks with the others. 'Can we all agree on that?'

Anna and Katarina nod. Erik, too, and finally Henrik.

'And you?'

'Can I have a bit more wine?' I say.

Erik gives a sort of start. Then he pours the wine, first for me and then for the others. I twirl the glass in my hand for a minute, watching the red wine dance round and round. It's not the colour of fresh blood but more like the old, clotted, dried variety. I drink deeply and put the glass down on the table in front of me.

'I accept the proposal,' I say. 'But I need somebody to carry the spade.'

Gunnar carries the spade. I thought that would be Erik's task, but for some reason it falls to Gunnar. Perhaps because he's a bit taller and stronger than Erik. You never know.

But I carry the woman. We don't say anything, and I walk

ahead, with Gunnar two steps behind. First we take a right onto the dirt track and then, after a couple of hundred metres, we go left towards Menez Rouz along the narrow path. It's the same way as last time, and the woman hangs over my right shoulder just as Troaë did, two days ago. Twice we have to stop, so I can put her down and rest a bit. I feel that I want to bury her close to the girl, not right alongside but within talking distance. It feels important for the girl to have her grandmother within reach even in death. But only within reach, because they clearly didn't always see eye to eye.

When we get to the little open area of ground, wanly lit by the hesitant moonlight, I signal to Gunnar to stop. I carefully lay the body down on the path and Gunnar passes me the spade.

'I'll go back,' he says. 'There's no need for me to stand about waiting.'

'You do that,' I say. 'This is going to take a while.'

He leaves me and is soon swallowed up into the gloom. I am alone with the body, the spade and the marsh.

And the bats. This is starting to feel like a habit.

By the time I get back to Erik's it is quarter past two, but they are all still there.

'We've been talking it over,' says Gunnar. 'And we've decided something.'

'Oh yes?' I say.

'We think it best if you leave now. Henrik and I will give you a lift part of the way, and you can continue by any route you like tomorrow morning. It'll be light in a couple of hours.'

I prop the spade against the railing that runs halfway round the terrace. 'So that's what you've decided, is it?' I say. 'Well, perhaps that's the best solution.'

'Glad you think so,' says Katarina.

'I've just got to clean up a bit first,' I add.

'Have a shower,' says Erik. 'I'll make coffee for you all in the meantime.'

'Whose car shall we go in?' I ask.

'You're welcome to take mine,' says Erik. 'No problem, I've only just filled up. There's enough in the tank to get you to Rennes and back if you want.'

I nod, and leave the others on the terrace while I go in for a shower. I wash the smell of earth and decay from my body.

We drive towards the dawn. Gunnar is at the wheel and Henrik is beside him in the passenger seat. I am in the back seat, sharing it with my big rucksack. The place names slip past in the thinning darkness. *Concarneau. Pont-Aven. Quimperle*, where we join the motorway and pick up speed. We say hardly a word, any of us. I wonder about the amount of alcohol in Gunnar's blood. It would be ironic if we were stopped by a police patrol and got caught for *that*.

But the roads are almost empty at this hour. *Lorient. Auray. Vannes*. They asked me if I preferred Rennes or Nantes. Both of them are a long way from Mousterlin; I realize that they really do want me properly removed. I told them I prefer Nantes. It's a larger city, and further south than Rennes.

I don't know what distance we've put behind us, but it is quarter past six when we turn into a motorway service station on the edge of Nantes. I have been dozing for the past forty-five minutes and I think Henrik has, too. Gunnar has black rings under his eyes and there's something about his look that reminds me of a lemur.

'Right then,' says Henrik. 'This is where our ways part.'

'I suppose so,' I say.

'Sometimes things just go wrong,' says Gunnar, and is overcome by a sudden fit of coughing. I understand that he's trying to say something universal and a bit conciliatory. About us all being victims of unfortunate circumstances, or something along those lines.

But the coughing puts paid to that. He brakes and pulls up right outside the cafe entrance. He doesn't unfasten his seat belt; he evidently doesn't even want to have a cup of coffee in my company before we part – even though he obviously needs one so he can cope with the journey back.

But maybe it's Henrik's turn to drive. Maybe they'll find another cafe as soon as they've got rid of me. Yes, I expect it's as simple as that; they don't want to see me for a second longer than necessary. Another ironic thought strikes me as I'm getting my rucksack out of the car: what if the one who's driving falls asleep at the wheel and they're both killed when the car crashes into a wall of rock? What a macabre postscript. I can't help wondering how the other three would try to explain away what the two men were up to, well over a hundred kilometres from Mousterlin so early in the morning.

'Right, we're off now,' says Henrik. 'No hard feelings.'

They don't even get out of the car. I walk round it and shake hands with each of them through the wound-down side windows.

'Drive carefully,' I say. I swing the rucksack onto one shoulder and go into the cafe.

I don't look back.

I sit at a table by the window, writing. I'm approaching the closing bracket after the latest events in Mousterlin. I've had an egg and bacon galette, and now there's a large cup of black coffee in front of me; I'm the only customer in the desolate place apart from a couple of lorry drivers hunched over vast breakfasts, each at their own window. Perhaps I could ask them for a lift – one or other of them – but I want to sit here for a while. Formulate these closing lines first, and maybe perform some rudimentary morning ablutions. It is still only a few minutes past seven, and I feel anything but ready for a new day.

I briefly consider the fact that in all probability they don't even know my full name, those holidaying Swedes in Mousterlin. In the eleven days we spent together I never revealed more than my first name. That very fact perhaps says something.

In some strange way, I am carrying the girl within me. Her grandmother, too, though her presence is not so palpable. I know I was dreaming about Troaë in those brief interludes of sleep I snatched in the car. Her vivacious innocence and intensity that first day on the beach and at Le Grand Large. Her helplessness in the waves. Her even greater helplessness as the earth closed around her body.

I am not sure I will ever be free of her. She is already eating into me, taking hold, and if there's anything that worries me about the future, this is it. If I had the chance to pass judgement in some utopian court of law, I would let her live in return for the lives of the other five. The grandmother's too, actually. I would do this without a second's hesitation; I am a little sorry that Dr L is not sitting opposite me, because it would certainly be interesting to hear his views on such an equation.

But I shall round this off now. With the concern I have

expressed above. These notes will find their rightful place at the very bottom of my rucksack. Later today, or tomorrow, I will buy a new exercise book to write in.

I finish my coffee and, deciding to forego the ablutions, I shoulder my rucksack and go out into the parking area. The sun is shining and it's going to be a hot day.

I have to move on. I have to head south.

Commentary, August 2007

There, now it is done. I had a plan, I followed it, and it succeeded.

All five are dead. I don't know if Gunnar has been found yet, and perhaps I will never find out. The only thing that made me slightly uneasy was that Katarina Malmgren floated up to the surface. That wasn't my intention. I fixed weights to both bodies but somehow the knots must have worked loose on hers. I wanted both of them at the bottom of the sea, where they could lie and reflect on Troaë's battle with the waves before she died. Those cowards who never left the boat to try to save her. Nor did Erik, in fact he just sat there in the cockpit, so I had to kill him first. I have already commented on the spanner, and that's now fittingly at rest on the seabed; I would have liked to use it on Gunnar, too, but it wouldn't have worked. I had to talk to Gunnar before I despatched him to the other side, and for that I needed a gun.

It proved an interesting conversation. It was particularly satisfying to see him crawling around at my feet, pleading for his life. He shed all his stature like some old, worn-out skin, just as I had hoped. He had already wet himself when I shot him.

I have stopped dreaming about the grandmother. For a while now I have been dreaming about the girl again instead, but now the dreams are good ones. Above all, I see her there on the beach, painting us with that smile of concentration on her face.

But I can't see the picture she painted. I never saw it then, and the people it portrays no longer exist.

The parenthesis is closed and it is high time for me to move on.

20–27 AUGUST 2007

32

When Inspector Barbarotti came into his office on Monday 20 August, it was almost exactly a week since he had left it.

It took him a few seconds to register the fact. Last Monday night he had shoved *Expressen* reporter Persson in the chest, then he had been suspended for three days, spent two up in Närke – plus a Sunday in Kymlinge under a cloud of thoughts, speculations and questions.

He had read *Notes from Mousterlin*, those sixty-four closely written pages, twice through, he had spent an hour and a half talking to Inspector Backman on the phone, almost as long to Astor Nilsson and at least twenty minutes to Jonnerblad.

The others had read the pages too. By nine on Sunday morning, Sorrysen had arrived at Barbarotti's flat to pick up the manuscript for copying and immediate delivery to the National Laboratory of Forensic Science in Linköping. They had all received a copy: prosecutor Sylvenius and Asunander, Jonnerblad, Tallin, Astor Nilsson, Sorrysen and Backman. And there was one for him, too.

'I'm braced for another sleepless night,' Astor Nilsson had confided to him around ten last night from Kymlinge Hotel. 'But at least there's some reading matter for me to get my teeth into. Bloody hell.'

Barbarotti hadn't slept particularly well either. He had been wrestling with a strange dream about combine harvesters sinking in mid-Atlantic, where he was part of a rescue team that failed to save all the distressed passengers from the angry waves. They were searching in particular for a little girl, and when he woke up around six thirty, it was a few moments before he realized his bed was not a raft and the only water around was the rain pattering on the bike shed roof in the courtyard.

He looked round his office. No one had cleaned up in his absence. He remembered the apple he had eaten the previous Monday afternoon, and the half cheese sandwich he had not finished, but neither object looked truly familiar to him. He had evidently drunk coffee from four different mugs, and there were two open bottles of a blackcurrant drink on the window sill.

At least the cleaner had emptied the bin – you had to be thankful for small mercies. He sighed and started to clear up, but less than a minute later Inspector Backman put her head round the door to say it was briefing time. Gunnar Barbarotti nodded, opened the little window vent to air the place, and went with her.

'I anticipate this briefing will last until lunchtime at least,' began Superintendent Jonnerblad. 'Coffee will be coming about quarter past ten.'

Barbarotti looked at his watch; he had found an old one in his desk drawer at home, an ancient wind-up model, but so far it had shown every sign of working properly. Just now, for example, it showed nine minutes past nine.

Everyone looked unusually calm and collected. People often did on a Monday morning, of course – it was a question of keeping your tail up and making an assured impression when Friday was still light years away, there was nothing strange in that. But today there was something extra. We look like a sports team that's been training for three years for a specific competition, thought Barbarotti. And now we're there. This is when it matters.

Why do I get these stupid ideas? was his next thought. I mean, we've been on this case nearly a month, and we're finally getting somewhere. It's hardly surprising everyone's determined and expectant.

'We've been working on this case for almost a month,' said Jonnerblad. 'For the first time, we've got some kind of handle on what it's all about. This is our most important meeting to date and it's vital that we stay focused today, I'm sure I don't need to remind you of that. Tallin.'

Tallin took over. 'Personally, I've read the murderer's account through twice,' he started. 'I know the rest of you have done the same. At least once. It's a gruesome tale he tells, I'm sure we all agree. He's clearly convinced we're never going to catch him. But we, naturally, must work on the opposite assumption. That is, that we're going to track him down and call him to account. Is there anyone with any immediate comment on this?'

Eva Backman raised a pen in the air.

'His ending?' she said. 'Before we go on, I'd like to ask you all what you think about the way he brings it to an end.'

'Same question from me,' said Astor Nilsson. 'He writes that none of the people in that painting are alive. Does he include himself in that?'

'Highly possible,' said Jonnerblad. 'But we certainly can't close the investigation just because we think the perpetrator might be dead. If we *know* he's dead that's a different matter, of course.'

'I've never said we should close the investigation,' said Astor Nilsson.

'It could be he's trying to make us *believe* he's dead,' said Sorrysen.

'But that's what's so damned odd,' said Astor Nilsson. 'Why is he writing to us at all? First all those letters and now this document. If he'd just killed these five people and gone off somewhere . . . well, why didn't he settle for that?'

'Significant point,' said Asunander unexpectedly. Unusually, the chief inspector was sitting with them at the table, not just observing proceedings from the sidelines like some silent, slightly disapproving shadow.

'He apparently feels the need to tell us why he did it,' said Eva Backman. 'I get the sense it's terribly important to him for his motives to be known.'

Jonnerblad cleared his throat. 'We'll go into the perpetrator's character in more detail this afternoon,' he announced. 'Lillieskog is coming over later with a forensic psychiatrist. We're dealing with an exceptionally tricky individual here, I'm sure we can all agree on that?'

He looked round the table. Tricky, thought Barbarotti. That was putting it mildly.

'He writes well,' said Astor Nilsson. 'You could almost call it literature.'

'Exactly,' said Eva Backman. 'That struck me, too. But even if we assume he's feeding us precisely the information he wants us to have, it's a ghastly story. And he doesn't portray himself in a particularly good light, either.'

'I don't think he puts himself in any sort of light at all,' said Astor Nilsson. 'I can't get to grips with him in the slightest.'

'Maybe it's his intention for us not to do that,' said Eva Backman.

'You reckon?' asked Astor Nilsson.

'I mean, it's clearly written as it was happening,' observed Tallin after a pause. 'Apart from these commentaries, that is. Well, hopefully we'll get verification of quite a few things in the course of the day. We already have confirmation that the Malmgrens did stay in that particular place.'

'But he must have done this fair copy,' Barbarotti pointed out. 'He wrote it all by hand in 2002, or so he claims. Since then he seems to have typed it up on a computer.'

'Yes, he does,' said Jonnerblad. 'But I don't see what difference that makes.'

'Probably none at all,' said Barbarotti. 'It would be interesting to know when he did it, that's all. Was it was five years ago or just before he started killing them?'

'Mhmm, er . . .' muttered Jonnerblad, leafing through a pile of papers. 'Well, as I say, there are a lot of issues to discuss. As you'll all have noted, we're recording this briefing. It's important not to overlook any individual question that comes up.' He indicated the diminutive tape recorder in the middle of the table. 'Any other comments at this point?'

'Have you been in touch with the French police yet?' asked Backman.

'We've got a call booked with them for this afternoon,' said Tallin. 'But any views on the information he gives about himself in these notes? We really don't find out very much, do we?'

'That's partly what I was driving at,' said Barbarotti. 'He doesn't tell us anything at all about himself, and I reckon any references like that in his original handwritten notes were removed when he typed them up.'

'Not impossible,' said Astor Nilsson. 'This Dr L he refers to a few times, how do we go about locating him?'

'I don't think we're meant to locate him,' said Eva Backman. 'And I still think the fact that our man hides everything, or almost everything, about himself is an indication that he hasn't taken his own life. If he was dead, it wouldn't really matter that much, would it?'

'Maybe he doesn't want it all to come out,' said Sorrysen. 'After his death, I mean.'

'But he tells the whole story,' said Backman. 'He wants to conceal his identity, but I don't get the impression he's ashamed of what he's done. Or feels any sense of remorse. On the contrary, he stands by what he's done.'

'Except in the case of the girl,' said Sorrysen.

'Yes, though he's actually innocent there,' said Backman. 'But he's got to kill these people because of what happened in Brittany five years ago – and he's got to explain why he's doing it. That's why he writes it all down. Isn't that the key here?'

'Some good points,' said Jonnerblad. 'We'll take them up with our psychiatric expert this afternoon. Backman, have you got that timeline I asked you for?'

Eva Backman nodded and brought out a sheet of paper. 'So this refers to his activities in the present, so to speak,' she explained. 'We've already ascertained that the murders and the letters to Barbarotti aren't particularly synchronized, and as for the potential role of this Hans Andersson, we still haven't the foggiest. Shall I go through the whole thing?'

'If you wouldn't mind,' said Jonnerblad.

Eva Backman cleared her throat. 'So, to take the sequence

of murders first, it starts with Erik Bergman on 31 July and continues with Anna Eriksson later the same day. Then we have Gunnar Öhrnberg, and we're not sure about this one, but sometime around 7 August seems reasonable, and lastly Henrik and Katarina Malmgren on the night of 12 August. If we compare those with the times at which Barbarotti's letters arrived, it's interesting to note that the famous Dead Man Gunnar letter arrives on Wednesday. It's postmarked in Gothenburg on the thirteenth, that is, last Monday, and it should have reached Kymlinge on the Tuesday, but I expect we can blame the slight delay on the Post Office.'

She took a sip of water and went on.

'Then there's the communication from Cairo, this recent one. It was sent from Cairo airport on Tuesday, the fourteenth, which means – correct me if I'm wrong here – that our perpetrator either went back to Sweden after he'd killed the Malmgrens on the ferry, or that he posted the Dead Man Gunnar letter before boarding. Personally I incline to the latter, especially as he's already in Cairo by Tuesday. Are you with me?'

'I think so,' said Astor Nilsson. 'But if he flew direct from Kastrup to Cairo on the Monday, then we'll have him on the passenger lists. There can't be that many planes a day.'

'I'm pretty convinced he didn't fly direct to Cairo,' said Eva Backman. 'He went to London or Paris or Frankfurt and bought his ticket for the next leg there.'

'Passport?' said Sorrysen. 'He must have shown his passport. Or ID card, anyway.'

'It's scarcely necessary these days,' said Tallin. 'For Cairo, perhaps, but not within the EU.'

Jonnerblad shook his head. 'If he's been carrying this story around with him for five years, then he's certainly had time to arrange a false passport, too. After all, he got himself a gun without any problem, we know that.'

'Not five years,' said Barbarotti. 'This trying to get some money out of them, which he refers to in his next to last commentary . . . that was only six months ago, or that's what I took him to mean, anyway. Don't you think it was after that he made his mind up?'

'It seems plausible,' said Jonnerblad. 'But that would still have left him plenty of time.'

'Enough, anyway,' said Barbarotti. 'I've got a completely different question. What are we going to do about releasing the photo to the papers now?'

Jonnerblad straightened up and put a pen in his breast pocket. 'Tallin and I have talked about that,' he said. 'And we don't really think this changes anything. The prosecutor feels the same, so we want to give the media the picture this afternoon. We know the pressure it's going to put on us, but as I see it, it's still the quickest way we can get him identified.'

'One important aspect,' put in Tallin, 'is that these photos are basically the only thing we have that the murderer didn't supply himself.'

'Significant point,' repeated Asunander, as unexpectedly as before, and the room fell silent for a second or two. A half-formed thought ran through Barbarotti's brain, one that somehow seemed familiar and strange at the same time as it flitted out of reach with the speed of a bat. But there was definitely something to it.

'Christ, yes,' said Astor Nilsson. 'I shall feel bloody sorry for the five hundred poor devils who happen to look like him, but

I'm sure we're right to publish it. If we're lucky, we'll have his identity within the week.'

'It would be nice to have his name, at any rate,' said Eva Backman. 'Even if we never track him down in person.'

'If it's possible to find old Nazis after fifty years, it's more than possible to find quintuple murderers after a month,' said Astor Nilsson.

'Six,' said Sorrysen. 'You forgot one.'

'Sorry,' said Astor Nilsson. 'Swedish steel found its mark on an old French lady too.'

'But he hasn't got the girl's life on his conscience,' Eva Backman reminded them.

'Not in the same way, it's true,' said Tallin. 'But it's a horrible story by any standards.'

They lapsed into silence again. Jonnerblad rustled through his papers and Asunander got up to open the window. 'Hot,' he said by way of explanation.

'I wonder whether they were questioned,' said Eva Backman.

'Pardon?' said Jonnerblad. 'Who?'

'Our victims. In France, after he left. And whether the police found out the girl had been with them, or not . . . and if they did, that would be another reason for interviewing them.'

'We'll get answers to that this afternoon,' said Tallin. 'Or very soon, at any event. Yes, I agree, one wonders whether they really did manage to avoid a visit from the police. Must have had luck on their side, if so.'

'They were actually innocent,' Astor Nilsson pointed out. 'We probably shouldn't forget that.'

'Innocent?' said Eva Backman.

'Of murder, at any rate,' specified Astor Nilsson. 'The question of their burden of moral guilt is worth discussing, though.'

'It weighed heavily enough to cost them their lives,' said Barbarotti. 'All five of them.'

'In the murderer's eyes, yes,' said Tallin. 'I just hope nobody round this table feels the same way. Or buys into his confessions unquestioningly. It isn't exactly a normal brain we're granted access to here, is it?'

His pen tapped the Mousterlin document, lying in front of him on the table.

'No,' said Eva Backman. 'I'd been expecting something pretty disgusting but this . . . well, in a way it's almost worse. So . . . so sad, too.'

Barbarotti glanced automatically at the sad-looking Inspector Sorrysen, and recalled that he'd been the one to pick up on a first little clue to lead them to France. The shade of blue paint on that litter bin.

It felt like a hundred years ago. He realized that in actual fact it was only about a fortnight.

'What's our approach?' he asked. 'Are we sending anyone down there?'

'It's not out of the question,' said Jonnerblad. 'Not out of the question at all.'

The latter part of the morning briefing played out in the minor key of the remaining unanswered questions, and Inspectors Barbarotti and Backman made time to slip away to the King's Grill in their lunch hour. They felt in need of a bit of traditional home cooking after all the takeaway frankfurters and instant mash.

'What did you mean by sad?' he asked, once they each had

the dish of the day in front of them: horseradish pike with melted butter and boiled potatoes.

'Don't you think so?' she asked in surprise. 'That it's sad?'

'Yes, maybe,' said Barbarotti. 'At least where the girl and her grandmother are concerned.'

'But I think there's a sort of sadness about the perpetrator himself, too,' said Backman. 'The whole thing's so . . .'

She hesitated.

'So . . . what?'

'So horribly random. It need never have happened. A little girl's hand slipped out of his grasp and seven people lost their lives for it.'

Barbarotti pondered. 'Eight, if he's also taken his own.'

'And do you think he has?' asked Backman.

'No,' said Barbarotti. 'For some reason I doubt it, actually. Don't ask me why.'

'OK,' said Backman. 'I don't think he's dead either. But who is he?'

'Good question,' said Barbarotti.

'Does he have any kind of profession? How's he been living for these five years since it happened . . . since he was sitting in that motorway cafe? And where?'

'What was he doing before all this?' put in Barbarotti.

'That, too. He walks and writes and talks about Dr L. I've stared at that picture of him when they're all sitting at the restaurant, and maybe it's that very day that he writes about? When they'd just met – what was the place called?'

'Bénodet,' said Barbarotti. 'The old harbour in Bénodet.'

'That was it. He looks so . . . well, so ordinary.'

Barbarotti nodded. 'I think so too. But then he does write that his inner life isn't visible in his outward appearance. He smiles and smiles, smiles and smiles, I think that's Hamlet actually . . . he must be pretty well educated, don't you reckon?'

'Yes,' said Eva Backman, and stared into mid-air for a few seconds, as if trying to capture some entirely new thought. But apparently she failed, because she shook her head and put down her knife and fork. 'Yes, that's the impression I get. It's like Astor Nilsson said, these notes have a definite literary touch. But where did he come from originally? Was he really in some kind of psychiatric care? He's hitching a lift on the motorway outside Lille, and then . . .'

'And after that he's at this place in Brittany for a couple of weeks,' supplied Barbarotti. 'But then he's gone again.'

'Heading south.'

'Heading south, yes.'

Silence again. It occurred to Barbarotti that he ought to have brought his list of questions along today, the one he'd drawn up when he was reading the Mousterlin document for the second time. To provide a bit of structure; it felt in a way as if they were just repeating the same questions and the same surprised reactions over again.

But the list was on his desk back home in Baldersgatan.

'His wife?' said Backman. 'What do you think about her? He writes that she died a few years back. But she and Dr L are the only people from his past that he mentions. Aren't they?'

'Correct,' said Barbarotti. 'We basically know nothing about him as he is today, but if we find him . . . well, you bet we'll get it all out of him. By the end, we'll have his first teacher's name and know what shoe size his disabled cousin in Bengtfors takes. And they'll all tell their stories in *Expressen*.'

Eva Backman laughed. 'Yes, I expect so. The picture of a murderer, it's . . .'

'Yes?'

'The most titillating thing imaginable, basically. And incidentally, it's been that way for hundreds of years, no, thousands, and it's still just the same today. Women are going to fall in love with him, just like they did with Clark Olofsson and Hannibal Lecter . . . one wonders why.'

'Isn't that why you're a police officer?' asked Barbarotti. 'So you get to meet that sort of individual and have your darker urges naturally satisfied?'

'The hell it is,' observed Eva Backman soberly. 'You've put your foot in it there, constable. Have you got another appointment with Olltman coming up, while we're on that subject?'

'I think she's declared me fit,' said Barbarotti. 'But I'd better check.'

'You do that,' said Eva Backman. 'Well, half-time's nearly up, don't you reckon?'

'Yep, better get back,' said Barbarotti.

33

The forensic psychiatrist was called Klasson and was a woman of forty-five. She and Lillieskog had been working well together for several years, she told them, but she doubted either of them would have a great deal to contribute to this case.

She had read all the material, nonetheless, especially the Mousterlin notes, and was prepared to offer a tentative analysis of the man they were hunting for.

Empathy deficit disorder was the first thing she wanted to put her finger on. His way of expressing himself about the people he went on to kill indicated that. The comments he had added later revealed an individual who found it hard to understand other people's feelings. And the murder of the girl's grandmother pointed to a pronounced lack of emotion in the perpetrator. He did not express any regret or remorse for his act, seeing it simply as 'a logical consequence', quoted Klasson.

'But he shows some feeling for the girl,' Backman pointed out.

'He does,' said Klasson. 'Very strong feelings, in fact, but it's interesting to note how he refers to them. He says she's "eating into" him, if I'm not mistaken. It's a process he doesn't seem to understand; it's beyond his control in the same way that all feelings seem to be external to him. He isn't really in contact with them.'

'It's his feelings for the girl that trigger everything,' prompted Lillieskog. 'Eventually. Perhaps we could say that his emotional life is out of balance?'

'A pretty typical disorder,' Klasson went on. 'Over-reactions and under-reactions. But I really do want to stress that we've remarkably little to go on in this case. The account he's left us with is extremely well written, in fact he seems to have the makings of an author. Which consequently means he gives us the image of himself that he wants us to have, of course. Not that he ever idealizes his image, I don't mean that. But I still think he writes with some kind of honest intent. He wants to tell this story and explain why he – as he sees it – has been forced to kill these five people.'

'So why does he stay with them, when he dislikes them so much?' Sorrysen asked. 'I find it hard to get my head round that.'

'Who knows?' said Klasson. 'But he's clearly used to not belonging anywhere, and indeed he tells us that at the outset. In his very first sentence. We're certainly dealing with a very lonely person, I think I can say that with confidence.'

'So it's not possible to make a psychiatric diagnosis of him on the basis of what he tells us?' asked Tallin.

'No,' said Klasson. 'We can speculate in various ways. He's obviously had contact with mental health services, perhaps even spent time in some institution or other. But I couldn't really guess what his medical notes say.'

'You're more used to diagnosing people face to face?' asked Astor Nilsson.

'Undoubtedly,' said Klasson, and allowed herself a fleeting

smile. 'Profiling is Lillieskog's territory, but we do collaborate, as I said.'

Lillieskog nodded. 'You always have to adjust the profile once you find the person behind the mask,' he said. 'And you often learn something new at that stage. One thing that brought me up short when I read his account was his wife. He mentions her twice, but only in the briefest of terms. We learn that she died. Five years before this Brittany interlude, as far as we can judge. How did she die? Is there some kind of trauma here? She can't have been all that old, after all, perhaps no more than twenty-five? There could be an accident involved, or something even worse lurking there.'

'Even worse?' queried Astor Nilsson.

'Yes,' said Eva Backman. 'I get this uneasy feeling whenever he mentions his wife. Could that have been where it all started?'

'It's entirely possible,' said Klasson. 'When you find him, I'll be happy to take him on for a couple of weeks, but until then I don't really know what to say about him. He's something of an enigma to me, as I presume he is to all of you.'

The briefing dragged on for a further half hour, but it seemed to Gunnar Barbarotti that nothing new emerged. Nothing that hadn't already been said, one way or another, and he took Klasson's term as the best summary of the perpetrator's character.

An enigma.

A little later that afternoon, two emails went off to the French police. A short one in French – Tallin turned out to have some acquaintance with the language – and then a longer one in English. Barbarotti and Backman, meanwhile, drew up a six-page outline of the case, in English, including a summary of the Mousterlin document; around four thirty, they emailed it up to the National CID for language checking, and at five it was time for the press conference and the release of the Sixth Man's photograph.

Gunnar Barbarotti didn't take part in the conference, but he knew they were going to stress that this didn't mean they were hunting for a murderer. Only that the police urgently wanted to contact the person circled in the picture.

It was taken in Brittany in France in the summer of 2002, and it was possible that he was in possession of information vital to the investigation into the five murders committed in various places around Sweden – with Kymlinge as a kind of grim hub – over the past month.

That was how it would be presented and then it would be up to reporters, readers, listeners and viewers to interpret the message as best they could.

Fat chance, thought Gunnar Barbarotti as he pulled his Crescent out of the cycle rack and set off home. For his part, he was under no illusions, and had no trouble visualizing the next morning's headlines:

THE MURDERER?

And the picture of Gunnar Öhrnberg, Henrik Malmgren and the Sixth Man at that restaurant table.

The first two of them murdered. Perhaps by the third, the one whose face was circled in white.

Not a halo. Just the opposite.

When I get home I'll ring Marianne, and Sara as well, Gunnar Barbarotti decided. I've got to stop thinking about this. Get it out of my head, basically, or it's going to burst.

But before he had time to ring either of them, he had a call from the third woman in his life.

Helena. His ex-wife. It took him a fraction of a second to remember that she existed, and he wondered what to put that down to.

'Hello,' he said. 'Nice to hear from you.'

'I hope it is,' she said, 'because there's something we need to have a serious talk about. But only if you've got time.'

'I've got time,' he assured her, and sank onto the sofa. He remembered the previous week's conversation with Helena after the Göran Persson incident, and assumed that was still on her agenda.

But it wasn't.

'Ulrich's had this amazing offer.'

Oh, he thought. And who the hell is Ulrich?

He didn't say it and that was just as well, because Ulrich was Helena's new other half, of course, and his sons' current father. When he came to think about it, he knew that was his name, of course – not Torben as he'd been imagining – and he'd just happened to repress it.

'They want to put him in charge of a completely new yoga centre in Budapest. He'll get a two-year contract and a flat in the middle of town. It's ideal, and we'll never get another chance like this again, but we've got to make our minds up within the week.'

What is she talking about? thought Barbarotti. 'Why is it ideal?' he asked.

'Because Ulrich speaks Hungarian, of course.'

'Why on earth does he speak Hungarian?'

'Because he's Hungarian, you daft idiot.'

'You've never told me that.'

'I'm sure I have.'

'I was convinced he was Danish. How the heck can a Hungarian be called Ulrich?'

'His mum's Danish. But he was born in Debrecen and he lived there until he was ten.'

'All right,' said Barbarotti. 'I believe you. So what has this got to do with me?'

He could feel himself getting tetchy and took a deep breath to try to calm down.

'The boys, of course.'

'The boys?'

'Yes. We've discussed all the options, and it doesn't seem very practical to drag them off to Budapest. I'm sorry about that, I really am, but the flat's too small. There's a wonderful view of the Danube, though.'

'So you mean . . .'

'Yes. I think it would be best for Lars and Martin to live with you for a couple of years. But only if you think so too, of course. Now Sara's moved out and everything, I thought it might suit all parties.'

All parties? wondered Gunnar Barbarotti. I know which party you represent.

But he took two deep breaths and thought about it. The maturity that had been afflicting him lately was continuing to make its presence felt. Keeping things nice and cool through all the phases of his life.

'I see,' he said. 'And what do *they* think about it?'

'We haven't told them yet. I wanted to sound you out first.'

'I thought you said you'd discussed all the options?'

'Ulrich and I have, not the children.'

'OK,' said Gunnar Barbarotti. 'Talk to Lars and Martin

tonight, then, and ask them to give me a ring. I might be getting married soon, but presumably that's not a problem?'

The line went very quiet and he thought they must have been cut off.

'Hello?'

'I'm still here. Why didn't you say anything?'

'I wanted to discuss it with my wife-to-be first.'

It sounded unnecessarily petulant and he bit his tongue.

'All right. If that's the way you want it, then fine. But I'll talk to the boys. And tell them that little bit of news as well. Has she got a name?'

'Marianne.'

'Marianne? That was the name of the girl you'd just broken up with when you and I met. It isn't her, is it?'

'No,' said Gunnar Barbarotti. 'It isn't her.'

'Good. We'll be in touch later this evening, then.'

'You can tell the boys I'd enjoy having them with me.'

Helena promised to do so and they ended the call.

I didn't mention that I might be moving to Helsingborg, thought Barbarotti, and went into the kitchen to put on a pan of water for some pasta.

But then again, Helsingborg wasn't in Hungary.

He had finished eating and was on the point of calling Sara when Tallin rang.

'Good evening,' he said. 'Tallin here. I'm sorry to disturb you.'

'No problem,' said Barbarotti. 'How did the press conference go?'

'Pretty well,' said Tallin. 'They got their juicy bone, didn't they, so it was all over in half an hour. How's your French?'

'I can count to twenty on a good day,' said Barbarotti. 'Why do you ask?'

'Because you and I are flying down there tomorrow morning. A female colleague who speaks fluent French is coming with us to be on the safe side. An inspector from Gothenburg.'

'You've spoken to the police down there?'

'Only by email. But it seems to work well enough. We're off to Quimper to meet a *commissaire* called Leblanc.'

'Oh yes?' said Barbarotti. 'Why . . . why isn't Jonnerblad going?'

'Because his wife's having an operation on Wednesday. Cancer. He's going up to Stockholm tomorrow evening.'

'Oh dear,' said Barbarotti. 'I didn't know . . .'

'Nor me. He didn't say a thing until yesterday. We'll just have to hope it all goes well.'

'Yes,' said Barbarotti, and was suddenly struck by how little he knew about his temporary colleagues. Nothing about their families, hobbies or leisure interests. Not even what football teams they supported.

Almost the same as with the murderer, he thought.

'We think three days should do it,' said Tallin. 'Back home on Friday. Does that work for you?'

'I've got something really important on Friday evening,' said Barbarotti.

'No problem,' said Tallin. 'We'll be home by then. The flight leaves from Landvetter at 10.50 tomorrow. A car will pick you up at quarter past eight. We'll leave our planning and so on for the way down. Right then, that's that.'

'Yes, I suppose it is,' said Barbarotti.

*

After this conversation with Tallin, he realized he didn't feel up to talking to either Sara or Marianne. So he put on some fado music, made a cup of tea and started reading the notes from Mousterlin for the third time. Just as well to be as prepared as possible, he thought. If we're going to be treading in the murderer's footsteps.

He carried on right to the end this time, too, and it was after twelve by the time he fell into bed. Just as he put out the light, he realized he'd heard nothing from Lars or Martin.

This simple fact kept him awake for at least another hour after that.

34

At Landvetter he caught sight of the first headlines, and they more or less matched what he had anticipated.

But none of the papers actually used the word 'Murderer'. They had gone with 'Wanted' and 'Who Are You?' instead. Thank heavens for small mercies, thought Barbarotti. Perhaps Jonnerblad and Tallin had made some impact with their appeal for self-control at yesterday's press conference, after all.

Or perhaps they had simply lied.

'Nice to get away, today of all days,' commented Tallin. 'Look, here comes our French companion.'

Carina Morelius didn't look very French. Barbarotti had unconsciously been expecting an elfin figure with short black hair, soulful eyes and sharp wits; Inspector Morelius was more reminiscent of a Norwegian women's skiing champion. Or a *former* Norwegian women's skiing champion; she looked to be in her forties and was tall, blonde and powerfully built.

'I'm glad you were able to make time for this,' said Tallin once the introductions were out of the way. 'Our *commissaire* supposedly speaks English, but you never know.'

'The pleasure's mine,' said Carina Morelius. 'On principle, I never turn down a trip to France. So you're the famous Barbarotti?'

She actually said it without irony or undertone, so he

accepted it at face value. 'Oui,' he said. 'The bloke who makes short work of jumped-up reporters and who's given police violence a face of its own.'

She laughed. 'There are all sorts, I assume. Police *and* journalists, I mean.' Her expression turned serious. 'This is an absolutely shocking story. I've only had it from the papers and TV, of course, but I expect you'll have time to put me in the picture on the way down.'

'We certainly will,' said Tallin, checking the time. 'It's six hours until we land in Quimper and you're going to need it all. We've got a document of sixty-four densely written pages for you to study, amongst other things.'

'I look forward to it,' said Inspector Morelius, and Barbarotti could detect no irony there, either.

At Quimper airport, it was raining.

They were met by a young policewoman in uniform, holding a sign that said *Talain*, and Inspector Morelius immediately engaged her in conversation in a French that made her sound more or less like a native. As far as Barbarotti could judge, at any rate. But then she had lived in Lyons for five and a half years and been married to a Frenchman, a professional cyclist, until she left him for a masseur from just outside Gothenburg. She had given them this and other assorted pieces of information on the plane from Gothenburg to Paris, where they had all been sitting together. From Charles de Gaulle to Quimper it was full to bursting and the seats unnumbered, so they had to sit apart.

Though of course the majority of their travelling time had been devoted to information and study material, just as Inspector Tallin had said.

Tallin also addressed the occasional comment to the young policewoman as she piloted them into the town; he had already shown that he knew a bit of the language. Barbarotti, for his part, spent the journey staring out at the rain through the side window from his back seat. What am I doing here? he thought. What are they talking about? I'm going to be the country bumpkin for three days.

But Commissaire Leblanc really did speak English. With a pronounced French accent, admittedly, but there was nothing wrong with his vocabulary. He was short and bald, and wore rimless glasses with little round lenses. He reminded Barbarotti of an actor whose name he couldn't remember. Leblanc greeted them eloquently and served coffee, announcing that the CID at the Quimper *préfecture de police*, of which he was head, would do everything in its power to support its Swedish colleagues in their work.

But he would require a fuller briefing on the case. He had read the faxes and Barbarotti and Backman's overview, but they needed a little more meat on those bones, yes?

For a good half hour, Tallin and Barbarotti did their best to provide this – with the occasional interjection in French from Inspector Morelius – and when they had finished, Leblanc took off his glasses, started polishing them with a little green cloth he took out of his desk drawer, and declared himself somewhat perplexed.

'*Dérouté*. Betwixted, yes?'

'Bewildered,' decided Carina Morelius. 'He says he's a bit bewildered.'

'Why?' asked Tallin.

'Because,' said Leblanc, checking the shine on his glasses by holding them up to the strip light on his ceiling, 'I do not remember a missing persons case that involved two people in the summer of 2002.'

The room went very quiet. Inspector Tallin raised his right hand and lowered it again.

'But there must have been a case,' said Barbarotti.

Leblanc gave an expansive Gallic shrug.

'I understand that you believe this,' he said. 'But I have checked in our archives and there is no record of any such report.'

'No missing girl, no missing grandmother?'

'No.'

'How strange,' said Tallin.

'We had a couple of Dutch tourists reported missing that summer, I do remember that,' Leblanc went on. 'A young man and woman, but they turned up later, somewhere near Perpignan. Drugs were involved in some way, if I'm not mistaken.'

'But surely it's impossible for the disappearance of two people to go unreported?' asked Tallin.

'Unfortunately not as impossible as we might wish,' said Leblanc somewhat apologetically, putting his glasses back on. 'There's also a chance that it was reported to some other police authority. But tell me, do you get the impression that this girl's grandmother had her own house near Mousterlin?'

'Definitely,' said Tallin.

'I'm not so sure of that,' objected Barbarotti, 'I actually think there could be other readings.'

'Other readings?' queried Leblanc.

'Yes,' said Barbarotti. 'The girl is the only one to mention the house, the first time they meet. But then it's implied at various points that the girl isn't really reliable. I read through his notes again last night, and—'

'I don't really know if I agree with this,' Tallin interrupted, but Leblanc ignored him.

'Could she have been renting a house?' he asked. 'If they were here on holiday, I mean?'

'Possibly.'

'But the grandmother is never referred to by name?'

'No.'

'And we don't get any idea of *where* this house is?'

'No.'

Barbarotti glanced over at Tallin, who gave a vaguely affirmative nod. 'This house question isn't entirely clear, it's true,' he admitted. 'Perhaps I assumed when I read the notes that the old woman and her granddaughter lived in a house somewhere near Fouesnant, and that the woman owned the house, but of course it's possible that Inspector Barbarotti is right.'

'He writes at one point that he thinks the girl is a compulsive storyteller,' Barbarotti pointed out. 'The first time I read his account, I thought for a while that there might not be any grandmother at all, and it was just something the girl made up. But then she appeared, so my suspicion was unfounded.'

'Appeared and met her death,' said Tallin.

'It's a horrible story,' Inspector Morelius said in French.

'All right,' said Leblanc. 'I think I'm starting to get a clear picture now. If a woman who has a house in Fouesnant goes missing with her grandchild, this matter will naturally come to our attention sooner or later. However, if we assume that it was not the grandmother the girl invented, but only the house, where does that leave us?'

Barbarotti scratched his head and exchanged another vacant look with Tallin. 'Yes, where does that leave us?' he repeated. 'It could even be the case that they weren't staying in a house at all, but . . . ?'

'At a campsite?' supplied Tallin. 'There are plenty of those in the area, aren't there?'

'Mais oui,' said Leblanc enthusiastically. 'Between Bénodet and Beg-Meil, the area behind Beg-Meil, that is, there are at least twenty of them. At that time of year, the middle of July to the end of August, we have enormous numbers of tourists here. Including thousands of campers. Mostly French people, of course, but also many from other countries. Britain, Holland and Germany. Some from Scandinavia, I really do hope there'll be some time for you to see our wonderful scenery, not just to work. Ooh-la-la, le travail, le travail, toujours du travail . . . that is how it is in the French police, and I assume you are tormented the same way in your country?'

'It happens,' said Inspector Morelius in French. 'Ça arrive.'

'We're staying until Friday,' said Tallin. 'So hopefully we'll find time to see a few things. But if we go with the idea that the girl was staying with her grandmother at a campsite . . . what does that change? Their disappearance ought to have been reported, in any case?'

Leblanc turned his hands palms up. 'Of course. It's bound to have been reported somewhere in the country. But going missing from a house and going missing from a tent are still two entirely different things.'

Barbarotti pondered this sobering truth for a moment. 'Could it be that they weren't even registered at a campsite?' he asked. 'Even though they were staying there, I mean?'

'I don't know,' said Leblanc, and gave a shrug. 'Of course

all campers are supposed to show their ID at reception when they pitch their tents or park their caravans, but . . . well, they are probably sometimes a bit lax about it. At that busy time of year there are farmers who open up a field or two to campers, as well, and it is not possible to keep checks on all that sort of thing. Perhaps not desirable either, and who can actually prevent someone putting up a tent on their field?'

Barbarotti nodded. 'But if we assume that was what happened,' he said, 'they must surely have left some belongings behind them. The tent, their clothes and so on?'

Leblanc thought for a while.

'Of course,' he said. 'Of course someone should have reported this to us anyway. But as I said, I can confirm that nobody did. Unfortunately, and I'm sorry about it.'

'A forgotten tent in a field isn't exactly a major police priority,' put in Morelius.

'Not a major one, no,' said Leblanc with a quick smile.

'But if that hypothesis is correct,' said Barbarotti with a sigh, 'then it just means the case is with some prefecture of police elsewhere in the country. Isn't that right?'

'Yes, most definitely,' said Leblanc.

'Where?' asked Tallin.

Leblanc ran a hand over his bare head. 'That depends entirely on who noticed they were missing,' he explained patiently. 'And *where* that happened, of course. If others did not know where the girl and her grandmother were spending their holiday, for example . . . well, then they would presumably have been reported in their home town. It was Paris, wasn't it?'

'Paris,' confirmed Barbarotti. 'At least if the girl is to be believed. But how did they get here, in that case? Wait a moment. Your people don't happen . . . didn't happen to find an abandoned car anywhere near Mousterlin that summer? It's asking a lot after five years, I know, but . . . ?'

Leblanc gave a short, gruff laugh. 'Ha. I can put a man onto it by all means, but I think it would bc foolish to expect anything. Maybe the farmer kept that too, for all we know? Why not?'

There was silence for a few seconds.

'You really think that could be the case?' Barbarotti asked sceptically. 'That the two of them were camping on a farmer's land, and when he noticed they were missing, he simply commandeered their car, their tent and all their things?'

'It's one theory,' said Leblanc, pushing his glasses up onto his forehead. 'I don't exactly want to believe it, but . . . well, what else are we to believe?'

Tallin cleared his throat. 'How did she get to Erik's place that evening?' he asked. 'The grandmother, that is. I didn't get the impression she was a driver.'

'Nor me,' said Barbarotti. 'No, she must have come on foot, otherwise her car would have been parked outside the house, and then . . .'

'Then one of the others must have taken care of it,' Tallin supplied. 'Well it's not impossible for them to have done that, is it?'

'No,' conceded Barbarotti, 'it certainly isn't.'

Good grief, he thought. That could be it. The Swedes had made certain to eradicate all traces of everything. The Sixth Man wouldn't have been aware of it, because he had left the area the morning after he buried the old woman in the polder.

'But if we assume she came on foot that evening,' resumed Leblanc, 'and if we assume she was a fairly old woman, then that would mean they were based somewhere nearby. And we know the holiday houses they were staying in, all the Swedes, don't we?'

'Yes, we do,' said Tallin. 'We had the last one confirmed late last night. Our plan is to visit all three of them tomorrow. But the fact that neither the girl nor her grandmother was reported missing in the area is certainly not something we were expecting. How long will it take for you to check this with Paris?'

'A couple of days, I should think,' said Leblanc, shrugging his shoulders again. 'It's a damn pity we haven't got their names, but I shall send out a countrywide alert.'

'Troaë,' Barbarotti reminded him. 'We've got that, at any rate.'

'If that really was her name,' said Leblanc, putting his glasses on his nose again. 'I've never come across such a name before. Oh well, if they have been reported missing anywhere in France, we should know by next week. Maybe even before you leave for home. Their full names, too.'

'Good,' said Tallin. 'We're grateful for that. Extremely grateful.'

'Have you any other questions that I might be able to answer?' asked Leblanc.

Tallin exchanged a look with Barbarotti before shaking his head. 'Not at present. But perhaps we can get back to you if we think of any?'

'Of course,' said Leblanc, and stretched. 'Crime must never be allowed to pay. Regardless of circumstances and of country.'

After these wise words, he turned his head and looked out of the window. 'The rain seems to have stopped,' he said. 'Can I suggest a soupçon of dinner in the old town before we drive you to your hotel? Mademoiselle?'

'Madame,' Carina Morelius corrected him, and smiled. 'Je vous en prie, monsieur le commissaire.'

They ate in the open air, on an unevenly shaped little square called Place Beurre. Even Barbarotti knew what that meant.

Goat's cheese au gratin. Moules marinières. Some kind of perfectly tender meat in a white wine and mustard sauce. A couple of cheeses; Roquefort and a well-aged Comté. Crème brulée.

An Alsace wine and a Bordeaux. A glass of Calvados and a small café noir. The meal took two and a half hours. Barbarotti decided there would be no more hot dogs from the Rocksta Grill for him.

Commissaire Leblanc kept the conversation flowing. He told them about the town of Quimper. Its artistic traditions, its architecture. Its beauty, particularly that of the old town where they were currently installed, enfolded by the moat and walls. The chequered history of the ancient cathedral.

But not a word about the case. Not a word about police work of any kind; this was the way to do it, thought Barbarotti. Shut the job out of your mind the instant you shut your office door behind you.

This was how he *had* to function in future, in fact, if he wanted to preserve his mental health, and wanted Marianne to put up with living with him. Not the way he was functioning at the moment – and not like Astor Nilsson, who clearly couldn't even sleep at nights.

Take an interest in other things, basically get a life, as the young people's TV programmes always put it.

Easy enough to say. Harder to put into practice, presumably. Once he got up to his hotel room – only five minutes' walk from Place Beurre, as it turned out – he unpacked his case and slid his finger into the Bible.

It was the first time he had ever taken it with him on a trip.

Proverbs 20: 5. He felt a sudden gratitude at being spared the evil eye.

> Counsel in the heart of man is like deep water;
> but a man of understanding will draw it out.

Ah, thought Barbarotti. So what's this telling me?

Whose counsel? My own or someone else's?

He sat on the edge of the bed weighing the words for a while, but the reference to the case felt so blatant that he decided to leave it. That was what he had learnt from Leblanc. He picked up his phone instead. Admittedly it was past eleven o'clock, but in love and war it was never too late.

'Hi there,' he said. 'Did I wake you?'

'No, don't worry,' said Marianne. 'I hadn't even got to bed. Jenny's started in a new form and she needed a bit of cheering up, which took a while.'

Goodness, yes, thought Barbarotti. The start of term.

'What about you, though? I hope you haven't changed your mind about Friday?'

'No chance,' said Barbarotti. 'But I'm in France.'

'In France?'

'I'm looking for the right wine to go with the lobster.'

'What?' said Marianne.

'Only joking,' said Barbarotti. 'I'm here for work. We think we're getting close now.'

'Yes, I saw the papers today,' said Marianne. 'And the evening news on TV. They seem to have had lots of calls to that helpline. Is it . . . is it the murderer, that man with the circle round him in the photo?'

'I don't know,' said Barbarotti, noting that he didn't feel as though he was lying as he said it. 'No, I honestly don't, it's a bit complicated. But anyway, I wanted to wish you good night, and tell you I love you while I'm at it.'

'Thank you,' said Marianne. 'That was nice of you. I'm looking forward to seeing you on Friday. Make sure you don't get held up there, that's the only thing, because we've got important things to talk about.'

'I'll be there to meet you with roses, milk and honey,' Barbarotti assured her. 'And wine, as I said. But you're welcome to wish me luck down here if you like, as well.'

'Good luck, my love,' said Marianne. 'Take care of yourself and you sleep well, too.'

But he didn't. Despite his good intentions. As soon as he put out the light, his head was full of everything that had emerged from their afternoon session with Commissaire Leblanc.

Never reported missing? What the hell could it mean?

And those speculations that the girl and the old lady could have been camping somewhere unofficial. How credible was that, in fact?

And how credible was Troaë? That idea the author of the document had had about her being a compulsive storyteller, well, he had undeniably found more to support it in the course of the day.

And the Mousterlin document as a whole? What was the point of writing it? And letting them read it? Wasn't that the underlying problem? The question they primarily needed to answer? From amongst the throng of other questions.

Counsel in the heart of man, in other words.

Inspector Barbarotti sighed and suddenly found himself thinking of what Axel Wallman used to claim when they shared digs in Lund. That the difference between a Nobel prize-winner and a dribbling idiot wasn't so huge when it came to it – it was just that the former had managed to amass about one per cent of the sum total of knowledge, whereas the idiot had stopped at a half.

Some slight consolation, perhaps?

The final time he was aware of raising his head from the pillow to look at the red digital display on the TV set, it had reached 01.56.

35

Leblanc had put a car at their disposal, a black Renault that made Barbarotti think of cognac. They drove out of Quimper at around nine and after half an hour's ride along winding roads through rich green landscapes, wild and tangled in places, they found themselves at Cap de Mousterlin. The headland protruded into the sea like a nose, with long sandy beaches extending on both sides; it was low tide and the water's edge was a good fifty to sixty metres from the grass-tufted dune protecting the polder behind it. It was not at all like the Brittany where Barbarotti had spent a few summer weeks fifteen years earlier. He had been up on the north coast on that occasion, Côtes-d'Armor, with its dramatic cliffs, small sheltered bays, caves and distinctive rock formations. The strangeness of the place names suddenly came back to him: Tregastel, Perros-Guirec, Ploumanach.

But here on the south side it was flat, just as the Mousterlin notes described it. And very warm, or today it was, at any rate; the sun shone from a remorselessly blue sky and the temperature must have been between twenty-five and thirty – even though it was only morning, and even though the schools had gone back in Sweden. The beaches were still virtually empty, but he didn't doubt they would be covered in people in a few hours' time. He regretted not having packed a pair of shorts after all, and felt uncomfortably hot in his black jeans – but there was something about police work and shorts that didn't go together.

Incompatible, as they said these days.

To the right, looking west, the beach ended at the little port of Bénodet; to the left, looking east, Beg-Meil could be seen about three kilometres away.

Barbarotti looked at the clock and Tallin nodded. Time to head to Le Grand Large, the restaurant which, according to their information, would be a couple of hundred metres away, towards Beg-Meil. It was here that the group of Swedes had come with Troaë that day they met her on the beach for the first time. Barbarotti realized it was a hopeless undertaking, and he knew Tallin and Morelius did, too. But they were going to talk to the staff there and give them copies of the pictures. Their business cards too, and a direct number to Commissaire Leblanc – in case their expectations were confounded and someone eventually happened to recollect something.

They were received with relative friendliness and interest, but also much apologetic shaking of heads. Only one current staff member had been working in the restaurant in 2002, and as she had seen no fewer than eleven summers come and go in this lovely place and, at a guess, somewhere between forty and fifty thousand punters passing through the restaurant and bar, she said she was sorry but she couldn't actually remember the people in the photograph.

They moved on to Bénodet and found the restaurant down by the old harbour. It was called Le Transat, and they also located what was in all likelihood the exact table at which the six Swedes had sat one Saturday five years ago, with the wall behind it – and they had quite a long talk to the owner of the place. He was two metres tall, had a brother who was in the Marseilles police force, and loved crime novels above all other things on earth. With the possible exception of his wife and children.

But despite all that, he was unable to help them. He studied the photographs of summer 2002 very thoroughly for a long time but, thought Barbarotti, even if he had had a sudden flash of inspiration and remembered that party of people and that Saturday, five years ago – what would they really have gained from it? Unless the Sixth Man had happened to leave his driving licence on the table or had trumpeted out his identity in some other way, they would be no further forward. Not necessarily right back at the starting line, but the finishing tape was definitely still nowhere in sight.

The owner asked them if they would at least stay for lunch, but since it was only half past eleven, they decided to leave that for their third restaurant of the day.

Le Thalamot in Beg-Meil.

This is where I'd live if I was rich, thought Gunnar Barbarotti as he was getting out of the car. And if I spoke French.

Well, not at Le Thalamot itself, but nearby. In one of the big stone houses, hidden behind tall garden walls, that seemed to constitute the heart of the Beg-Meil community. Turrets and towers, blue shutters and deep foliage; splendid isolation and the sea just a few metres away.

But I never will be rich, he thought. And I'll certainly never be able to learn to speak French. You'd have to be married to a cyclist from Lyons to pull that off.

They presented their questions and were answered for the third time with apologetic smiles and shakes of the head. They ordered salads and omelettes and, since they were there, took the opportunity of sampling the local cider, too.

It tasted like old apple juice that was starting to ferment. Barbarotti remembered it had been just the same on the Côtes-d'Armor fifteen years earlier, and none of them asked for a refill.

'The names match, at any rate,' said Tallin once the coffee had arrived. 'The places and the restaurants do exist. And the people, it all tallies. We've no call to doubt the story itself.'

'Maybe not,' said Barbarotti. 'You're right that everything seems to be where it should be. But there are a young girl and an old lady buried out in the marshes, too, and they seem to have vanished without anybody giving a damn. It's a bit frustrating. That's what I think, at least.'

'We haven't heard yet whether Leblanc's appeal for information has yielded any results,' Morelius pointed out. 'With any luck, we'll have their names by tonight or tomorrow.'

'Let's hope so,' said Tallin.

Barbarotti noted that even the doughty detective inspector was starting to look tired.

'Troaë,' he said. 'Leblanc said he'd never heard that name before.'

'I've never heard it either,' said Morelius.

'The Root of All Evil,' sighed Tallin. 'Christ, too right.'

'Anything new from back home?' asked Barbarotti, changing the subject. 'There hasn't been a peep out of my mobile since last night.'

Tallin drained his coffee cup and looked as though he was making an effort to buck up. 'Yes, I spoke to Asunander this morning,' he said. 'Four hundred and fifty-five names, just yesterday. That must be a record, and about ten of them are going to sue us for defamation. But they're busy sorting through them all, so we'll have to see what we end up with.'

Barbarotti nodded. 'Hope they've whittled it down to seven or eight by the time we get home. That would be a bit more manageable.'

'No harm in hoping,' said Tallin. 'Right then, shall we pay and venture out for a look at the property market?'

This, too, proved to match the Mousterlin document, as they had somewhat reluctantly started to call it. The house the Malmgrens had rented through the agent in Gothenburg was a few hundred metres west of the cape of Mousterlin, just inland from the dunes. They had not arranged with the owner to search the place, mainly because it was not in the same hands as five years ago. Monsieur Diderot – that sounded somewhat familiar, Barbarotti thought – who had rented out his house to the Swedish couple, had died in 2004, and it had then passed to his heirs and been sold to a Swiss banker.

But there it stood, a pleasant whitewashed house surrounded by a low stone wall. Slate roof, like almost all the roofs in the region, a large terrace, a few cypresses and lots of rhododendron bushes and hydrangeas. Barbarotti didn't feel entirely au fait with the flora, but Morelius put even that into Swedish for him.

Gunnar Öhrnberg and Anna Eriksson's holiday accommodation took slightly longer to locate. It turned out to be roughly halfway between Mousterlin and Beg-Meil, and they went round in circles for a good while on the dirt roads that criss-crossed the polder area before they found the right place. They had not arranged to meet the owner here, either; Leblanc and Morelius had spoken to him on the phone early that morning, but he claimed to have rented his place out to so many crazy tourists over the years that he couldn't tell them apart any longer. What was more, he was about to go out fishing and he didn't intend to let the police get in his way. Des flics et des touristes! Jamais de la vie!

Cops and tourists, not on your life, translated Morelius.

When they arrived at Le Clos, which was the name of the third and – on the basis of all their well-founded hopes – most important house, it was four in the afternoon and there still wasn't a cloud in the sky. The owner, a Monsieur Masson, had promised to show up around five, but had also said that if they happened to get there earlier, they were welcome to just go in through the gate and take a seat. There was a bakery a stone's throw away, just as it said in the document, and it was about to open again after its lunch break; they trekked over and bought water, fruit, a newspaper and three pains au chocolat. They returned to Le Clos, sat down under the sun umbrella on the terrace and waited. Barbarotti judged it to be at least thirty-three degrees in the shade, and if they hadn't had a female inspector with them he would have stripped down to his underpants.

Because no one could have seen in. A rhododendron hedge, tall and dense, surrounded it on three sides. On the remaining side, facing the sea, a meadow stretched away, with grass a metre high. Barbarotti noted that you could hear the sea, even though it must be several hundred metres away. He guessed the tide must be on its way in.

The house itself was not unlike the Malmgrens'. White, two-storeyed, with gable ends of grey stone. Blue shutters. A terrace with white plastic furniture, a blue and yellow sun umbrella. As though IKEA had laid claim to yet more territory. The gate was exactly the same shade of blue as Sorrysen's litter bin.

'This is the actual murder scene, then?' said Inspector Morelius, breaking the neck of a banana.

Barbarotti looked around him. 'Presumably,' he said. 'Yes, this must be where it happened, on this terrace . . . and over there,' he pointed, 'we have the tool shed.'

It was half hidden by the overhanging branches and leaves of a tree. To Barbarotti it looked like a chestnut, though the leaves were slightly the wrong shape. He drank some water, got up and went over to take a look. It was cooler in the shade beneath the lattice of branches and he lingered there; a slight breeze found its way in, too. He thought that if he lived here, he would undoubtedly spend a day like this in a deckchair under this very tree, whatever kind it was.

So this was where the old woman's body was lying, he thought next. While the Swedes sat over there on the terrace and discussed what to do with her.

A frail old woman, her head smashed in by a Swedish spanner. He stared down into the grass by the corrugated iron wall of the shed. Just here, he presumed, on this little patch of grass and soil, this was where she was lying, a Frenchwoman dressed in black, with a straw hat of blood-red, and . . . a sudden light-headedness came over him, or perhaps it was sunstroke, a result not only of the heat but also of this whole story, incomprehensible yet somehow so tangible, with a protagonist who . . . well, who what?

Who eluded any attempt to make head or tail of him, thought Barbarotti. That was surely the least one could say? Who had spent a few weeks in this peaceful little house, one summer five years ago, and who had seven people's lives on his conscience. Maybe his own, too.

Who are you, he wondered. Or who *were* you? What is the point of your story?

Yesterday's passage from the Bible came back into his mind.

Counsel in the heart of man is like deep water; but a man of understanding will draw it out.

Or perhaps it wasn't that complicated when all was said and done? He had felt obliged to take revenge in order to find restitution, and he had felt obliged to explain himself. Just as he had written in his document. Wasn't that sufficient explanation?

His mobile rang. He gave a start, fished the phone out of his breast pocket and answered it.

'Hi Dad! It's Lars.'

'Hi there, Lars!'

'What are you doing?'

For one brief second a possible continuation of the conversation played out in his head. If he were to stick rigidly to the truth.

'I'm in France, Lars.'

'What are you doing there?'

'I'm standing on a lawn looking at a spot.'

'What sort of spot is it?'

'It's the spot where some people put a murdered woman, five years ago.'

'Why?'

'I don't know, Lars.'

'Why did they? Have they taken her away now?'

'Oh yes. Now the sun's shining, and it's all sweetness and light.'

But no, the truth wasn't always the best medicine when you were talking to your children.

'I'm on a little trip at the moment,' was what he actually said. 'What are you and Martin up to?'

'We just got in from school. Dad, we want to come and live with you. Can we?'

'Of course you can. It would make me very happy to have you here, you know that, don't you?'

'Oh good. We'll come then. I'll tell Mum and Martin you're happy about it.'

'You do that,' said Gunnar Barbarotti. 'And ask Mum to ring me, so we can arrange when you're coming and so on.'

'Great. Thanks, Dad,' said Lars, and ended the call.

So there it was, thought Barbarotti. Life and death.

He put away his mobile and went back to the terrace.

Henri Masson arrived a few minutes after five, bringing with him a bottle of local cider and a Breton cake as refreshments for his guests from afar.

He was in his seventies, and sported a straw hat and a moustache of such audacious proportions that you could even see it when his back was turned.

But his back was only briefly turned, while he closed the gate and checked the mailbox. After that, he was all sociability and bonhomie. And very willing to do his bit. Leblanc had given him a rough outline of the matter at stake, and perhaps it was Leblanc he was quoting once he had filled four tall glasses and was proposing a toast.

'Pour la lutte contre la criminalité!'

He didn't have a word of English, but took an instant liking to Inspector Morelius and clearly enjoyed having his every word interpreted by such a delightful and striking woman.

'So,' said Tallin. 'We're interested in a Swedish man who rented this house from 27 June to 25 July 2002. His name was Erik Bergman. He may well have had someone else sharing the place with him, too, and we'd be grateful for any information you're able to give us.'

'I remember,' declared Henri Masson, not without a hint of pride. 'I've been renting out this house for many years, since the 1970s, but the summer of 2002 was actually the last time. I only had one more tenant after Monsieur Bergman.'

Finally, thought Barbarotti once Morelius had finished translating, finally a bit of good fortune in this recalcitrant mess.

'Naturally I always leave my guests in peace,' Masson continued, twirling the tips of his moustache between finger and thumb. 'But I come and cut the grass and take out the bins once a week. My wife and I live in the centre of Fouesnant, you see.'

'Why did you stop renting the place out in 2002?' asked Barbarotti.

'I won the football pools,' announced Masson, even more proudly than before. 'I didn't need the money any longer. These days I let my children and their families come and stay here. A group of them left yesterday, but some more are coming on Friday. I've got five children and thirteen grandchildren, and as long as they clean up after themselves, I don't care what they get up to here.'

'This Monsieur Bergman,' Tallin prompted him. 'What do you remember about him?'

Masson shrugged. 'Not all that much, of course. I was here

to meet them when they arrived, I saw them when I came to cut the grass one week, and I checked up on the cleaning and so on when he left. My wife was with me on that last visit; women have a better eye for that sort of thing than we men do, naturellement.'

He gave Inspector Morelius a knowing wink, which she calmly returned.

'You say "them"?' queried Tallin. 'So there were two of them staying here, then?'

'There were two of them to begin with,' said Masson. 'But Monsieur Bergman was alone when he left.'

'This other person, was it another man?' asked Barbarotti.

'Oui, it was a man. I suppose they must both have been in their thirties. I've never cared about any sexual preferences but my own, so . . . well, it doesn't bother me.'

Another wink at Morelius. Another one from her in return.

'So you think they were a gay couple?' said Barbarotti.

'No, far from it. That's to say, I didn't bother to think anything.'

'All right, we understand,' said Tallin. 'What was the other man's name?'

Barbarotti found himself closing his eyes and clenching his fists. This is it, he thought. Yes or no?

Henri Masson gave a shrug of his broad shoulders. 'No idea.'

Morelius's translation was superfluous but she gave it to them anyway. It's no more than I expected, thought Barbarotti. Why would he have been so careless as to leave his name behind? This, too, matched what they had learnt from the Mousterlin document.

'You're sure you never found out his name?' asked Tallin, and cautiously sampled his cider.

'Absolutely sure,' Henri Masson assured him. 'I never knew what his name was, so I haven't forgotten it, either.' He tapped the top of his straw hat with one finger. 'Monsieur Bergman was responsible for the house. And everything was in good order when he left.'

'You didn't notice whether there was an adjustable spanner missing from the tool shed?' Barbarotti asked.

'An adjustable spanner? No, I didn't. But there's so much junk out there that it wouldn't be missed.'

'I see,' sighed Barbarotti.

'This other man,' said Tallin. 'Would you recognize him if you saw him again?'

Henri Masson took a large glug of cider and thought about it. 'Probably,' he said. 'Yes, I think so.'

Inspector Barbarotti carefully took one of the photographs out of the folder. He slid it across the table to Masson.

'Is he in this photograph?' asked Tallin.

Henri Masson begged their indulgence while he extracted a pair of glasses from a shiny metal case and positioned them very deliberately at the end of his substantial nose. He took the picture between finger and thumb and studied it for five seconds.

'Oui,' he said, and pointed. 'This is him. I don't recognize the other two.'

Gunnar Barbarotti realized he had been holding his breath throughout the proceedings.

36

When Gunnar Barbarotti woke up on Thursday, the sky was swathed in dark clouds, and he remembered it had been just the same, that summer in the 1990s. Brilliant, cloudless days interspersed with storms and cold Atlantic winds. Somewhat reminiscent of Helena's mood swings, in point of fact. As he showered and dressed he wondered how their life together would have looked now, if they hadn't got divorced nearly six years ago.

It didn't feel like a particularly appropriate line of thought for a new, optimistic day, and he soon knocked it on the head. He realized he had got up far too early; he had arranged to have breakfast with Tallin and Morelius at about half past eight, but it was barely eight by the time he was ready. Pointless to sit there on his own over the croissants for half an hour, he decided, and then another thought popped into his head.

He hadn't spoken to Sara for . . . well, it must be a fortnight now. He'd been on the point of ringing her several times, but something else had always got in the way.

Now, though, he had a bit of time on his hands. Admittedly she would probably still be asleep but surely that consideration was outweighed by the chance of starting the day with a considerate and loving father as her alarm clock?

He called her number. He heard it ring, six times, before her recorded message cut in. He rang off and tried again.

This time, she answered.

At least he thought it was her. It sounded roughly like treading on a meringue. Not that he ever did such a thing, but it was that sort of brittle shattering.

'It's me,' he said. 'Your loving dad.'

'Dad?'

'Yep, it's me.'

'Why . . . why are you ringing . . . what time is it? Seven! Why are you ringing me at seven in the morning? Is anything the matter?'

'It's eight,' he told her.

'But it's seven over here,' objected Sara. 'You know that, don't you?'

'Er yes, of course,' Barbarotti had the presence of mind to say. 'Well, it occurred to me that I hadn't heard from you for a while, and I had half an hour to spare.'

'Half an hour to spare? Are you *that* busy?'

He considered this for a moment. 'Yes, actually,' he said. 'Things have been pretty hectic. But we can hang up if you need to sleep. I'll ring you tonight instead.'

'Well you've woken me now,' said Sara. 'And there was something I wanted to tell you, as it happens . . . I was going to call you today.'

'Oh yes?' said Barbarotti. 'What sort of thing?'

'I . . . I need to borrow a bit of money.'

Christ, thought Barbarotti. Something's up.

'Why?' he said.

Sara wasn't in the habit of asking for money. He had good

reason to suspect there was a problem. It didn't mean he was an over-protective dad.

'Why?' he repeated.

'I don't want . . . no, I don't want to tell you,' she answered slowly, her voice full of remorse. 'But I thought I could pay it back over the autumn. By Christmas, say?'

Christmas, he thought with foreboding. 'How much were you thinking of?' he asked.

'Four thousand kronor,' she said. 'Or five, if you can.'

'Five thousand? What on earth do you need five thousand for, Sara?'

'It's just something,' said Sara, and she sounded really unhappy, he noted. Not just tired. 'But I can't tell you what it is.'

'Sara, love . . .'

'It'll only be this once. You know I'm not always asking you for money, and I promise I'll pay it back. I don't want to ring Mum, because—'

'I'd prefer to know what you need it for,' he said. 'You must see that?'

'If you're going to insist on that, I'll have to try somewhere else,' said Sara.

'For God's sake,' he said. 'Of course you can borrow the money. How are you feeling?'

'So-so,' said Sara. 'But it'll sort itself out. There's no need for you to worry, Dad.'

'Have you still got your job?'

'Oh yes.'

'At that pub?'

'That's right.'

'And that musician? Have you still got him, as well?'

Why am I asking, he wondered. I only want to hear the answer if it's no.

'Can I call you in a couple of days, Dad?' she said. 'It's a bit hard to talk right now.'

Why, he wondered. Why was it hard to talk? Because Malin had woken up and was listening in? Or that . . . what the heck was his name . . . Robert? Richard?

Right, that's bloody it, thought Gunnar Barbarotti. I'll give her the money and a week, and then I'll go over and fetch her.

'I'll transfer the money today,' he said. 'I've got your account number, it's no problem.'

'Thanks, Dad,' said Sara. 'I love you.'

'I love you too,' said Gunnar Barbarotti. 'Try to get back to sleep for a while.'

He rang off. Then he checked the time. Quarter past eight. He hadn't even told her he was in France.

But he had enough time to ring his bank and transfer five thousand kronor. When he asked the friendly sounding woman at the other end how much that left in his account, she told him he had sixty-two kronor and fifteen öre.

Leblanc was engaged in crime fighting of his own that morning, so they had a couple of hours for sightseeing – but as the rain started pouring down just as they finished breakfast, they shelved the idea. They gathered in Tallin's room instead, ordered a pot of coffee and sat down to mull things over.

'Anybody come up with any new ideas during the night?' asked Tallin. He had asked the same thing at breakfast, but something had happened to Tallin, thought Barbarotti. He seemed to have deflated since they got to Brittany; it had struck Barbarotti yesterday and he seemed the same today. As if he had toothache or had just lost all his savings at poker.

'Afraid not, as I said,' said Carina Morelius, pouring coffee. 'But I see myself more as an observer in all this. And interpreter, obviously. You've been working on this case for the best part of a month now, haven't you? It was on the twenty-fifth it all kicked off, wasn't it?'

'The twenty-fourth or the thirty-first,' said Barbarotti. 'It rather depends how you calculate it.'

'New ideas?' persisted Tallin.

'Well, what can one say?' said Barbarotti. 'At least we've been able to confirm that the Sixth Man really was staying with Erik Bergman . . . and that he's the one in the photo. Haven't we? And that certainly ought to count as a breakthrough, but I just find it a bit hard to actually see it as one.'

'Did you have doubts about it all tying in?' asked Tallin.

'No,' said Barbarotti. 'Not really. Well, we'll have to see how it goes this afternoon, but if neither the girl nor her grandmother have been reported missing anywhere in France, then the whole story looks . . . pretty convoluted. In my view, at any rate.'

'Mine too,' said Tallin. 'Damn it, I've been in this field of work for more than thirty years and I can't remember anything like this, I have to say.'

'That bit about the grandma's accent,' said Barbarotti after a few moments of oppressive silence. ' . . . and the girl's too, at one point . . . it doesn't bear thinking about really, but if they came from some other country, that would throw the whole thing wide open.'

'I know,' sighed Tallin. 'No, I agree with you. Let's leave that alternative out of it for the time being.'

'How are they getting on with the identikit picture back home?' asked Morelius. 'Has any new information come in?'

'Over five hundred calls,' said Tallin. 'But we're not talking identikits here, remember. This is an actual genuine photo.'

'Sorry,' said Morelius.

'Not to worry,' said Tallin. 'But anyway, all the tip-offs are being checked and prioritized. One, two or three. In the first group, the most plausible leads, they'd got forty-five when I checked this morning. They're starting the interviews after lunch today. So with any luck, that's where we could see our breakthrough. Regardless of what this trip to France yields, I mean.'

'It wouldn't take much to come up with an alibi though, would it?' Inspector Morelius put in.

'The same thought had occurred to me,' said Barbarotti. 'Apart from the summer of 2002, you'd have to have been at four different murder scenes all over Sweden in the past month. That includes being aboard a ferry to Denmark on the relevant night . . . well, if we find some poor devil without an alibi for that lot, things aren't going to look very good for him at all.'

'Especially if he happens to look like the guy in the picture?'

'That too, of course.'

'But glamour boy Masson seemed credible enough, anyway?' said Morelius with a smile.

'Yes, I got that impression,' said Barbarotti. 'Not that he had that many to choose between, of course. We should probably have handled it a bit better when we showed him the photo.'

'Why's that?' asked Tallin irritably. 'You reckon he's going to be our star witness at the trial, or what?'

What's the matter with Tallin, wondered Barbarotti. He's starting to lose his touch.

'I just need to make a couple of calls,' he lied. 'See you down in reception in an hour, then?'

'So do I,' announced Inspector Morelius, and they left Tallin's room together.

'He seems in a bit of a grump,' she said when they were out in the corridor. 'Your friend the chief inspector, I mean.'

'Yes,' said Barbarotti. 'But I don't really know him. He's come from the National CID.'

'I'm aware of that,' said Carina Morelius, and lowered her voice to a confidential whisper. 'But *I* know him. We were in a relationship a few years ago, in fact.'

'What on earth . . . ?' said Barbarotti, and stopped in his tracks.

'Yeah, but it was only for a few weeks. Relationship's the wrong word, really. Fling would be better, we had a *fling*.'

'He must be at least fifteen years older than you?'

'Thirteen,' said Morelius. 'But age wasn't what it hinged on.'

'So you mean he . . . he had certain expectations of this trip?'

'That's your interpretation,' said Morelius, and slipped into her room.

Well well, thought Inspector Barbarotti. We learn something new every day.

'Every year, around sixty thousand people are reported missing in this country,' explained Commissaire Leblanc. 'Six zero zero zero zero.'

Barbarotti jotted this down.

'It's a huge number, of course, but it's still only a tiny percentage of the population. The vast majority don't disappear. To put it simply, we could say one person in every thousand goes missing. And to continue with the statistics, this means that in round numbers we have around five thousand disappearances every month.'

'The statistics for this are quite high in our country, too,' Tallin pointed out. 'I read in an article not long ago that the percentage per capita is pretty similar in most countries across western Europe.'

'Yes, that's right,' confirmed Leblanc. 'But what we have to remember is that, of these five thousand missing persons a month, only a fraction are still missing a year later. Around fifteen per cent in fact. People turn up, come back home or are found dead. Crime is only involved in about ten per cent of cases, and the figure for those still missing after five years is about the same – barely ten per cent. What I'm trying to say is that around six thousand individuals vanish into thin air every year. It's generally assumed that roughly half of them have died, and of the remaining three thousand, there's little doubt that only around a hundred are still in the country. People do a runner, basically, and they do it for any number of reasons. Unpaid taxes are probably the most common one.'

Barbarotti turned the page of his pad and decided to stop taking notes. 'How many went missing in July 2002?' he asked.

'That's what I'm coming to,' said Leblanc with a quick smile. 'Excuse the statistical exercise, but I wanted to give you the background.'

'Excellent,' said Tallin.

'If I've understood you correctly, the girl Troaë and her grandmother are thought to have died at the start of July, so to be on the safe side I looked at the two months between 5 July and 4 September that year, by which time school would have started again in most places, and in that period 12,682 reports of missing people were filed – across the whole country. Statistically average, in other words. More people tend to disappear over the summer, but that year the figure only rose marginally.'

He paused briefly, polished his glasses and consulted his papers.

'Of those individuals, one thousand and thirty-five are currently still unaccounted for.'

'Still missing, you mean?' asked Barbarotti.

'Precisely,' said Leblanc. 'And of that thousand or so, no two were reported by the same person.'

'Hang on,' said Barbarotti. 'So you're telling me no one reported the girl and her grandmother missing together?'

'Correct,' said Leblanc.

'But that must mean nobody reported their disappearance at all, mustn't it? Why would two *different* people have told the police they were missing?'

'We would certainly expect just one person to have reported both, if we really are dealing with a grandmother and granddaughter,' agreed Leblanc, referring to another sheet of paper. 'But if we assume for a minute that we're talking about two separate reports, and if we cast our net wide as regards their ages . . . let's say the girl is between ten and fifteen, and the grandmother between fifty and eighty . . . well, do you agree that builds in enough of a safety margin?'

'Definitely,' sighed Tallin. 'So how many does that leave us with?'

Leblanc cleared his throat. 'In the whole of France, I stress the *whole* of France, for that two-month period of July to August 2002, we have sixteen women still missing in the older age range and eleven girls in the younger one.'

'And we've got all their names?' asked Barbarotti.

'Naturally,' said Leblanc. 'But we have no family links between any of them, and none of the girls is called Troaë.'

There was silence for five seconds. Chief Inspector Tallin leant back in his chair and glared at the ceiling. Barbarotti realized he was biting the inside of his cheek so hard that it hurt.

'One question,' he said. 'Does this include people discovered missing by an institution of some kind . . . like a school, say, or a tax office?'

'Yes,' said Leblanc, 'it includes them as well.'

'But in principle,' said Barbarotti, 'there's nothing to rule out the girl and her grandmother being amongst these . . . how many was it . . . ?'

'Twenty-seven,' said Leblanc.

'Amongst these twenty-seven people?'

'Nothing at all,' said Leblanc. 'I've asked for the details of all these cases, and I'll send the material up to you in Sweden as soon as I get it. Early next week, I hope.'

'Merci,' said Tallin. 'Merci beaucoup.'

'Just one more thing,' said Barbarotti. 'I assume there are a lot of people in your country without residence permits. The sort the authorities have no information about?'

'Probably about a million and a half,' said Leblanc. 'The vast majority from Africa.'

'And if a couple of those . . . ?'

'Of course not,' said Leblanc. 'They fall outside all the statistics. But they were white, weren't they, the girl and her grandmother?'

'Yes,' said Barbarotti. 'There's nothing to indicate not, at any rate.'

'Arabs,' said Tallin, pulling a face. 'Why not? The girl had dark hair, it says so several times in the notes.'

More silence. Leblanc took off his glasses and started to polish them. Barbarotti glanced out of the window and saw that it was still raining.

'Well then,' said Tallin in Swedish. 'I guess we've got all we can out of this.'

He was still of the same opinion six hours later, after they had dined at a restaurant called Kerven Mer. This was a stone's throw from the hotel and it was just him and Barbarotti – Inspector Morelius had asked for the evening off to visit an old friend of hers in Brest – and they had drunk two bottles of Burgundy. It was a delicious, full-bodied wine, but one bottle would have been enough.

'If you can tell me how the hell all this fits together, I'll make sure you're a chief inspector come January the first,' said Tallin. 'By God I will.'

Barbarotti was well aware that this sort of advancement scarcely lay within Tallin's gift, but he didn't quibble.

'Thank you very much,' he opted to say. 'Well, I suppose it isn't really that complicated. Either the girl and her grandmother will be in the paperwork we get next week . . . to put it simply. Or . . . er, or they were tourists in a caravan.'

'What?' said Tallin.

'Or gypsies with no residence permits,' said Barbarotti. 'Or Arabs, why not? The girl was dark-haired and so was the granny. Even if they weren't dark-skinned.'

Tallin pondered this. 'Are they the two alternatives you can think of?'

Barbarotti also pondered for a moment. 'There is a third, of course,' he said. 'That he's lying.'

'Lying?' said Tallin.

'Yes, that he invented the whole story. If the girl and the old lady ever existed at all, then they didn't die.'

Tallin raised his glass and set it down again without drinking.

'What the heck do you mean?' he said.

'It's not out of the question, is it?' said Barbarotti. 'He made up the whole story . . . well, not the part about the Swedes, obviously, but about the girl and her grandmother . . .'

'And what conceivable reason can you think of for him making up a story like that?' said Tallin, suddenly seeming entirely unaffected by the amount of wine he had consumed.

'None at all,' said Barbarotti. 'I take it back. I set more store by my two other ideas.'

But Tallin wouldn't leave it at that. 'So he could have killed these five people for some *other* reason?' he said. 'A reason he wanted to conceal for purposes unknown. Is that what you mean?'

'No,' said Barbarotti. 'I don't mean anything. It sounds insane.'

'But he must have realized we would check up on all this,' Tallin went on doggedly.

'Maybe it doesn't make any difference to him whether we do or not,' suggested Barbarotti.

Tallin scratched his head. 'Do you think that makes all this any more intelligible? What would be the point of coming up with a story that he knows we're going to see through?'

'I'm a bit drunk,' said Barbarotti. 'And I'm telling you, as I said, that Germans in a caravan seem a much likelier explanation to me. They told their friends and family thcy were going up to the North Cape, and then tricked them all by going to Brittany instead. And then they fell into the hands of our Swedes. When was it you said I'd be a chief inspector?'

'I think I'll treat myself to a coffee and a cognac,' said Tallin.

'Is that strictly necessary?' said Gunnar Barbarotti.

They had just checked in at Quimper airport on Friday morning when Barbarotti's phone rang. It was Dr Olltman.

'How are you feeling?' she asked.

He cast about for another pig metaphor but failed to find one. 'Oh, fine,' he declared. 'I'm down in France at the moment. I left you a voicemail message about last Friday, I hope you got it?'

'Yes I did,' Olltman assured him. 'But I'm ringing to arrange an alternative date.'

'Things have changed a bit,' said Barbarotti.

'For the better, I hope?'

'Definitely,' said Barbarotti. 'But it's all been pretty hectic.'

'I do still read the newspapers,' Olltman informed him. 'Ring me when you can find the time. I think it would be a good thing for us to have another session or two.'

'Of course,' said Barbarotti. 'I'll be in touch next week, once things calm down a bit. I've just got to go through security now.'

'Have a good trip home then,' said Olltman.

'Thanks very much,' said Barbarotti.

Calm down a bit? He considered this once he had switched

off his mobile and started fishing all the metal out of his pockets. Well, he could always dream. But I'm the kind who won't get any rest until I'm in my grave, if then, he thought.

As he followed Tallin and Morelius to the gate a minute later, he remembered he'd got to make time for the duty free shop at Charles de Gaulle and find a nice wine.

Friday had come round, in spite of everything.

37

It took two hours to prepare the lobster and four hours to consume it.

The unusually protracted eating period was the result of the break they took in the middle to make love. They sort of just couldn't stop themselves.

There was a lot more they couldn't stop, either.

'I've decided,' said Marianne. 'I want to live with you.'

'That's settled then,' said Gunnar Barbarotti.

Marianne laughed. 'I shall always remember those words,' she said. '*That's settled then.* When we're walking hand in hand along a beach at sunset, forty years from now, I'll remind you of them.'

'I'll be eighty-seven by then,' said Gunnar Barbarotti, 'and probably in need of reminders about quite a lot of things. But you think we ought to have a proper wedding and all that stuff?'

'Don't you?'

'Oh yes,' Barbarotti assured her. 'Of course. Do you want a bit more wine?'

They had reached the dessert. Just ice cream with warm cloudberries, but the lobster had taken so long that he hadn't had time to do anything more complicated. Still, as it happened, in Gunnar Barbarotti's world there was no nicer dessert than vanilla ice cream with warm berries. Not even that crème brûlée in Quimper.

'No need,' said Marianne. 'I'm drunk on love.'

'I shall remind you of that when we're on that beach,' said Barbarotti.

'Good,' said Marianne. 'But you're sure you'd be happy with a church wedding and so on?'

'Well, a small church would be big enough for me,' Barbarotti suggested. 'Not five hundred guests and tons of confetti.'

'Just you and me, then?' said Marianne.

'Well, maybe a vicar, too?'

'OK, a little one. What do you think about our children?'

Barbarotti considered the matter. He hadn't told her about the latest manoeuvre from Copenhagen, and he didn't really know why. Perhaps because he wasn't entirely sure things would turn out as intended, when it came to it. Not sure he would be looking after Lars and Martin. He had been through this sort of thing before. But perhaps it was because he didn't want to talk to Marianne about Helena. For whatever reason.

'We'll have to tell them, I assume,' he said. 'Maybe we can say they're welcome to come if they want?'

She looked serious for a moment. 'You realize you're going to be a dad of teenagers?' she said, her green eyes fixed on him. 'Johan and Jenny live with me and that's the way it's going to be in future, too.'

'Of course I realize,' said Barbarotti. 'I shall teach them everything I can.'

She laughed again. 'You know what?' she said. 'The best thing about you is that I can laugh with you. I never laughed with Tommy.'

'Never? Surely you must have larked about together sometimes?'

She shook her head. 'No, we never had a laugh together, not towards the end anyway. He would laugh *at* me, but that's not really the same thing. The depressing thing is, I think he laughs at his new wife as well.'

'Do you ever meet her?'

'Only when I drop the kids off and collect them again. But she doesn't look very happy. They've got two of their own, as well.'

'You're not thinking that we . . . ?'

'Not on your life,' exclaimed Marianna, administering a punch to his belly. 'You've got three, I've got two, and if you want any more you'll have to pick someone else.'

'Excellent,' said Gunnar Barbarotti. 'We're entirely in agreement.'

'Though there is one other thing,' said Marianne after a spoonful of ice cream.

'What's that?'

'Well, you've got to stop getting into fights with reporters. Johan's actually thought about becoming a journalist. He writes really well and it would be a shame if he thought . . .'

'I'll sit down and talk it all through with him next time I see him,' said Barbarotti. 'If he's going for that as a career, I actually think I could be of some use to him.'

'Good,' said Marianne. 'We're agreed on that as well.'

'So you'd like Helsingborg?'

'Sorry, what was that?'

'I asked whether you'd mind living in Helsingborg.'

'Not at all.'

Still only Friday.

But late. Long gaps between each conversational gambit, and a gentle breeze from the open balcony door. Stretched out on the floor by candlelight. Cristina Branco playing faintly in the background. He had discovered fado music, Portugal's blues, less than a year ago, but he already had fifteen CDs in his rack.

A state of grace, thought Gunnar Barbarotti. There was no other word for moments like these.

'Hmm.'

'What do you mean by "Hmm"?'

'Well, I've lived there for ten years, you know,' she said, running her hand over his chest and stomach. 'And I reckon I could be ready for a change. So it's like a new start for us. But I'd have to talk it all over with the children, of course.'

'You haven't dropped any hints to them that we might be . . . moving in together?'

'No,' she said, sounding slightly concerned. 'I have to be sure I know my own mind first. And getting married is my decision, not theirs. But I've got to give them some say in where we're going to live.'

'Of course,' said Barbarotti. 'On that note, shall we go for a stroll? Then you can see what this town looks like on a warm night in late summer.'

'Absolutely,' said Marianne. 'Do you think we ought to put a few clothes on first?'

'I think that would be a good idea,' said Gunnar Barbarotti.

She stayed all of Saturday and half of Sunday. On the Saturday evening, he told her about his three days in Brittany, and eventually about the case as a whole. It was not something he had planned to do but, after all, everything had started when he opened the first letter, that lovely summer morning at Gustabo in Hogrän, so she had a point when she claimed the right to be informed.

'So what do you think then?' she asked when he had finished. 'Deep down.'

'That's the worst of it,' he said. 'I don't think anything, basically. We generally get some sense of where things are leading, but not in this case. Though I have to admit I've never come across any business quite like this before.'

Marianne frowned. 'There could be something in that idea of them being caravanning tourists, couldn't there? There were a couple of references to the girl and her grandmother having a foreign accent, weren't there?'

'The grandmother, at any rate. Well yes, that could be right. But the murderer himself seems so . . . well, what can I say? Unlikely?'

'You mean the way he's provided a written account of it all?'

'Yes, amongst other things.'

Marianne considered this. 'But don't you think there's a certain logic to it? He was made into a scapegoat and forced to take responsibility for everything – though it was really just an accident that started it all off. I don't think it's particularly odd for all that to have given him a restless soul.'

Gunnar Barbarotti gave a quick smile. 'A restless soul? It sounds a bit old-fashioned, but it pretty much sums him up.'

'Perhaps we can see this written account of his as a healthy sign,' suggested Marianne. 'In spite of everything. The fact that he feels a need to explain himself?'

'Well yes,' said Barbarotti. 'That's occurred to me as well.

But what about these letters? It's a bit harder to see them as a healthy sign, wouldn't you say?'

'You're right, of course.'

Half a minute passed in silence and he could see she was brooding on the puzzle. Then she pulled her fingers through her hair and shook her head, as if trying to banish all these bizarre speculations and replace them with something brighter and more normal. 'It's a terrible story, that's one thing for sure,' she said. 'Do you think the police will be able to solve it? By which I mean, do you think you'll catch him?'

Gunnar Barbarotti gave a laugh.

'I put my finger in the Bible and asked for a bit of guidance while I was down there,' he said. 'Can you guess what came up?'

'No.'

'Proverbs 20:5. Do you know it?'

She thought for a few seconds. 'Something about man's heart and deep water, isn't it?'

'Christ Almighty, that's impressive.'

'I do read it sometimes, you know that. And I quite often read Proverbs. What's the full text?'

'Counsel in the heart of man is like deep water,' said Gunnar Barbarotti, 'but a man of understanding will draw it out.'

'Well, off you go, then!' laughed Marianne. 'It doesn't come much plainer than that. Draw out his counsel! Discover his plans.'

They parted on Sunday afternoon. They agreed to tell all the children involved, plus ex-spouses and anyone else directly affected, and promised one another they would celebrate

Christmas together as man and wife. That was four months away, but surely quite a small wedding in quite a small church, presided over by quite a small vicar, couldn't involve that many preparations?

Once Marianne had gone, he couldn't help feeling it had been foolish of him not to tell her how things stood with Lars and Martin – though he could always pretend he had just heard the news when he rang her in the week. Nor had he said anything on his thoughts about changing jobs, but then he hadn't been thinking along those lines himself this past week, either, so that, too, was probably just as well.

It was four o'clock when he switched on his phones, which had been off since Friday evening. He had four messages. Two from journalists who wanted to interview him, one from Helena, and one from Eva Backman.

He took the journalists first, his promise to Marianne fresh in his mind: that he would cultivate his relationship with the press. They were from *Dagens Nyheter* and the family magazine *Vår Bostad*. He told them both, politely but firmly, that he was more than willing to make himself available for interview, but only once the current case was over.

Then he called his former wife. It struck him that those were precisely the terms in which he preferred to think of her. Not *Helena*. Not *My children's mother*. More was the pity.

'Lars called,' he said. 'He told me he and Martin are prepared to live under the same roof as their old dad.'

'Ha ha,' said Helena. 'Yes, I think they'll cope with that.'

'Glad to hear you think so,' said Barbarotti, and took a deep breath. 'So you've definitely decided on Budapest, then?"

'Oh yes,' she said. 'Ulrich's going over on Wednesday, and

I'll be following on as soon as we've sorted things out for the boys.'

'What's all the hurry?' asked Barbarotti.

'What do you mean?' she retorted. 'If they're changing schools, it's just as well to do it as near the start of term as possible. Isn't it?'

'When were you thinking of?' said Barbarotti.

'Could you manage it by next Monday?'

'Next Monday? Hey, that's only a week.'

'I know, but it'll be best for all parties not to spin it out. I'll talk to their school here tomorrow, and you can do the same in Kymlinge, I hope? Then we can get back to each other tomorrow evening, OK?'

I'm surprised she's not just going to ring the doorbell and dump the two of them on the mat with their suitcases, he thought. But then he remembered his new, grown-up approach, shut his eyes, counted to three, and said he thought that sounded a first-rate plan.

Once he had hung up, he thought for a while about how they would organize themselves in the flat. Would the boys insist on a room each, or could they share Sara's old room, as they did whenever they came to stay for a few days? Sara had generally slept on the living-room sofa while they were there, or gone to stay with one of her girlfriends.

Oh well, it would work out somehow. And he would call Kymlingevik School the next morning. A week from now he would be responsible for a ten year old and a twelve year old again; say what you liked about life, it was full of variety.

He rang Eva Backman's number. She was busy getting dinner and asked if she could call him back two hours later.

*

And she did.

'I heard what happened with the French police,' she said.

'I bet you did,' said Barbarotti.

'So what does it mean?'

'I don't know,' said Barbarotti. 'I just don't understand it.'

'Nor me,' said Eva Backman. 'And I don't like things I don't understand.'

'I know,' said Barbarotti. 'For me, it's pretty staple fare.'

'I can imagine,' said Eva Backman.

She seems on good form, thought Barbarotti. 'But you lot haven't exactly been covering yourselves in glory here at home either, I gather?' he said.

'It's a right old mess,' conceded Backman. 'I don't get why we had to publish that picture. Hundreds of innocent Toms, Dicks and Harries are now suspected of being mass murderers, and that's the only thing we've achieved. If we don't find the right man, the whole lot of them will be under suspicion for the rest of their lives.'

'But most of them won't have any problem establishing an alibi?'

'Of course not. But you think the papers are going to bother publishing pictures of the ones we've ruled out of our enquiries? Kenneth Johansson in Alvesta didn't murder five people, nor did Gustaf Olsson or Kalle Kula in Stockholm. The damages claims are going to go on for ten years, believe me.'

'You sound a teensy bit furious.'

'You bet I am. And I've had to sit through six unihockey matches thinking about it.'

'Ah? The season's started again?'

'The pre-season,' said Backman. 'But never mind that. This

girl and her granny are what interest me. You must have uncovered *something*?'

'Not much,' said Barbarotti. 'Well, one thing. I think the girl's name was made up.'

'Who by?'

'Either the girl or the murderer.'

'And what makes you think that?'

'The fact that Inspector Leblanc had never heard of the name. And then . . .'

'And then?'

'Then there's that play on the letters. The Root of All Evil. It's too much of a construction, that's all.'

Backman thought for a moment. 'If it's a construction, it could hardly be the girl who constructed it.'

'No, hardly,' said Barbarotti. 'But there's something in all this that doesn't add up. And I've also been thinking about what happened between Erik and the girl when they took that walk on the island.'

'That's pretty easy to work out, I'd have thought. He screwed her, that's what. And maybe she wasn't entirely unwilling, either.'

'A twelve year old?' said Barbarotti.

'That might not be correct either,' said Backman. 'But don't think I'm defending him.'

Barbarotti had no comment.

'So why haven't they found them in the archives?' Backman went on. 'Regardless of whether all the details are right or not.'

'There are various possible explanations for that,' said Barbarotti. 'In a few days' time we'll be getting material from France about people still recorded as missing and if we don't find them there, well, then we'll need to come up with some other solutions.'

'Other solutions?'

'Yes.'

'Such as?'

'Can we do this tomorrow?' asked Barbarotti. 'And there is one thought I'd very much like to discuss with you.'

'It's good to know you've still got some thoughts in that skull of yours,' said Eva Backman.

'Oh yes?' said Barbarotti.

'Yes. Because tomorrow morning you're going to solve this case. You're going to go through all the Sixth Men who've come in and remember one of them from your past. That's the general plan.'

'Oh is it, indeed?' said Barbarotti. 'In view of the letter writing, you mean?'

'Yes. And once you've done that, I can finally take my holiday.'

'I promise to do my best,' said Barbarotti, and they ended the call.

At half past nine that evening he had a small whisky. It was something he hardly ever did, especially not on a Sunday evening. But the purpose was medicinal. There was just too much going on in his head, and he needed something to help him get it under control.

And he needed a bit of fire in his belly, too. He sipped his drink and tried to sort out what was most important.

Marianne? In a month or two they would be married and living together. Was he really ready for that step?

Stupid question. Of course he bloody was.

The boys? Next Sunday, a week from now, he'd be putting them to bed on the eve of their first day of school in Kymlinge. It felt so odd. But it was the same as with Marianne: if there was anything that wouldn't help here, it was hesitation and doubt.

Sara, then? This one really got to him. What on earth did she need five thousand kronor for? What had happened? He made a huge effort and submerged her in his subconscious again.

And Johan and Jenny? He scarcely knew them, having only met them five or six times, and yet he was going to assume parental responsibility for them. The cop who brawled with journalists, what sort of replacement dad was he going to make?

Ah well, thought Gunnar Barbarotti. He could only do his best, and put his hope and trust in things turning out all right. He took another sip of his whisky and closed his eyes.

And finally, *the case*. This whole damned case that he couldn't make head or tail of. Troaë, a drowned girl, who felt more and more elusive and inaccessible – and her grandmother, an old woman who turns up one evening outside a house in Finistère and gets herself killed with a Swedish spanner. Where did the pair come from? Were they ever going to find out their true identity?

Or, as Marianne had asked, were they ever going to solve this?

His whisky glass empty, he prayed an existence prayer.

O Lord, send a beam of clear, pure light into a befuddled copper's brain. Never mind all this idle talk of counsel and deep waters. You've got twenty-four hours to sort this, but if enlightenment isn't forthcoming by tomorrow evening, you'll lose a point. Help me out, though, and I'll award you three. This is important, are you listening? Three points!

Our Lord, who was currently at plus eight in the existence stakes, replied that despite it being strictly against the rules – because this involved an ongoing police investigation and they were not part of the deal – he would think it over.

Gunnar Barbarotti expressed his gratitude. Then he found an old Michael Caine film on one of the cable channels. It started at ten and by quarter past he was fast asleep on the sofa.

38

'How can I be expected to recognize him today, when I didn't recognize him in the Brittany photos?' objected Barbarotti.

'It's not his face you're supposed to recognize,' Superintendent Jonnerblad patiently explained. 'It's his name. In any case, we haven't got photos of most of them.'

'Ah, right,' said Barbarotti. 'How's your wife?'

'My wife?'

'Tallin said she was having an operation on Wednesday.'

'Thanks for asking,' said Jonnerblad, his eyes and mouth suddenly assuming a softer look. 'Yes, the operation went well, but they don't know if they got it all out.'

'I see,' said Barbarotti. 'Well, we must hope for the best. OK then, I'll take these lists to my room and get down to it. Shall I start with the top priority group?'

Just for a moment, Jonnerblad looked as if he couldn't really remember where he was.

Then he said, 'No. And we're not telling you which of them has an alibi, either. It'll be better to leave you to work without any preconceptions.'

He passed over a sheaf of paper in a soft, transparent plastic folder.

'Do you really think there's a link between me and the murderer?' asked Barbarotti from the doorway.

'Well we can't exclude the possibility, that's all.'

'How many have we got here?'

'Only five hundred and fifteen,' said Jonnerblad. 'We weeded out a hundred and fifty loonies, so it wouldn't be too much for you.'

'Thanks,' said Barbarotti.

He sat at his desk and spent two and a half hours going through the names. Jonnerblad had told him to work calmly and methodically, and he did. He studied the details provided: name, year of birth, domicile and profession, keeping the photographs of the Sixth Man in front of him as he did so, and when he finally got to the end, his conclusion was that he knew who three of them were.

They were all from Kymlinge. One of them worked at the gym where he went to work out, all too infrequently; one lived on the same staircase in the block of flats on Baldersgatan; and one was a police officer.

He couldn't help being taken aback by the last two. A neighbour and a colleague? What could it signify? Their names were Tomas Jörnevik and Joakim Möller. He tried to summon up their appearances and compare them with the restaurant scenes in Bénodet, but couldn't make anything match particularly well. Jörnevik was more powerfully built, he seemed to recall, with a much rounder face, and Möller was darker-haired, much darker, and didn't have the same sort of eyes, either. No, Barbarotti found it hard to see any similarities.

So his slight surprise was more to do with the two individuals' links to himself, and that, after all, was the whole point. This was what Jonnerblad was after. He wondered who had rung in about them. No doubt this had been recorded somewhere, but not on the lists he'd been given. He tried to recollect what he knew about Jörnevik and Möller, but soon realized it amounted to virtually nothing. They were both thirty-six, the information was next to their names; he thought Jörnevik worked as a taxi driver, and they would say hello when they saw each other on the stairs, but that was basically all. Maybe he was studying for something, too, and Barbarotti had an idea he lived alone. Möller worked in the youth task force, mainly on mapping and combating the flow of drugs. Married to a local councillor, wasn't he? He seemed to think she was with the Social Democrats, and blonde and quite pretty, in fact.

If you were allowed to think about councillors in those terms? But perhaps you were. Hadn't some female minister stuck her head above the parapet a few years back and said politics was the sexiest thing she knew?

He closed his eyes to banish such thoughts. Focused in on the three names again and tried to think of any unfinished business he might conceivably have with any of them, but to no avail. He gathered up all the sheets of paper, put them back in the plastic wallet and glanced at the time. Twenty past eleven. He had agreed to see Jonnerblad after lunch, at one o'clock.

Time to put his parental hat on for a little while, he thought, and rang the number of Kymlingevik School.

It was no problem at all. There were plenty of spaces in years four and six. Barbarotti didn't bother going into the reasons for the sudden move, simply explaining that an unexpected change of circumstances meant Lars and Martin would be living with him from now on.

The deputy head, whose name was Varpalo, didn't enquire, either. Perhaps it was normal for kids to move from one place to another just any old how these days, thought Barbarotti. And the school was glad to have two new pupils, of course, because apart from anything else it must mean a chunk of extra money in the budget.

If his understanding of the current school funding system was correct. At any event, Varpalo promised to find suitable forms and form teachers for them and to be back in touch the next day.

He had just hung up when Inspector Backman knocked on the door and stuck her head round it.

'I'll treat you to lunch at the King's Grill,' she said. 'If you tell me the murderer's name, that is.'

'The King's Grill sounds good,' said Barbarotti, 'but I'll pay for my own lunch.'

I've got sixty-two whole kronor in my bank account, he thought but didn't say.

'Negative, then?' said Backman.

'I reckon so,' said Barbarotti. 'Do you know which of them have got alibis?'

'I haven't got it all in my head,' said Backman. 'But in principle. Can I guess which ones you picked out?'

'I've got to report back to Jonnerblad at one o'clock. Won't you be there?'

'Depends if you've got anything interesting to say. Shall I guess, then?'

'Fire away,' said Barbarotti.

'Three of them,' said Backman. 'Your neighbour, the guy from the gym, and Möller.'

Barbarotti stopped chewing. 'Christ,' he said. 'I spend all morning slogging over it, and then you come along and just . . .'

'Sorry,' said Backman. 'I got it right, then?'

'Yes,' said Barbarotti glumly. 'You got it right. And I assume you've checked these three out?'

Backman nodded. 'Jonnerblad doesn't know about it, but I did it yesterday. Möller had already been checked, of course, but I did the other two during the unihockey matches. Only on my mobile, you know, but I'm pretty sure I can rule them out as well . . . though I don't want to disappoint those National CID types, so let them do it again, that's my advice.'

'So you're not coming to the meeting?'

'No,' said Backman. 'I'll give it a miss. Got a few other old leads to follow up instead.'

'And what are they?'

'The beef stew wasn't bad at all,' said Eva Backman.

'Right, that's you cut out of my will,' said Barbarotti.

'People are crazy,' said Astor Nilsson. 'Somebody rang this morning and said his brother could be the perpetrator.'

'Nothing wrong with shopping your brother,' said Tallin. 'A murderer's a murderer, after all.'

'Fair enough,' said Astor Nilsson. 'But this brother happens to be seventy-five and lives in Los Angeles. Blind from birth, what's more.'

'I suggest we cross him off the list,' said Sorrysen.

'All right,' said Jonnerblad, looking a little bewildered again. He cleared his throat and turned to Barbarotti. 'So you know who these three people are, I assume?'

Barbarotti nodded.

'Möller's already in the clear,' said Jonnerblad. 'What about that neighbour?'

He looked at Tallin. Tallin looked at Sorrysen. Sorrysen consulted a sheet of paper in his hand. 'It can't have been him,' he said. 'He was in Greece for the last two weeks of July.'

'The fellow at the gym?'

'Hasn't been checked yet,' said Sorrysen. 'I'll do it this afternoon.'

'Who reported him?' asked Barbarotti.

Sorrysen looked it up. 'His wife. They're going through a divorce, I gather.'

'Good grief,' groaned Astor Nilsson.

Inspector Barbarotti left Kymlinge police station just after five on Monday, in a frame of mind reminiscent of . . . well, what exactly? The depression that readily presents itself when you find you've just failed the same exam for the sixth time?

Or not passed your driving test at the tenth attempt?

Or proposed and just been laughed at?

Despite having done everything in your power to get it right. We're not going to solve this, he thought. Not ever. We're . . . he searched for the words as he unlocked his bike and pedalled off . . . we're in the hands of a murderer so much smarter than we are, so many steps ahead, that in actual fact it's pointless to carry on. He toys with us. He sends us letters and entire narratives, he lies or doesn't, as he sees fit, and we dance to his tune like marionettes with no will of our own, our thoughts paralysed. He's murdered five people in the space of a month and he's going to get away with it. At least five people. Maybe seven, maybe eight. Shit.

And now he had finished. If there was one thing that

seemed clear, it was that. The last sign of life from him had been two weeks ago, when he posted the Mousterlin document from Cairo. Barbarotti had read somewhere that if you wanted to vanish into mid-air, discreetly disappear from the surface of the earth, there was one city in the world that particularly lent itself to the procedure. Cairo.

Since the Tuesday before last he had been silent. Case closed. The killer was done with killing and had nothing more to say on the matter. Bloody hell, thought Barbarotti, I almost wish there was another letter waiting for me on the hall rug. Even if it meant a new name to deal with.

Just so he had another lead. A fresh opening, a chance to start from a different angle. Leblanc's promised report had not arrived by the end of the day, but Barbarotti sensed that when in due course it did, it would constitute another blank. And the long shot about the girl and her grandmother being foreign tourists with a caravan . . . well, however would they be able to investigate something like that? Or what if they were Romanian gypsies and not on any register anywhere on the planet? Why not? It wasn't hard to imagine the whole case expanding endlessly in space and time – nor to see himself and his colleagues in his mind's eye, still poring over the same papers and lists and documentation in five or ten or fifteen years' time. Shit was the word for it, all right.

On the other hand, I gave Our Lord twenty-four hours, he reminded himself. Though there was plenty to indicate it would be a tough deadline to meet.

A new coffee place had opened on the corner of Skolgatan and Munkgatan. Aware that no one was waiting for him at home, he applied the brakes, propped his bike against the wall and went in. He ordered a cortado, half espresso, half milk, picked up a local listings magazine and started idly flicking through it. Got to do something else, he thought. Got to be like Leblanc, leave my work at work. He had managed it for the two days of Marianne's visit, but now he was back to the usual. Everything simmering away inside his head like some old ragout nobody would ever want to eat, and if he didn't do something about it, it would presumably bubble away all evening until he finally managed to get to sleep. Sometime way past midnight, he was sure of that.

And it would all still be there in his dreams. The case, the investigation and the mocking murderer in some fiendish 'new' confection – or ragout, indeed – to add to the other ingredients in his muddled life.

Marianne. The boys. Sara. Göran Persson.

Göran Persson, he thought. No, fuck it, not Göran Persson.

His mobile rang.

It was Asunander.

What in hell's name? thought Barbarotti. Asunander? He *never* rings.

'Sorry to bother you,' he said.

And that was equally unusual.

'Just having a coffee in town.'

'When will you be home? There's something I'd like talk to you about in peace and quiet.'

Barbarotti was suddenly aware of all the racket going on around him. And of the fact that he was double the age of the next oldest customer in the cafe.

'What about?'

'I'll tell you later. If it's all right to ring you at home, that is?'

'Yes,' said Barbarotti. 'Of course. I'll be home in fifteen minutes.'

'Good. I'll speak to you then,' said Asunander, and hung up.

Gunnar Barbarotti drained his cup and left the cafe.

'There's something I wanted to talk to you about.'

'Uh huh?' said Barbarotti.

'To do with the case.'

'Yes?'

'I wasn't at work today. I stayed at home to read and think. I've got a theory.'

Gunnar Barbarotti pinched himself. He seemed to be awake. He was talking to Asunander. He thought back over the day and realized he hadn't seen the chief inspector at all.

But a theory? *Asunander*?

'I suggest you come round to my place, so we can discuss this. If you're not busy, that is?'

'Er, no, I mean yes,' said Barbarotti. 'No, I'm not busy. When shall I . . .'

'Can we say eight o'clock? I'll mix you a grog. I'm in the high street, number fourteen, and the front door code is 1958. Year Sweden hosted the World Cup.'

'OK,' said Barbarotti. 'I'll be there.'

After he rang off it suddenly struck him that he had not heard a single click of false teeth for the duration of the call.

39

A grog, thought Gunnar Barbarotti as he headed for the high street on foot. It was only ten minutes from his own flat, and quite a narrow road, but perhaps it had been more of a main thoroughfare in the past. Why on earth is Asunander offering me grog? And presenting me with a theory?

About the case.

He had never been to Asunander's before, and he doubted any of the others had, either. Not Backman, Sorrysen or Toivonen. Possibly one of the other departmental chiefs, but he didn't really think so. Asunander wasn't the sort to invite people round. Or at least, not with the way things had turned out. Since the accident. The baseball bat and the unfortunate new teeth.

Barbarotti calculated. It was eleven years now. 1996. Asunander had just taken over as their chief; he came from Halmstad and hadn't been in post more than six months when it happened.

Bellas Gränd, the alleyway behind the station. An evening in November, four thugs, a hefty blow. He had been on duty but not in uniform, but the perpetrators claimed at trial that it had not been mere coincidence that the victim was a high-ranking police officer.

After that he had been on sick leave for four months. Then

his wife had left him. They'd had a house over on the Pampas side of town, and after the divorce Asunander had bought this flat in the old high street.

To cut a long and dismal story a little shorter, he hung onto his post as head of the CID and grew increasingly isolated as the years went by. But he stayed on. He never went into the field. If you'd got your teeth knocked out on active service, you could at least be sure of one thing. You'd never get fired.

What a bloody depressing fate, thought Barbarotti. Why have I never thought about it before? Has *anybody* ever cared about Asunander?

But there was another side to it, too. Asunander wasn't an easy person to get along with. That had been true even in the short time before the baseball bat, and it certainly didn't improve afterwards. Barbarotti remembered Backman doing her best to get a bit closer to him, and perhaps there were others who had tried. But it had proved essentially futile.

This was how Barbarotti summed it up in his mind as he emerged from the railway underpass and turned right along the high street. And if he had thought they had come to the end of all the remarkable features in this investigation, he had been proved wrong: there was one strange thing still to come.

A grog and theory session at Asunander's.

Asunander shook him by the hand and bade him welcome.

'Thank you,' said Barbarotti. 'You know what, I think this is the first time I've seen where you live.'

'I know,' said Asunander. 'I've become a bit of a recluse, unfortunately. That's just the way things have turned out.'

It was the most personal comment Barbarotti had ever heard the chief inspector make. And there was more.

'There was the dog, of course, but I had to have her put down in the spring. She only made it to eight.'

'I'm sorry to hear that,' said Barbarotti.

'It was her hip joints, she could barely walk by the end. She'd had too many puppies, you see. Oh yes, I know you all think I'm a bit odd. And I'm well aware I have my strange ways.'

Gunnar Barbarotti nodded and followed Asunander into a large living room. Bookshelves ran from floor to ceiling along three of the walls. Just a single picture on display. A large oil painting between the two windows, its subject a lone, wind-swept tree on a desolate, yellowish plain.

'But it's still three years before I can draw a reasonable pension, so I'm afraid you lot won't be rid of me before then.'

'Look, I've never—' began Barbarotti, but the chief inspector waved his hand and interrupted him.

'No need to protest. I know how the land lies and so do you. That's not what this evening's about. Would you like whisky or brandy?'

'Whisky,' said Barbarotti. 'And just a drop of tap water with it, please.'

'Excellent,' said Asunander. 'We're on the same wavelength there. I'm sorry I called it grog.'

'It doesn't matter,' Barbarotti assured him.

They each took a baggy leather armchair. The little table between them was of a wood that looked almost black, ebony perhaps? How could both the armchairs have got so well worn, wondered Barbarotti involuntarily. Did he swap over each evening? Or had one of them been his wife's . . . yes, that seemed more likely, they looked a fair age. Asunander had already set out bottles, glasses and a carafe of water. Two little bowls, as well, one of olives and the other of nuts. An ashtray with a pipe and matches. He poured a few centilitres into the glasses and indicated that Barbarotti should add his own water to taste.

'You said you had a theory,' said Barbarotti.

'Correct,' said Asunander. 'By the way, did you notice that my teeth aren't clicking today?'

'Yes, I did,' said Barbarotti.

'I'm trying a new adhesive. Seems to work pretty well, touch wood.'

'Why don't you bring it up with Jonnerblad and the others,' asked Barbarotti. 'The theory, that is.'

Asunander was quiet for a moment. Then he said, 'Two reasons. I don't like Jonnerblad. I like you and Backman better. But you can't invite a woman round for whisky.'

'Hmm,' said Barbarotti.

'And I had a feeling we'd need a drop of the hard stuff.'

'Oh, Backman's fine with a whisky,' said Barbarotti.

'Is that a fact? Anyway, the other reason is that I'm not entirely convinced by it. My theory. And I don't feel like getting laughed at by those damn goons from Stockholm. I wanted to try it out on you first.'

'You're making me curious now,' said Barbarotti.

'Good,' said Asunander. 'You'd be a bloody bad policeman if you weren't. Cheers!'

'Cheers,' said Brabarotti.

They drank. The chief inspector pulled his face into a grim sort of smile and set down his glass. Barbarotti looked at the windswept tree and waited quietly for Asunander to light his pipe. He took a few pleasurable puffs and blew a cloud of smoke up to the ceiling. Barbarotti suddenly felt unsure whether he was awake or lying in bed asleep. The whole situation felt distinctly like the opening scene in a nightmare.

'I've been making a few discreet checks during the day, as well,' explained Asunander. 'And I'm pleased to say they point in the right direction.'

'You really had better tell me the whole story now,' said Barbarotti.

'Willingly,' said Asunander. 'So, my starting point is that there are a damn lot of weird things about this case.'

'Agreed,' said Barbarotti.

Asunander leant forward with his elbows on his knees. 'Now listen and let me recapitulate a little. The murderer writes you letters. He communicates with the press. He announces whom he's going to kill, though in most cases they're already dead by the time you get the letters. He doesn't kill one of the people he names. He writes a long screed about some strange events in Finistère five years ago. He posts it to you from Cairo. So the question is: why does he do all this?'

'He kills five people as well,' Barbarotti reminded him.

'He certainly does. But why bother with all the other things? What's his motivation?'

'I don't know,' said Barbarotti.

'You don't know?'

'No.'

'Yet we've been trying to identify that motivation from the very start,' Asunander observed, putting his pipe down on the table. He tossed a couple of olives into his mouth. 'And his motivation has been correctly identified several times in our discussions.'

'Has it?' said Barbarotti, starting to wonder if the chief

inspector was having him on. Or had received another baseball bat to the head, maybe.

'Several times,' repeated Asunander. 'We've dropped it into the conversation every day.'

'Get to the point,' said Barbarotti.

'To mislead,' said the chief inspector, spitting the olive stones into his hand. 'He does it to mislead us. To distract our attention and make us look the wrong way. I'm right, aren't I? That's what we've been saying?'

'Of course,' said Barbarotti. 'I've certainly had that feeling all along.'

'Me too,' said Asunander. 'The problem is that we've found it hard to keep focused on that. As soon as he made another move, we started analysing right, left and centre, and taking measures.'

Barbarotti pondered this.

'Instead of seeing that it's all entirely pointless,' went on Asunander. 'There's no logic, there's no reason for these letters. Nor for the fact that they were addressed to you. He never intended murdering any Hans Andersson. He never let a girl slip out of a boat and there's no grandmother buried anywhere round Mousterlin.'

'What?' said Barbarotti.

'The whole thing's a fabrication.'

He took up his pipe again but didn't light it. Barbarotti shook his head and tried to understand what Asunander was actually driving at.

'But he murdered the others . . .'

'Oh yes. And he has an actual motive for that. At least for a couple of them.'

'A couple of them? You . . . you've lost me now,' said

Barbarotti, taking a gulp of whisky. As he put down his glass, he noticed that his hand was shaking.

'But you agree with my reasoning so far?' asked Asunander, peering at him with an intent and appraising look that Barbarotti had never seen from him before.

'Yes,' he said. 'I think so.'

'Good,' said Asunander. 'Let's have a bit more whisky then, and I'll tell you how I reckon it all fits together.'

By the time he left Chief Inspector Asunander's flat on the high street it was quarter past eleven and rain had begun to fall. Cold and penetrating autumn rain, what was more, but he was oblivious to it. The theory Asunander had advanced – which they had then chewed over very thoroughly for two hours while they polished off the bottle of whisky, a ten-year-old Glenmorangie Highland Single Malt – absorbed his thoughts and consciousness so completely that he probably wouldn't have noticed two metres of snow or the town hall going up in flames.

It's not possible, he thought. Bloody hell, it's just not possible.

And yet he knew that it was. That this was exactly how it all fitted together, and that the only thing left to do was to tie up the ends so the murderer couldn't fall out of the sack.

Strange are the ways of the Lord, thought Inspector Barbarotti, pushing open the front door of 12 Baldersgatan. Truly. Was it three points they'd agreed on?

SEVEN

29–31 AUGUST 2007

40

Barbarotti and Backman conducted the interview. Jonnerblad, Tallin and Sorrysen sat on the other side of the two-way mirror and observed.

The interview was recorded, too. On audiotape and on DVD, to make completely sure. Asunander had insisted on that, too, and he himself chose to sit in a different room and watch proceedings on a TV monitor.

The woman's name was Ulrika Hearst. She was thirty-seven, her maiden name was Lindquist, and her husband was English. They had found her the previous day.

'Hoss and Boss?' queried Barbarotti.

'That was what they called themselves,' said Ulrika Hearst. 'Even when they were small. It might have been somebody else who came up with the names, I don't know.'

'And you've known them all your life?'

'Yes. We're cousins. Our mothers are sisters. They lived in Varberg, and we lived in Kungsbacka. We saw quite a lot of each other. I'm an only child, and Hoss and Boss are my only cousins.'

She tucked a strand of her blonde hair behind one ear. Her blue eyes shifted back and forth between the two DIs, as if she were trying to decide which of them she was really meant to be addressing.

'It's Hoss we're particularly interested in,' Backman said, taking her turn to speak.

'So I understand,' said Ulrika Hearst.

'Can you tell us a bit about him?'

She thought for a moment.

'He was . . . difficult,' she said. 'They both were.'

'Difficult?'

'I don't really know how to describe them,' said Ulrika Hearst. 'I didn't have all that many friends when I was a child. Solitary at school and that sort of thing. Hoss and Boss were sort of part of my world and you just accept things as normal there, don't you? When you're a child, at any rate. That's what growing up involves. Seeing your childhood delusions and myths for what they are.'

Backman nodded. 'I understand what you're saying,' she said. 'So when was it you became aware of how difficult they were?'

'We moved to Stockholm when I was sixteen,' Ulrika Hearst told them. 'I started at a good upper secondary and found some new friends. My cousins were at more of a distance, and that was when I started to realize they were a bit odd.'

'In what way were they odd?' asked Barbarotti.

'They were always such know-alls, for one thing,' said Ulrika Hearst, almost breaking into a smile but instantly suppressing it. 'I think they competed with each other to be the one who knew everything, but whenever I came to visit they would, like, gang up against me instead. I was their dumb cousin who didn't understand a thing . . . I was ten months younger, as well, with a December birthday, whereas theirs is in February. Sometimes they would compete to see who could fool me the best.'

'Competed to see who could fool you?' said Backman. 'That doesn't sound very pleasant.'

'No, it wasn't,' said Ulrika Hearst. 'Once, I must have been about eight, Hoss claimed he'd dropped a wallet full of money down a well, but neither he nor Boss could climb down and get it because they suffered from some strange ear condition that meant they couldn't go into confined spaces. But if I did it, they'd give me half the money. There were metal rungs set into the side of the well, but of course there was no wallet and as soon as I reached the bottom, they put the cover on. They made me sit down there in the dark for over an hour. I remember wetting myself, but I never dared tell my mum why.

'What little bastards,' said Backman.

'So they're identical twins?' said Barbarotti.

'Oh yes,' said Ulrika Hearst. 'They've always been impossible to tell apart, unless you know that Hoss has a little birthmark under his left ear. He's a centimetre taller and twenty minutes older, too, but apart from that they're identical.'

'And no other siblings?' asked Backman.

'No, it was just them. And they were as thick as thieves. I know that Maud and Yngve, their parents, did what they could to discourage it. They tried separating them in various ways, but it was no good. They always insisted on sharing a bedroom, for instance, even though they lived in a big house. And at school, putting the twins in different classes just made them refuse to work at all. They never had any other friends, either, only each other.'

'How did things go later on?' asked Barbarotti. 'When they got older?'

Ulrika Hearst slowly shook her head and a strange look

came into her eyes. She tidied away another stray strand of hair and took a drink of water.

'I'm not really sure,' she said. 'But there was definitely something wrong. They finished school together in 1989. Same class, same grades, and I went to their graduation party. It was a strange affair. Ten or twelve people. I'd had my own party up in Stockholm two weeks earlier and there were at least fifty of us. That was the first time it really came home to me how weird they were. They both got top grades in their exams, they'd both applied to study medicine in Gothenburg and of course they got in right away. Then their parents bought them a small flat in Aschebergsgatan, thought it was a relief to get rid of them I expect, and the boys had never shown any attachment to *them*, either. So they moved in there and started their medical degrees.'

'Go on,' said Barbarotti. 'This is the autumn of 1989, right?'

'Yes,' said Ulrika Hearst. 'The first three or four terms it all ran like clockwork, I think. They passed their exams and vivas and all that stuff. I went to see them a couple of times when I was in Gothenburg on other business. They really were wrapped up in themselves and their studies, with skeletons and anatomical charts all over the place. They treated me with slightly more respect once we were adults, didn't spin me lies and send me down wells and so on, but I was still always happy to leave their flat. I remember I . . .'

'Yes?' said Barbarotti.

She gave a laugh. 'Err, yes, I'd stop outside and just stand there taking deep breaths on the pavement outside the flats. Drinking in the normal world out there, it was . . . well, it was a purely physical sensation. I was studying economics in Uppsala, and there was lots of talk about who was duller, economists or medics, and I remember thinking that if they ever met my cousins in Gothenburg they'd have no trouble making their minds up.'

Eva Backman allowed herself a fleeting smile. 'But then something happened, did it?'

'Yes.' Ulrika Hearst braced her back and was suddenly serious. 'Boss met a girl. That was in May '91. I went to see my mother in Nacka for her birthday, and she broke the news to me. It would have been entirely normal in any other family, of course, but for us it was pretty much a sensation. And it was even more sensational when it emerged in the course of the summer that they were getting married and moving to Australia. She was an exchange student from somewhere outside Brisbane.'

'And that was what happened?' asked Backman.

'Yes it was. Boss and Bessie, that was her name, got married and moved to Australia around Christmas 1991, and they've been living in a suburb of Sydney ever since.'

'Have you been to visit?'

'I have, actually. I spent a month in Australia with my boyfriend in . . . well it must be twelve years ago now, so we went to see them while we were there. They had a baby daughter and everything seemed rosy. Boss had softened up a bit, not that he was as laid-back as your average Australian, of course, but by his standards. It was a big change.'

'But you only saw them the once?'

'Yes. And we weren't there particularly long. We only spent one night with them, so I can't really say. But Gustaf, my boyfriend at the time, thought they were nice, I remember.'

Barbarotti nodded. 'And what about Hoss? How did he react to his brother going off like that?'

Ulrika Hearst took a sip of water before replying. She ran the tip of her tongue over her lips.

'Well that's just it,' she said. 'It's like, we don't know. I mean, Hoss has never confided how he's feeling to anybody. My mother didn't know a thing. His parents just reported that Boss had got married and moved to Sydney; when I met up with Hoss in June 1992, we went for a coffee in Haga, and he said everything was fine. But that autumn he gave up his medical course and started studying philosophy instead. He never told anybody why. I was more or less out of touch with him for a couple of years. I lived in England for a while, but when I got back to Sweden, in 1997, he'd got married and had nearly finished his PhD. I gather he rose to the top as a logician in record time. He got his doctorate in 1999 and was given an academic post at the university the same year.'

'Did you meet his wife?'

'Yes. A couple of times. The first was just after New Year, 2000. She was pregnant and they'd just bought a house in Mölndal. She worked at Sahlgrenska hospital, I assume they met there when he was a medical student. She lost the baby a few months later and . . . well, they never had any children.'

'What sort of impression did you get of their relationship?' asked Eva Backman.

She hesitated, but only for a moment.

'I could see he was the dominant one,' she said. 'She seemed terribly shy to me, and later on I found out she grew up in a strictly religious home, and Hoss pretty much uprooted her from there.'

'Uprooted her?' said Backman. 'Ah, I think I see.'

'I met her again a few years later,' said Ulrika Hearst. 'Just her, we bumped into each other in Stockholm completely by chance, and I hardly recognized her. She'd . . . grown, somehow. Become her own woman, you could say, if it weren't such an overused phrase.'

'There are reasons why some phrases get overused,' said Eva Backman.

'Yes, I suppose so.'

'When?' said Barbarotti. 'When was it you met her in Stockholm?'

'I've thought about that,' said Ulrika Hearst, 'and I reckon it must have been January or February 2006.'

'About eighteen months ago, then?'

'Yes.'

'And Hoss? Have you seen anything of him in the past few years?'

'I only met him once,' declared Ulrika Hearst with an apologetic shrug of the shoulders. 'The Gothenburg Book Fair last year. Well, met isn't really the right word . . . I saw him on a seminar panel. I don't remember the subject, but I saw his name and went along because I was a bit curious. He didn't make much of an impression. We didn't say hello; I saw him notice me in the audience but when it was over he slipped out the other way.'

'Do you know anything more about their relationship?' asked Eva Backman.

'Not really,' said Ulrika Hearst. 'But I remember my mother saying a couple of years ago that she wouldn't want to be in her shoes.'

'In Hoss's wife's shoes?'

'Yes.'

'And did she say why?'

Ulrika Hearst gave a sort of smile. 'My mother liked

analysing relationships,' she said. 'She divorced my father when I was fifteen, and after that it was one of the most important interests of her life, I think I can safely say.'

'When did your mother pass away?'

'Last year. Cancer, it was all over in a few months.'

'But she worked as a family therapist?'

'Yes. She used to say she'd married her profession in place of my father, and this time round it really was true love.'

Eva Backman nodded. 'So when she said she wouldn't want to be in Katarina Malmgren's shoes, she knew what she was talking about?'

'I should think so,' said Ulrika Hearst.

'I'm sorry to have to ask,' said Astor Nilsson, 'but I'd be bloody grateful to know how all this fits together. And how we arrived at it.'

Astor Nilsson hadn't been present at the interview with Ulrika Hearst. He'd been busy interviewing a couple of other people at the University of Gothenburg.

But now he had arrived at Kymlinge police HQ. It was three in the afternoon and all those involved were gathered in Jonnerblad and Tallin's office.

'Yes, things did speed up rather, towards the end,' conceded Jonnerblad. 'But there doesn't appear to be any doubt. Henrik Malmgren is our man. We also have to take our hats off to Chief Inspector Asunander, because without his perceptive analysis we'd still have been getting nowhere.'

'Don't mention it,' said Asunander.

'Can we start with the method?' asked Astor Nilsson. 'How the hell did he do all this? If we forget the writing part for a minute and just look at the MO itself, I mean?'

'Let's save the motive for a while, too, come to that,' said Tallin.

'OK,' said Eva Backman. 'Now that we know, it isn't that complicated, in actual fact.'

'Oh really?' muttered Astor Nilsson.

'Yes really,' said Backman, opening her notepad. 'He comes up here from Gothenburg and kills Erik Bergman and Anna Eriksson. That's on 31 July. He must have been a bit familiar with Bergman's jogging habits, but that sort of knowledge is easy enough to acquire. He lurks in the bushes and jumps him when he comes tootling past, it's as simple as that. Sticks the knife in a few times and leaves him there.'

'A few hours later he goes to Anna Eriksson's, after arranging to call round,' Barbarotti took over. 'We can assume he did that, at any rate. They'd met down in Brittany, after all, and maybe he says he's got something for her.'

'How can you know this?' asked Sorrysen.

'I'm only guessing,' said Barbarotti. 'But anyway, she lets him in and he kills her, possibly even with an adjustable spanner like the one he writes about, but we can only speculate. He wraps her in plastic to keep in the smell, because he wants it to be a few days before she's found, and then leaves.'

'OK, got it,' said Astor Nilsson. 'Jesus Christ. And then?'

'Then he sends off some letters and lies low for a few days . . . contacts the press, comes up with the Hans Andersson red herring and a few other things, partly to confuse us, but maybe also so the remaining two victims won't twig there's a link to the holiday in France. They actually did meet and socialize a bit down there five years ago, but remember the Mousterlin document is fiction from start to finish. Especially where the girl and old lady are concerned.'

'Especially that part, yes,' said Eva Backman.

'But how the hell could he—?' Astor Nilsson managed to exclaim before Asunander broke in.

'We'll take that later. Go on, Barbarotti.'

'So, about a week later he goes up to Hallsberg. He takes a gun with him this time, because he hasn't quite got the measure of Gunnar Öhrnberg. It's Öhrnberg and Henrik's wife who are the important victims; he kills Anna Eriksson and Erik Bergman to make events fit the Mousterlin notes. To make us swallow the whole story, in other words.'

'Good God,' said Astor Nilsson. 'So he's going to kill Gunnar Öhrnberg because . . . ?'

'Because he's having an affair with Katarina, yes,' said Barbarotti. 'And to think I actually got a bit of a lead when I talked to that diving mate of his. He told me Öhrnberg was paying a secret visit to a married woman in west Sweden. But how the heck could I know it was Katarina Malmgren?'

'Yes, how?' said Tallin. 'Go on.'

'He undoubtedly takes his time killing Gunnar Öhrnberg, and maybe it even happens the way he describes it in his notes. Or anyway, I get the impression he enjoys this killing. But that's something for the forensic psychiatrists to get their teeth into.'

He took a gulp of water. Backman turned to another page in her notepad and took over.

'Having positioned his third victim in the famous wheat field, he drives home to Gothenburg and he and his wife pack the car ready for their week's holiday in Denmark. They catch the overnight ferry on Sunday evening, as planned, they take a stroll on deck, he strangles her and chucks her overboard. He goes ashore as a foot passenger in Fredrikshavn, makes his way to Copenhagen and boards a plane at Kastrup. Twenty-four hours later he's in Cairo, posting off his Mousterlin notes.'

Five seconds' silence followed.

'Unbelievable,' said Astor Nilsson at last. 'Totally unbelievable.'

'Excuse me asking,' said Sorrysen, 'but what about passports and that sort of thing?'

'We've checked that out,' said Backman. 'There's a passenger Malmgren from Copenhagen to Athens on 14 August. Bertil Malmgren. I think we can assume his brother sent *his* passport from Australia. Bearing in mind what Ulrika Hearst told us. Don't you think?'

'That would seem to be the case,' said Jonnerblad.

'All right,' sighed Astor Nilsson. 'Smart. Yes, I accept that all this works, purely technically. But for the whole thing to be triggered by his wife finding another man . . . well, it feels rather petty, if you'll pardon me saying so.'

'He must have relished the planning part,' said Eva Backman. 'Devising a plan and then putting it into operation. I was with a bloke like that once, when I was young. We went on a road trip, driving all round Europe, and the map was much more important than Europe.'

Silence descended again, and then Asunander cleared his throat. 'We have to remember one thing,' he said. 'Namely the fact that motives are rarely in proportion to crimes.'

'Expand on that,' requested Jonnerblad.

'Except in the perpetrator's head, that is,' clarified Asunander. 'From outside, the reasons are nearly always small and insignificant, and they're nearly always the same. Jealousy, revenge, greed. Though they can express themselves in very different ways.'

'You can say that again,' said Tallin. 'How did you hit on the solution, in fact?'

Asunander sat with his head bowed, apparently contemplating his clasped hands for a while before he answered.

'Reduction,' he said. 'It was the only thing left. The only remaining possibility.'

'I've been trying to reduce,' said Astor Nilsson. 'All along. The only problem is that there's never anything left. Not a blessed thing.'

'There is one other detail,' said Asunander after a short pause.

'A detail?' said Tallin.

'Yes. In his notes.'

'What sort of detail?' said Jonnerblad. 'I've read them . . . read them I don't know how many times. At least four.'

'I think I'll keep it to myself,' said Asunander.

'What the . . . ?' began Astor Nilsson, but Asunander stopped him by raising a warning finger.

'That's my business,' he said. Then he folded his arms across his chest and let his eyes scan the entire company, emitting a sort of faint vibration that made Barbarotti think of a purring cat. He's bonkers, he thought. He's bloody bonkers.

But he solved the case. One detail? What goddamned detail could that be?

'And you ran some kind of . . . check?' asked Tallin cautiously.

Asunander nodded. 'Nothing special. But I've got an old friend who knows his way round the banking world. Malmgren sold all his shares at the end of May. Almost a million and a half, and no new purchases after that. Well, I expect he needed a bit of seed capital down there. Backman's quite right, there was planning behind all this. A lot of planning.'

'He could have made things easier for himself,' Astor Nilsson pointed out.

'Perhaps,' said Asunander. 'His aim was to kill his wife and her lover, but I think there were other aims as well.'

'Such as what, precisely?' said Sorgsen.

'Something happened down there in Brittany,' said Eva Backman, once Asunander had given her a nod of approval. 'Anna Eriksson and Erik Bergman were involved somehow, but we don't know how. I suppose we'll have to see whether he tells us.'

'The Sixth Man?' asked Astor Nilsson.

'We don't know who he is. Some guy who stayed with Erik Bergman for a week or so, but he may not play any part in this story at all.'

'He's in the photos, though.'

'And where did we find the photos?' said Eva Backman. 'Have you forgotten? In the Malmgrens' album.'

'Fuck,' said Astor Nilsson. 'Them too?'

'Yes,' said Barbarotti. 'Them too.'

Two hours later, he was out by the bike rack with Backman. There was a threat of rain in the air, and he noticed to his surprise how chilly he was, and hoped the heavens would resist the urge to open.

'It was no exaggeration of yours, back there,' he said.

'Which one?'

'That something happened down in Brittany. In Henrik Malmgren's eyes, at least, it must have been something really crucial, mustn't it?'

Backman paused to think. 'Yes,' she said, 'but at least there were no girl and grandmother to lose their lives. So what do you reckon happened?'

'Have you read the notes from Mousterlin since you found out Henrik Malmgren wrote them?'

'No,' said Eva Backman. 'I haven't had time. And I've no idea what detail it was that made Asunander hum like that.'

'Nor me,' conceded Barbarotti. 'But I reread the whole thing last night. There are loads of peculiar keys in that text, once you know that it's Henrik Malmgren wielding the pen. And that he's intending to kill the lot of them . . . err, it kind of turns it into a completely different story.'

'A completely different story?' said Backman. 'Well it would, wouldn't it? Do you know what I can't wait for?'

'Your holiday?'

'That, of course. But above all I can't wait to sit down and interrogate him. Can you?'

Gunnar Barbarotti pondered. 'Maybe not,' he said. 'But they haven't got their hands on him down there yet. I'm not so sure you're going to have the pleasure of looking him in the eye.'

'Killjoy,' said Backman. 'They've had barely eight hours, and I do believe it's only morning in Sydney, you know.'

'Quite right,' said Barbarotti, looking at his ancient but fully functioning watch. 'But if there's a time you should be able to find people in it's at night, surely? No, I reckon he's going to slip away, and you'll only have the pleasure of talking to Boss.'

'Hoss and Boss,' snorted Backman. 'Some men get off to an unfortunate start. And then it just keeps going. So you think there's some element of truth in the Mousterlin document, then? Apart from Asunander's detail, that is.'

'Read it for yourself and you'll see,' said Barbarotti.

Backman gave a shrug and stuffed her briefcase into her bike basket. 'If I do get to talk to him, I shall ask him about his need for control,' she said. 'That's the loosest screw.'

'You reckon?' said Barbarotti.

'Oh yes. First he's abandoned by his brother, who's probably the only person in the world who means anything to him. That must have felt little short of an amputation. He somehow contrives to find a woman, all the same, but she gradually grows past him and wants to get out. That's presumably what dawns on him that summer. And once it's actually happening, he sets this whole black circus in motion in order to be avenged, disappear and start a new life in Australia. It must have given him one hell of a kick and the awful thing is that there's actually some sort of logic to it.'

'Logic, ah yes,' said Barbarotti, suddenly remembering what Marianne had said. He took his bike out of the rack. 'Well after all, he is a senior lecturer in philosophy, mother of all the sciences. Makes you feel a bit sorry for the sciences.'

Backman smiled. 'But you know what?' she said. 'What's almost the weirdest thing about this whole weird business?'

'No,' said Barbarotti.

'That you've started drinking whisky with Asunander.'

'I think it was only a one-off,' said Barbarotti.

'I hope not,' said Backman. 'Because I'd like you to ask him a question next time the two of you are sitting there over your grogs.'

'What question?' said Barbarotti.

'Why he's making do with false teeth at all. I've been

wondering for ten years but I've never dared to ask. All the pensioners are getting dental implants these days. False teeth are so Stone Age.'

Barbarotti considered this.

'I don't know him all that well yet,' he said, 'so it'll have to wait, I'm afraid.'

'Coward,' said Eva Backman. 'OK then, see you tomorrow. And I'll read the document tonight, one more time. Are we going the same way?'

'I don't think so,' said Barbarotti. 'I'm taking a detour via the school first.'

'The school?' said Backman. 'Why's that?'

'I'll tell you another time,' said Barbarotti.

41

'Can you speak up?' said Barbarotti. 'I can't hear you very well.'

It was Thursday morning, and ten past nine. He wasn't entirely sure what time it was in Australia.

'Sure, mate!' yelled DI Crumley, suddenly sounding as close as if he were squatting on Barbarotti's shoulder. 'We got 'im! We got 'em both, in fact!'

'You've got them both?' asked Barbarotti in his best school English. He felt DI Crumley's school English left a certain amount to be desired. 'Is that what you're saying? That you've got both Malmgren brothers safely in custody?'

'You bet!' shouted Crumley. 'Hoss and Boss Malmgren. He was staying at his brother's, like you thought. Do you lot want both of them or just the one? We find it a bit hard to tell them apart, to be honest.'

'I think we need both,' said Barbarotti. 'You can stop shouting now, the line's much better. Well, there won't be any problem about bringing our perpetrator over, but I'll go right now and look into how we have to handle . . .'

'Boss Malmgren's coming voluntarily,' interrupted Crumley. 'He's told us that seventy times since we brought them in. He wants to come to Sweden and be at his brother's side. Come what may.'

'But he's got a family, hasn't he?' asked Barbarotti. 'Boss Malmgren?'

'Not any longer. He got divorced three years ago. They seem to have missed each other quite a lot, the two brothers. They're behaving a bit like chimps they forgot to separate when they were babies, if you know what I mean.'

Barbarotti wasn't quite sure he did, but he got the gist.

'I see,' he said. 'OK, we'll make arrangements to bring them both over. I'll get all the paperwork ready and send it down. Make sure they don't escape or kill themselves in the meantime, that's all. Hoss has actually got four people's lives on his conscience.'

'He doesn't look as if he's *got* a conscience,' said DI Crumley. 'But maybe that's the problem?'

'I imagine it is,' said Barbarotti. 'Have you asked that question I wanted you to ask?'

'The Sixth Man? Yes mate,' said Crumley, and cleared his throat loudly. 'I asked him in total ignorance of what I was asking for, but I'm used to that. He didn't say anything for ages, as if he couldn't make his mind up whether to answer or not. Then he kind of nodded to himself and said his name was Stephen.'

'Stephen?'

'Yep. And that he was a hitchhiker on holiday in Europe. He came from Johannesburg, South Africa. Does that make sense?'

Barbarotti thought about it. He assumed Swedish criminal cases didn't command much space in the South African newspapers, and said it did. Make sense.

'Anything else?' Crumley asked him.

'I'll email it down to you,' said Barbarotti, and they said their goodbyes.

'So you got hold of her friend, too?'

'Yeah,' said Astor Nilsson. 'She was pretty keen to talk to the police, actually.'

'And why was that?'

'Because she got such a shock when she heard they'd been murdered. But she'd no reason for thinking it had anything to do with what Katarina had confided about this lover of hers.'

'And what precisely had she confided?'

'That his name was Gunnar and that she loved him. That was about it, I think. Plus she wanted to leave Henrik but didn't know how to pluck up the courage.'

'Was she scared of him?'

'I should have thought so,' said Astor Nilsson. 'Jessica, this friend, claimed she'd been trying to psych her up for over a year so she'd be brave enough to take the first step.'

'So it wasn't common knowledge, then? That Katarina Malmgren had a lover?'

Astor Nilsson shook his head. 'No, I pressed her quite hard on that, and she was pretty sure she was the only one who knew. Katarina Malmgren didn't have a large circle of acquaintances. Not the flock of friends some women seem to surround themselves with. He kept her under the microscope, if you know what I mean?'

'I see,' said Barbarotti.

I wouldn't mind working with Astor Nilsson again, he thought suddenly. You could have a constructive conversation with Astor. Things always progressed, somehow; with certain other people it was just the opposite, unfortunately. You had to put yourself in isolation for an hour after you'd talked to them, simply to get your brain going again.

Though for all he knew, there might be people who wanted to go and hide after an encounter with Inspector Barbarotti, as well. He couldn't claim to be any better.

'Katarina Malmgren and this Jessica were work colleagues, weren't they?'

'That's right,' said Astor Nilsson. 'And something really did happen that summer in Brittany. Katarina told her it was there that she and Gunnar first saw each other. Not that they got it together or anything, but that summer was when she realized, or so she claimed.'

'Realized what?'

Astor Nilsson shrugged. 'Well, I don't know. But it's not that hard to speculate. What a stunted life she was living, perhaps. And who she was married to. There in Brittany she got some inkling of how it *could* be, or that was how she described it to her friend, anyway. There were five of them in that group of Swedes, four having a good time, and then Henrik Malmgren.'

'But she didn't know her husband had found her out? Recently, I mean.'

'Jessica didn't think so. And Henrik certainly hadn't said anything. But he's a peculiar guy, she confirmed that much. She only met him the once, but things Katarina told her sounded scary. He wanted to control her utterly, but at the same time she was growing away from him with every passing day. That was how she put it. *Growing away from him*. It's insane the way people live their lives, when you take a little look behind the facade.'

Gunnar Barbarotti sat there with his chin in his hand and reflected. 'When was the last time she saw Katarina Malmgren?'

'A week or so before they were due to go to Denmark. Katarina had spent a night with Gunnar, while he was at his diving camp I suppose, and . . . well, Jessica sensed Katarina had made up her mind.'

'To explain the situation to her husband? To tell him she was leaving?'

'Yes. She didn't say it in so many words, but her friend got that impression.'

'And by then he'd already started murdering the others?'

'Yep. But she suspected nothing. She had her plan, her husband had his.'

'Christ almighty. It sounds almost choreographed.'

'Quite a sense of timing, at any rate. She went on a week's holiday in Jutland intending to tell him she wanted a divorce. He went intending to kill her and dump her overboard. You could say he was a few steps ahead. And Jessica Lund's convinced Katarina was oblivious to it all. She knew he was crazy, of course, but not *that* crazy.'

'No,' said Barbarotti. 'How could she have done?'

'I expect she'd got a bit too used to it,' said Astor Nilsson, looking grim. 'It's hard to see the insanity when you live with it. I had a period like that in my life, in fact. But one of Malmgren's colleagues told me something interesting. He would willingly shorten his life by thirty years in exchange for fame and distinction.'

'Henrik Malmgren?'

'Yes.'

'That's a bloody desperate kind of bargain.'

'Seems that way to us,' said Astor Nilsson. 'But there are

people like that, of course. You'll get the Nobel Prize if you agree to die at fifty-two. No prize and you'll get to eighty-two . . . though I don't know that he was right, that colleague. The lives that Malmgren cut short weren't his own, after all.'

'He'll be here by the middle of next week,' Barbarotti began to wind up the conversation. 'We'll have to see what we've got to say about him after we've been face to face with him for a while.'

'I suppose so,' said Astor Nilsson. 'Well I'm making fucking sure I'm part of it, come what may. Pitiful, isn't it, being so eager to scrutinize monsters like him? Or to get to see them, at any rate.'

'It's an urge you share with the rest of humanity,' said Gunnar Barbarotti.

'Yes, I know,' said Astor Nilsson. 'And it doesn't make it any better, the fact that everybody else is as perverted as I am. Though Henrik Malmgren's sort are pretty rare, luckily.'

'What do you suppose his brother's like?' asked Barbarotti.

'His wife seems to have left him with his life intact, so I'm sure he's a great guy,' said Astor Nilsson. 'Yeesh, I don't want to talk about this any more.'

'Nor me,' said Barbarotti. 'You get to a point where enough's enough.'

After his chat with Astor Nilsson, Gunnar Barbarotti went to the window and stared out. That was what the clever cops in the books always did. They looked out between the strips of their Venetian blinds onto a rainy grey Paris or a vermilion-coated sky that presaged snow in Gothenburg. Allowed the external space (the city, where the crime played out) to correspond to the internal (the cop's brain) in some sublime literary fashion. Barbarotti's problem was that four fifths of his view was taken up by the side of Lundholm & Sons' defunct shoe factory. It had stood empty and disused for over twenty years, all the windows were broken and he just wished the decision-makers of the town would make their minds up to pull down what was left of it. Preferably replacing it with a park or some kind of low-growing development, so he finally had a bit of a view.

Though if he went right up to the window and looked sideways, up and to the left, he could actually see the top of a tree and a patch of sky. But Backman was right when she said his balcony was a much better place for analysis and reflection. A damn sight better.

On the other hand, open views probably weren't the right inspiration for comprehending Henrik Malmgren. More the opposite: the ability to penetrate a very cramped space, stunted, a sort of inverted universe. Why not a well, even, like the one Ulrika Hearst had told them about? But of course, thought Barbarotti, if you'd constructed your world view out of so few building blocks, you really wanted them all to be in their proper places. If a block the size of a brother or a wife suddenly vanished, there was obviously a serious risk the whole thing would come crashing down.

Could he be understood in those terms? Astor Nilsson had said he was quite a big name in philosophy circles. Great philosophers normally reached the height of their reputation after fifty – or indeed, once they were dead – but Henrik Malmgren had been a precocious star. Especially in the fields of multivalent logic and deductive mathematico-logical systems. On the subject of his human qualities there had not been much to say,

Astor Nilsson reported from his interviews. Some slightly awkward silences had ensued.

But the very idea of fabricating a story like that? A drowned girl and her grandmother? And the girl's name? The Root of All Evil.

And describing himself through the eyes of his fictitious murderer. Was that where he had given himself away, wondered Barbarotti. Was that where Asunander had sensed something wasn't right? He didn't know. Barbarotti himself had suspected nothing. Asunander said it only struck him something was wrong on his third or fourth reading of the Mousterlin document. That was when he detected his crucial detail. Perhaps he'd say a bit more on the subject if they had another whisky session – or perhaps he really did intend keeping it to himself. Asunander was a tricky devil, and maybe he was just the kind of person you needed when trying to understand other tricky devils. Like Henrik Malmgren.

The previous evening, another remarkable thing had happened. When Barbarotti popped out to the local shop, he bumped into Axel Wallman, who had business in town, unusually for him. He had clearly read Henrik Malmgren's name in some newspaper – in his capacity as victim, not perpetrator; he stopped Barbarotti and told him about it. 'You lot ought to fish that dead philosopher out of the sea,' he said. 'He's the type who needs a stake through the heart before he's really dead.'

When Barbarotti – without revealing the latest developments in the case – had asked what he meant by that, Wallman had thrown up his hands and related how he had once taken part in a seminar with Malmgren, who had shown what rotten stuff he was made of.

But even when the full story had emerged, he never made the point of having been right about Malmgren coming from Halland; Barbarotti remembered that one for himself.

There was a knock at his door. He turned his eyes from Lundholm & Sons' shoe factory, and that was the end of his analysis.

'Jonnerblad's bought in a couple of smorgåstårta,' Backman informed him. 'It seems there's going to be some kind of wake for the case.'

'I'll be right there,' said Barbarotti.

But the real summing-up didn't take place at the party.

No, it was achieved in an exchange between himself and Eva Backman just before they went home for the day. That was the way things usually happened.

'So what have we learnt from all this, then?'

She had been sitting in his visitor armchair, ruminating for quite a while before she said it.

'I don't know,' said Barbarotti without looking up from his paperwork. 'But I assume you've got the answer, since you're asking. So you tell me, what have we learnt?'

'Well if that's the tone you're going to adopt, I almost feel like not telling you anything,' said Backman. 'But OK, you look as if you might be a teensy bit receptive after all.'

Barbarotti looked at her. 'You know I never forget a word you say,' he said. 'And I record your wisest pronouncements in a notebook I bought specially for the purpose.'

'Good,' said Eva Backman. 'Well, the way I see it, even if ten cops slave away for a hundred days and interview a thousand people, it doesn't always help.'

'Great introduction,' said Barbarotti.

'I know, don't interrupt. So when we're trying to hunt

down a solitary perverted brain, it could very well be more important for us to have a brain on our side that works the same way. That has what it takes to understand the killer. If Asunander hadn't spent a day thinking instead of coming to work, we wouldn't have solved this.'

That's exactly what I was thinking an hour ago, Barbarotti silently noted to himself. 'You mean we need Asunander because he has a perverted brain?' he said. 'Isn't that what *Silence of the Lambs* was about? I shall ask Asunander next time we're on the whisky whether his first name happens to be Hannibal.'

'It's Leif,' said Eva Backman. 'I checked. No, what I mean is that there are cases that demand a different kind of input, not just broad detection work.'

'Philosophizing as you sit on a balcony at sunset?' suggested Barbarotti, and he was struck by how much chatter there was in his head about his balcony at the moment.

'If I'd had your balcony, I'd have solved this case in three days,' said Backman.

'Well I won't have it very much longer,' said Barbarotti.

'What? Why not?'

'I . . . I think I'm expecting additions to the family.'

At first, Eva Backman looked totally nonplussed. Then she gave a crooked smile and heaved herself up out of the armchair. 'Congratulations,' she said. 'How many?'

'I don't know exactly,' said Barbarotti. 'But my little flat's going to be too small however it works out.'

'Aha,' said Backman. 'You'll have to tell me more about your life in three weeks' time. I'm off on holiday now. Though I might just drop by briefly for a look at Malmgren.'

'You do that,' said Barbarotti. 'And have a lovely time. But what am I supposed to put in my notebook on this occasion?'

'Never trust a writer,' said Eva Backman. 'I thought I'd made that abundantly clear.'

42

He emerged from Dr Oltmann's surgery at just after five on Friday afternoon. They had been talking for almost three hours, though the consultation was only supposed to last forty-five minutes. No follow-up appointment had been booked, but she promised Barbarotti he could ring her any time, if the need arose. As he thanked her it was on the tip of his tongue to say he would have liked to be married to a woman like her, but he resisted saying it. Maybe, he thought, maybe Marianne is a woman like that.

And he didn't think the need would arise. Something's happened to me these past few weeks, thought Gunnar Barbarotti as he passed the coffee shop in Skolgatan and didn't go in.

He wasn't quite sure what had happened, but definitely something.

The fact that they'd solved the case was a factor, of course. The brothers Malmgren were due to arrive at Kastrup airport on Tuesday; according to Crumley, assorted confessions had been made, so presumably the rest was a matter for the prosecutor, lawyers and legal psychiatrists – but that deranged philosopher had set some kind of mechanism in motion in him, too, hadn't he?

Some kind of correspondence that wasn't at all easy to put into words, but he could sense it and weigh it. Perhaps it was mere mental froth, but he should probably try to define it better.

Well, the fact that one couldn't perceive life the way Henrik Malmgren had done, perhaps that simple observation got to the heart of it. If life was a game, and presumably it was – at least some aspects of it – then human beings had to accept the role of humble pieces on the board, not leaders of the game. Which wasn't to say they had to give in to other pieces, or accept rules, decrees and acts of folly that curtailed their own existence.

The old AA prayer, in other words. They had discussed these things, he and Olltman, not in exactly the terms that went waltzing round in his head afterwards, but still; this was what it was all about. Freedom and responsibility, those worn old cornerstones. The 'I', its surroundings, its neighbours, its presence; above all the last of these, the being present in every moment, or at least as much as one possibly could; he had often been neglectful of that. He went into the little ICA supermarket in Frejagatan and prayed a swift prayer of existence.

O Lord, thank you for an instructive summer. If you keep me in decent shape and let things go without a hitch – you know what I'm talking about – you'll have your three points all sewn up. What's more, you've actually existed for eleven months at a stretch now, which is a record and bloody good going, bearing in mind all the circumstances, internal and external. Fresh pasta, with olives, capers and parmesan cheese will have to do on a day like today, don't you think? It's a heavenly combination, but maybe I don't need to tell you that?

Our Lord made no reply, except for a low and inarticulate murmur emitted by a slightly dodgy freezer cabinet – but it sounded friendly and reassuring, and as Inspector Barbarotti started to fill his basket he couldn't help feeling a certain degree of confidence.

He was just in the middle of his pasta when Sara rang.

She didn't even ask him to ring back, but simply burst into tears.

'What on earth is wrong, Sara?' he asked. 'What's happened?'

She sobbed for a while and he repeated his question in a variety of different ways, several times. My God, he thought. She must be pregnant. At the very least. She's got AIDS, I knew it. She's dying.

'I want to come home, Dad,' she said when she was finally able to produce words rather than sobs.

'Of course,' said Gunnar Barbarotti. 'You do that. Catch a plane first thing tomorrow.'

'Will you let me?'

'What?'

'Will you let me come and live with you again?'

'Are you crazy, Sara? Of course you can come home. I'd like nothing better.'

'Thank you.'

'But what's the matter, my darling girl? You've got to tell me. Are you ill?'

She gave a laugh. A feeble little laugh. 'No Dad, I'm not ill. And I'm not pregnant either, which I expect was your next question. But I don't want to stay here any longer. Can we leave the explanations until I see you?'

'Of course,' said Barbarotti. 'Do you want me to check

flight times for you, and so on? Have you got enough money for your ticket?'

'I'll sort it out myself. And I think I've got enough money. Can I borrow some from you if I haven't?'

'Any time,' said Gunnar Barbarotti. 'I've still got sixty kronor in my account. You start packing, and ring me again when you know what time you'll be here.'

'Thanks Dad,' said Sara. 'I'm sorry it turned out like this. I didn't mean it to.'

'Never mind, it doesn't matter,' said Gunnar Barbarotti. 'Shit happens. Err . . . there are going to be a few changes here at home, too, by the way, but I'll explain when I see you.'

'Changes?' said Sara. 'What sort of changes?'

Gunnar Barbarotti thought for a moment. About how much mobile phone calls from abroad cost, amongst other things.

'No, we'll do it face to face. Same as yours.'

There was a brief silence at Sara's end, then she accepted the situation, and they rang off.

He polished off his pasta as he thought everything over. And counted.

He made it seven. There would be seven of them. Marianne and her two children, he and his three.

Seven? Christ.

He cleared away, washed up, then took the newspaper out onto the balcony with him and sat down. It being Friday, there was a property supplement. He started leafing through it.

Seven? If they all gathered on this balcony, they'd have one and a half square metres each. It wasn't much, and would probably bring the whole balcony crashing down, anyway.

A house, he thought. A house is what we're going to need.

With quite a lot of rooms.

About fifteen seconds later, he found it. An old detached house, a former summer villa, out on the point at Kymmens Udde. Ten rooms plus kitchen, it said. In need of renovation. Large garden and private jetty. Only a million and a half.

A snip. And a use for his sixty kronor.

He rang the number, spoke to a friendly old man for ten minutes and was invited to a viewing on Sunday at 1 p.m.

He had just moved indoors to the computer on the desk to see his future in pictures, when Marianne rang.

She sounded cheerful.

Basically she almost always did, but there was something extra this time.

'You know what?' she said with a laugh. 'I've been getting on with things.'

'Oh yes?' said Gunnar Barbarotti. She's found that little vicar, he thought. 'What sort of things?'

'I had a chat with Kymlinge hospital. They can offer me a permanent post there from the first of November. What do you say to that?'

'The first of November?'

'Yes.'

'I knew it all along,' said Barbarotti. 'No one can resist you.'

'Go on with you,' said Marianne. 'And Johan and Jenny are still fine with moving, so what I'm really ringing to say is that it's decision time for us.'

'I thought we'd already decided,' said Barbarotti. 'Though we're going to need a slightly bigger place than we talked about.'

'Bigger? Why's that?'

'Hrrm,' said Gunnar Barbarotti. 'Stuff's been happening on

the children front. It seems . . . well, it actually seems as if I'm going to have all three of them with me.'

'What?' said Marianne.

'Yes, that's right,' said Gunnar Barbarotti, feeling a sudden shortness of breath. Or perhaps it was more like a kind of inhibiting viscous membrane that refused to let through the words that had to be spoken. 'That's how it's turned out,' he said with some effort. 'Lars and Martin will be here tomorrow, in fact, and Sara just called from London to say she was on her way home, so . . . well, including yours too, that actually makes seven of us.'

'Seven?'

'Seven, yes. But I'm going to look at a house on Sunday and . . .'

There was silence at the other end of the line. He raised his eyes and saw a gaggle of jackdaws land in one of the elms outside Cathedral School.

This is it, thought Inspector Barbarotti. Right now. The churchyard, the cows, the field of rape, the forest. In three seconds' time I shall know.